"Each story can stand alone. Dunmore can write as chillingly macabre an ending as Roald Dahl at his best or add a poignantly ironic twist worthy of O. Henry." – *Toronto Star*

"Spencer Dunmore is a good example why fiction based on the Second World War continues to be popular 46 years after the fighting stopped . . . . He can hold his own in the front ranks of today's writers of war stories." – *Edmonton Journal*

"It's hard to believe, when reading Dunmore's novels on the war in the air, 1939-45, that they are not based on first-hand experience. . . . Dunmore's characters are superbly drawn." – *Calgary Herald*

"Well-paced stories, several of them quite cleverly constructed, that fit well into the mainstream of war fiction. . . . the carefully-written dialogue crackles with tension at the right moments and slows into the sort of forced casualness of wartime at others." – *Hamilton Spectator*

ALSO BY SPENCER DUNMORE

Bomb Run (1971)
Tower of Strength (1973)
Collision (1974)
Final Approach (1976)
Means of Escape (1978)
Ace (1981)
The Sound of Wings (1984)
No Holds Barred (1987)
Reap the Whirlwind
[with William Carter] (1991)

SPENCER DUNMORE

Squadron

An M&S Paperback from
McClelland & Stewart Inc.
The Canadian Publishers

An M&S Paperback from McClelland & Stewart Inc.

First printing August 1992
Cloth edition printed 1991

Canadian Cataloguing in Publication Data

Dunmore, Spencer, 1928-
Squadron

"An M&S paperback."
ISBN 0-7710-2919-5

1. World War, 1939-1945 - Fiction.   2. Great Britain.
Royal Air Force. Bomber Command - Fiction.
I. Title.

PS8557.U54S75 1992   C813'.54   C92-093703-9
PR9199.3.D85S75 1992

This is a work of fiction.

Cover illustration by Wes Lowe
Cover design by Stephen Kenny

Printed and bound in Canada

McClelland & Stewart Inc.
The Canadian Publishers
481 University Avenue
Toronto, Ontario
M5G 2E9

for Jeanne Claire

Squadron Personnel

Aircrew

The Fry Crew

Squadron Leader Colin Fry, DSO, DFC and Bar, *pilot and "A" Flight Commander*

Flying Officer Maurice Staples, *navigator*

Flight Sergeant Donald Flinders, *bomb-aimer*

Sergeant Thomas Buckle, *flight engineer*

Sergeant Samuel Cooper, *wireless operator*

Sergeant Leonard Hodgkins, *mid-upper gunner; replaced by* Sergeant Albert O'Connor

Sergeant George Hall, *rear gunner*

The Pettigrew Crew

Flying Officer Nigel Pettigrew, *pilot*

Flying Officer Guy Venables, *navigator*

Sergeant Forbes Morris, RCAF, *bomb-aimer*

Sergeant Duncan Glossop, *flight engineer*

Sergeant Daniel Carter, *wireless operator*

Sergeant Bernard Betts, *mid-upper gunner*
Flight Sergeant Ernest Thwaites, *rear gunner*

The Sinclair Crew

Pilot Officer Ross Sinclair, RCAF, *pilot*
Sergeant Roland Hibbert, *navigator*
Flight Sergeant Harold "Chalky" White, *bomb-aimer*
Sergeant William Perkins, *flight engineer*
Sergeant Gordon Wallis, *wireless operator*
Sergeant Andrew Shaw, *mid-upper gunner*
Sergeant Tynan Marshall, RAAF, *rear gunner; replaced by*
   Sergeant Geoffrey Flynn

The Harker Crew

Flying Officer Neal Harker, *pilot*
Flight Lieutenant John Caldwell, *navigator*
Flight Sergeant Joseph Hobbs, *bomb-aimer*
Sergeant Raymond Mitchell, *flight engineer*
Sergeant Owen Bryce, *wireless operator*
and gunners

The Warren Crew

Flight Sergeant (later Pilot Officer) Christopher Warren,
   pilot
Warrant Officer Roger Birch, *navigator*
Sergeant Norman Sims, *bomb-aimer*
Sergeant Robert King, *flight engineer*
Sergeant Edward Buckman, *wireless operator*
Sergeant Martin Finch, *mid-upper gunner*
Sergeant Cornelius "Lo" Brand, RCAF, *rear gunner*
Sergeant Vernon Snook, *temporary rear gunner*

The Tuttle Crew

Pilot Officer Thomas J. Tuttle, *pilot*
Pilot Officer John Pitt, *navigator*

Sergeant Frederick Boxley, *bomb-aimer*
Flight Sergeant Ernest Crocker, *temporary flight engineer*
Sergeant Alistair MacRae, *wireless operator*
Sergeant Roy Gilpin, *mid-upper gunner*
Sergeant Sidney Partridge, *rear gunner*

and ...
Sergeant Gwyr "Taffy" Williams, *a bomb-aimer*
Sergeant Brian Stroud, *a pilot*
Flight Lieutenant Clifford Holden, *a pilot*
Flight Sergeant Philip Baldry, RAAF, *a gunner*
Flight Lieutenant Ronald Darby, *engineering officer*
Squadron Leader Victor Stevens, *"A" Flight Commander
    replacing* Fry
Flight Lieutenant Patrick Swann, *a pilot*
Aircraftman Bertram Snell, *a former gunner*

Administrative and
Ground Crew Personnel

Wing Commander Thorbert Davis, *squadron commander*
Squadron Leader Roderick Fawcett, *administrative officer*
Squadron Leader Simon Coombs, MC, *adjutant*
Flight Lieutenant Michael Coates, *medical officer*
Flying Officer Kenneth Freeman, *catering officer*
Flight Sergeant Percival Pudwell, "Chiefie" *in charge of "A"
    Flight aircraft maintenance*
Leading Aircraftman Nigel Slattery, *clerk*
Aircraftman Eric Shufflebotham, *batman*
Aircraftman Cyril Pollard, *batman*
Aircraftwoman Phoebe Webb, *clerk*
Aircraftwoman Beryl Phipps, *clerk*
Corporal Cuthbert Hardy, *leader of station dance orchestra*

Contents

The Flight Commander

DAWN BROKE WHILE THE BOMBERS WERE OVER THE North Sea on their way back to England. At first the light was timid and uncertain, slowly revealing the bombers as if in a poor black and white photograph, scores of them scattered about the sky, the loose cohesion of the stream abandoned as the coast appeared in the distance. The undersides of broad wings glinted dully. The aircraft descended. The crews could relax a little; the worst of the trip was over. Oxygen masks were unclipped; coffee flasks were passed around the draughty, trembling metal tubes of fuselages. Cigarettes were surreptitiously lit in machine gun turrets, the fag ends hidden in flying boots to be disposed of after landing.

Far behind the others two aircraft flew at sea level. Both were damaged. Feathered propellers stood silent and still before fire-blackened engines. Both aircraft bore the scars of flak and cannon. One, a Stirling, trailed an undercarriage leg like a wounded limb; fuel leaked from the trailing edge of the starboard wing in a fine mist. The second aircraft, a Halifax, flew with bomb doors agape, its tail unit a sorry assembly of buckled and battered metal and ripped fabric.

The two bombers had been limping homeward in the darkness, unaware of each other's presence until the first glimmer of light. The Halifax pilot, a twenty-four-year-old Squadron Leader by the name of Colin Fry, edged his aircraft closer to the Stirling. He gave the pilot an encouraging wave. He could see the fellow clearly, a slight figure in a brown flying jacket, his helmeted head straining forward as if urging his crippled mount to greater effort.

Colin Fry flipped his intercom switch.

"Tom, how's Len coming along?"

"He seems pretty comfortable, Skipper. The bleeding's stopped. He's swearing at me so I think he's feeling better."

"Coffee, Skipper?"

It was a well-established routine: Sam Cooper abandoned his radios to take the coffee flask to every member of the crew, from George Hall in the tail turret to Maurice Staples, the navigator, and Don Flinders, the bomb-aimer, both of them huddled in the narrow nose.

Tom Buckle, the flight engineer, burly in bulky flying gear, came forward to stand beside Colin in the tiny passageway beside the cockpit. He peered across the sea at the Stirling.

"I don't think he'll make it, Skipper."

Even the crackle of the intercom couldn't disguise Tom's Cornish twang.

The Stirling kept drifting, wobbling as it made its uncertain way home. The pilot was clearly having to work like the devil.

"More coffee, Skipper? There's a drop left."

Colin nodded. It was vile stuff as usual, but a treat after nearly eight hours without a drop of anything. His insides felt dry and dusty. He made a practice of touching nothing liquid for at least two hours before take-off on ops; it was just too much of a bind to relieve oneself in the air. He finished the coffee. He would be glad to get this trip over and done with. It had been one of the dicey ones. The fighter had caught them as they turned away from the target. He was a good shot, peppering the fuselage and wings. Within seconds they had lost two engines. The miracle was that no one was dead. Len's wound wasn't serious. Colin himself had had a close shave. A shell had torn through the fuselage just behind the cockpit. It had nicked his helmeted head, ripping through the leather earphone holder, failing to decapitate him by a mere centimetre or two. Lucky. Again. But he still had to get across the sea. He feared the sea. Always had. Huge and bloody merciless. And every op began and ended with endless treks across its malevolent expanses.

Tom caught Colin's sleeve. He pointed.

The Stirling was going down, half banking, half skidding.

"He's going in . . . ditching!"

Colin winced as he watched. Damn one's total inability to do a single thing except radio the position and hope that the message would get through to Air-Sea Rescue in time . . .

"Poor old bugger," commented Don Flinders from the nose. He was right; the Stirling did look old; a decrepit shell of its former self wearily looking for a place to die. Everyone pitied Stirling crews. Even Halifax crews.

The Stirling flattened out just above the water. Its great shadow danced across the restless surface of the sea. It started to turn back on to the course for home.

The end came quickly, suddenly. One wing struck the water; the big aircraft cartwheeled in an explosion of spray.

Colin turned and dived over the spot. Damn it, damn it, all he could do was watch the poor devils. A dinghy bobbed to the surface. But it was empty. A head appeared, an arm outstretched, reaching for the dinghy.

He passed over the crash site again. Just in time to see the front of the Stirling going down. And, God almighty, the pilot was still in there, trapped beneath the transparent canopy, struggling to escape, white face looking up, pleadingly, as the waters closed in on him . . .

The odd thing was, the reaction waited until later, after they had crossed the English coast near Hull and had traversed the quiltlike pattern of East Yorkshire's fields and had landed back at Rocklington. The orderlies had carted Len off to sick bay, assuring him and everyone else within earshot that the wound was minor and that Len was a lucky blighter. Then it was off to debriefing, to tell the intelligence bods all about the raid, about the weather and the flak, the fighter opposition, the accuracy of the Pathfinders' marking, the bombing... the Stirling.

It was during the post-op meal that it happened. He had been looking forward to having a snack before going to bed. He was hungry. Yet he managed only one bite. He couldn't swallow. The damned stuff lodged in his throat and he found himself thinking of that poor sod in the Stirling, trapped in the cockpit, the sea pouring in on him ...

He muttered something about having forgotten to attend to an important matter, got to his feet, hurried outside and was sick between two of the clustered Nissen huts. After the eruption he leant against the corrugated metal wall and savoured the cool morning air. His legs felt as if they had turned to rubber. His head pounded. His innards writhed. Damn it, he couldn't get the sight of that Stirling pilot out of his mind. What tortures did the wretch suffer in his last minutes? How long did it take him to die? He shook his head as if trying to dislodge the memories. He had seen plenty of men get the chop; once, during his first tour, he saw a man burn to death as he struggled to get out of the gun turret of a crashed Wellington. Horrible, but such things happened – although always to other fellows. It was the basic tenet of one's faith, the essential belief that enabled one to go out night after night to offer oneself as a target for flak and fighters.

He looked about. Thank God, no one in the immediate vicinity to witness his shame. Hell of an example, a Flight Commander heaving up behind the Officers' Mess. He dabbed at his battledress tunic. Did he feel better? He wasn't sure. Such a thing had never happened in two years of operational flying. His mouth tasted vile. He needed a glass of water. Cautiously he made his way around to the side door. He encountered no one until he got into the corridor leading to his room.

Simon Coombs, the Adj, materialized, pink and toothy as ever.

"Hullo, old chap. Heard you had a spot of bother."

"Nothing to speak of."

"They tell me Rawlings had to land somewhere in the south. Manston, I think. Hydraulics gone and almost out of juice. Good show for a young chap." The Adj wore RFC pilot's wings and had an inexhaustible fund of stories about the Western Front. "Ah, but Rawlings isn't in your Flight, is he? Of course not. Silly of me. Got them mixed up. They say the memory starts to go first," he added, his middle-aged choir-boy's face crinkling into a smile.

Colin said good night and headed for his room. You couldn't afford to let an exchange with the Adj die a natural death; you had to put it out of its misery.

The Adj waved a limp hand. "Good night, old man. Or rather, good morning."

Colin glanced down at his front as he walked away. Two or three suspicious-looking patches dotted his blouse. Did the Adj notice them?

He flopped onto his bed, but when he closed his eyes the room revolved about him. He opened his eyes and found his hand gripping the iron bedstead as if it were a lifebelt and he were trapped in that Stirling with that poor bastard. . . . He sat up and ran his hand through his hair. His innards quaked. He dragged himself to his feet and washed his face at the basin. His reflection was ghastly, a death-bed grey, with the oxygen mask still outlined on his cheek.

Shaken. That's what you are, he told his reflection, bloody shaken. Admit it. These things happen.

He took off his clothes and tossed them on a chair. Pollard would put them away later.

Muggles claimed you could only do so much operational flying before the stresses and strains started telling on you and it was time to stop. But some men could fly a hundred ops before getting the twitch; others could manage only a handful. The trouble with the twitch, he used to say, was that it forced you to realize what a sodding dangerous business flying was. Dear old Muggles with his funny ugly-yet-appealing face, his odd twisted grin, his rumpled uniform and his cap always stuck on the back of his head. A New Zealander, Muggles had been flying since the dark ages, the futile days of '39 and '40 when it was a major achievement for an RAF bomber to find its target at night let alone hit it. Bomber Command seemed to exist to bolster British morale more than to dismay the enemy. Posted to a Wellington squadron in Lincolnshire, Colin had found himself in the second pilot's seat next to Muggles. Muggles was his mentor; he taught Colin the tricks of the trade: how to maintain a gently weaving path over enemy territory, dipping your wings so that your gunners could spot any fighters coming up from below; how to time your run over the target to take advantage of other pilots' ill fortune; a favourite Muggles trick was to wait until the defenders' attention was concentrated on one hapless soul coned by the lights and then slip through. Muggles was dedicated to the proposition that to take anything for granted was to ask for it to go wrong. He knew as much about the Wimpy as the mechanics; he could handle the radio, he could manage the guns, he could navigate at least as well as most navigators on the squadron.

He had a theory that everyone started out on ops with a ration of luck. Lots for the lucky ones. A mere pinch for the unfortunates.

He also claimed that one knew when one's luck was running out. There were warning signs: twitches of the testicles and palpitations of the bowels.

Muggles's luck ran out one February night shortly after Colin had been promoted to command his own aircraft. Over the target Colin saw a Wimpy on fire. It broke up, a searing tangle of metal and fabric that went fluttering away into the darkness. Was it Muggles's kite? Possibly. A dozen Wimpies went missing that night. A couple of days later the Red Cross sent word that Flying Officer Clarence Potter – Muggles – and his crew had been killed and were buried at Nienburg. Why the nickname? Colin never knew. Muggles once claimed that it was a Maori name of admiration for warriors possessing appendages of magnificent proportions; another time he said it was an appellation bestowed by an instructor who described him as a muddled Biggles, hence Muggles.

Colin eyed his reflection. Pasty skin, dull eyes, a mouth that appeared to have slackened in the last couple of hours.

Was it the face of a man whose luck was running out?

The Flight Office door was stuck again. A couple of muscular airmen burst it open, ripping the lower hinge off the jamb. Hilariously good sport. It was their considered opinion that Colin should have the building demolished and a new Flight Office built replete with bar, cinema, and dance floor.

"Whole place is dangerously out of whack, sir," said Nigel Pettigrew.

"Definite bias to port," observed Venables, Pettigrew's navigator.

"Be glad to do the job with a couple of 250-pounders, sir," Pettigrew added.

"You couldn't hit it with a couple of hundred," someone said.

Air Ministry bulletins and posters papered the Flight Office walls; dusty black aircraft recognition models turned endlessly at the ends of lengths of thread. On one, a Manchester, someone had painted the legend PANTON'S PERIL. But no one remembered who Panton was or why his name was linked with the awful Manchester. He was just another of the passing parade of aircrew personnel. Even the lucky ones who survived their tours seldom stayed more than four or five months. Most crews were on the station a matter of weeks, in some cases just days. The only permanent residents were the administrative and ground staffs.

Colin sat down at his desk. He felt fragile. His head throbbed, his stomach stung as if he had been kicked. No ops tonight, thank God.

Without enthusiasm he tackled the serviceability reports, the memos, the bulletins, the infuriating and generally valueless bumph that filled his in-tray day after day.

But he worked only a few minutes on his paperwork.

"Morning, sir. I'm Sinclair."

A tall, well set-up fellow, Sinclair, in a well-tailored Pilot Officer's uniform with CANADA flashes on his sleeves. He had a lean, intelligent face and that air of easy confidence possessed by so many North Americans. He took a chair and relaxed at once, as if he was joining an old chum. None of that awkward, first-day-at-school, edge-of-the-chair business for friend Sinclair.

"Settled in?"

"Sure have, thanks."

"Quarters are a bit cramped, I'm afraid."

"No sweat . . . sir."

Sinclair and his crew had arrived the previous day. Sinclair was replacing Coburn who had bought the farm over Hamburg.

Colin glanced through Sinclair's log book. Elementary flying in Alberta, advanced work in Texas, then off to England for operational training and the gathering of a crew. A couple of "Above average" entries; small wonder he exuded confidence.

"What part of Canada do you come from?"

"Winnipeg, Manitoba . . . sir."

"How long have you been in England?"

"A little over three months." ·

"Terrible grub, what?"

"Sure as hell is."

With feeling.

"Some people say it was even worse in peacetime."

Sinclair grinned and accepted a Player's from Colin, producing an expensive-looking Ronson lighter.

Colin asked him about his crew. Great guys, all of them, was the response. Colin judged him to be the sort to have confidence in his crew for the simple reason that he picked them. Friend Sinclair trusted friend Sinclair's judgement. Sometimes sprog skippers came to the squadron full of doubts about navigators or gunners; such types seldom lasted long.

Colin gave him the standard introduction to the world of operational flying. The first few trips were critical, he explained, because it was during this time that a crew picked up the essentials of survival. Or didn't. Sinclair would go on a few "second-dickey" trips so that he might see how experienced crews coped. A dozen second-dickey rides were desirable but it was unlikely that he would get more than two or three; the war wouldn't wait. He concluded with the standard wise words about training, navigation exercises and fighter affiliation, dinghy drills and bombing practice, about the necessity for the crew to act as a team and not as seven individuals.

Sinclair kept nodding, taking it all in. A good sort by the look of him; it was to be hoped that he might be numbered among the lucky few who beat the odds and completed their tours. Not a single crew had reached the magic thirty in the last couple of months. Among the recent casualties were four crews who were on their last half-dozen ops. Which did little for morale. How much of his luck ration had Sinclair used up during his training? His log book didn't say; log books were notoriously lacking in such vital gen.

"Can I ask you something . . . sir?"

Sinclair had trouble remembering that "sir."

"Ask away."

"What's your honest opinion of the Halifax?"

"Why do you ask?"

"I've heard a lot of talk about structural failures, engine vibration trouble, flaming exhausts, all that kind of stuff. To tell you the truth I was kinda hoping I'd get posted to Lancs."

We all were, Colin thought. But he said:

"I think you'll find the Hally is a pretty good kite when you get to know her. She has her faults but so do all aeroplanes. The main thing to remember about the Hally is not to overdo the rudder at low speed, while corkscrewing, for example. The rudders lock, overpowering the ailerons, and you're into a spiral dive before you know it. Apart from that little idiosyncrasy, she's a good kite. Treat her well and she'll treat you well."

When all else fails fall back on clichés.

He wished Sinclair good luck. "Get your crew together and we'll do a little flying later on today."

Sinclair got up. "It was good talking with you, sir. One of the guys was saying you've done nearly a hundred ops."

"A bit of an exaggeration. I'm a dozen trips into my third tour." Between his second and third tours he had done a spell at Boscombe Down helping to find out why Halifaxes kept crashing without apparent cause. Unkind of the authorities to follow this up with a posting to a Halifax squadron.

Soon Sinclair's name would be added to the list of skippers on the Flight Office wall, the chalked names protected by a sheet of Perspex. God knows how many names had been there, to be wiped off when, in officialese, they failed to return – a curious expression, suggesting that it was their fault, a deliberate choice. Colin sighed. His stomach stung. He had spent the night dreaming of the sea splashing into his cockpit, rising, bubbling, the Stirling pilot beside him, struggling, his white face staring up, eyes imploring, hands reaching through the water, clutching for God knows what. What a hell of a way to die, gasping for air, lungs filling up with water ...

A skipper named Harker came to see him. Normally a cheerful chatterer, he was downcast, his voice not much more than a whisper.

"Sir ... it's about what the CO said."

"Which was?"

"He just about ... said I was a coward for returning to base last night."

Colin stared. "Didn't you have carburettor trouble and a coolant leak?"

"That's right, sir. The Engineering Officer examined the engines when we landed. He said if we'd gone on another fifty miles we'd have had a fire. I tried to explain it to the CO but he didn't give me a chance." The young man's voice was husky with emotion. "I didn't want to turn back but when Ray – that's Ray Mitchell, my flight engineer – when he said we simply wouldn't keep going much longer ... well, what choice did I have?"

Christ. Christ all-bloody Mighty.

Colin's headache became a pounding sledgehammer. Harker had had a rough tour so far; a few weeks before he had lost half his crew to a direct hit by flak, then one of the survivors refused to fly again.

"Leave it with me. You did the right thing – in fact, there wasn't anything else you could have done. All I can think is that the CO has got hold of some duff gen. I'll have a word with him, Neal. Don't worry about it."

When Harker had gone, Colin telephoned the CO. The Adj, Coombs, said he was in conference with the Station Commander. He would ring back.

"It's urgent," said Colin.

Damn him. Bloody career officer.

He had half a sandwich for lunch, some indefinable slice of something trapped between two chunks of bread and margarine. It lay in his stomach like a lump of lead as the crew van transported him to S-Sugar's dispersal. He felt slightly sick. The question was, did he feel slightly sick because of the luncheon sandwich or because of the imminent prospect of climbing back into an aeroplane? Who felt worse, the Flight Commander or the crew under scrutiny? Fortunately there was little to say. Sinclair proved to be a competent pilot and his crew seemed to have the makings of a good team. Colin had to meet them all: the diminutive but dapper Lancashire flight engineer, the self-possessed navigator, the wireless operator with the Cockney accent, the bomb-aimer, the gunners. They all regarded him with the same mixture of deference and envy, their eyes inevitably dropping to the ribbons beneath his pilot's wings. So this was the Squadron Leader Fry they'd all heard about. DSO and DFC and Bar. Two tours over and done with, another well along. Living proof that it was possible. You could see them wondering what it was that set this bloke apart from the rest. A large ration of luck, he wanted to tell them, but I think it may all be gone now . . .

The CO was sitting in Colin's office looking at an old copy of *Flight*.

"Heard you were in the circuit, old chap. So I popped over. You said you wanted to confer."

The CO had been putting on weight, which was probably why he never wore battledress these days. His dress uniform bulged about the middle, tugging at its brass buttons. A Cranwell type, a regular, the CO had spent the first three years of the war in Training Command. Since arriving at Rocklington he had flown on a handful of ops; no one expected him to do more; he was, after all, an ancient of nearly forty.

"Pleasant day, what. Bracing. Something about the Yorkshire air that agrees with me. Keeps me regular," he added with a chuckle. He had grown a moustache recently and he kept touching it as if to make sure it was still there.

"Neal Harker came to see me this morning."

"Harker. Yes, I had a word with him myself."

"He said you tore a hell of a strip off him."

The CO smiled and shook his head as if constantly perplexed by the peculiar reactions of people.

"Wouldn't say that, wouldn't say that at all. Merely getting a point across. These early returns are a vexing problem. The fact of the matter is, Group simply won't tolerate them."

"Harker had no choice."

"I wonder."

"I don't."

The smile didn't waver. "Look, old chap, I can understand how you feel. Your sympathies lie with your crews. Perfectly understandable. In fact, there'd be something wrong if that wasn't the case. But the statistics are alarming; and they're not getting better. Let me add that this unit's record is not impressive in that department. We simply can't have it, old chap."

"Harker did the right thing."

"Possibly."

"No doubt about it as far as I can see. Darby examined Harker's aircraft the moment he landed. He was in full agreement with Harker's actions. He said they would have had an engine fire if they had flown much longer."

"Darby could be wrong."

"Then what's the point of having an Engineering Officer? Why ask him if we doubt his opinion?"

At last the smile faded, leaving just the merest angling of the lip at one corner. The CO sighed. He lowered his voice. "Don't think for a moment that I enjoy this sort of thing. But Group is hounding me on this one. Absolutely hounding me. Demanding the most exhaustive report on every case. And if they're not totally satisfied they demand more information, numbers, records, every bloody thing. They pestered me about young Coburn. Great pile of bumph arrived yesterday. Demanding more gen. I sent it back and told them that Coburn had gone for a Burton over Hamburg. That should shut them up. For the moment at least."

He sounded like a sales manager who had cleverly side-stepped a complaint from head office. Colin shook his head. Regular officers saw everything in terms of their careers; ops and crews were just assets and liabilities. The only thing that mattered was how the numbers would look on their records when the time came for promotion and knighthoods.

"Harker did the right thing."

The CO stroked his prominent nose between thumb and forefinger as if shaping it. "Believe me, old chap, I understand how the men feel. I sympathize. In this business one's chances aren't encouraging even when things are working perfectly. So it's all too easy to convince oneself that an engine doesn't sound as healthy as it might. But it's a pattern we can't afford . . ."

"Would you rather Harker killed himself and his crew? Would that make the records look better?"

The CO looked pained. "It's an attitude that has to be inculcated in the chaps' minds. Take the last lot. Troops going over the top. Day after day. Couldn't let them go *back* to the trenches if they'd got a bit of mud in their rifles, could you? Same principle here. In a way. See what I mean, old man? Young Harker may be thoroughly cheesed off at me. No doubt he'll tell all his pals what a swine I am. Good. His pals will tell theirs. That old bugger of a CO won't tolerate early returns. Splendid. We're in a war and our job is to win it. Only the end matters. And as far as we're concerned the end is to get this squadron the best record in the Group. I won't be satisfied with anything less. I make myself clear?"

"I can't agree to treating aircrew like . . . *cannon fodder.*"

"Don't expect you to agree, old chap. That's why I didn't want to get you involved directly. Don't want to jeopardize your relations with your crews. Perfectly all right if they hate the sight of me. But not you." Another sigh. "Nasty, what? Command can be perfectly dreadful sometimes. Often envy junior officers. Blighters don't know how lucky they are." The smile returned. "You can tell Harker that no further action will be taken on this occasion . . . "

"Further *action* . . . ?"

The CO got to his feet. "Pleasant chatting with you. Always is. Good show last night, by the way."

The aircraft sat on its haunches, its blunt nose angled up as if to sniff at the air. In its original form the Halifax had possessed bluff, double-chinned good looks with a gun turret and a jutting bomb-aimer's blister. But in a desperate attempt to improve its performance the heavy front turret had been ripped out, the hole being faired over with sheet metal; the result was an abbreviated nose that some likened to that of a haughty camel. A new Halifax was said to be in the works with a redesigned nose, a bigger, safer tail section, and better engines; but it would be the autumn before the squadron would be re-equipped. A lifetime. Many lifetimes.

Colin watched Tom Buckle as he diligently checked that the pitot head cover and control locks had been removed, that the cowlings were secure, that the control surfaces were in good order, and that the tire tread was sound. He had handled the CO poorly. Didn't stand up to him, that was the truth of the matter. And in turn the CO had failed to stand up to those pompous sods at Group. And who suffered? The poor devils of aircrews, of course.

Chiefie Pudwell came wobbling along on his bicycle, a portly man with the purple-hued nose of the indefatigable drinker. In his deliberate way he leant his bike against the Halifax's tire before snapping to attention and saluting Colin.

"Just wanted to let you know, sir, we've given the 'ydraulics a real going-over. A bugger, some of them 'ydraulics jobs. Bloody isolating valves and accumulators. Mind you, 'ydraulics has been a weakness all along with the Hally."

"I'm sure we'll find everything on top line."

"You just let me know, sir, if you don't."

Chiefie Pudwell was responsible for the maintenance of the Flight's aircraft. He treated most of the aircrew as not very bright infants who should never be trusted with expensive aeroplanes, but in Colin's presence he positively oozed respect.

Tom emerged from beneath the fuselage.

"Everything okay?"

Tom nodded. "On top line, Skipper."

"Got your elastic wound up?" asked someone.

Tom ignored the crack.

One by one Colin's crew squeezed up through the hatchway in the rear of the fuselage. The narrow metal tubular body possessed its own aroma: aluminum, oil, and fuel, subtly combined with a dash of sweat and a drop of fear. You had to clamber uphill as you made your way forward, pushing past ammunition tracks, flares, oxygen and nitrogen bottles, hydraulic pumps, tank valves, the mid-upper turret. Colin eased himself into the pilot's seat. It was warm; the sun had been shining since noon, and some nitwit had closed the sliding window panel at his left shoulder. In the nose compartment Maurice, the navigator, was complaining that he couldn't find the correction card; Sam Cooper found it stuck beside his radio set.

Colin fastened his harness. His innards stirred uneasily. Where was the delight he had once known in preparing an aircraft for flight? Had he simply done it all too many times? Or was this another sign of a running-out of luck? Automatically his eyes roved the instrument panel. Blind flying panel, engine gauges, throttles – great tubular projections that looked as if they had been borrowed from a railway signal box – propeller speed controls, mixer, superchargers. Flap and bomb door levers at his right hand, neatly positioned side by side for maximum confusion. It seemed not to occur to the designers that someone might have to select the correct lever rapidly in an emergency: bomber pilots didn't always have time to look down and make sure which lever was which.

Beside him, Tom Buckle planted himself on the jump seat hinged to the starboard side of the fuselage. An ample type, Tom, with the ruddy glowing face of the countryman; incongruously he possessed a tiny button of a nose.

Up front, Maurice was telling Don what was wrong with the capitalist system. Maurice never discussed; he declaimed. He intended to be a teacher after the war. Through the side window Colin could see Chiefie Pudwell and a couple of erks standing, hands on hips, gazing up at the Hally. One yawned.

Tom was rendering "Three Blind Mice" between his teeth, a sort of hiss-cum-whistle. A cheerful type, Tom. All the crew were. Poor bastards, they considered themselves lucky to have crewed up with him; if anyone could get them through their tour it was him. Fry, the expert, the skilled practitioner of the strange form of Russian roulette practised by Bomber Command, in which the crews strapped themselves into flimsy metal vehicles overloaded with thousands of gallons of fuel and tons of bombs and ammunition, and took off to fly into enemy territory to be fired at both from the ground and from the air. You won the game if you could drop your bombs before the enemy knocked you out of the sky.

He taxied the Hally clear of the dispersal, turning on the perimeter track. The control column vibrated gently in his hand. This morning's clouds had dispersed; a perfect summer's day.

He waited beside the runway while another aircraft landed, bumping gently from main wheels to tailwheel and back again.

A burst of power dislodged the Hally once more. Colin taxied onto the black strip that stretched away, disappearing from view over the slight hump in the middle of the field.

"Pilot to crew, stand by for take-off."

Did his voice tremble just a little? He felt as if something was nibbling away at his vitals.

His right hand eased the four throttle levers forward. The aircraft trembled like a hound straining at its leash. He released the brakes and pushed the throttles all the way, leading with the left-hand levers to counteract the Hally's tendency to swing to port during the take-off run. The runway began to unroll before him, slowly at first, then with increasing speed. The sun sparkled on the cockpit canopy. Tom's hands hovered behind his own, ready to take over the throttles if the vibration made them slip back during the take-off run. Bomb bays empty, the bomber picked up speed rapidly. The tail rose. Colin left the throttles to Tom. Now he could steer with the rudders, the notorious rudders that were such an aid and comfort to the enemy . . .

The white strips in the centre of the runway became a solid line; the Hally's nose gobbled it up. Gentle back pressure on the control column; a touch of rudder. The runway fell away.

"Undercart up," he ordered, touching the brake lever to stop the wheels turning as they disappeared into the nacelles.

Whereupon the dinghy suddenly popped out of its compartment in the port wing, its hatch cover whirling away in the slipstream.

Then, while Colin was still reacting to the sudden departure of the dinghy, the port engine stopped with a bang and a streak of flame. The aircraft lurched, abruptly robbed of power and lift when both were most needed.

There followed a succession of oddly extended moments. Moments of clutching controls and thrusting levers, moments in which instinct seemed to play the dominant role. It was almost as if he were observing someone else wrestling the Hally back onto an even keel and getting it to return to the runway in one piece. The crew considered it a splendid show, further proof of their skipper's matchless skill and complete indestructability. Magnificent airmanship, said the CO. An example to one and all.

Colin and the crew took up another aircraft for a night-flying test but the op was scrubbed before briefing. They got out of their flying gear and went to the camp cinema to see *Destry Rides Again* with James Stewart and Marlene Dietrich. Colin had to leave the cinema halfway through the performance to be sick on the camp vegetable garden.

Colin made his way along the cinder path toward the cluster of wooden huts at the north side of the airfield. He wondered if he should go and see Coates, the MO. He felt wobbly and fragile. Had Muggles felt similarly wobbly and fragile during his last days? Was it a symptom of a dwindling supply of luck? The near-thing of the previous day kept haunting him; they had all come within a hairsbreadth of getting the chop. A split second more and it would have been too late. Lucky. Damned lucky. Was that the last bit of luck being used up? As yet the experts hadn't explained why the engine stopped and the dinghy popped out. They were working on it, they said. He sighed. Once he had been able to accept the inevitable dangers of operational flying with equanimity. No more. Was that another symptom of running out of luck? Or was it guts that he was running out of? A dwindling of intestinal fortitude?

As a Flight Commander Colin was expected to pay regular visits to the NCO aircrew quarters. To hear their complaints. To answer their questions. To show that he cared. Usually it was a duty that he enjoyed. The NCOs were good company and invariably had a cup of cocoa to offer him. Why was it that today he found the prospect of visiting the NCOs such a bind, an onerous duty to be completed as rapidly as possible? Yet another symptom of diminishing luck?

The NCO aircrew occupied wooden huts with half a dozen bunks on either side and a solitary stove to provide heat. In the winter the NCOs complained about the draughts and the damp.

They had a new complaint.

"Bloody rodents," said a gunner, a ginger-haired fellow with a peppering of freckles on his snub nose. "They're taking over, sir."

"What sort of rodents?"

"Mice. Little brown buggers."

"I saw a rat. Dirty grey colour. Nose like a Heinkel III."

"One of them ran by when I was in the bog this morning. Plump sod, he was."

Colin promised to have someone investigate.

The flight engineer in Cliff Holden's crew, a Flight Sergeant named Crocker, complained that the workmen who were putting up new billets nearby made too much noise early in the morning.

"It's not bleedin' fair, not when you've been out on ops all bleedin' night. Some noisy bugger wakes you up at seven o'clock shouting to his mate about bleedin' mortar or wood or something."

"I'll take it up with the Admin Officer."

Jutting jaw. "You said you'd do that last time."

"And I did . . ."

"Didn't seem to do much bleedin' good, did it?"

Colin had to agree. He felt stupid and witless – at a loss for words. Why did they have to make him a Flight Commander? Some people commanded instinctively. Some didn't. Colin knew in which category he belonged.

Lamely he told Crocker he would do what he could.

The Flight Sergeant didn't bother to thank him. You could see the contempt in the man's eyes; he made some comment about it being nice and quiet in the officers' quarters, he bet.

An Aussie named Baldry saved the day.

"Hear you've been pushing your luck, sir."

"Not intentionally, I can assure you."

"Take it easy, will you? Bloody bind having to break in a new Flight Commander."

It was a relief to get out of the billet. What a bloody awful leader he was. Why didn't they sack him and get someone the men could respect?

"Skipper?"

Don Flinders came hurrying after him, light brown hair flopping across his forehead.

"Could I have a word, please?"

"Of course."

"It's a . . . it's a *personal* thing." The young bomb-aimer looked away, cheeks pinkening. "I wanted to know how you'd feel about . . . "

"About what?"

"About having a married man in your crew."

"Married? You?"

The pink turned to tomato red.

"No . . . no, we're not married . . . yet."

"But you're thinking about it."

"Yes."

"Seriously?"

"Quite seriously, sir."

"You kept very quiet about it."

"It . . . well, it only just sort of . . . happened. The thing is, I'm not going to get married if you or the others say no. You know, some skippers feel strongly about married men in their crews."

Colin nodded. Such skippers reasoned that a man on ops had enough to worry about without a wife and babies and rent and God knows what else. But the real reason was the upsetting of the delicate equilibrium of the crew, with who knew what awful consequences. A rapid consumption of the crew's supply of luck, for example.

"Have you talked to any of the boys about it?"

"No sir. And if anyone objects we'll wait."

"Wait?"

"Until we've finished our tour."

Marvellous, his confidence. Not a doubt in his mind that they would get through the tour safe and sound with the redoubtable Squadron Leader Fry in the pilot's seat. Colin wished he shared Don's confidence.

"Please accept my congratulations, old man."

Nods and awkward shuffling of feet. "Thanks, sir . . . and you'll talk to the others, will you?"

"I promise. Who's the lucky lady?"

"A WAAF, sir. Stationed here at Rocklington. In Sick Quarters. Phoebe Webb. We've got a lot . . . in common."

"I'm sure you have."

He walked back to the Flight Office. Damn command. It meant having people depending on you. Flying Officer Harker and now young Don. And no doubt he would fail Don just as he failed Harker.

A pilot named Stroud went off in Y-Yorker to practise evasive tactics with Spitfires from Church Fenton. Fighter affiliation was the official term. It was considered good sport to take Air Training Corps cadets on such trips, for it was a rare stomach that could retain its contents when the Hallies went into their corkscrewing manoeuvres.

It was as well that Stroud took no ATC lads on that particular trip. It ended after fifteen minutes when Y-Yorker spun vertically into a beet field a couple of miles outside the village.

Colin went to the crash site in an ambulance. But there wasn't much to see. The bomber and its crew had been reduced to a pathetic collection of fragments.

"Rotten luck, buying the farm like that," observed the Station Commander. "Can't imagine what happened."

Colin could. Most of the port rudder had been found a mile away, suggesting that it broke away during the corkscrewing, just as test kites had broken up at Boscombe. Bloody overbalanced rudders; the same old dismal story. All the tests proved that the average service pilot stood a distressingly good chance of killing himself and his crew if he followed recommended evasive procedures. How many poor devils had heard the shout "Corkscrew!" from one of the gunners, had slammed the throttles shut on one side, simultaneously applying full rudder and diving, then rolling to the other side and climbing, only to plunge again in the original direction a moment later . . . and had ended up in an uncontrollable spiral dive? It was all because of speed. At less than about 120 mph the rudder completely overpowered the ailerons. How many Jerry fighter pilots had watched in astonishment as their prey fell to bits without a shot having been fired?

Pilot Officer Tuttle was a problem. Bad luck followed him around like an ill-tempered barracuda. On his first second-dickey trip he managed to catch the valve of his Mae West, inflating the thing during the take-off run. He completed the op but the MO grounded him with a cracked rib. He was no sooner back on flying status than he destroyed the Station Warrant Officer's greenhouse. It wasn't exactly his fault, but it was typical Tuttle. Coming in to land after a night cross-country, he encountered an errant patch of mist over the threshold of the runway, a not unknown phenomenon in that part of Yorkshire adjoining the Wolds. Levelling out, flaps and undercart down, Tuttle saw another aircraft hurtling at him out of the mist. Tuttle's reactions were rapid, commendably rapid. He threw the Hally out of the way, slamming on full power. It could hardly have been done better. Indeed, Tuttle's splendid reactions probably saved the aircraft from total destruction. But they didn't save the SWO's greenhouse. A wing-tip smashed through it, ripping the roof to bits, scattering shards of glass and slices of tomato in every direction. There was no doubt that Tuttle could handle himself in an emergency. But in this case there was no emergency. The lights that Tuttle had seen hurtling at him were his own, reflected in the mist. Only a few days later a propeller sheared while he was taking off. The blade scythed through the port outer engine and part of the wing, setting off a raging inferno. Again, Tuttle was to be commended for getting the aircraft down in one piece without killing anyone. His navigator broke his arm in his haste to get out of the wreck. His rear-gunner developed an acute case of the shingles.

"Simply a spot of bad luck," said Tuttle. He looked about fourteen. Put an Eton collar on him and you could lose him among the grammar school boys in the village.

He spoke casually about luck, as if it was something to do with chance and fate. The poor devil still didn't know that it was a resource to be husbanded with the utmost frugality. Colin sent him on seven days' leave.

Tuttle was dismayed; he looked as if he had been told he couldn't play rugby for the First Fifteen. "But, sir, I just got here. I really don't want to go on leave, not until I've put in some operational time."

Colin wanted to tell him not to be so eager. But instead he said it was a firm squadron rule to give a pilot a few days' rest after any experience that might be termed harrowing.

"But I really don't feel I *need* to rest, sir."

But we do, Colin was tempted to reply.

He saw Coates that evening in the Mess turning the pages of *Punch*, his thin lips cracking into an occasional frosty smile.

"I understand you have a WAAF named Phoebe Webb working for you."

"Webb?" A nod and a narrowing of the eyes behind those rimless glasses. "What about her?"

"A chap in my crew is thinking of marrying her."

"Really?" The MO shook his head as if he considered the notion outlandish. He was only a year or two older than most of the aircrew, but he seemed middle-aged with his spectacles and his thinning hair. "She hasn't said anything to me about it."

"I think it's still in the planning stages."

"Ah." Coates's eyes narrowed again. He peered at Colin. "You look tired. Having trouble sleeping?"

"None at all. Sleep like a top."

"I can give you something to help you sleep."

"No need of it. Thanks anyway."

Why this refusal to admit to a problem? Was poor sleep something to be ashamed of?

Oddly enough, he fell asleep quickly that night. But he

woke early, before dawn. He had been dreaming that he was in a fun fair, fastened to a huge iron wheel. The wheel revolved at a deliberate pace, squeaking, groaning. At first he was in total darkness, then he was in daylight. And half a dozen idiots were blazing away at him with rifles. He woke up. Another stupid dream. A memory of Muggles must have triggered it. Muggles likened operational flying to being a moving target at a fun-fair rifle range. No sharpshooter was fast enough to knock down every target that passed his rifle's sights. It was the same with bombing. Send a solitary bomber to Cologne and it stood an excellent chance of being shot down. But send a thousand and most of them would get through. Swamp the defences. Push forty bombers through every minute, a thousand in twenty-five minutes. Far too many for the searchlights, the flak and the fighters. You could therefore guarantee that the majority of bombers would escape the defenders. But what you couldn't guarantee was which bombers would be the lucky ones and which the unlucky.

Stroud's parents arrived on the 10:42 from York.

Pale-faced, middle-aged folk with moist eyes and uncertain lips, they looked dully at the airfield and the aircraft and the hordes of young men and women in air force blue. Were they looking for their son? Did they still secretly cling to the hope that it was all a ghastly mistake and that he would suddenly break into view and come running to them and ask them what they were doing here?

The Adj shepherded the Strouds about, making the necessary introductions. He was good at it; he'd had practice.

"Squadron Leader Fry was your son's Flight Commander."

"You knew him well, then."

Stroud's father spoke in a monotone, like a bad actor.

"Yes, we . . . all liked him so much." Colin tried – and failed – to recall Stroud's face.

"It was an accident, then."

Mr Stroud sounded as if he had uttered the statement a thousand times in the past few days.

"I'm afraid so, one of those totally unpredictable things that happen in wartime no matter how diligently everyone tries to avoid them."

His Hally's tail broke off because someone in a design office didn't do his sums properly.

"It wasn't something Brian did wrong, then." Mr Stroud ran a finger inside his stiff white collar. "He worked so hard at his flying. It was what he'd always wanted to do. He was so proud when they accepted him for pilot training . . . and when he got his wings I remember it was a bitterly cold day in the winter but he wouldn't wear his greatcoat; it would hide his wings, you see. What was it that . . . went wrong?"

"I'm afraid I can't divulge the details, Mr Stroud. Security, you know. Secret equipment."

"Did he suffer?" Stroud's mother asked the question, her soft brown eyes pleading.

"It was over in a flash," Colin assured her. "I shouldn't think any of them had time to know what was happening."

Except, he thought, for the lifetime it took the Hally to spin in minus fin and rudder. What did Stroud and his crew think about as they watched the earth revolving, rushing closer and closer?

"And this is Phoebe." Face pinkening, Don held the girl's arm as if determined never to let go. He cast a quick, slightly self-conscious glance across the crowded Saloon Bar of The White Rose, then at the members of the crew jammed around the tiny circular table, finally at Phoebe herself, his pleasant, open features becoming even pinker, until he looked as if he had been left out too long in the sun. "And this unruly mob is the crew . . . not the Skipper, of course, he's never unruly."

She smiled and extended a hand. "Hullo, sir."

Colin said it was a pleasure to meet her. It was. An unusually attractive girl, young Phoebe, with thick black hair and intense jade eyes. Her broad, good-humoured mouth was set in a chin that combined delicate form with determined angle.

Don held his arm out like a ringmaster at the circus. "And this is Maurice Staples, our navigator. An Oxford type.

Always spouting Latin and Greek to make the rest of us feel ignorant."

"And succeeding brilliantly," Maurice murmured.

"Tom Buckle is our flight engineer. He has the loudest snore on the squadron. Sam Cooper is our wireless operator. You'll see him running around the peri track in his underwear sometimes."

"Just keeping fighting fit – and it's not my underwear, it's my athletic attire, I'll have you know."

"George Hall sits in the tail turret and falls asleep. He's a beer-swilling reprobate, a danger to every unmarried girl in Yorkshire."

"And a lot of married ones too," muttered someone.

Bert O'Connor, a diminutive Liverpudlian with a great explosion of ginger hair, was the new mid-upper gunner, the replacement for Len Hodgkins who was recuperating from his arm wound.

It was a pleasant party. George recounted improbable tales of his cousin Albert's experiences as a burglar in Plymouth. Tom did his imitation of George Formby. Sam had brought Susie, a WAAF from the parachute section, who giggled. The White Rose filled up; the air became layered with tobacco smoke. Air force personnel outnumbered civilians four to one.

Colin found himself sitting next to Phoebe while Maurice – who tended to carp after a drink or two – declared that the endless delays in opening the Second Front were part of Churchill's and Roosevelt's cynical plans: "Sit back while the Russians and Germans destroy each other, wipe each other out . . . then we'll stroll in and pick up the pieces."

"Sounds like a bloody good idea," commented Sam.

Quietly yet earnestly, Phoebe told Colin how glad she was that Don was flying with such an experienced skipper. Her steady gaze was a command to bring her fiancé back safe and sound.

"He said he asked you if you minded having a married man on your crew. Some skippers are against it, aren't they?"

"So I'm told. Superstitious nonsense."

Like believing that people possess finite amounts of luck. The idiocy of such beliefs was directly proportional to the amount of bitter one had consumed. Just as one's confidence in oneself was directly proportional to one's proximity to this delicious creature with the eyes that seemed to promise so much.

"Did you and the crew have a conference?"

"About what?"

She grinned. "About Don getting married."

He nodded. "They all thought it was a good thing. It might get his mind back on his job."

For a moment she took him seriously; a shadow touched her brow. Then she laughed and the laugh carved neat little dimples on either cheek. She had a way of looking at you when you spoke that seemed to say that she found your words to be among the most profound utterances of our time. And gazing into those superb eyes made you think of desertion and finding thatched cottages to hide in.

"How long have you been in the WAAFs?"

"Six months."

"Do you like your work?"

"Not much. I'm just a clerk really. But I suppose it's important in its own way. Not like your work of course."

"I'm a chauffeur, that's all. Don's the only one who really matters. He drops the bombs."

"You're very nice," she said. "Are you engaged? Or anything?"

"Not even anything."

She clicked her tongue. "Shame."

Maurice informed Don that the Skipper was trying to steal his girl.

Damn Maurice for telling the truth.

He knocked. His mother opened the door. Her eyes lit up when she saw him; what a marvellous surprise; she had no idea he was coming home on leave.

"This is Phoebe," he said.

"How do you do, Phoebe," said his mother, shaking her

hand. "Please come in. I'm happy to welcome you to our home."

His father met them in the hall, pipe in mouth, newspaper in hand.

"We've deserted," said Colin.

"What? Both of you?"

"Both of us. Silly, flying all over the place and getting shot at. No future in it. So we got married and came here."

"We've got your room ready. What time would you like your morning cup of tea?"

"Half-past seven. No . . . dash it all, one doesn't get married every day. Eight o'clock and not a moment before!"

"Henceforth it shall be known as Muggles," she said when they were in bed and wrapped in each other's arms.

"Whatever made you pick that name?"

"It appeals to me. And *it* appeals to me, therefore it's an eminently suitable name."

He laughed. He was still laughing when they came bursting in, the service police with their side arms drawn.

And Don, with a rifle and fixed bayonet.

Quivering with fury, cheeks crimson, eyes full of hate.

He lunged – but the bedroom door opened and took the bayonet, snapping it off at the hilt.

Colin's father entered carrying a tray with tea things.

"What the devil are all of you doing in here?"

"Morning, sir. Ops are on."

Pollard materialized, prim little smile pasted on his doleful features.

The usual flurry of night-flying tests, of urgent conferences with Chiefie Pudwell about the port outer on B-Beer and the electrical problems with L-London's bomb-release mechanism. Too much waiting. Too much thinking. Another round of Russian roulette, Bomber Command-style. Play the game long enough and you were bound to lose. The odds had to catch up with you. No wonder some men were obsessed by statistics. The squadron was currently losing aircraft and crews at an average rate of 3.1 per cent per operational sortie. But some targets were more costly than others. In May, 3.6 per cent losses could be expected on Düsseldorf trips. Essen was currently costing an average of 4.15 per cent, down a few precious percentage points from April. If you were a navigator, gunner, wireless operator, engineer, or bomb-aimer you had a 19.8 per cent chance of surviving in the event your aircraft was shot down. But if you were a pilot, your chances were only 9.78 per cent. A sprog crew had slightly more than one chance in five of coming back from their first half-dozen ops; if they got through a dozen, however, the odds of their completing the tour jumped to one in three.

Old Friend Fear started prodding and probing during briefing. The Intelligence Officer – "Dim" to the crews – rambled on about the defences of Gelsenkirchen. Memories flooded back, unbidden, unwanted. Burning aircraft. Mid-air collisions. Men tumbling to certain death. Old terrors that had lain dormant for years, springing up like frightful corpses in a horror film. He felt the sweat beading his body; his shirt clung to him like an offensive second skin.

God, how many times did he have to listen to Dim on the Ruhr? He knew the place all too bloody well: the hundreds of searchlights, the flak emplacements, the industrial haze that obscured the targets, forcing you to drop your bombs on flickering flares as you hoped that they were the ones dropped by the Pathfinders and not decoys set off by the Jerries . . .

The CO got up to nag everyone for the umpteenth time about the unsavoury subject of "creepback" and how it was every crew's duty to push on all the way to the aiming point, resisting the despicable temptation to dump the load early and get out of the target area . . .

At last the briefing was over. A brisk "Good luck, chaps!" from the Station Commander, and the crews filled out on their way to the Crew Room.

"Phoebe thought you were smashing, Skipper." Don beamed. "Easy to talk to, that's what she said."

"I liked her too."

"Did you, Skipper? I thought you did. Super girl, isn't she?"

If Don had been a puppy his tail would have wagged like a windscreen wiper gone mad.

"Will you be able to come to the wedding, Skipper?"

"I sincerely hope so."

The crew van arrived to take them out to the aircraft. It was still daylight, a gentle evening with a warm breeze, an evening meant for cricket on the village green and snogging in haystacks, not clambering into bombers and setting off to be shot at.

"It'll be in September, I think," said Don.

"What will?"

"The wedding."

"Of course."

He followed the others into the van: seven young men and their assorted appurtenances – navigation satchels, parachutes, helmets, oxygen masks – and George's .38 Smith and Wesson; George always took it on ops, insurance against the day when he might be on the run in Injun country. The van set off with a creaking of weary springs.

"Haven't seen that one before," commented George, nodding meaningfully towards the driver's compartment. "Lovely pair on her. Did you notice?"

"Bloody hard to miss 'em," sniffed Tom.

"I could get into a lot of trouble over *them*. I wonder what her name is."

"Circe," said Maurice.

"Bloody funny name."

"It's Greek."

"She doesn't look Greek to me."

Maurice smirked in Colin's direction, a we-officers-get-the-joke-don't-we smirk.

The Halifax, O-Orange, awaited them, broad black wings outstretched, bomb doors agape, motionless propellers looking too frail to move this monster.

Colin breathed deeply of the evening air. His legs felt

rubbery; perhaps it was nothing to do with luck or guts, perhaps he was simply sickening for something. Hell of an irony if one survived two and a half tours only to expire of natural causes in one's so-called prime.

The sun-warmed fuselage was clammy; he sweated freely as he settled himself into the pilot's seat and fastened his harness. Tom squatted on the jump seat beside him, puffing as if he had been for a run. On the ground, in summer, flying togs could be a curse.

The starboard inner wouldn't start.

While they laboured to coax the recalcitrant engine into life, the bombers emerged from every corner of the field, waddling like overfed birds, undercarriages straining beneath their burden. More than one gunner sat on the edge of the mid-upper escape hatch enjoying a few minutes' fresh air before take-off. The bombers assembled at the runway, a great line of them, their propellers dicing the fading light.

O-Orange's engine still refused to start. Sweating, scrambling, the crew transferred to the spare aircraft, G-George. The first of the squadron's bombers were already taking to the air.

Colin and Tom ran through the checklist while they taxied G-George out to the runway, hurrying along the peri track to catch up with the others. A tricky business, taxiing rapidly; it was all too easy to let a wheel run off the concrete and get stuck in the soft, rain-soaked grass on either side.

"Skipper."

Colin turned. Tom's eyes were dark with foreboding.

"What's up?"

"I've left the garter in O-Orange."

Colin shrugged. What did Tom think could be done about it? Taxi all the way back to O-Orange's dispersal to get a bloody garter? The war wouldn't wait. Tom shook his head as he peered back. He looked like a man who had abandoned all hope. According to Tom, the garter was a gift from a Windmill girl, a lovely creature with a saucy smile and a shape that would drive a man mad. The garter had accompanied the crew on every op, dangling from a fuel pump lever. It was

Tom's amulet, his good luck charm. It had brought him safely through a dozen trips; now it was in one Hally while the crew set off in another.

Colin cursed. One damned thing after another. Don talking about getting married, now Tom and his bloody garter . . . and the inexplicable case of the collywobbles . . . and this strange kite that rattled as it trundled along the peri track. Something was loose behind the cockpit. There had been no time to check the aircraft as thoroughly as good sense dictated.

The other aircraft had already gone.

But the usual assembly of well-wishers still stood beside the runway.

"She's there!" Don cried.

Indeed she was, pretty as the proverbial picture, hatless, dark hair bobbing in the wind, waving with both arms. Colin stuck his left arm out of the window and wagged it in reply.

"You've got a green," Tom announced, voice flat and tight.

"Pilot to crew, stand by for take-off. All clear at the rear end, George?"

"All clear, Skipper."

The usual tension of total absorption; too busy for funk right now. Time enough later.

Power on, building against the brakes, the bomber shivering, trembling, eager to be on its way. Brakes off. With a sigh the bomber began to roll, weighed down by its huge burden of bombs and fuel. It would need every foot of the 6,125 feet of runway that stretched ahead, disappearing over the hump in the middle of the field.

The damned rattling started again as the bomber began to pick up speed. A spot more throttle on the port side to keep the kite heading straight. It sounded as if half a dozen pots and pans were bouncing about under the flight engineer's station.

The tail had just begun to rise when the port outer cut.

The Hally veered; the runway came angling like a knife edge. Wrench the kite back with brake and rudder. A thump and a rattle and the kite swung off the active runway.

"Lost an engine," he reported. "Stand by." Anyone would think the poor sods had any choice. What the hell was wrong with the squadron's engines these days?

He caught Tom's eye. Odd expression. As if he had known that there would be trouble; it was all due to the missing garter.

Balls, Colin told himself. Several times in a row.

He taxied back toward the hangars. He brought the aircraft to a squeaking halt.

A van appeared; an officer and a couple of erks jumped out, gawking, pointing at the port outer's stationary propellers as if they had never seen one before. Heart trying to thump its way out of his chest. Sweat pouring out of him as if he'd just done the hundred yards. Hands not quite steady on the controls. Was this sort of thing that happened when your luck started running out? To hell with luck.

"Let's give it another try."

No response. Tom took a deep breath.

With a bang and a puff of smoke the port outer started.

No time to wonder why it had cut on the take-off run. Pressures okay. Mags okay.

"We'll make it this time," he told the crew.

"Promise?" grunted someone.

He taxied back to the runway. It was empty and quiet now. An immediate green from the control van.

"Pressures still okay," Tom reported without enthusiasm. Full power.

A frenzy of clattering to the rear; had someone stowed a set of drums back there? Before him the needles shivered in a couple of dozen gauges. Engines sounding healthy enough.

Tail up. Steer with rudders now. Tom was clutching the throttles, his mouth set in a tight-lipped line, head angled back a little, as if he anticipated a sudden stop.

The trees came bounding, growing in the windscreen. Engines still bellowing away. Steady easing back of the control column. Up and away. The runway fell behind. Trees merged with the lengthening shadows. The village slid beneath the port wing.

"Undercart up."

Then the flaps, a few degrees at a time, exchanging lift for airspeed.

Tom busied himself with the isolating cock and the mechanical locks.

The rest of the squadron aircraft had disappeared from view; the leaders would already be over the sea, the crews taking their last looks at the English coast and trying not to wonder whether they would see it again.

Damn the port outer; it kept slipping out of synch, creating an odd pulsating tone to the din of the engines. What's more, the bloody thing was delivering something less than full power, although the gauges indicated normal pressures and temperatures.

There was none of the usual post-take-off chit-chat on the intercom. The crew's uneasiness was almost palpable.

The earth disappeared beneath a layer of wispy cloud; the aircraft wobbled. The sky was assuming a pretty, pinkish hue; the clouds in the distance looked as if they had had their undersides painted.

"It's working, that's all you can say for the sod," commented Tom from the engineer's compartment behind the cockpit. "Could be a gasket or a seal, something like that."

"Is it going to keep going for us?"

"Couldn't say, Skipper. It might. It might not. You can never tell."

Please conk out now, Merlin, so that we might go home with clear consciences. Why the hell did you start up again after conking out the first time? No sign of any other aircraft.

"Pilot to navigator. If we stay at this speed how late will we be at the target?"

"Twelve minutes, give or take thirty seconds or so," Maurice answered.

"That'll put us right under the Lancs," put in Sam Cooper.

"I'm aware of that," said Colin.

A nice prospect, arriving at Gelsenkirchen just as the

Lancs were unloading from their lofty perches. A month ago a Hally had returned to Rocklington with an enormous hole in the fuselage and part of the wing. A Lanc's 2,000-pounder had hit it fair and square. How the aircraft remained in one piece was beyond anyone's comprehension. The Hally might possess fatal flaws and might be a heavy lump of an aeroplane to fly, with a pathetic operational ceiling, but it did possess a fair degree of structural strength.

The cloud cleared. The sea was a sheet of smoky glass.

"Grimsby coming up," reported Don from the nose.

If you're going to conk out, Merlin, for God's sake do it now.

Every few seconds the engine seemed to miss half a beat, then try to catch up. Colin kept adjusting the throttles and trim. But, blast it, it kept going.

The light was fading fast. Purple intermingled with the pink, worming its way through the texture of the sky.

The gunners tested their weapons, firing short bursts into the gathering darkness. Their Brownings were no match for the 20 mm cannon carried by the Jerry night-fighters. Rumour had it that the Jerries would soon be carrying 30 mm weapons; a single hit from one of those aerial blunderbusses would blow a Hally apart. One wondered at the celerity with which Fighter Command's aircraft had been equipped with cannon when the Battle of Britain revealed the inadequacy of their .303 machine guns. But no one in high places seemed to give a damn about the inadequacies of the guns on board Bomber Command's aircraft.

The last glimmers of daylight faded high in the heavens.

He checked on the crew. Everyone responded. No one had fallen asleep or passed out due to lack of oxygen.

Old Friend Fear sat beside him, keeping him supplied with disquieting memories, a pageant of disasters, lest he forget for a moment how good were his chances of getting killed.

The minutes ticked by, every one bringing the enemy coast three miles nearer.

Night cloaked the land ahead. The rest of the squadron's

Hallies were somewhere in that darkness, slogging their way to the target. The Lancs were probably right overhead, but so far he hadn't seen any.

"Any good news on the port outer, Tom?"

"No better, Skipper."

"No worse?"

"No worse."

"Enemy coast in ten minutes," Maurice reported.

A thin layer of cloud had formed. Nasty stuff, thin cloud. When the searchlights played on the underside of the layer they created a semi-translucent surface against which the bombers were silhouetted, lethally visible to the high-flying night-fighters. *Please, God, make the cloud disappear over the target. And please, God, make sure the fighter controllers are too busy worrying about the main force to concern themselves about the progress of a single Halifax. Do these things, God, so that we may drop high explosives and incendiaries upon the citizens of a city called Gelsenkirchen.*

Swaying searchlights ahead, like luminous bullrushes in the sky.

Colin cursed himself for not abandoning the op after the engine failure. Stupidity, that's what it was. Damn it, had he lost the ability to make an intelligent tactical decision? Was it one of the symptoms of running out of luck? Muggles hadn't mentioned it.

Tom was busy switching tanks, dutifully writing reams of numbers on his log sheets, the pencil almost disappearing in his great lump of a hand.

Maurice called with a change of course. As usual, he sounded bored with the whole tiresome business.

Trim and re-trim. Not only was there the bloody port outer to contend with, the whole kite seemed to be out of trim, a hangar queen, a rogue that should have been written off months ago.

The damned cloud persisted.

No sign of activity ahead, but Maurice had said the target was ahead, therefore it was.

Sam Cooper called, "Skipper, shall I come aft now?"

"Okay, Sam."

"Going off intercom."

It was routine: near the target Sam left his radio and went back to the astro dome, the transparent blister on the top of the fuselage, to be an extra pair of eyes on the lookout for fighters. He emerged from the nose, bulky and awkward in his flying gear. He raised a gloved thumb. Colin nodded. Sam disappeared aft.

The Hally flew on, apparently alone in the hostile sky.

"There it is," said Don. "Where the hell are the markers?"

Colin stared. A silent fireworks display. A confused one at that.

"Bloody Pathfinders . . ."

"Kites right overhead," reported Bert from the mid-upper turret.

"They'll be the Lancs."

"Christ . . ."

A Lanc went tumbling by, wreathed in flame, one entire wing missing, the tail section breaking up, the red, white, and blue fin stripes clearly visible in the glare of the fire.

"Poor sods."

"No chatter, please. Keep your eyes peeled."

Firm, incisive tone. Not bad, considering. Odd, the feeling of detachment, of being a spectator not really involved in these lunatic proceedings.

"Fighter flares . . . look at the sods."

Damn them, they had lit up the target like Oxford Street on Christmas Eve. The flares hung in the chutes, rows of them, creating flickering, wobbling avenues in the sky. Above, the shadowy forms of bombers hurried on their way. No flak over the target: the Jerry fighters had the show to themselves. They were up there in the darkness, stalking, killing.

Another bomber went down, disintegrating as it fell, sections of fuselage and wing fluttering free. A man fell from the wreckage, somersaulting neatly, expertly; he vanished in the blackness below.

It took Don a lifetime to satisfy himself that he was aim-

ing at the right markers and not decoys. Now it was necessary to fly straight and level so that Don could make his
adjustments for wind and speed before dropping the bombs.

"Left, left, Skipper . . . hold it . . . steady as you go . . . bombs
gone."

Another lifetime: thirty more seconds of waiting for the
photo flash to light up the target as the bombs landed. A
crew returning to base without a snap of the night's work was
liable to be accused of not carrying out its collective duty.

George Hall's voice squeaked with alarm:

"Fighter! Port quarter! Corkscrew port . . . *now!*"

Left-hand throttles back. Hard port rudder. Nose down.
The world tipped. A plunge. Now an opposite bank with a
wrenching, stomach-grinding turn . . . describing crazy convolutions in the darkness but maintaining an approximation
of one's original course.

Colin gulped, tasting the sharp, rubbery taste of the oxygen mask while his imagination painted a picture of the
enemy: narrow-eyed, merciless-mouthed, supremely skilled,
with scores of Lancs and Hallies to his credit.

"Did we shake him?"

"Dunno, Skip . . . can't see him."

"There!"

George's voice, harsh and urgent now.

"Yeah, keep corkscrewing! Port! Go!"

At such times a skipper had to obey the gunners' commands, for only they could see what was happening behind.
The thump-thump-thump of the fighter's cannon cut
through the bleat of the engines and the light rattle of the
Brownings. The kite kept shuddering as the shells walloped
home, ripping through the fragile skin. Colin winced, imagining the aircraft disintegrating behind him, great chunks
flying off until the Hally became so much scrap metal tumbling through the air.

Tom was at his side, clutching a strut for support, his eyes
wide above the snout of his oxygen mask.

Thinking about his garter?

No time to worry about the crew. Every fibre of his being

was devoted to hurling the great lump of the bomber into its torturous manoeuvres. Arms aching, shoulders numb, but somehow feeling as if they belonged to someone else.

Sod the bastards who kept ordering more and more of the Hally's armour-plating removed so that it could carry greater bomb loads.

"Port outer, Skipper!"

A lick of flame battered by the slipstream.

"Feathering port outer."

"I think he's lost us . . ."

"Starboard inner's missing, Skipper."

Damn the disloyal contraption for choosing this moment to conk out.

George called, "He's coming in again, Skip! Prepare to corkscrew port."

"Christ! What the hell – "

"Got him!"

The explosion seemed strangely distant and innocuous, a harmless pop at a fireworks display. But its impact was startling. Its force caught the Halifax beneath the tail. No time to react. Or think. The bomber flipped onto its nose and plunged, slicing through the cloud layer, diving vertically, suicidally.

A screaming, semi-solid torrent of air froze the controls.

Colin heaved with all his strength, one foot braced against the instrument panel. Nothing budged. Helplessly he watched the city growing larger in his windscreen.

A few more seconds, mere moments; it would all be over – an instant of blinding light, then darkness for ever.

But wait – what about the trim tabs? Would they work at this crazy speed? Could they coax the elevators to shift?

If they did, the wings would undoubtedly come off.

It was a fact to accept as the earth came hurtling at you, as the howl of the hurricane past your cabin windows overpowered the noise of the engines, while you worked at the trim tab wheel. Persuading it to turn, pushing the small elevator-within-an-elevator up, a fraction, then a fraction more . . .

Going to go now, Colin told himself as the ground grew

hideous and huge in his windows. Wings can't stand it. Won't . . .

But they did. And suddenly the aircraft was streaking over the city at rooftop height, grey shadows of streets, shops, and factories rushing by like images in a film run too fast.

The speed dropped away quickly as the momentum of that insane dive faded. Bless Mr Handley Page's muscular wings.

Light flak pestered them, little balls of fire streaking by, falling, bouncing, dying.

Maurice appeared in the entrance to the nose, oxygen mask dangling at one side. He grinned and shook his head as if to say what a naughty fellow Colin was, frightening them all like that.

He bellowed something in Tom's ear.

Tom turned to Colin and mouthed the message: No intercom. Then he went aft, squeezing through the narrow bulkhead. It was his job to report casualties and assess damage.

Thank God Tom remembered his emergency drill. Sometimes men's brains were paralysed by catastrophes. One knew the feeling well, the complete inability to reason, the fingers around one's throat, the shackles pinioning every limb.

Sam Cooper's head appeared in the nose entrance. He nodded when he saw Colin, then withdrew. Had Maurice neglected to mention that the Skipper was alive and functioning?

Bloody awful, not knowing what was happening aft. One's imagination worked overtime. One saw scores of fighters on the tail, lining up to attack.

It was a full-time job, trimming and re-trimming her, trying to persuade her to fly in a reasonable approximation of a straight line; the poor old tattered thing felt as if it was about to flop over on one wing and go cartwheeling into the ground. The whole structure was rattling, vibrating, emitting mechanical death rattles.

Maurice re-emerged from the nose and gazed at the repeater compass, then scribbled something on a pad and went forward again.

Colin asked himself whether he really thought he could fly this wreck all the way back to England. And if he couldn't, what action did he propose to take?

He shrugged. God knows. It was hard to think beyond the next moment.

Tom returned. He scribbled a note:

GEORGE HAS FOOT WOUND. EVERYONE ELSE OK. HYDRAULICS U/S. FUEL OK.

All right. So that was the situation. Bloody awful but not hopeless. Kites had been coaxed home in worse condition.

Maurice appeared again. He held up a note:

STEER 310.

Colin nodded. Gentle persuasion from the rudders and ailerons to nudge the great blunt nose round to the correct heading without upsetting the aircraft's tenuous balance in the air.

310.

Needle quivering as if it were as scared as the rest of them. Maurice waited until Colin had the course set, then he withdrew into the nose. Thank God for a navigator like Maurice; the aircraft's position and course were two things the pilot didn't have to worry about.

They flew over open country, traversing an endless patchwork of fields and little boxes of houses that came speeding out of the shadows before disappearing to the rear. With any luck the Jerries weren't aware of the solitary Halifax at rooftop level. Radar had its limitations, thank God.

A man on a bicycle looked over his shoulders and shied away in alarm when he saw the Hally; he skidded, lost his balance; he was tumbling to the ground when they hurtled over him. Colin hoped the fellow didn't hurt himself.

It was semi-hypnotic, the endless parade of fields, taking form in the darkness growing large, then vanishing behind to be replaced by another and another.

Lucky chap, Don, having a girl like Phoebe to go home to. An unusual girl, Phoebe; pretty enough, but it was really the intelligence and the intensity in those eyes that captivated one.

The damned countryside was endless. How many hours had they been flying?

Maurice appeared, holding up another note:

COAST IN FIVE MINUTES.

Colin grinned.

Maurice shrugged an it-was-all-too-easy shrug, then went back into the cramped nose compartment that he shared with Sam Cooper and Don.

Searchlights away to starboard. Five miles at least.

An airfield! For God's sake, they were flying right over the hangars! Grey squat buildings, small aircraft dispersed around the field. Training types, by the look of them. No sign of life. Everyone asleep presumably . . .

Tom puffed his cheeks in relief. He turned to grin at Colin.

Then the flak opened up, the night erupting in a blizzard of darting, dazzling lights. Something hit the canopy over Colin's head; the fuselage quivered, taking more shots through its fragile skin.

The earth tumbled to one side as Colin skidded away from the flak. Hellishly accurate, the bastards. Damned near thing. How many more near things were in store?

The sparkling lights vanished aft.

Colin breathed again. They had run the gauntlet. Aircraft still flying. Engines functioning, more or less. Casualties? Oh God, Tom was in the nose compartment, looking grim. He emerged in a moment. Bad news. Maurice had been hit. Bleeding badly. They took him back to the rest bunk amidships.

Five minutes later Don came forward to report that Maurice was still breathing and the bleeding seemed to have stopped.

Was he conscious?

Partly, was the reply.

All right. The plan was simply to maintain the last course Maurice had provided. And hope.

Colin narrowed his gaze ahead. Was that the glint of water?

He edged the nose down a fraction. It was as well to depart the enemy coast with as much speed as one could muster.

A small village . . . a cluster of vehicles, military-looking things . . .

Gone in a flash.

Colin gulped as the sea slid below. They were striking out over the sea in an aircraft that exhibited all the signs of imminent disintegration.

No, unfair. The kite was still in one piece, wasn't it? . . . in spite of the most disgraceful treatment. Treatment that would have torn lesser aircraft to bits. He hereby took back all the nasty things he had ever said or thought about the Halifax.

The sea looked semi-solid, like molten lead.

Tom came back to the cockpit. He held up a note. More bad news: Flak had holed a fuel tank and had damaged the fuel distribution system. According to his calculations they would be out of fuel before they reached England.

God, God, God . . . it was coming true, his worst night-mare. A ditching. He was going to join that poor bastard in the Stirling. He winced as he imagined the sea splashing in, choking the life out of him. He didn't want to die like that. It wasn't fair . . . it wasn't right . . .

Despair was a lump in the pit of his stomach.

He gripped the control column until his hands ached. *Control yourself. You're not dead yet. Think.* Number one, the crew must dump everything not essential to flight – the Brownings from the turrets, the ammunition, the bunk, the Elsan, anything that could be ripped out and tossed overboard. Every pound saved meant a few more moments of flight . . .

The bloody sea. Endless acres stretching away, frigid, indifferent, an enormous graveyard.

But at least it was fairly calm.

If you had to ditch you needed calm conditions. In rough weather you could bet the kite would break up the moment it hit the water . . .

A freezing gale suddenly burst through from the nose. Shocked, Colin had visions of structural failure at the front end. But no, it was just Don and Sam opening the forward escape hatch.

The Hally limped on, torn wings still supporting the two of her four engines still functioning.

Tom scribbled another note:

ABOUT FIVE MINUTES FUEL LEFT.

His beefy face wore an apologetic expression as if the situation were somehow his fault.

Five minutes.

About five minutes.

So it could be six minutes.

Or four.

If Maurice was conscious he would be able to say where five minutes' fuel would take the Hally. But Maurice wasn't conscious, so what the hell was the point of thinking about it? All that could be done was to keep on the same heading and hope for the best.

Christ, Muggles had been right . . . you know when your luck is running out, when everything is coming unstitched.

An Aussie pilot had told him ditching was like flying into a brick wall – "Big bloody wave caught the port wingtip, just about ripped the sod off . . . bloody kite fell to bits around me." Half of the Aussie's crew had gone down with the wreck.

Fear seemed to move within him, prodding, digging here and there, like some foul little creature.

Beside him Tom was shaking his head, no doubt ruminating about the stupidity of taking off without the garter. Colin found himself thinking about the CO and what his reaction would have been if his "A" Flight Commander had abandoned an op because of a missing garter.

Twerp! Stop wasting your time thinking such things! Try to think of something useful, something that might save your crew and your own miserable hide.

Below was black emptiness.

It was to be hoped that the dinghy's emergency transmitter was in good working order, for it was the only means of making contact with the Air-Sea Rescue boys.

He kept seeing the Stirling pilot, trapped, doomed, reaching for God knows what. *Please God, not like that . . .*

An army officer had once observed that the great advantage of fighting one's war on solid ground was that when things got desperate there was usually somewhere to run to.

I would run if I could, Colin thought. Like a bloody rabbit.

Tom went aft to his instruments, reappearing a moment later. His thumb and forefinger indicated a zero. He leant over and tightened Colin's harness, tugging at the straps until they threatened to crush every bone in his body.

Colin nodded, innards freezing over. With a gloved hand he instructed Tom to go aft and make sure the crew was prepared, sitting with their backs to the wing's main spar, knees up, hands behind heads.

It was time. Far better to ditch while the engines still worked, providing some control over the last few moments. Ease back on the throttle levers; nose up; trim. Airspeed was falling off with unseemly haste. A spot more power. Now the kite was descending in good order, like a sheep going obediently to slaughter.

Nothing to be seen but darkness. It was like descending into a gigantic ink well. Ah, there was something – a change in the texture of the blackness . . .

According to the altimeter the aircraft was only twenty feet above sea level. Then where the hell was the sea? He stared until it hurt.

Then he saw it. A furry layer like a black cloud. Fog!

Damnation, ditching was bad enough in the dark but it was infinitely worse if you didn't know just where the surface was. How thick was the fog? A hundred feet? A dozen?

There was, he decided grimly, only one way to find out.

The bloody rattling started up again as he descended, skimming along the surface of the mist before letting the kite sink into its clammy embrace.

A lunatic urge came over him. Shove the stick forward. Dive the kite straight in. Get it over and done with.

He shook his head. *No, sod you.*

Then he saw the sea, mist and water moving sluggishly as if the mess were solidifying.

An ever-so-gentle easing of the throttles. The Hally sank a few more feet, slicing its way through the mist; it was like flying through ten billion cobwebs.

Nose high. Speed falling off. Rattling behind.

One heard of floatplane pilots flying straight into still lakes because the transparent surface provided no visual reference for them to judge their altitude. If you're not careful you'll stall her in, he informed himself. Old Friend was of the opinion that under the circumstances he was almost certain to do so.

Down into the shadowy world, eyes leaping from the instrument panel to the outside; one's instincts played tricks under such conditions, warning you that you were sliding to the left when in fact you were going the other way.

Christ! The sea took form. Instantly. Like the product of some chemical experiment. Stick back. Bang! Shuddering, the Hally rebounded from the surface.

Then it hit again.

Cataclysmic sound. Sound that burst from within him . . . a monstrous wall of sound surrounding him, crushing him . . . bursts of orange and red splashing over him . . .

"C'mon, Skipper, let's get you out of there."

Distant voice, oddly hollow-sounding.

Hands clutching, tugging, hurting.

He was in a wading pool at Bournemouth and his mother was calling to him, telling him it was time to collect his bucket and spade . . .

"Soon have you out of there, Skip."

A moment, an hour, a week – God knows – of wavering between reality and fantasy. Eventually the realization that the water lapping about his feet wasn't in a wading pool but was the North Sea, and it was rapidly filling the cockpit.

"He's stuck. Get something to pry him free."

"And bloody hurry."

Colin started to speak, then the pain hit in great searing waves. He couldn't think; the pain paralysed his brain.

He felt the hands under his armpits, tugging.

He opened his eyes and saw Don, frowning. Grimacing.

"Can't budge him . . . "

Numbly, he realized what had happened. The front of the aircraft had folded in on him, the instrument panel, the remains of the nose compartment. A great crumpled mess, a metallic cocoon, a coffin . . .

He couldn't move. Were his legs still there? Could they have been sliced off in the crash? No . . . he *felt* water, didn't he?

Tom was dragging at the tangle of metal with his bare hands; blood streamed from a slash, spattering on the remains of the instrument panel.

The aircraft lurched.

"Christ, she's going."

The sea was up to his waist.

"Where's the axe?"

"We threw it out like the Skipper said."

"Jesus."

Tom kept working, cursing, half sobbing in his frustration.

The water slopped like some greedy monster, licking its evil lips.

"You chaps get out while you can."

Remarkably calm, almost matter-of-fact voice.

"Can't leave you."

"You must."

"Go to hell, Skipper. We're not bloody leaving you – there's got to be something we can do. We need a bloody crowbar . . . "

Another heart-stopping lurch and a sloshing of water into the cabin.

"You've got to go now," he said. "There's nothing more you can do. No point in you getting yourselves caught in here too."

For an instant he thought Tom was going to cry. But it was rage that contorted his normally amiable features, impotent rage. He kept saying that he wouldn't abandon Colin, he couldn't, it was unthinkable . . .

"Even more unthinkable for you to stay here," Colin said. Matter-of-factly. Afterwards, they would shake their heads and say how brave he was. Not true of course. He was just a better actor than he knew. He managed a half turn. Tom, Don, George: they were crammed into the narrow space beside the cockpit, gazing at him like visitors at a hospital. "Get into the dinghy. That's an order . . . a direct order. You're good fellows, all of you, but there's no point in you going down with the kite. Can you get Maurice out?"

"Yes, but – "

"Skipper – "

"Don't argue. George . . ."

"Yes, Skip?"

"Did you bring your six-shooter with you?"

The gunner nodded, tugging the weapon out of its holster and handing it to Colin.

"Is it ready to fire?"

"Just release the safety catch. That thing there."

"Thanks." Colin nodded to them calmly. He had the odd feeling of playing a part in a school play. He should have gone on the stage. Too late now.

The aircraft lurched again; the water splashed up to his chest. The bloody sea was going to get him just as it got that Stirling pilot. Cursing, Tom and George tried once more to pull him free of the debris. They succeeded only in shifting him slightly so that something sharp stuck into the side of his leg. But the pain seemed distant now. Was he already on the way out?

"For God's sake get going. I absolutely insist. Good luck all of you."

He turned his head away from them as the aircraft settled another foot or two. The water splashed onto his face then receded a few inches as the kite wallowed to one side. He heard the boys scrambling out of the hatch on top of the fuselage and sliding across the wing. Lucky sods. They would see tomorrow. They had some luck left; his was all gone. He'd known it for days. In a moment the Hally would be submerged. He was alone now. But he wouldn't wait for the sea. He would cheat it with George's gun. A bullet in the head was better than having the sea choke the life out of you.

Dear God, I'm sorry for . . . everything.

He said goodbye to his parents. And to Phoebe.

And to Muggles.

You were right, you old bastard.

He had no fear now. Regret was the emotion that permeated his whole being: regret at not having done so many things ... damned shame ...

He released the safety catch on the revolver. The water was gurgling in through the cabin window, filling the cabin inch by inch. It was time.

He wondered if he would shortly be seeing Muggles. And Stroud. And God alone knows how many more.

He placed the muzzle in his mouth. It had a metallic, oily taste.

No, not through the mouth. Horrible, the thought of the bullet smashing through the roof of his mouth, blowing the back of his skull out. The forehead was preferable; cleaner, somehow. But perhaps the soft bits at the sides were best. He seemed to remember people in films and plays pointing guns in that area. He breathed, greedily. Never before had he realized how delicious air was. Head back more. One more deep breath. Savour it for an instant.

"Cheerio," he muttered to the world in general.

His finger tightened on the trigger. He looked down at the weapon; close at hand it was enormous, the barrel huge, like a length of oil pipe.

It seemed a pity that the revolver would be the last thing he would ever see. He glanced ahead. Nothing but wispy, shifting fog. Above was blackness. No sign that there was anything in the world outside this wreck and the sea ...

Get it over and done with, chum.

One last deep breath.

He pulled the trigger.

Two bangs. The gun and something below.

The aircraft had jerked, shifting the gun as Colin had fired, spoiling the aim.

The bullet whizzed past his brow and smashed through the metalwork to his left.

"Bloody hell," he muttered.

He had to steel himself to do it again.

Then he noticed something. The water wasn't rising. The aircraft wasn't moving. It took a moment for the truth to sink in.

The Hally had run aground.

They told him that he had been unconscious and half dead from exposure when the rescue team had cut him out of the wreckage. His legs were a bit of a mess, they said, but he was alive, that was the main thing, wasn't it?

He was incredibly tired. He craved sleep but there was something he had to say first.

"The crew didn't want to leave me," he told the MO, who possessed an uncommonly prominent Adam's apple. "I ordered them to go. A direct order. I want that clearly understood. No blame must be attached to them."

"It won't," the MO told him.

"How can I be sure?"

The MO sighed. "Because I'm afraid they're all dead. Their dinghy failed. Battle damage perhaps. You were the only survivor. A very lucky fellow indeed."

The Flight Engineer

THE HOURS DRAGGED. SOON THERE WAS LITTLE LEFT TO say that hadn't been said before. They read *John Bull* and *Picture Post*, looked at their watches, and yawned. Then Harry said:

"This squadron has lost three sprog pilots on second-dickey trips in the last two and a half months."

"Trust you to find that out," said Andy.

"I am a seeker after knowledge, you know that."

"What if he doesn't come back?" said Roland. "He will, of course, but what if he doesn't?"

"They reclassify us as a headless crew and ship us back to OTU to get crewed up all over again."

"They wouldn't break us up."

"They might," said Gordon gloomily. "They can do with us what they will. We are their property. Chattels, that's all we are, bloody chattels."

The two gunners, Andy and Ty, played cards. They played cards by the hour, usually a form of Australian patience introduced by Ty.

Willy Perkins shifted in his wicker chair. Ross would come back all right. You just couldn't imagine Ross getting the chop on a second-dickey trip. Which was daft when you thought about it. No one, not even Ross Sinclair, was immune to a direct hit by an eighteen-pound 88 mm shell in the bomb bay or a fighter's cannon fire in the wing tanks. According to the experts that was the way most Jerry fighters attacked. They came from below, manoeuvring to get under the bomber where the gunners couldn't spot them, since some bright spark had decreed that RAF night bombers didn't need belly gunners like the Yank bombers. It was a safe bet that that particular bright spark hadn't tested his theory personally. The Jerries could hardly miss. Bloody great expanse of wing just sitting there full of petrol. One burst would usually do the trick. Enough to give you the shivers just to think about it. A nasty world over there. And Ross was in it. Or over it. No, he was on his way home by now or. . . . He was on his way home.

Earlier that evening they had clustered beside the runway and had waved to the Halifaxes taking off into the gathering twilight. Strange how vulnerable they had looked, those bellowing monsters, as they rolled away. Any one of ten thousand things could go wrong (Harry claimed to have listed them all) to reduce a Hally to so much scrap metal in a scintilla of a second.

Ross was flying in R-Robert. When he had scrambled aboard the crew van clutching his helmet, yellow Mae West unfastened, trailing tapes, he had waved to Willy, grinning. You'd think he was a lad from the mill off on a Bank Holiday ride to Blackpool. Never seemed to cross his mind that he might not come back. Typical Ross.

Willy had met Ross at HCU – the Heavy Conversion Unit – where newly trained crews went to learn to operate the four-engined bombers they would fly on ops. Funny how it happened. The clerk told Willy to report to a Flight Lieutenant Holden in "A" Flight office. But when Willy got there Holden said he already had a flight engineer – and pointed him out to prove the point: Crocker, a lofty bloke with black hair that looked as if it had been painted on his skull. So Willy returned to the clerk – who frowned and mumbled and riffled through sheafs of papers, then glared at Willy as if he was the one who had erred. With a self-important flourish, he scribbled a name on a piece of paper: Pilot Officer Ross Sinclair, "B" Flight. Willy went on his way and because he was nervous he began to whistle. He was still whistling when he entered the shack that housed "B" Flight.

"Big John's Special."

A tall lad with a dazzling grin. A pilot, a Canadian.

"What?" Willy had to think for a moment. "Yes, that's it. Benny Goodman."

"Big John was a guy who ran a gin mill on Seventh Avenue between 131st and 132nd Streets in Harlem."

"I didn't know that," said Willy.

"Fact," grinned the Canadian. He was an officer. "Name's Sinclair. Ross Sinclair. From Winnipeg, Manitoba."

"I'm Willy Perkins, from Manchester . . . well, Droylsden, it's near Manchester . . . and I'm your flight engineer."

"Well, I like the way you whistle, Willy. Any guy who can whistle like that must be a helluva engineer. Welcome aboard."

Within minutes Willy had met the rest of the crew: a soft-spoken navigator, a Londoner named Roland Hibbert; a cocky bomb-aimer, Harry White, who had raced motor cycles in peacetime and seemed to be splendidly informed on every aspect of human existence; a wireless operator by the name of Gordon Wallis who looked harassed, as if he was worried about missing a bus; and a brace of scruffy gunners, Andy Shaw from Bristol and Tynan Marshall, an Aussie from some place with an unpronounceable name.

By the time the crew was posted to Rocklington, Willy and Ross had become the best of friends. They were an unlikely pair. Ross the officer, strikingly good-looking and six feet one; Willy the sergeant, barely five feet seven and possessing what he freely admitted was a "mass-production" face, pleasant enough but duplicated by the thousands in Manchester or any big industrial city. Ross, brimming with self-confidence, never at a loss in any sort of company; Willy, chronically shy, often tongue-tied among those whom he classified as "posh." Ross the notorious spendthrift, splendidly disinterested in the value of money; Willy the scrimper and saver, conditioned since childhood to regard cash as a commodity that was destined always to be in short supply, to be squandered on frivolities like taxis and restaurant meals only in the direst of emergencies. Yet the curious fact remained: They were friends, always together, usually chatting about King Oliver or Jimmy Lunceford, Bechet or Beiderbecke. Willy's knowledge of jazz was encyclopaedic; he knew who played what on the legendary Basie sessions of 1938; he could reel off the dates of the Hot Five and Hot Seven recordings without a moment's hesitation. But he knew these performers only through their records; Ross had heard them in person, in hot spots from Chicago to New York, Toronto to San Francisco. Thus they complemented each other admirably, Willy providing the statistics and discographical data, Ross the first-hand experiences. They could discuss jazz for hours on end to the bewilderment of anyone else within earshot.

Ross's kite was the second to land.

"Piece of cake," he said. "You guys shouldn't have stayed up."

"We were waiting for you to come back and tuck us in," said Harry White.

Ross grinned; his fair hair was flattened by hours under a tight-fitting helmet.

They asked him about the op. The flak. The fighters. The weather. The searchlights. Did he see any aircraft getting the chop?

He answered their questions with his usual ebullience. Fantastic "firecracker" show over the target. Flak thick enough to walk on. You could smell the explosive even through your oxygen mask.

Ross did another second-dickey trip two nights later, returning with a hole in the starboard aileron.

The following day his name was on the battle order as a skipper. He was to fly B-Beer; the aircraft's regular crew was on leave.

They flew for over an hour performing all the usual nightflying tests and practising every emergency procedure time and time again. The crew had to be a team, Ross insisted, not a bunch of individuals. There should never be any doubt as to who was supposed to do what at any given moment.

That evening, just before boarding the aircraft, he told them:

"You're a hell of a good crew. So let's go out there and prove it."

It all sounded a bit like a basketball coach exhorting his team to greater effort. But Ross could say such things; his infectious enthusiasm seemed to make them acceptable; even Harry the cynic nodded without comment.

It was still light when they took off, sweeping low over the York Road with their load of high explosive, incendiaries, and fuel. The evening sky was dotted by aircraft from the score of airfields in the vicinity of Rocklington, all climbing slowly, laboriously, laden to their limits and beyond. Bomber Command's chiefs were as passionate about tonnages of bombs as accountants about profits and losses, but their insistence on bigger and bigger loads sometimes backfired. Many a 4,000-pound "cookie" ended up in the North Sea on the outward journey; relieved of the weight, the lumbering bombers – notably the Stirlings and Halifaxes – could attain a little more height and thus improve their crews' chances of survival.

Willy's job as flight engineer was to assist Ross with take-offs and landings, after which he was responsible for the workings of the aircraft's systems: fuel, hydraulics, electrics, and its four Merlins. Willy had volunteered for pilot training but the authorities had turned him down. Not enough education, they said. But he might be considered for flight engineer training. He said yes before they changed their official minds. But he still yearned to be a pilot. And he was learning. Ross had already taught him to fly straight and level and to handle simple turns. The crew was notably patient at such times; everyone recognized the desirability of having someone capable of taking over the controls should Ross be killed or injured.

Cologne was the target that night. Since the beginning of the war Bomber Command had attacked it more than fifty times. After the Thousand Bomber raid more than a year ago, many airmen thought the city had been wiped off the face of the earth. But the reconnaissance photographs told a different story. The fires that had seemed so all-engulfing at night had inflicted grievous damage, but it was scattered. The city still functioned. It made one wonder. Would Bomber Command ever have enough bombs or aircraft to destroy the place? And how many more cities had to be demolished before Germany collapsed?

As B-Beer arrived over the target a Stirling went down in flames, describing a great fiery spiral in the sky. Flak laced the night; searchlights probed the darkness, great swaying columns of light. One caught a Halifax a hundred yards away to port. A blue-tinted light. The most dangerous type, according to the experts. Blue-tinted lights were radar-controlled, master lights, to be avoided at all costs. And yes, just as the experts had said, the other lights – the "slaves" – came to join the master, coning the unfortunate Hally. It turned and dived in desperation, but it didn't have a chance. Every flak battery blazed away. A wing glowed, then erupted. Trailing flame, the Hally continued its agonized convolutions. The wing suddenly folded. A man jumped as the aircraft plummeted. For riveting moments he tumbled straight down the beam of a searchlight like a circus performer whose every move was being followed by a spotlight.

He disappeared.

Ty Marshall said, "No sign of a chute. I wonder if the poor bastard had time to clip it on."

Ross snapped, "Forget him. No chatter. Keep your eyes peeled. And that means everyone."

They unloaded their bombs and turned for home. Roland announced the course in his subdued way, sounding as if he was apologizing for interrupting Ross. A quiet bloke, Roland; funny how Ross seemed to have surrounded himself with opposites. Except for Harry, the bomb-aimer. Harry White – nicknamed "Chalky," of course – was as self-confident and brash as Ross, always talking about Brough Superiors and Squariels, Cottons and DOTs. If the war hadn't come along, he kept on telling anyone who would listen, he would have made fifteen hundred quid "easy" in '40; everything was coming together for him in the racing game, then the bloody war put a spanner in the works.

Over the sea they had coffee and sandwiches. The first glimmers of the new day brushed the English coast. The fields looked like green velvet.

A sense of accomplishment fairly tingled through Willy. He had done it. He had become operational.

Ross touched down as sweetly as could be, the tires emitting an obsequious little squeak at the moment of impact. First op successfully completed. A milestone.

"Nice work, guys," Ross commented as he taxied the Hally to its dispersal. "Knew I'd be proud of you."

No ops the next day. Willy and Ross went off to explore York. On the way Ross talked about going to a dance in Minneapolis to hear Bunny Berigan and his band. Ross said he drove there after school – and back the same night – some eight hundred miles in all. "Borrowed Dad's Caddy. Great car for a long trip like that, but I didn't get home till after eight a.m. – then had to go straight to school!"

Willy listened, awestruck by the notion of driving eight hundred miles to hear a band – even one led by Bunny Berigan. It was the equivalent of driving from Droylsden to the *Shetlands* – if that were possible – plus the ruddy return journey! Ross seemed to have an innate contempt for distances; miles existed to be gobbled up by those monster cars they drove over there.

What an engaging fellow he was, bubbling over with enthusiasm for York Minster. His eyes lit up at this tomb or that. "Imagine, four hundred years old; some guy actually carved this way back then! And those kings and queens and bishops walked right here where you and I are walking, buddy!"

The idea fascinated him. It gave him "goose bumps," he said.

Ten minutes later he was telling a waitress that she possessed a better figure than Betty Grable. She regarded him with the narrowed gaze of someone who had been the recipient of lines from every branch of the Allied services, from the marines to the military police.

"I don't need your sauce," she declared.

"It's not sauce," Ross replied. "It's a fact. A self-evident truth!"

Never at a loss for words, was Ross.

Before the sausage and chips were gone, he had made a date with the waitress for the following Thursday, provided Bomber Command didn't have other ideas for the evening.

"Always stick to the truth," Ross advised. "If she has a great shape tell her so. Okay? Besides, it makes it easier later. If you've made up a bunch of lies, it could be real tough to remember what you told her. Sure you don't want to come along? She said she had a cute girlfriend for you."

Willy said, "To be honest I've never been much of a one for blind dates." Which was true in a way; no one had ever asked him to be involved in one.

Within the hour Ross was chatting to an ATS corporal at a bus stop. This time it was her eyes. Such subtle colouring, such depth and warmth.

He was shameless! Half a dozen citizens happened to be lined up at the bus stop with the ATS girl; they listened with interest. Willy squirmed with embarrassment but Ross seemed unperturbed, shrugging philosophically when the ATS girl told him she was engaged to a captain in the West Yorkshires.

"He's a lucky guy," Ross told her. He turned to the others in the queue. "You win some, you lose some, right?"

Fortunately the bus arrived at that moment.

Ross waved to the ATS corporal as the bus pulled away.

Willy said, "I don't know how you had the nerve."

"Nerve? I just told her the truth. She does have great eyes. Sort of hazel with flecks of green and brown. Real pretty. Remember what I said, always stick to the truth. It's easier in the long run."

He talked about sticking to the truth as if it was a subject he had studied at university between the civil engineering classes that he had abandoned to join the air force.

Willy had never met anyone like Ross. He loved to listen to him talking about Canada and its enormous spaces, its colossal mountains, its endless lakes, its lousy beer parlours, and its stupid Sunday laws. Ross's family was comfortably off. You only had to hear about his father's consulting firm, his Cadillac "automobile," the winter place in Georgia, and the annual theatre and shopping trip to New York to guess how comfortably. It all sounded like a Mickey Rooney-Judy Garland film with open sports cars full of laughing boys and heartbreakingly pretty girls, of skiing and skating, of cocktails and cabins in the country. A ruddy sight more fun than Droylsden, Willy thought.

Over Gelsenkirchen the following night the squadron lost two aircraft. Three nights later another one over Aachen. Essen, Hamburg, Remscheid. The ground crew diligently painted little red bombs on the Halifaxes' flanks to indicate the number of ops they had completed.

It was shortly after the Remscheid trip that Ross had the encounter with the Station Administrative Officer. A WAAF named Elsie was involved. A pretty fresh-faced girl from Dundee, Elsie worked in the parachute section. Ross took her to York for dinner, then to The White Rose in the village. For several days he could talk of no one else. She was the perfect girl for him – sensitive, humorous, intelligent, perceptive. Willy listened, nodding automatically. He was becoming accustomed to Ross's grand, but usually short-lived, passions. Ross charged into relationships in the same enthusiastic, no-holds-barred way he approached every other facet of human existence.

One Wednesday morning Pilot Officer Sinclair was informed that it was not considered seemly for officers to be seen consorting with non-commissioned WAAFs.

"So it's okay as long as we're not seen?"

The Admin Officer, a bristly old chap of forty-five or more, wasn't amused.

"I must ask you to conduct yourself in a manner befitting an officer."

"I guess we Colonials don't really know the form, do we?"

"Obviously not."

Typical British bullshit, Ross said. The class system would be the death of the whole place. He had no intention of listening to such blatant nonsense. He was going to see Elsie. But Elsie had been spoken to; fond as she was of Ross she thought it better if they didn't see each other again. Ross was furious. He told the Flight Commander and the CO so. They told him that rules were rules and he wasn't going to change anything.

They went to Mannheim. Flak blew a chunk out of the port rudder. Ross said it improved the kite's handling.

The next morning the crew was sent on leave.

Ross forgot about Elsie. London! He'd been looking forward to London ever since he'd been shipped over; he was going to see everything and do everything. Willy had to come too. They could have one great time, the two of them, catching some good music and some cute girls . . .

Willy was flattered, though he cringed at the thought of the cost of such goings-on. Fortunately he had the perfect excuse.

"I can't, Ross. I'm sorry. I have to go home. To Droylsden."

Ross grinned. "Sure you do. Clean forgot you've got yourself a family here. No sweat."

Willy had an idea. "Tell you what, you must come home with me. The family would love to have you. I've told them all about you. Mum's a terrific cook. Wouldn't you like some home-cooked meals after all this air force muck?"

"Listen, I couldn't impose . . . "

"Tell you what" – Willy was getting excited about the notion – "we can catch the train to Manchester. We'll be at home by half past two or three. Spend Saturday with us and if you want to go down to London on the Sunday, well, that's up to you, but why anyone would want to go to London when he's in Manchester is beyond me."

More grins from Ross; the thought of spending a little time in a real home clearly appealed.

"You're sure your folks won't mind what with rations and

all – but, say, I could bring a couple of cans of ham or Spam or something."

"That's the ticket," said Willy.

"You're sure?" said Ross. "Real sure?"

"Positive," said Willy.

They took the train to Manchester and walked to Stevenson Square. There they caught a 27 tram that trundled and clattered the five miles to Droylsden past endless rows of tiny terraced houses; the funny thing was how interesting they were to Ross; he was glued to the window throughout the ride, as captivated by the sights as if he had been journeying through Baghdad.

It was a few minutes' walk from the tram stop to Union Street.

Willy walked with a jaunty step. Anticipation bubbled within him. He could hardly wait to see the family, Dad, Mum, and sister Gwen. The last time he had been home was just before he joined the squadron. Since then he had undergone a sort of transformation. He had seen action. He had become a real fighting man. The family was bursting with pride of course, no question about that. He would be deluged with questions, all of which he would answer with commendable patience, dismissing their more flagrant flatteries with modest shrugs.

He remembered Ross, striding along at his side.

How did the street look to him? Did the houses seem small and shabby? Was he wishing he had gone straight to London? Was he counting the minutes until he could escape? Perhaps it wasn't such a good idea bringing Ross here, after all. What was the poor sod going to *do* . . . ?

He didn't have time to wonder about it. They were home. Number 21. With a shriek his mother burst forth from the front door, apron fluttering from her waist like a pennant. She embraced her son and his friend with equal enthusiasm. Ross, she declared, was just as nice as our Willy had said he was and where was Manitoba and did he have relatives in England and what about brothers and sisters and what were they both doing outside and weren't they going to come in? She fired broadsides of questions as she bustled about the kitchen "brewing" tea and finding boxes of biscuits and bottles of sherry that were kept for special occasions.

"You're just like our Willy said you were."

"So are you," said Ross. Which seemed to cause Willy's mother no end of amusement.

After several cups of tea and a quantity of substantial biscuits Willy and Ross went for a stroll. Willy nodded to neighbours and acquaintances, stopping to exchange a word with Alf Corbett and Mrs Sugden, popping in to Sinden's on Market Street to buy an evening paper and introduce Ross. Grand, to observe the raised eyebrows and the glances; causing quite a stir, the two of them were, as they toured Droylsden.

Ross liked the way people called each other "loov."

When they got back to the house, Willy's father was home from work, his hands still grubby from the printing press he operated all day. A stocky little man with bright blue eyes and very little hair, he declared it to be "right champion" to have both of them under his roof. But, he asked, hand under chin, could they really get *all* of Ross inside an aeroplane? They grew them big over there in Canada, didn't they? To Willy's relief Ross took it all in good part. He seemed to be enjoying himself. He even managed to show interest in the family, peering at the portraits on the mantelpiece as if they were of royalty.

"A distinguished-looking gentleman."

"My cousin Selwyn. Forty years with the railway, he did."

"How about that. And this lady?"

"My Aunt Bernice. Married Fred Broadbent on the Saturday and he was gone on the Tuesday. Never saw hide nor hair of him again."

Uncle Shepley, Cousin Oswald, Aunt Winifred: Ross had to hear about them all. He had digested about half of the story of Mrs Perkins's niece Polly who became a nurse and married a Polish corporal when Gwen came home.

"Willy!" She carolled from the hall.

She burst into the living room.

Then stopped. Her mouth dropped open.

"You didn't say there was company. You should've told me."

"He's not company," said Willy expansively, "he's just my skipper, Ross Sinclair. He talks a bit funny but he can't help that because he's a Canadian. Skipper, my baby sister Gwen."

But she wasn't a baby any more. Incredible what a difference those last few months had made. Something *basic* had happened. She had almost become a woman. And unless Willy was mistaken she had accorded Ross something that could only be described as the glad eye – and after a few months with Ross, Willy knew a glad eye when he saw one.

Ross was all charm, at his courtly best, *standing*, saying how delighted he was to make her acquaintance and shaking her hand one hell of a lot longer than was strictly necessary. He told Gwen that Willy had often talked of her – which was a bit of a tall one, in Willy's opinion, for he had no recollection of ever mentioning her existence.

Mrs Perkins handed out glasses of sherry.

Mr Perkins got to his feet, his glass raised high. He called for "a bit of hush," directing his outstretched arm at everyone in turn like a magician with a wand.

"I propose a toast to welcome my brave son back from the war and his friend Ross who probably isn't quite as brave but I'm sure is no disgrace to his country."

"Put a sock in it, Dad," said Willy.

"*And*," went on his father, rocking slightly as he spoke as if swayed by the intensity of his feelings, "to my daughter Gwen who, you may just be interested to know, has only this week been accepted by the Wrens."

"*What!*" Willy could hardly believe his ears. Little *Gwen*?

"Terrific," said Ross.

"Why didn't you tell us?"

"Didn't have time, did I?"

"My only regret," declared Willy's father, "is that no one has seen fit to follow my footsteps into the army."

"What? After all those stories about mud up to your you-know-what! You put us off, Dad, that was the truth of it!"

"Well," was the response, "you can buzz around in your aeroplanes and bob about in your boats but in the end it'll be the P. B. I. – the Poor Bloody Infantry – who'll have to finish the job."

"We can do without that sort of language," said Willy's mother.

"It's a *term*, Vera, a *term*."

"And not a very nice term."

Ross got to his feet. "I'd like to toast you, Mr and Mrs Perkins, for your hospitality to a stranger. I used to think about England a whole lot before I came here. I often wondered what it'd be like in an English home with an English family. And you know, this is just like I figured it would be – only a darn sight better!" Good old Ross, he could turn it on at will. "And let me add just one thing. Your son Willy sits beside me in an airplane, and I want you to know there's no one I'd rather have beside me than him. Now your daughter is going off to serve her country. You're just the sort of folks that the people back home think about when they think of an English family, and it's a privilege and a pleasure for me to be here with you. So I'd like all of you – yeah, and you, Willy – to remain seated while I drink your health, all of you, all by myself."

They applauded him as if he had done a clever turn – and in a way, Willy supposed, he had. Quite a gift of the gab, had old Ross. And he'd certainly had an effect on Gwen. She kept asking him questions about Canada. What was the population of Winnipeg? Where was Hudson Bay? How long did it take to get from Toronto to Halifax? To hear her prattling on you'd think she made it her life's work to study the country. On the other hand you couldn't get away from the fact that Ross had a way of talking about it; he made it sound exciting, an adventurous sort of place with its wild bears and snakes and Indians living on reservations. About as unlike Droylsden as you could imagine.

After a meal of cottage pie, Ross insisted on helping with the washing-up – he called it "the dishes"; then he sat down at the old upright in the front room and played everything from

"Knees Up, Mother Brown" and "There'll Always Be an England" to "Sweet Georgia Brown." Willy listened in amazement. Not once had Ross ever mentioned touching a piano.

"I'll tell you why," said Ross. "One night I sat and listened to Art Tatum. At The Three Deuces, I think it was. Had a ringside table. Great. Before then I thought I could do a thing or two with the keys. But the more I listened the more I realized I wasn't on the same planet as that man."

"You play beautifully," said Gwen.

"No, he doesn't," said Willy. "I know what he means . . . adequate, you might say . . . that's all . . . in comparison with a Tatum . . . "

But she wasn't listening. She had gone across the room to help Ross wind up the gramophone and select records from Willy's collection.

Just like a female. Gwen had always hated jazz – "a lot of noisy rubbish," she had said so many times. Now, miraculously, she was a fan, listening wide-eyed when Ross talked about the Condon band at Nick's in Greenwich Village, Count Basie in Chicago, and Bob Crosby in Indianapolis. Willy shook his head to himself. What a hypocrite she was! If Ross had discussed mountaineering there's little doubt that she would have remembered a lifelong ambition to become the first woman up Everest. Later they rejoined Willy's parents for a goodnight cup of cocoa; it was almost midnight when they finally turned in, Mr Perkins noting with satisfaction that tomorrow was Saturday with only a half-day's work waiting for him. Mrs Perkins made up the couch in the front room; Ross would be as snug as a bug, she declared.

Willy went to his room, the room that he always seemed to associate with being eight or nine years old. He was home. He should have been content. But he wasn't. Irritation bubbled within him like an ill-digested meal. He didn't know why. Yes he did. It was Gwen. And Ross.

Gwen had a *crush* on Ross. She was *infatuated*. Daft kid. Did she really think a bloke like Ross would be interested in her? What a hope! Something else ruffled him. He had to admit it: the spotlight had shifted. He had become a sort of spectator instead of the star turn. Yes, it was childish to be upset by it, but he was upset and that was the ruddy truth of it. How could Gwen possibly have become old enough to be a Wren? Wrens were grown-up, hot stuff, according to the connoisseurs. And Gwen – *their* Gwen – was going to be one of them? It didn't make sense. But then nothing had made much sense since he got home. Barmy, bringing Ross. The maddening thing was that the whole family thought him marvellous, handsome, charming, rich. Thank the Lord he was going to London the next day.

At breakfast Ross was in good form, regaling the family with chatter about the Calgary Stampede and Niagara Falls. Gwen was dressed to the nines and looking as if she were going to meet the royal family that morning instead of going off to work at the mill office.

"You should stay another day," she told Ross.

"He's going to London," said Willy. "He's booked a hotel."

"It's nicer here than some old hotel," said Gwen – with a smile that was downright provocative. How was it that no one else seemed to notice? Mother grinning indulgently, Dad munching toast as if all was well with the world!

"I couldn't put you folks to the trouble . . . "

"There's a big dance on tonight at the Co-op Hall," said Gwen. "Al Bogley's band will be playing."

"Not *the* Al Bogley?" said Ross.

"Yes . . . " Gwen started to giggle – hand on mouth as if it was suddenly unladylike to laugh. "Oh you, you're having me on."

"Bogley's got a corny band," Willy pointed out. "Besides, it's just a rotten little dance in a poky little hall . . . "

"If you want to stay, lad, you're more than welcome," said his father.

"*Please*," said Gwen.

"But the hotel . . . " Willy put in.

"No sweat, buddy," Ross reassured him. "I can call them and cancel one night. They're not going to have any trouble getting rid of the room."

"I think you'd best stay one more night," said Willy's mother. "If only to keep the rest of them from nattering."

"Gee," said Ross. "I hope I can return the favour to you folks one day."

"Aye," chuckled Willy's father, "we'll all come trooping out there for a Bank Holiday."

"I sure hope you do," said Ross.

That afternoon they went for a walk in Daisy Nook; Ross and Gwen chattering and chuckling, Willy following in frowning silence. Later, Ross insisted on taking all the family to eat at the Midland in Manchester. The meal cost the earth – the best part of a fiver, Willy calculated. But Ross didn't turn a hair when he got the bill; the pound notes came tripping out like cards in a game of pontoon. Overpaid, the Canadians, just like the Yanks. And as Willy well knew, if Ross ran a bit short he simply wired daddy in Winnipeg for a few extra quid.

"A really grand lad," Willy was told by his father when the two of them went to the gents. "Glad to see you chumming up with the likes of Ross, a gradely lad."

"He's all right," said Willy.

"Funny thing is, I think our Gwen's taken a bit of a shine to him."

"You don't say."

"I do," grinned his father. "You should keep your eyes open so you can see what's happening in t'world."

The prospect of going to the dance at the Co-op Hall filled Willy with a sour sort of irritation. He couldn't dance. He had tried countless times. Gwen had done her best to initiate him into the mysteries of the foxtrot and quickstep, to no avail. And he loathed Al Bogley's band; it played a syrupy sort of Guy Lombardo style; Al himself was a simpering presence on the stage, resplendent in white evening suit with sparkling lapels; he spent the evening bestowing soppy smiles upon the dancers, occasionally picking up his violin and scraping out a whining chorus of something or other inconsequential. If it hadn't been for Ross, Willy wouldn't have

gone near the dance. Now there seemed to be no way of
getting out of it; besides, with the interest Gwen was taking
it seemed unwise to let them be unchaperoned. Not that his
mother and father seemed concerned; have a nice time,
you're only young once, they kept on babbling; daft stuff like
that.

It was even worse than he had anticipated. Packed, the
rotten place was. You had to fight to get a tasteless lemonade.
The dance floor itself was invisible beneath a forest of feet;
God knows how many hundreds of young men and women
there were, locked in each other's arms, shuffling around,
bumping into one another, while loathsome Al Bogley and
his well-lubricated minstrels puffed away and produced
nothing. Umpteen Yanks were there, all sounding like Ross
and displaying the same maddening self-confidence – and
succeeding in drawing forth adoring glances from the females. Silly cows. If only they could see themselves, Willy
told himself. Ross and Gwen came into view from time to
time, grinning, waving like holiday-makers in one of those
wish-you-were-here snaps. Entwined in each other's arms,
they were clearly having a whale of a good time.

After a ponderous but noisy attempt at swing by the Bogley aggregation, Ross and Gwen coasted in for a quick glass
of lemon-something.

"Not dancing, buddy?"

"He can't," said Gwen, whose forehead was pink and shiny.
"Never learnt. Tried to teach him. But it was hopeless. He's
not like you," she added. "You're a lovely dancer."

You bloody well would be, Willy thought.

"Try; it's easy," Ross told Willy as Gwen tugged him back
into the rabble.

Off they went, the crowd absorbing them as if it were a
vast, roisterous sponge. Willy exchanged promising glances
with a pale-eyed girl; then she was whisked away by a sailor.
He had a couple of words with a Tank Corps corporal; the two
of them had been at council school together and neither was
overwhelmed to see the other. After a few minutes the brown
job went off in pursuit of some popsy. Willy hated dances –

and envied those fellows who could casually invite total strangers to dance, then go whirling around, arms about them, holding them as tight as could be. A thoroughly smashing way to meet girls! Willy wished fervently that he could participate. He had studied charts showing disembodied feet positioning themselves on sheets of paper; he had even managed to make a few moderately successful attempts alone. But it was hopeless when he tried with a girl in his arms. He tripped and trod and plodded like a cart-horse. He would never get it right. Now he wanted nothing more than to get out of this steaming, smoky hell-hole . . .

He needed a breath or two of fresh air. Urgently. He elbowed his way through herds of perspiring humanity. A pimply-faced youth at the door gave him a pass-out and told him not to lose it or else he wouldn't be let in again. A fate worse than bloody death, Willy thought. He started down the steps to the street below. Then he wished he had stayed put. It was almost as crowded on the stairs as on the floor; but now the figures were stationary, like statues, all engrossed in one another, kissing, caressing, murmuring things in low, urgent tones. Willy winced. He had no business *there*; he was an aberration, a solitary male in an area reserved for couples. He turned to go back. And stopped. There, between the Royal Marine and the blonde and the Yank corporal and the brunette was an air force officer and a girl who were absolutely unmistakable even in the dim light. Ross and Gwen. And how fervently they embraced, how passionately they kissed, hands moving, grasping, exploring. Instinctively, Willy retreated.

In his haste to get back inside he almost knocked over a GI and his partner. Muttering apologies, he stumbled into the hall, shaken. Gwen! His sister! A child, no matter what the Wrens thought. And Ross! He felt dizzy. He had a glass of something horrible and listened to a Yank telling a girl about the wonders of Noo York City. It could have been Ross. God, the daft place was stifling, a sort of Dante's *Inferno* with Al Bogley and his shimmering lapels as a sort of limp-wristed devil.

At last Ross and Gwen reappeared, chuckling, clinging. Was Willy having a good time? Oh, just ruddy perfect, he assured them.

It was the same on the walk home. Lots of laughs. A real fine evening, according to Ross. Simply grand, agreed Gwen. She had a purry quality to her voice that Willy had never noticed before.

The parents were still up, waiting to provide the merry-makers with a goodnight cup of cocoa. Willy had to listen to Gwen regaling Mum and Dad with an account of every dreary minute, who was there, who wasn't, who was wearing what, who was with whom. It went on and on. Then Gwen said:

"Ross is going to stay until Monday."

"You are?" Willy was caught off guard.

"I am?" Ross seemed surprised too.

"It's all right, isn't it?" Gwen wanted to know. At once.

"You're welcome to stay as long as you like, lad," said Willy's father while his mother nodded her agreement.

"I'm imposing," said Ross. Willy was inclined to agree.

"Don't give it a thought, love. You're as welcome as a day in May."

"Told you," said Gwen.

"What about your hotel?" Willy asked.

"No problem. I'll call them in the morning."

There were walks and pictures, glasses of watery beer at The Butcher's Arms and endless yap about Winnipeg and Cadillac cars, about Gwen's hitherto unrevealed passion for skiing and camping.

It was a considerable relief when Ross caught the London train on Monday afternoon. He was a good chap, well-meaning, but to Willy's way of thinking it was possible to have too much of a good thing.

"A grand lad," said Willy's mother that evening. "Just like one of the family."

"He might be the way he and our Gwen were carrying on," Willy said.

His mother frowned as if he had said something improper.

"Well set-up lad," contributed his father.

"Lovely manners. Opened the door for me. Called me ma'am."

Willy sighed. They were all bewitched by Ross-magic. Then Gwen came home from work, looking as forlorn as any young girl whose love has run away.

The place seemed empty without Ross, she declared. She became quite snappish when Willy remarked how pleasant it was to have a little elbow room in the house.

The rest of his leave was vaguely unsatisfactory. The conversation invariably seemed to shift to Ross: what a grand lad he was, what a fine pal for Willy, how good-looking, how well-mannered. Gwen was constantly quivering on the brink of tears – why did he have to go to London? Why couldn't he have spent the rest of his leave at the house? When would he get leave again?

"You're going to bring him home again, aren't you?" It was more demand than question.

Willy shrugged. "He won't want to come back here again. He's seen it. There's nothing for him to come back to."

Whereupon Gwen burst into tears and fled upstairs.

"You didn't have to say that," his mother pointed out.

"It's the truth," said Willy.

"That's not the point."

"It's time our Gwen realizes that Ross has got girls all over the place. He collects them just like some lads collect stamps."

"I don't think that's very nice."

"I'm just trying to be realistic."

"Think of your sister's feelings."

It was almost a relief when the time came to return to Rocklington. The lines were clearly drawn there; you knew what was expected of you; you could say what was on your mind.

Ross was a trifle wan but cheerful enough. Willy asked him about London.

"That London," Ross said, "is one hell of a town. A guy could kill himself with pleasure there and it'd be a real nice way to go. How are your folks?"

"Grand."

"Swell, all of them. I wrote home and told them all about your family and how they'd treated me. Fine weekend, wasn't it, a great start to a leave, a sort of warm-up." He grinned then yawned. "Got to get some shut-eye, buddy. We could be on ops tomorrow and it won't do to sleep all the way there and back. Say, she's new, isn't she?" He nodded in the direction of a pert, red-headed WAAF who went by. "Will you get a load of the swing on that rear end!"

They were briefed to raid Emden. They bundled themselves in their flying gear, carted maps and refreshments, parachutes and assorted paraphernalia out to the aircraft, nerves tightening and innards loosening; they went through the agony of waiting and trying to make casual conversation to prove to their crewmates that they viewed the proceedings with equanimity. Then the op was scrubbed. Typical. The crew went down to the village. There was time for a couple of pints before closing. Ross and Willy argued most of the way about Harry James, Willy dismissing him as a mere exhibitionist, Ross claiming that he was a good jazz musician beneath all the syrup – and he had the advantage of having heard James in person and on records never released in England. No sooner were they in The White Rose than Ross started talking to a couple of leathery-faced old locals, the sort who hated the air force filling up their pub and drinking their beer. But Ross beamed; it was just great to make their acquaintance; he was Ross Sinclair from Winnipeg, Manitoba, and he would be real happy if they would join him and his buddies in a drink. In a moment they were all chatting away like old school chums. Ross and his silver tongue. Willy sighed.

"Great institution, your pubs. We don't have them back home. Got to do something about it, seems to me. Create nice warm meeting places where a guy can have a glass of something and exchange a word or two with his neighbours. Civilized, I call it. I bet the idea would catch on like wildfire back home. May have some trouble with the liquor laws. Weird laws we've got, believe me. So we'll have to get 'em changed."

Typical Ross. Anything was possible. If it needed doing, there had to be a way of doing it. If pubs didn't exist in Manitoba, create them.

Willy said, "I think the family quite missed you when you went off to London."

"I missed them too. Great folks."

"Our Gwen was sorry you didn't stay longer. But I told her, he's got half a dozen popsies waiting for him down in London . . . "

"Hell of a girl, your sister."

Willy was on the point of asking Ross whether he wanted to come to Droylsden on the next leave. Gwen had insisted that he find out. She must know, she said. Willy cleared his throat and drew a breath. Then he stopped. Ross had turned away. He was gazing at a WAAF who had just entered the bar in company with an RAF sergeant. A pretty girl, the WAAF, with a delicate mouth and soft green eyes, and prominent cheek-bones that gave her face an almost Oriental cast. Her black hair was pulled back severely beneath her cap.

She and the sergeant sat down near the door.

"She's a doll," said Ross.

"I remember her," said Harry. "She was engaged to one of Colin Fry's crew. Poor bugger bought it when they ditched."

"How come I never noticed her before?"

Ross asked the question in a slightly aggrieved tone, as if one of the crew should have pointed out the girl to him.

"The bomb-aimer."

"What?"

"That's who she was engaged to. Can't remember his name, though."

"You see what she's got?" Ross asked Willy.

"Aye, a shandy, I think."

"*Class*, my friend, that's what she's got."

"They're all the same in the dark," yawned Harry.

Ross shook his head. How, he asked, did he ever get crewed up with such a bunch of soulless clods?

"Don Flinders," said Gordon.

"Huh?"

"That was his name."

"Whose name?"

"The chap she was engaged to. Her name's Phoebe."

"She reminds me of a sheila I knew in Brisbane," said Ty. "Very passionate. Bit me once. I'm too much of a gentleman to say where."

"I thought you said it was in Brisbane," said Ross.

"She puts me in mind of a chorus girl I met in Leicester," said Harry. "Charming little bitch. Stole a fiver from me."

"Was she worth it?"

"No woman is worth five pounds."

"Betty Grable is," said Ty. "I'd pay a fiver for her any day. Maybe even ten."

Willy was inclined to agree, but he said nothing.

The next night they went to Mannheim. Shortly before they arrived at the target Andy Shaw glimpsed a Ju 88 night-fighter.

"Corkscrew starboard!" His voice snapped like the crack of a whip.

Ross's reaction was instantaneous. The world went mad, whirling, revolving, sending senses reeling. You clung to bulkheads. And prayed. A stream of darting lights went sailing away into the night.

"We've lost him."

"Don't be so sure. Eyes open wide, everyone."

Over the target the Hally indulged in its usual little buoyant bounce as the bomb load fell away. At almost precisely the same instant another fighter attacked – this time an Me 110, according to Andy. Its fire riddled the rear of the fuselage, sounding for all the world like someone hitting a toy metal drum. The acrid stink of cordite filled the twisting, plunging metal tube while the guns rattled in sharp bursts.

"I hit him!" screeched Andy from the mid-upper turret. "I saw bits fall off. Big bits!"

"Nice work, Andy," acknowledged Ross in his unhurried way. "But keep on the lookout. Everyone all right? Report in."

Ty Marshall in the rear turret had been wounded in the

exchange. Willy and Gordon went aft and helped him out of his turret. He had been hit in the thigh; his flying suit was black with blood; he kept muttering and Willy kept nodding although he couldn't hear what was said because Ty wasn't plugged into the intercom. They settled him on the rest bunk and applied dressings and administered a shot of morphine.

On touch-down, the lacerated fuselage buckled, the tail twisting, the rudder sending up showers of sparks as it scraped along the runway. The medical orderlies swarmed aboard and carted Ty away. He had lost a lot of blood, they said, but with a bit of luck he should be all right.

The crew went to visit him the next morning. He managed a weak smile, then dozed off. The MO, Coates, wanted them to leave.

"Needs lots of rest. Regaining his strength. Supremely important, this period of his recovery, with the body still grappling with the trauma of it all."

Coates always sounded as if he was quoting from a medical book.

"How long will he be out of action?" enquired Ross.

"Hard to say, old man. Depends so much on the individual."

It was on the way out of Sick Quarters that Ross suddenly stopped, his shoes sliding on the polished lino floor. Willy almost collided with him, so abrupt was his halt.

"Hi there," said Ross, opening a glass-panelled door.

It was the WAAF they had seen in the pub.

She looked up from the filing cabinet.

"Yes sir?"

"I saw you in The White Rose the other night."

She smiled that same thoughtful smile.

"Were you there, sir?" Very correct, very cool.

"Sure. You work here?"

"Yes."

"I'm Ross Sinclair."

"I know. We've got one of your crew. He's going to be all right, I'm sure."

"Someone said you knew a good friend of mine. Don Flinders."

Willy winced. There were times when Ross went a ruddy sight too far. On tiptoes, he glimpsed the girl over Ross's shoulder. She stood perfectly still, her eyes on Ross, her mouth slightly open as if she had been turned to stone while speaking.

Then she took a quick breath and seemed to come back to life.

"I don't remember him mentioning you."

"Why would he? I was just another guy he knew at OTU."

Another quick breath.

"He . . . bought it," she said. The familiar term sounded odd coming from a woman.

"I know. I heard. Tough break."

For the rest of the day Ross wouldn't stop talking about her. Such a quality in the voice. Such eyes.

"Cute name, Phoebe, don't you think?"

Really, he could be the most insensitive sod. He seemed to have completely forgotten that he was talking to Gwen's brother – Gwen, who had been the focus of his entire being a few days ago.

Before the day was out Ty Marshall's replacement had reported in. His name was Geoff Flynn, a solid, round-faced youth from Ludlow who was the sole survivor of a crew lost in a cross-country accident.

They went to Leverkusen. It was a quiet trip until a Lancaster was blown to bits immediately in front of them. A large chunk of the stricken aircraft smashed into the Halifax's port outer. It burst into flames. Seconds became stretched, distorted, tortured into lifetimes while gloved hands fumbled for the Graviner fire extinguisher and the feathering buttons. The wind-beaten flames played like a torch on the tail until it created a monstrous beacon for every night-fighter and flak battery in the area. Then the flames flickered and disappeared. Blessed darkness cloaked the Halifax once more. It limped back to base.

The next morning a letter arrived for Willy. It was from

his mother. She hoped the letter found him well and eating properly and keeping warm now that the weather was beginning to turn. It was so lovely having him home on leave. And what a grand lad Ross was. Would he be coming home with Willy on the next leave? Willy sighed. His mother's guess was as good as his.

The crew went out to look at their aircraft. It was a sobering sight. The fire had done more damage than any of them had realized. The wing could have folded up at any moment during the trip home.

"I'm glad I didn't know," said Ross.

"You fly better when the kite's falling to bits," said Harry.

That afternoon they took a replacement aircraft for a test, turning and diving in the sunlight high above the layers of grey that hid the earth from view. It was another world up there, a world of sparkling brightness, a clean, uncomplicated world. On the way back to Rocklington, Willy took over.

He revelled in these moments, feeling the pulse of the aircraft through the controls, observing the horizon tilt at his will. He could handle turns now, keeping the rudder and ailerons coordinated to prevent the aircraft skidding. Ross had taught him that the kite had to be coaxed not forced, that flying was a sort of partnership. Willy piloted the Halifax all the way home, until the field was in view; then Ross took his seat once more and landed with his usual flair, slipping off speed and altitude so that the big bomber touched down at the end of the runway with barely a squeak from the main wheels and the tailwheel.

Ross always maintained that aeroplanes wanted to do the right things: it was idiotic, ham-fisted pilots who made them err.

Later, in the Crew Room, Ross remarked that he had received a letter from Gwen. "Writes well. Constructs a proper sentence; people do here, I've noticed. Folks are too sloppy about grammar and stuff back home."

"Does she know when she's going in the Wrens?"

"Not yet."

"She seemed to enjoy that weekend when you came home."

"So did I," Ross responded with a grin. "Had a whale of a time. Gwen sure was a great gal."

Was. Past tense. Had Ross so filed her in his mental black book? Willy shrugged to himself. He couldn't tell Ross how to pursue his love life. Gwen would get over it.

The mist rolled in the next day. The Halifaxes sat immobile, engines, wheels, and canopies shrouded in covers, propeller blades damp with beads of moisture that looked like ice.

That evening Willy was adjusting his tie when Ross came bursting in, in a hurry as usual.

"Glad I found you, buddy. Doing anything?"

"Going to see *The Maltese Falcon*. Told you this afternoon."

"So you did. Well, listen, I know how you feel about blind dates, but there's this cute WAAF who works in Sick Quarters, Phoebe – you met her, didn't you? Sure you did. I suggested we go down for a couple of drinks in the village. But she wants this friend of hers to come along."

"And the friend doesn't have anyone to go with."

"You catch on fast. I've always said that about you."

"No," said Willy. "Thanks for the offer. But I'm going to the pictures."

"Her friend is really cute," said Ross. "You'll have a whale of a time. You need a night out."

"No, I need a nice quiet night at the pictures. Blind dates aren't my cup of tea." Besides, there was a question of loyalty to Gwen, wasn't there?

Willy was never quite sure afterwards when and how he agreed to go along. But soon he found himself shaking hands with a substantial Birmingham girl called Beryl. She was as tall as Willy and her sole topic of conversation for the first half-hour was how the mist was taking the natural *spring* out of her hair.

Phoebe hailed from Surrey; her father, she said, was a musician, a violinist – whereupon Ross declared himself to be a lifelong lover of the violin, reeling off names like Stern and

Menuhin in the same reverent tones usually employed for Armstrong and Bechet. Willy had to admit that Phoebe was formidable competition for Gwen, an amusing and intelligent conversationalist. Beryl was less delightful. She gulped down gin after gin, and with each one she became slightly more surly and opinionated. With the topic of her hair exhausted, she now expounded on every other conceivable subject. Stalin had been dead two years, but to maintain morale the public hadn't been told; a stand-in was being used for public appearances. Bomber Harris had to clear every target with the Americans. Britain would be a colony of the United States after the war. Howard Hughes was Jewish. So was Anthony Eden. Greta Garbo was a man. The Jerries tried to invade in September 1940; bodies littered the beach at Porthcawl, bloated and burnt.

At closing time the four left together in company with a crush of air force types; it was like walking in a forest of blue trees. In minutes Willy and Beryl were walking alone in the mist.

"Crafty sod," commented Beryl. "I know what's on his dirty mind. But Sinclair won't get anywhere with her. She knows how to look after herself, she does. Bloody men."

There seemed little for Willy to say, so he remained silent, concentrating on keeping up with Beryl – no mean task, for she maintained a telling pace.

When they were halfway to the camp, Willy remarked that despite the mist it was a pleasant night for a stroll.

She turned on him, startling him.

"You mean it's a good night for some hanky-panky behind the bushes. That's what you mean, isn't it?"

"No – "

"You bloody men are all the same. Always thinking of *that*. Always wanting to *paw*. Make me sick, all of you."

"But, honest – "

"Just forget it. A couple of drinks and you think you've *bought* someone."

"I didn't think – "

"You try any funny stuff and you'll be sorry."

Mercifully, a creaking Austin Seven came along, bulging with members of Bob Shipton's crew. Somehow they found room for Willy and Beryl.

The next day the mists cleared. The sun shone. Ross was in a cheerful mood. Strange, wasn't it, what happened at closing time? The fog. Son-of-a-gun how you could get separated in fog. Wasn't Phoebe a delight? A unique quality. Never met anyone remotely like her. Doubted that there was anyone like her anywhere. And wasn't that Beryl a character?

They had a relatively quiet trip to Nuremberg, landing at three minutes past four in the morning. A scant six hours later an airman was waking Willy up.

"C'mon, Sarge. Rise and shine. Ops on again."

Willy muttered something, but the man was already moving to the next bunk, rousing Gordon; his voice had a maddening lilt; he enjoyed waking people up, you could tell. Willy dragged himself out of the warm bedclothes. The linoleum floor was like ice. Where the hell were his slippers? He had slept badly as he often did after an op. It had taken him hours to drop off; every time he began to sleep he saw a collision between two bombers in the darkness, the violent cataclysmic transformation from neat, well-balanced mechanical devices to a welter of tangled metal and flesh, spinning propellers and vomiting fuel tanks, tumbling, turning, becoming a fireworks display. . . . Why was it that all the terrors of night bombing were for him embodied in collisions?

There was a letter for him.

From his father. Unusual, that. Dad usually left the letter-writing to Mum, always saying she had more time for that sort of thing.

"Dear Son, I hope this finds you well. It is a difficult thing to write about but you are a man now and in a sort of a way it involves you, not that you're to blame, nothing of the sort. It's about our Gwen. She has a problem. I don't think it's necessary for me to go into details. And why I say it involves you is because it was your friend Ross, you see, nice lad though he was . . . "

Strewth! Willy sat back, blinking at the words.

He had to go back and read the opening paragraph again. It was true; he hadn't imagined it. He read on:

"I have written to Ross, so has Gwen. He has to know, of course. But seeing you're so close to him, we felt you had to know too, and of course it was your right to know, if you follow my meaning. There is only one thing for Ross to do. He must marry our Gwen. And he has to be quick about it. I will leave you now. Sorry to burden you with this when we know how much you have on your plate, but we all agreed you had to know and that you would want to do your best to look after your sister's interests. Your loving Father."

Strewth again! Willy kept looking at the letter as if to remind himself that it was real and not something left over from a dream. *Gwen*? And *Ross*? He stuffed the letter in his pocket and went to breakfast. He sat beside a gunner named Bannerman who had the twitch. Poor sod, he had flown too many ops. He kept heaving huge sighs; then he would say:

"Nice day to go flying, isn't it?"

And chuckle as if he had said something immensely witty. He belonged in a mental ward. Or did he? Perhaps it was part of a campaign to get himself taken off flying duties. A lad named Summers was reported to have kept on peeing in his bed until he was grounded. Someone said he was a big cheese in the public relations group at the Air Ministry now . . .

What to say to Ross? How to behave? How did he *feel*? Presumably, as a brother, he was supposed to be outraged. But, upon reflection, he came to the conclusion that he was annoyed with Gwen as much as he was with Ross. Silly buggers, they had made a right mess of things. Would he feel differently if the villain were someone else, a stranger? He wondered. He wasn't sure, about anything. Was Ross at this moment sitting at breakfast in the Officers' Mess reading his morning post? Had he suddenly lost his appetite? *You daft sod, Ross.*

Harry planted himself beside Willy, yawning and scratching his ribs. Did Willy hear those bastards with their lorries at half past seven? No bloody consideration, that was the truth of it. Did they give a damn that the occupants of those huts had been up all night at *war*?

Gwen!

No, he still couldn't believe it. Yet he knew it was true; the fact was inescapable. But somehow it had no *substance*; it couldn't be taken seriously, not yet.

When had the dirty deed occurred? After the dance? Hanky-panky during the night? Creeping about the house from bedroom to front room?

But why would Ross go to so much trouble . . . for *Gwen*?

Like most brothers, Willy found it difficult to accept the fact that his sister was alluring enough to tempt a normal man to foolish excesses.

After breakfast Willy made his way to the Flight Office. Ross was there, talking to an Aussie pilot named Harding. He nodded to Willy. Willy nodded in return. Mechanical, ill at ease nods. Did Ross *know*? Did he get his letter from Droylsden too? Was it in fact that slight lump in his battle-dress pocket? What a ruddy turn-up for the books. He wished he knew what he was supposed to do. And feel. Wasn't life complicated enough without *this*?

"We've got a new kite," Ross announced.

Harry grinned like a man whose long-awaited sports car has finally arrived at the dealer's.

"Let's call it ROSS'S RESPONSIBILITY," Willy suggested.

Ross frowned but said nothing.

Roland shook his head. "I do think we should be able to do better than that."

"Just a suggestion."

"What d'you think?" Harry asked Ross.

"About what?" Had Ross paled a bit?

"The name."

"*Name!* Whose name . . . ?" Definitely a shade paler.

"The kite's name."

"Oh . . . *that*."

They collected their gear and went out to the dispersal. Ross said little. Hardly surprising, Willy supposed, under the circumstances. He found himself grappling with a curiously disturbing mingling of emotions: outrage and empathy, embarrassment, and something vaguely resembling jealousy, that any bloke could be so downright *successful*.

The new kite awaited them, its paintwork fresh, its metal parts pristine, its great tires unblemished.

Ross and Willy walked around the aircraft followed by the ground crew chiefie, Pudwell, who kept pausing to point here and there and make knowing comments. But it was obvious that Ross's mind was elsewhere. His features wore a dazed, slightly bewildered expression, a how-could-fate-be-so-cruel look. Willy wondered how one broached such a subject in such circumstances. One didn't, he decided. One waited until a suitable moment presented itself. If it ever did.

Ross boarded first and disappeared forward, his flying boots thumping within the metal structure. When Willy joined him in the cockpit Ross didn't look up. No question now; he knew. The fact that he didn't look up was proof. He always looked up with a grin, a carefree grin. No more of those for a while. Willy tugged the leather helmet over his head and gazed through the window at his side. The ground crew stood, hands on hips, watching, looking as if they regretted handing the kite over to the doubtful skills of this lot.

Willy and Ross went through the start-up litany like two strangers.

The engine clattered into life, generating the familiar vibrations, the drumming through the feet, the excited trembling of the airframe; it felt as if the kite couldn't wait to get going. Ross taxied out with little bursts of power. At the threshold of the runway he ran up the engines one by one, thrusting the throttle levers forward until the engines threatened to drag themselves out of the wings.

With no bombs and only a partial fuel load, the Halifax became airborne little more than halfway along the runway. She climbed with considerably more enthusiasm than her predecessors.

It was good to leave the complicated earth behind. The

familiar countryside dropped away below. You always breathed a little easier when the kite had successfully parted company with the runway and gained a decent height; trouble close to the ground often meant the chop for everyone concerned.

As the Halifax's broad wing traced a half-circle around the village, Willy wondered what Ross expected from the outraged brother. And how would King's Regs deal with such a situation? Did they make allowances for NCOs whose sisters had been violated by officers? Would a court martial be understanding if Sergeant Perkins biffed Pilot Officer Sinclair on the nose?

But what if Ross still didn't know? He might not have received the news yet. His mood might be the result of a couple of drinks too many in the Officers' Mess the night before.

Up through scattered cloud, the blunt nose thrusting into sparkling, umblemished sunshine. Ross put the bomber into a steep turn, circling around a fluffy cumulus cloud, slicing bits off with his wingtip. Willy wished he would stop it. What if there was another Halifax doing exactly the same thing on the other side of the cloud, coming in the opposite direction? In some ways it was preferable to fly at night when you seldom saw another aircraft and were blissfully ignorant of how many near-misses you had miraculously survived.

They tested the aircraft and its systems, then headed back to Rocklington. Ross didn't suggest that Willy take over the controls for a few minutes; he grunted his way through the approach check list – fuel, gear up-locks, flaps . . . auto-pilot off, superchargers in M ratio . . .

Perched on the jump seat, Willy watched the village sliding toward him. Toy houses. Dinky Toy cars. The railway line swept below, looking like one of those Hornby train displays in Lewis's at Christmas, so appealing but so impossibly expensive. Over the grammar school, the deserted playing field, a boy's cap lying there in the grass . . .

Lor! They barely missed the rugger posts! The trees went sailing by. Far too bloody low! Willy turned to Ross.

At that moment Ross seemed to wake up to the danger. He thrust the throttle levers forward. The aircraft surged, shuddering, brushing through the topmost branches of the trees that bordered the field.

It was a rotten landing. A thumping, banging, bouncing landing.

"Are we down yet?" Andy asked after three bounces.

Ross didn't respond. He taxied the Hally back to its dispersal and switched off. No one had anything more to say about the landing.

Later, outside the Crew Room, Ross muttered quietly, "What can I say?"

He shook his head and sighed, puffing his cheeks.

"You got a letter from our Gwen?" Willy asked.

Ross nodded, taking off his cap and running a hand through his hair. "Sure, I got a letter from your Gwen. You too?"

"My dad wrote to me," said Willy.

"Son of a bitch," said Ross. "I'm real sorry . . . I mean, well, you know . . . especially after your folks were so nice . . ."

"They liked you too," said Willy. "But what are you going to do about this?"

"Do?" Ross scratched his forehead. "What d'you have in mind?"

"For a start, I'd say it'd be a good idea if you got in touch with her."

"Huh?" Ross scratched his chin. "Think so? Yes, maybe I'd better."

It would have been more reassuring had he declared his intention of sending her a telegram or writing a long letter or placing a trunk call to the next-door-but-one neighbours who had a telephone. But the news seemed to have made Ross strangely indecisive.

Willy said, "Ruddy good job you're not married already."

"Married?" Ross frowned at the word.

"What I mean is, it would be awkward if you already had a wife. But you haven't, have you?"

"No," Ross murmured.

"You're sure?"

Ross glared at him. "Of course I'm sure."

"That's good."

Ross continued to glare as they made their way past the hangars.

"I hadn't figured on this," Ross said, sounding like a man whose bill is much larger than he had expected. "It's not . . . right. You enjoy yourself and . . ."

"Aye, it's unfortunate."

"Unfortunate? It's one hell of a lot more than unfortunate."

"I suppose you'll be writing to her."

Ross scowled. "I said I would."

"Good. When?"

"When? Do you want a goddam timetable?"

"Just asking."

Ross glanced at his watch.

"Got to go."

"But . . ."

"But what?"

"Is that all you've got to say about . . . it?"

"What else do you want me to say?"

Willy wanted him to declare unequivocally that he would do the right thing, that he would send telegrams, that he would go to see Gwen and indeed the whole family at the first opportunity, that he wasn't really all that sorry about the turn of events because it meant that he and Gwen would be together always . . .

But Ross hadn't said any of those things.

The padre. Wasn't he there for precisely this sort of problem? To advise? To offer a suggestion or two? A bespectacled man with a perpetually surprised expression, the padre was to be seen at briefings and post-op interrogations, bestowing vague smiles on one and all.

The padre's office was somewhere in the administration block. Willy went into the Orderly Room to find out just where.

He found Beryl looking important behind a typewriter.

Willy asked her if she could tell him where the padre's office was.

"Certainly can. But will I, that's the question." Big, self-satisfied smile; she seemed to be in better humour than the last time he had seen her. "Just joking. On the left down the corridor. Arranging the wedding, are you?"

"Wedding?"

Another grin. "Your friend Ross and Phoebe."

A lump of something rough and heavy seemed to thud into Willy's stomach.

"Ross? Wedding?"

"Well, I'd say they've clicked, wouldn't you?"

"Clicked?"

She shook her head impatiently. "You know what I mean. On good terms. *Very* good terms."

She winked.

"I didn't know that," Willy muttered.

"Mind you, I told her, I said, 'You'll be getting into hot water, going out with an officer. They don't like it. Don't like it a bit.'"

"That's true."

"Even aircrew. But they can't do anything about it if she marries him, can they?"

Every time she used the word the lump in Willy's stomach grew rougher and heavier. He said, "It's my understanding that he's already engaged . . . to a very nice girl in the Manchester area."

"*What!*"

You heard, Willy replied in silence as he left the Orderly Room.

Marry! Had he already *asked* that Phoebe woman? Was it *official?*

An LAC clerk sat in the padre's office, smoking and reading the *Mirror.*

"Can I see the padre, please?"

"Sorry, Sarge, he's away."

"Hell."

"Not that far," said the clerk, "just over to Spodworth. Goes there every Wednesday. They don't have a padre there, see. Back tomorrow. Can I help, Sarge?"

Willy shook his head and returned to his billet. He would see the padre the next day. This was the sort of thing padres were for, wasn't it? He started a letter to his father. And abandoned it after a couple of paragraphs. He had nothing to say, that was the truth of it. He had talked to Ross but might have saved himself the trouble for all the good he had done. There was no point in writing until he had news to impart, news of a positive nature. Dad had written to him because he was here, on the spot, to look after Gwen's interests. But it was easier said than done. He couldn't take Ross by the scruff of the neck and make him write telegrams and letters. He couldn't *order* him. But he could hear his mother and Gwen carolling: "You could've done *something*. The family was depending on you and you let us all down . . ."

He went to the ops meal with Flight Sergeant Crocker who related in grisly detail an operation his uncle had recently undergone on his bowels. In the middle of this saga Roland walked over to the table. Had Willy seen Ross? Where could the stupid sod be? Had he forgotten they had an op to fly?

Willy shook his head. Had Ross ended it all in the Rocklington Canal?

After the meal the aircrews shuffled into the briefing room and sat down at the long dark tables. Roland kept looking around, frowning, biting his lower lip, looking like a bridegroom waiting for his bride.

Willy sniffed. Roland only had to find another pilot; finding another husband for Gwen would be a ruddy sight harder.

Ross came rushing in a moment before roll-call. He nodded to Roland but avoided everyone else's eyes. A moment later the Station Commander and his entourage strode in, briskly, importantly.

The familiar map. The red areas indicating enemy defence concentrations. The route: a tape that stretched for ever across Germany, all the way to . . . Berlin. A groan from the assembled crews, although they knew by the fuel and bomb loads that a distant target had been selected. But Berlin was so bloody far way and you could reach it only by flying endless miles over just about the most hostile territory on earth.

But the briefing officers were enthusiastic.

"We're going to burn Berlin to the ground just as we did Hamburg!"

They sounded as if the job was going to be jolly good fun. The route had been masterfully planned; the diversionary raids were brilliantly conceived; the weather was going to be ideal. The raid would be a major blow to Jerry; the utter destruction of his three major cities, Berlin, Hamburg, and Cologne, could well prove to be more than he could bear. Codswallop, of course; the experienced crews had heard it all before; the rhetoric was aimed at the sprogs who didn't know any better.

Willy waited while Gordon gathered his code sheets with the lists of frequencies to be used for communications and for jamming.

They collected their gear, parachutes, rations, helmets, oxygen masks, and drifted outside, an untidy gaggle of them, bulky and hot in their flying suits and wool-lined boots, smoking, peering up at the darkening sky, chatting and chuckling a trifle too loudly.

Willy heard Roland say something to Ross, something about wondering whether he was going to get to briefing in time.

"I got there, didn't I?"

"Just."

"Better than not at all."

Roland looked concerned, but didn't reply.

At last the vans arrived; the crews bundled themselves and their luggage aboard. Willy found himself sitting beside a gunner named Keegan who talked about a certain WAAF driver who was rumoured to be supplementing her pay by servicing the ground crews while ops were on, travelling from dispersal to dispersal, dispensing her favours according to a rigid price list; the gunner claimed that she was saving up for a house for her parents who had been bombed out.

"The way she's going she'll be able to buy Buckingham Palace."

There was a light rain falling when the van deposited the crew beneath the nose of their aircraft.

Ross said quietly, "We'll talk some more when we get back, okay?"

Willy nodded. "I've got to look after . . . Gwen's interests."

The term seemed cold and mercenary but he could think of no alternative.

"Sure you do, buddy. I understand."

Ross grinned, half-heartedly, shrugging. He looked like a schoolboy who had run out of excuses and was going to take his punishment.

They took off as darkness enveloped the field. Ross used every last foot of runway, pulling the kite into the air moments before the York Road swept below. He kept the nose down until the speed built up, then heaved back on the control column. The shadowy ground fell away; the aircraft lurched as the undercarriage folded back into the inner engine nacelles.

After take-off, Willy spent the early part of every trip with his head in the astro dome, looking out for other aircraft. The Vale of York was cluttered with airfields. Navigation lights punctuated the darkness, each pair representing one bomber filled with fuel and loaded with bombs. Hundreds of eyes probed the night.

What was Gwen doing at this moment? What *did* girls do under such circumstances? Cry? Did she feel sick already? Girls were supposed to feel sick, weren't they? He still couldn't believe it.

When they reached ten thousand feet everyone went on oxygen. Willy positioned the rubber mask across his face, fastening it by means of a press stud on his helmet. Nasty rubbery-smelling things, oxygen masks; they came in three sizes, none of which fitted him; his face was invariably chafed after a few hours' flying.

"Aircraft right behind us," reported Geoff.

Willy could see its shadowy form between the wingtip lights. The aircraft soon dropped away to the rear; it couldn't climb like Ross's brand new Hally.

He settled down to his log, entering rows of figures: fuel consumption, air temperature, airspeed, engine revs, boost, oil temperature, coolant temperature, supercharger, oxygen. . . . Did anyone ever do anything useful with all the reams of data brought back by droves of flight engineers from every trip?

Over the sea the gunners tested their Brownings, firing short bursts that sounded like popguns against the din of the engines.

He looked forward, over Ross's shoulder and through the windscreen. The weather had cleared. The sea shimmered faintly far below. On either side the exhausts of the Merlins glowed. The makers had tried various devices to cut down the glow but still it persisted, inviting the attention of Jerry night-fighters.

You've got a responsibility, lad, he told himself. To Gwen. To the whole family. You've got to do the right thing.

He wished someone would tell him what the right thing was.

Perhaps the padre would do so in the morning. Words of wisdom from the Sky Pilot. The Right Thing, King James Version. But what if Ross simply said that he loved Phoebe and that he wouldn't marry Gwen, no matter what? What then? He shrugged. A proper bugger. And yet he, Willy Perkins, was expected to put it all to rights. The whole family was depending on him, which meant that everything would be his fault if it went badly. Why didn't he do that? Or this? Or the other? Didn't he care about his sister's welfare? Didn't he understand his responsibilities? He shook his helmeted head, perplexed.

Every fifteen minutes on the dot, Ross ordered every member of the crew to check in. It was a sensible practice; a crew member could easily be in difficulties without anyone knowing about it. Willy heard of a crew who brought back a dead gunner. His oxygen had failed during the trip home and he had died in his turret; his death was undiscovered until the aircraft was close to England.

"Enemy coast in five minutes."

A tightening of nerves and sinews, a bracing of one's self for the familiar ordeal. Like entering the dentist's office.

"Flak ahead."

Willy peered forward. Flak was pretty at a distance, reminding you of fireworks on Guy Fawkes Day. The pity was, you couldn't keep flak at a distance; you had to plod on through it, your only protection being the fact that it was statistically certain that the vast majority of aircraft would get through.

Searchlights sliced the darkness, restlessly searching for prey. Why didn't the fighter boys go in and shoot the ruddy things out? The lazy bastards were enjoying themselves in pubs when they could be out here doing a useful job of work.

Ross instructed everyone to keep their eyes peeled. Unnecessary, because everyone was all too conscious of the danger from predatory night-fighters. But one of the reasons the crew had survived this long was that Ross didn't leave things to chance – at least not in the air.

More numbers for the log. Willy copied them in his neat hand. Engines humming nicely, gulping fuel at the approved rate, not like R-Robert; a ruddy thirsty kite, R-Robert. Willy was convinced it had a leak, but the erks never found it. Now they never would.

Geoff announced the failure of the electrical heating system in his flying suit.

"Check all your connections."

"I have. I'll check 'em again."

Ross should finish his engineering studies when he got back to Canada. A married man with a family needed a profession.

The aircraft rocked and swayed as it drifted into someone else's propwash. Disquieting yet comforting to know that you were in the bosom of the stream. Safety lay in its numbers, an enormous convoy in the night; if you wandered away you were easy meat for the Jerries.

"Enemy coast coming up."

A mile or two ahead someone bought it. A sudden, blinding flash; a great eruption of light as high explosive and fuel converted a bomber and its seven occupants to fiery particles zigzagging across the night. No one had a prayer.

Willy found himself huddling against the fuselage wall. Silly, really. There was no protection to be found there; he was standing in a box made of thin, fragile metal; flak fragments sliced through it like a hot knife through butter.

Now the bombers were striking out across the heart of Germany; there simply was no other way of reaching the target. Not fair; London was a piece of cake to reach. Turn left at the Thames Estuary. Follow the fog.

The flak subsided. A peaceful cross-country by night. But no one was deceived; down below the Jerries were as busy as little ants, calculating where the bombers were headed, scrambling their fighter squadrons, sounding the air raid sirens.

Did Jerry air raid sirens sound like ours?

No sooner had he asked himself the question than the first fighters attacked the stream. Harry reported from the nose: Bomber going down in flames to port. No sign of chutes.

Willy watched from the astro dome. He never liked having his head stuck in the thing. He felt so horribly vulnerable there. No doubt he was equally vulnerable in the interior of the fuselage but at least there was a *feeling* of security inside. Sticking one's head in the astro dome was like poking it out of a trench and asking the enemy to try and shoot it off.

Flickering lights darted upward almost vertically. Tracer. A great smear of flame stretched out behind a Hally. Down the aircraft went, turning, twisting, the fire following it until it disappeared from sight, thank God. You didn't want to watch the poor bastard going down, yet you couldn't tear your eyes away . . .

It was quiet again. A night cross-country; but the wrong country. The bombers droned on. Far away to starboard there were searchlights and flak. A diversionary raid probably. A dozen Mossies making the Jerries think it was a full-scale op. Lucky sods, the Mosquito crews; in their speedy, agile little kites, they had the lowest casualties in Bomber Command. Too bad they didn't need flight engineers in Mosquito squadrons.

Ten minutes later the flak started again in earnest. Flashes burst around them; one was near; something hit the wing.

Willy gulped. A nasty night. The natives were bloody rest-less. Best not to peep out of the window. Best to pretend there wasn't anything happening outside.

Geoff Flynn's voice came from the rear turret:

"Start weaving, Skipper. Looks like the flak's forming up on us."

"Thanks, Geoff." Ross flew an erratic path, climbing, de-scending, sliding from port to starboard.

"Rear gunner to Skipper. They've given up on us."

"Nice work."

None of that captain-to-rear-gunner stuff with Ross.

They flew on, rocked by flak explosions but untouched.

Time to go aft to change tanks. It was lonely amidships. The fuselage swayed, vibrating as if scared by the din. Fur-ther aft Andy sat in his turret, turning, always turning. In the tail Geoff would be doing the same thing. Best not to try and calculate how many heavy bombers occupied the sky all around you. The bomber stream was like a great school of metal fish all buzzing along with their eyes closed, hoping they wouldn't bump into one another.

As soon as the flak eased off the fighters swarmed in again. Willy saw the tracer as he made his way forward.

Ross kept dipping one wing then the other so that the gunners could check below. Why didn't the Hally have a belly turret like the Yanks put on their Forts and Libs? No doubt some committee – well-fed, pot-bellied types puffing on ci-gars – had sat down and decided that such devices were too costly and heavy and, after all, adding them would mean a corresponding reduction in bomb loads, so, when the pros were bounced against the cons, it was clear that the best course of action was no action, and although it would mean increased casualties, the losses would be borne with true British fortitude . . .

An endless journey . . . could this be the one when the Jerries finally managed to get every one of the bombers? Daft, cruising along in the middle of Germany, asking for trouble . . .

He had to marry her, didn't he? It was the only proper thing to do. Good job it was Ross and not some others one could mention. Ross had his faults, but he was essentially a grand lad.

Which should have provided a certain comfort.

And didn't.

The bombers droned on. An hour. Two. The fighters got a Stirling. It broke up when its fuel tanks exploded. The final leg to the target. Ross gave the Pathfinders' flares a wide berth; although they were a helpful signpost in the night and tended to concentrate the stream for its assault on the target, they were an invitation to the fighters. Many a sprog crew bought it near such clusters of flares.

"Target in five minutes."

Another glance forward. Flickering pinpoints of light ahead. Back into the astro dome; he would do his log on the way out of the target area.

Ah, some poor bugger was coned, the searchlights joining forces, trapping him in their confluence. Down he went, trying to shake the lights while every flak battery in the area blazed away at him.

"Target coming up."

Now Harry's voice controlled the bomber, instructing Ross . . . right, left-left . . . steady . . .

It was the now-familiar dirge that marked the pivotal moments of the operation, the justification for it all.

"Bombs gone."

Thirty more seconds of exquisite agony to be endured: the price of getting a good picture of the bombs doing their stuff. A nice little snap for Butch's album; something to show Winston during the bargaining for another thousand aircraft and crews . . .

Someone got the chop off to port. A flickering of flame, an erratic twisting path, then a sudden plunge. And another, behind, the burning bomber turning away gently, as if the pilot and crew had all the time in the world; it descended, still turning until it went out of sight. Would the BBC be reporting that *all* our aircraft failed to return?

"Fighter astern," reported Geoff.

"I see the bugger too," said Andy. "Keeping his distance, so far."

Heart thumping, Willy turned to go rearward. He couldn't see the fighter.

"Could be a decoy," said Andy.

"I know," said Geoff, shortly. Any gunner worth his salt knew about decoys; the Jerries were fond of trying to get all a bomber's gunners concentrating on one fighter while another sneaked in from the side or below. Only sprog crews fell for that sort of thing.

"He's gone after someone else," reported Andy.

Thank God for that – although bad luck for that someone else. But that someone else was anonymous, a shadowy form in the night, so you couldn't feel too sad about him, could you?

Ross turned away; the glowing clouds and the wandlike searchlights tilted. An aircraft went spinning earthward, blazing, disintegrating, to join the glowing patches below.

The umpteenth kite going down off to starboard. God only knows what the missing rate would be for this raid. Berlin was just too bloody far away and too heavily defended. Leave it for the Russkis . . .

The long trip home. A repeat of the journey to the target, but the kite handled better now that the bombs had gone and much of its fuel had been consumed. The minutes dragged by as the bombers headed for the coast; the weary aircrews tried to be as alert as ever because the flak and fighters were a threat all the way; indeed, often more aircraft were lost on the homeward trip than on the run in to the target.

"Coast in five minutes," Roland announced.

Lovely words. You could let a bit of the tension slip away when at last the enemy coast fell behind.

"Flak up ahead," said Harry.

Willy glanced forward, over Ross's shoulder.

At that instant the world went mad.

A direct hit in the nose just ahead of the cockpit. Willy saw it explode, ripping the flimsy metal skin.

The aircraft staggered, skidded, lurched.

Simultaneously a wind of cataclysmic ferocity smashed into the narrow metal tube of the fuselage.

Stunned, Willy fought for breath. The awful hurricane screamed around him. He couldn't move. He couldn't think. Life consisted solely of hanging on to the bulkhead. Something solid, something of substance. This was it, he told himself numbly; this was what getting the chop was all about . . .

The fiendish wind was battering the life and sense out of him. He was squashed, powerless, his brain whirring like a runaway motor. He clutched at the bulkhead and pulled himself forward; he was partially protected from the wind. He could begin to think, to consider the dilemma. Where was his parachute? There, stowed away in the corner. He clipped the pack in position on his harness. Simultaneously he felt the kite fall away on one wing. The beginnings of a spin. Straight into the ground it would go, just like countless others before.

Clutching, clawing, he dragged himself back into the freezing hurricane. Ross. Was he wounded? Dead?

He couldn't move.

Couldn't budge himself. Had he lost a limb without knowing it? Such things happened. Then he saw why he couldn't move. His flying boot was jammed between two stringers, part of the fuselage structure. He reached down and freed it, whereupon the hurricane took the boot and sent it slithering aft like a bit of newspaper on a windy city street.

No time to try and retrieve it. No time to do anything but clutch at Ross's seat and pull himself forward with the freezing gale blinding him, numbing his brain.

Flames roared into the fuselage from the nose.

Christ.

Ross lay slumped, blood soaking his flying suit, arms flopping loosely in the screaming, killing wind.

Dead? Not much doubt . . .

A nightmare. The aircraft out of control, skidding, diving,

wallowing madly in its unbalanced state. God only knows why it hadn't already spun in. God knows why it hadn't broken up. God.

Got to jump, he told Ross. Not a hope otherwise. In a moment the kite will go.

Now!

A few steps would take him back to the escape hatch.

But he thought of Gwen.

Gwen! He had forgotten about her! Completely! Utterly!

But what could he do? Ross was dead. The kite was about to crash. Should have crashed already. It would fall to bits any instant.

Panic coursed through him like an electrical charge. Survive! Nothing else mattered! He had to get out of this thing while he still could.

The aircraft dipped and pitched while the unholy hurricane ripped through its vitals, the controls shifting. *George!* That was it; Ross must have had the auto-pilot on when the flak hit; that was why the kite didn't go straight in. But how long could it maintain control? Didn't Ross once say that the device could easily be upset; wasn't it just a lot of gyros?

No flames coming from the nose now.

He leant across Ross's inert form and grasped the stick. It twitched in his hands. He could keep the wings level. But without rudder control the aircraft skidded about the sky like a lorry on an icy road.

What if Ross was still alive? He looked dead, but perhaps . . . . It was possible, wasn't it? He seemed to hear Gwen. And his parents. He saw them, their disappointed expressions. Was it true that he abandoned Ross? Jumped? And left Ross to his fate without making sure he was dead?

A lunatic conversation in a crazy, quivering place.

His father informed him that his sister was depending on him.

Gwen was nodding, one eyebrow raised in that irritatingly helpless look she sometimes wore.

Unfair! Bloody unfair!

He was alone. Everyone had gone, everyone with any sense.

He was fumbling with the ruddy controls, not knowing what the hell he was supposed to do . . .

Bloody madness, this was.

He hit Ross's harness release. The straps slackened. With the strength of desperation he dragged Ross's body out of the seat; it slumped to the floor like a sack of potatoes.

Sorry, Willy heard himself saying for some ungodly reason.

Head down against the wind, he grabbed the controls, thrusting his feet on to the rudder pedals.

To his surprise the aircraft responded to his control movements. It kept wanting to slip away to the left but he was able to level the wings and to get the thing flying on an even keel. A miracle, with the nose a great tangle of wreckage. A miracle the controls still functioned. A miracle the engines still worked. Crazy, he told himself, madness!

You're dead, he silently bellowed at Ross. I'm going through all this for a corpse. And your corpse at that, you randy sod!

The aircraft was sliding away to the left. It felt as if it was falling to pieces, ripped apart by the wind. How much could it take?

Most of the windscreen had gone. He had to put his head on to one side to escape the worst of the biting, cutting torrent of freezing air.

Now the faint horizon was disappearing behind wispy cloud. Where was it among all those gauges? He had never had to refer to the altimeter during those training jaunts in the sunshine over Yorkshire. The ground or layers of cloud had always been comfortingly present. What was it Ross had said? As long as the altimeter and airspeed indicator were steady you were flying more or less straight and level. But God knows in what direction.

The fire in the nose was out. Something to be thankful for. *Christ!*

He found the altimeter. Sorted out the significance of the needle's position. Two hundred feet! In the same instant he saw something solid sweeping below. He heaved back on the control column. Shuddering, complaining, the aircraft levelled out and began to climb. But now the speed was falling off, frighteningly. Lose your speed, Ross used to say, and you'll lose one hell of a lot more. Hastily Willy thrust the column forward. Too much! Back again; nervous experimentations until the altimeter and airspeed indicator steadied.

Still the kite wanted to turn. Keep the wings level. Artificial horizon, next to the ASI. Left wing sagging, nose wobbling; none of that nice solid feeling that the kite used to have when he took over from Ross. Trimming! Ross was always trimming, wasn't he? Balancing the bird, he used to call it. Poor old Ross. Dead? He certainly looked dead. If the explosion didn't kill him the wind probably froze him. So this is daft, isn't it? he asked himself. Probably. But if the sod's got any life left in him, he's going to marry Gwen – no one plays fast and loose with *my* sister.

He glanced quickly along the broad expanse of the wings. Engines were still going well.

All right. A moment to review the situation. Kite more or less stable and making progress. But in what direction? North-east, according to the compass – although God knows whether the thing was still working properly. So the first priority was to get the kite turned in the right direction. Due west was good enough. Careful with the aileron and rudder; remember, one engine out . . .

A timorous turn; the compass needle obediently twitched its way around the dial. Willy was sitting with his body angled to the left so that he was looking along the left-hand edge of the fuselage; but he was avoiding the worst of the hurricane. Although it hurt his eyes he had to keep watching the airspeed indicator and altimeter. *If the altimeter starts to move to the right you're climbing and your speed will drop off and if you let it drop off too much you'll stall the kite and fall out of the air and it'll serve you bloody well right for your incompetence and stupidity . . .*

Ross lay in an untidy heap beside the pilot's seat.

Sorry, Willy said to him.

Wind-blasted tears blurred his vision. He dashed them away with his gloved hand. How far to England? Was he even heading in the right direction? He shook his head as if admitting his ignorance to some invisible examiner. How much fuel remained in the tanks? Did the gauges still record their contents accurately – or as accurately as they ever did? What tanks were they on when the kite was hit? He couldn't remember. It was like trying to recall something that happened six months ago. But now it was no use worrying because he couldn't do anything about the ruddy tanks even if he wanted to.

His shoulders and arms were aching, the pain tearing at every sinew. Agonizing, trying to keep the aircraft heading in an approximation of a straight line. But the port wing kept dragging no matter how many times he corrected it. Was there a way to trim, to compensate? He shook his head again. He didn't know and this wasn't the time to experiment. The poor shattered Hally was on a sort of aerial tightrope; any disturbance of the balance could mean disaster.

You'd ruddy well better not be dead, he informed Ross, his words a curious echo inside his head, *after I've gone to all this trouble. You're not going to get out of anything that way, dear me no . . .*

Was this really happening? To *him,* Willy Perkins from Droylsden? The moments passed in an oddly dreamlike way, and yet he had to concentrate totally on the aircraft's controls, correcting, coaxing, never letting the big machine have her way for an instant.

Altimeter, airspeed indicator . . .

Compass.

Christ!

The kite had drifted away to the south, back toward the bloody enemy . . .

Come on, girl, a spot of rudder and a bit of aileron; nose coming around nicely. Well done.

That was when he became aware of a presence at his side. For an instant he thought Ross had recovered and had scrambled to his feet. He glanced. Geoff! Ruddy lovely sight! The gunner half stood, half knelt in the torrent of freezing air, clutching at the fuselage structure for support. Behind his goggles, his eyes were wide with alarm. Willy in the pilot's seat! Ross a bloody lump on the floor! He kept mouthing questions at Willy. Daft sod, did he think Willy could drop everything he was doing and scribble a note in reply?

Willy indicated Ross and pointed a thumb to the rear.

Get him back to the centre section where the main spar and the rest bunk were to be found.

Geoff mouthed the question: Is he dead? Willy shrugged. Geoff stared, then set to work to drag Ross's inert form to the rear.

It was an odd sort of relief to have Ross looked after. Not that it did anything for the general situation; perhaps it was just the presence of Geoff, knowing that there was someone else aboard. If Geoff reported that Ross was dead, then the sensible thing to do would be to climb to a decent altitude as soon as they crossed the English coast – if they ever did – and jump.

But his father's voice put a stop to any such line of thinking. Remarkable, the steely edge he could add when the occasion called for it.

You abandoned him! Your sister's intended! And you didn't really know, you weren't absolutely positive that he wasn't still alive! I call that muddled thinking, very muddled indeed. And indicating a sad lack of concern for your sister's welfare.

Willy could hear him, above the din of the engines.

His back and shoulders were aching because he was half on and half off the seat. The rudder pedals were too far away, having been adjusted to accommodate Ross's six feet. How to re-adjust them? He didn't know. He would have to put up with the discomfort. How long had he been flying? What was the time? For some reason it seemed important.

If the kite is badly damaged, land her wheels-up; simply fly her low and chop the throttles and let nature and gravity take care of the rest. That was what Ross used to say. But Willy kept remembering the Lanc that had attempted a landing at Rocklington early one morning; wheels-up it had approached the field in good order, but moments before touchdown, one wing had suddenly dropped. In an instant the great machine had cartwheeled, ripping itself to pieces and disappearing in a monstrous bonfire. Only the rear gunner had survived the crash – and it was questionable how lucky he was, considering his unspeakable condition when they dragged him out of the flames.

Willy gnawed at his lip, as he wrestled with the controls, correcting for the umpteenth time.

"Won't be long now, lad," he informed Ross. Then remembered that Ross was no longer lying on the cockpit floor.

Ross wouldn't stand a chance if it came to a ditching. Poor sod, he'd be wiped out the instant the kite hit the water. Ruddy difficult, successfully ditching a complete kite; ruddy impossible, trying to do the same thing with the nose gone.

Hard to gauge how much fuel was left; the needles kept fluctuating as if they couldn't agree among themselves. Not much point in worrying about it. No point fretting about problems he couldn't control. Concentrate on what he could do. Which wasn't much.

Those daft buggers who turned him down for pilot training should see him now. A ruddy natural, he was. Altitude a thousand feet, according to the altimeter. A thousand feet above sea level. Christ, his arms were going to drop off. No feeling left in them; they were like chunks of wood attached to his shoulders. No feeling there. Was it damaged when the flak hit? Was gangrene setting in already?

Nose tending to veer off to the left again. *C'mon back, love. That's it. Lovely.*

Geoff reappeared. He leant across; Willy thought he was going to shout something in his ear but he simply took Willy's intercom lead and connected it to the socket. The familiar intercom noise crackled in his earphones.

"It works," said Geoff.

"Grand," said Willy. "How's the Skipper?"

"Dunno. I thought he was dead but I think there might be a bit of a pulse. Hard to tell with the kite vibrating. Mind turning off the motors for a bit?"

Ha bloody ha.

"Where's Andy?"

"Still in the mid-upper. The tail turret's U/S, so we thought he should stay here."

"Good idea."

"We didn't know if there was anyone up front. Kept calling on intercom but no one replied. So I thought I'd come and have a look-see. Bloody mess in the nose. Roland's hit but alive. Harry jumped."

"Did you see anything of Gord?"

"There isn't much to see."

The radio compartment was directly below the pilot. Willy thought Gord might have escaped the full force of the explosion; apparently not.

"You all right there?" Geoff enquired.

"So far. But we've got to check on the fuel situation. So go and have a look at my panel, will you. You'll see a row of dials about halfway down. 'Fuel Tank Contents,' it says; you can't miss it. Tell me what they say. And tell me if the fuel pressure warning lights are on. All right?"

"Okay."

A minute later he reappeared and read off the contents of the tanks in the wings and fuselage. No fuel pressure warning lights. Willy gave him instructions on changing tanks.

"And do it exactly as I told you. It's important."

"Okay."

"Sure you've got it?"

"Piece of cake."

Geoff gave him a thumbs-up and went aft.

According to the altimeter the aircraft was at fifteen hundred feet above sea level. But could the altimeter have been upset by the explosion? Could it be out by a couple of thousand feet? Or more?

Should he climb? Or descend? Or just keep going?

He peered ahead through narrowed eyes but there was nothing to see.

Jesus!

Suddenly, shockingly, a great slab of cliff came looming out of the darkness like some huge barricade . . .

A glimpse of trees, of a cow lying in the grass ignoring the noisy thing bellowing overhead . . .

A church spire sped past on the right.

A cluster of trees. A pond.

But they appeared – and disappeared – so quickly that he hardly had time to acknowledge their presence. What now? Look for an airfield?

He didn't have to wait.

One engine coughed, roared, stopped.

"Bloody hell . . . sorry . . . I buggered it up."

Geoff's voice.

No time to fix things. "Get set!" Willy yelled, chopping the throttles.

The wind howled through the shattered nose section.

No time to do anything but hope – and try to aim the kite between those two tall elms.

Do it if all else fails, Ross said once; go between two big trees. The wings would rip off but the fuselage would be more or less okay provided there wasn't a brick wall on the other side of the trees.

But how did you make sure that there wasn't a brick wall?

You hoped. And squeaked a prayer.

And glimpsed the port wing crumpling and tearing away, a complete Merlin spinning overhead, a twelve-cylinder projectile, the world turning upside down, the canopy disintegrating, bits of trees flying in every direction, noise enfolding you, burying you.

Afterwards, Willy couldn't remember much of what the King had said.

"He was very nice, though," he assured his parents. "Quite friendly, and easy to talk to."

"I should hope so," said his father. "Not every day he gets to pin a VC on a chap." Tears glistened in his eyes; tears of pride and happiness. He kept patting Willy on the shoulder and glancing down as if to make sure that the purple ribbon was still in position beneath Willy's flying badge. There were photographs – thank goodness it was a bright day – with Buckingham Palace in the background; then a lunch at a posh restaurant, all paid for by one of the important-looking officers who kept materializing at opportune moments.

In the afternoon they went to see Ross in the hospital. He was coming along well, though he would never fly again, not with his one arm gone. But Gwen didn't seem to mind about the arm. She was just happy that he was alive; they had been married at his bedside; now the baby's presence was beginning to become apparent. Ross was getting some of his old energy back; the facial scars were improving day by day, the doctors said he would be as good as new by Christmas – well, almost as good as new – which they kept saying was a very good show indeed, considering his appalling condition when he was dug out of the Hally's remains. Clearly they all thought they had done a remarkably fine job of work on him.

A reporter from one of the big dailies came along to the hospital, jotting down a lot of silly notes about the reunion of the VC and the man he saved. Daft stuff, because he made it sound as if this was the first time they had met since the crash. Nonsense of course; there had been lots of visits; but presumably it made a better story and that was all the reporter cared about. Then there were more photographs: Willy shaking Ross's left hand, Willy and Ross with Gwen, Willy and Ross and the parents and a huddle of nurses who had baked a cake in honour of the occasion; everyone wanted to be photographed with a VC.

Willy still found himself calling Ross "Skipper"; he couldn't quite accept the fact that the two of them were now brothers-in-law. As for Ross, he seemed enchanted to be alive and to be an expectant father. He kept saying that you had to be three-quarters dead to know how good it was to be alive.

At last it was time to go. Willy was on fourteen days' leave; he and his parents were returning to Droylsden. Ross would soon be shipped back to Canada (from where he promised to send Willy a collection of the latest jazz records). Gwen would be following Ross, according to the various government departments who wrote endless letters on the subject;

Gwen and her mother kept discussing whether the baby would be born in England or Canada – or in the middle of the Atlantic. The remarkable thing was how they could occupy so many hours on the subject.

"So long, buddy." Ross grasped Willy's hand. "Congratulations on your gong. You sure as hell earned it."

"It was your flying lessons that did it. And a heck of a lot of luck."

Ross's old grin came through in spite of the scars. "I'm just glad I slept through it all. If I'd known you were flying the kite I'd have died of fright right there and then."

On the way back to the Regent Palace Hotel, a boy of ten or eleven leant across the aisle of the bus and pointed at Willy's ribbon.

"That's a VC ribbon. You just got it from the King. Read about it in the paper."

"Aye," responded Mr Perkins before Willy could utter a sound. "Sergeant William Herbert Perkins, VC. My son."

Suddenly the whole busload of citizens knew about it. There were handshakes and congratulations, plus a couple of requests for autographs, which embarrassed Willy.

A thin lady with a blue hat said, "You must have been very nervous meeting the King."

Willy nodded. "But he was nice. Put me at ease in no time."

"Marvellous man," sighed the woman.

"The King or our Willy?" Mr Perkins wanted to know.

"Both of them."

Willy smiled. He felt as if he were participating in a fairy story with kings and queens and palaces and total strangers shaking his hand. Yet how near he had come to jumping out of that tottering, burning wreck of a Hally. He could still hear those voices screaming at him to jump while he still had time. *Now!* Ross was dead. It was obvious. There was nothing he could do for him . . . and any lingering doubts were blasted away by that shrieking, screeching wind. Yes, he would have baled out if he hadn't thought at that instant of Gwen and her problem and his dad and the family assembled, demanding to know why he abandoned the father of Gwen's child without making absolutely, totally certain that he was beyond help.

The King had said that Willy's actions were particularly commendable because they were directed solely at saving the life of a comrade.

Willy replied, "Well, sir, in a way you might say I didn't have any choice."

The King had nodded understandingly.

The Wireless Operator

THE SMELL OF THE TIN ROOM HAD ACCOMPANIED BRYCE onto the bus. He slid the window down a few inches. The stink refused to be blown away. Before leaving that morning, he had soaked his hands in hot water and scrubbed them with carbolic soap until they felt raw. A waste of time. Sour old grease from those foul pots and pans, congealed gravy and the bricklike baked remains of God knows what animate beings: the reek permeated every pore. When an elderly lady with a large shopping basket sat beside him Bryce thrust his hands into his pockets.

The bus stopped. A couple of air force types came clattering up the stairs. Bryce looked out the window. Only when the bus was moving again did he glance forward. The airmen, both corporals, had deposited themselves half a dozen rows further forward. Bryce didn't recognize them. He relaxed.

The familiar countryside slipped by: bright green fields and dour walls of grey Yorkshire stone, righteous little villages and sturdy folk with rosy cheeks and eyes that met yours unwaveringly. Bryce had disliked Yorkshire when he first arrived; now he found himself absorbing every sight like a native son returning after a lifetime's absence.

The George came into view. Neal liked The George. Always had. Said it didn't try as hard as The White Rose to be hearty; nothing worse, the Skipper claimed, than a pub that is too deliberately hearty. Neal knew.

A Halifax appeared, climbing, tucking its wheels into the inboard engine nacelles. Bryce tried to read the identification letter on the side of the fuselage but the bomber disappeared behind trees.

Not long now. Exciting, seeing a Hallybag again. Calm down, he told himself. Important to be level-headed. Vital to make the right impression.

The bus turned into the High Street and passed the war memorial and the post office. The place looked just the same. He smiled to himself. A place like this didn't change much in a hundred years. What change did he expect in a few weeks?

"Rocklington!" bellowed the conductress as the bus squealed to a halt.

Bryce collected his side pack and hurried down the steps to the street. The two corporals followed him. He saw them glancing as they stepped off the bus, their eyes drawn to the tell-tale patches on his sleeves and chest.

He turned to look into a shoe shop window.

The corporals went on their way, thank God.

Another Halifax flew over the village, flaps and undercarriage extended, lining up for a landing on number 4 runway, the one with the bump two-thirds of the way down its length.

No sign of Neal. No doubt he'd been held up at the field. He had said he would meet the bus if he could get away. No firm promises.

The cloud cover was dispersing; the sun glimmered, brightening the village street. Bryce watched, giving the two corporals time to turn the corner by the station; then he followed. He knew the way; he had done this trek a hundred times.

His boots sounded like a blacksmith's hammer on the pavement. He had the odd feeling that everyone was watching him, that everyone knew his business.

Had Neal started things rolling yet? He didn't say as much

in his last letter but that had been written almost a week ago. Neal wasn't the sort to let grass grow under his feet when something needed doing.

The road led past the grammar school. The boys, resplendent in whites, were busy at the cricket practice nets; the last time he had come this way they had been playing rugger. Incongruous, the backdrop of Hallies squatting at their dispersals, brooding, looking as if they were stretching their wings in preparation for flight.

Runway number 2 ended at the road. During the winter a Halifax had crashed on the road, just missing an East Yorkshire bus on its way to Hull. The impact had blasted an enormous hole in the road. It had been repaired but the scar was still conspicuous, telling its story. Like the patches on his tunic.

He watched a Hally approach; it thundered overhead and touched down, bouncing gently from its left wheel to its right, then settling. A minute later another Hally taxied onto the runway. Bryce braced himself against the blast from its four Merlins as it began its take-off run. The din of the engines was deafening. But exciting. His spine tingled.

Everything was going to be all right; it had to be.

The last clouds moved away; a hot day was brewing.

He was sweating freely by the time he reached the main gate. He mopped his forehead with a handkerchief while a skinny SP eyed him from the Guard Room window. Was there a glimmer of recognition in those dull eyes? Bryce hoped not.

"My name's Bryce. I have an appointment to see Flying Officer Harker ... "

"Do you now? Harker, you say?" An automatic clicking of the tongue and a looking up and down of the newcomer to check that his appearance was suitably airmanlike. A bony finger travelled the length of a page. "Yes, it's here." A sniff. "You're Bryce, are you?"

"Yes. 606."

"Yes." The SP tugged at the loose flesh of his neck. "Trouble is, he's gone missing, Flying Officer Harker, that is ... "

"*Missing?*" What was the idiot talking about?

" 'Fraid so, old son."

"Have you got the right Harker? *Neal* Harker?"

"That's him."

"But . . . " He almost said it was impossible. But it wasn't impossible. "I got a letter from him just yesterday."

"Sorry, old son. Happened last night. Remscheid, it was."

Bryce kept staring at the man, his mind in a whirl. He heard the SP asking if there was anyone else he wanted to talk to. He didn't reply. He turned and started along the road back to the village. Somehow he couldn't quite grasp the thought that Neal was missing: Neal was *vital*; he was the link to everything. Without Neal . . . God knows. Neal with his pipe and his grave courtesy; his quotations from Shakespeare, his opinions on everything from organized religion to holiday camps. A gentleman, a real gentleman. He had come within two or three trips of the magic thirty. He of all people deserved to complete his tour.

A car slowed beside Bryce. An officer hailed him from the driver's seat. An admin type; he wore no flying badge.

"Want a lift?"

Bryce nodded and got in beside the officer.

"I can drop you off at the railway station. That all right? Going on leave, are you?"

"No sir, I'm already on leave. I'm not stationed here, you see, not anymore. I came to see a friend of mine, Neal Harker – Flying Officer Harker. But I've just heard that he went missing last night."

"Ah. Yes, they said we lost someone. Bad night." As he put the car in gear the officer glanced at Bryce, no doubt wondering how it was that a mere aircraftman was on friendly terms with a Flying Officer. "Known Harker long, have you?"

"Several months."

On the way to the village Bryce wrestled with the dilemma. What should he do? What *could* he do?

"Bad luck about Harker," said the officer when he stopped at the station to let Bryce out.

"I thought so," said Bryce.

"You all right?" the officer asked.

"Yes sir . . . thanks for the lift."

He went into the station and had a cup of metallic-tasting tea at the snack bar. The place was deserted but for a chubby girl behind the counter. She said the weather seemed to be looking up. She wanted it to stay nice for the weekend; she planned to go to Knaresborough with a friend and take a boat on the Nidd. She giggled as if there was something slightly naughty about the notion. Bryce hardly heard her; he kept thinking about Neal. And the others. In all probability they were dead; there was a chance – a slim chance – that they were prisoners; an even slimmer chance that they had escaped capture and were on the run. Some blokes made it back to England. About one in a thousand. It took months sometimes.

He shook his head. He didn't know what to do. The stench of the Tin Room assailed his nostrils when he raised his cup to drink. He was going to be stuck in that foul Tin Room in the Transit Camp for the rest of the war. Neal had been his only hope. Neal would have managed things. Somehow. Without him it was hopeless. Or was it? What about Neal's Flight Commander? Fry? A good sort. Everyone said so. If Neal had discussed the matter with anyone it would have been with Fry . . .

As he drank the tea he rehearsed his approach. Important to get the story out as simply and cleanly as possible, with no fumbling for words.

There was a telephone box outside. He inserted the pennies and dialled the operator. She said she was connecting him.

"RAF Rocklington," announced a pert female voice.

Bryce cleared his throat.

"Squadron Leader Fry, please – 'A' Flight."

"One moment, please."

A man's voice: " 'A' Flight."

"May I speak to Squadron Leader Fry, please?"

"Who's calling?"

"I'm . . . a former member of the Flight."

"I'm afraid Squadron Leader Fry . . . isn't available. Perhaps I can help."

"No, I have to talk to Squadron Leader Fry."

"I'm sorry . . . Squadron Leader Fry isn't here at the moment."

"It's important. Very important."

A sharp little sigh. "Just a jiffy."

A new voice came on the line. A crisp, incisive voice.

"Stevens."

"Sir . . . my name's Bryce."

"And?"

"I was supposed to meet Flying Officer Harker today. I was told he had gone missing."

The man's voice softened a fraction. "True, I'm afraid. We have no more news at present. Are you a relative?"

"No, a friend." The moment of truth. "Actually I'm a former member of his crew. He and I have been corresponding about the possibility of my . . . being reinstated."

"Reinstated?"

"To flying duties, sir."

There was a puzzled silence. Then: "Your name again?"

"Bryce, sir."

"Bryce." He snapped the word out. "I know who you are. You were Harker's wireless op."

"That's right, sir."

"Went LMF, refused to fly."

"Yes sir – but I was in a state of shock. I didn't know what I was saying. Or doing. But I'm over that now. I know that if I was given another chance I could be a good member of an aircrew again – "

"And are you trying to tell me that Harker told you you could get back in his crew?"

"Well . . . sir, he didn't think it was *impossible*. I think he may have discussed it with Squadron Leader Fry."

Stevens said, "I don't care if he discussed it with Jesus Christ himself. It's too late. You had every opportunity to reconsider your decision."

"But I – I wasn't thinking properly, sir."

"We're not running a bloody Boy Scout camp here. You can't refuse to fly one day then change your mind the next. You volunteered for aircrew, Bryce, no one forced you. It was your decision. So was your refusal to fly. And now that you've done it, who the hell would want you in his crew? You've branded yourself, Bryce. For your information, Squadron Leader Fry is in hospital. Badly injured. He may not pull through. I have no way of knowing whether he and Harker ever discussed your case. And I haven't got time or the inclination to find out. There's nothing I can do for you."

"Sir – "

But the line was dead. Stevens had hung up, no doubt glad to be rid of the coward and his petty problems. And why should he waste his time? There was no shortage of volunteers for aircrew; the recruiting offices bulged with patriotic types eager to become air force heroes.

He became aware of a rapping on the glass door of the telephone box. A portly man in a brown suit was waiting, fretting and frowning, tugging at the tie in his stiff white collar.

Bryce opened the door and stepped out.

The man in the brown suit brushed past him with a sarcastic tone. "Sure you're done?"

Bryce nodded. "I'm done all right."

He wandered away from the station back into the centre of the village. Steven's words kept stinging. He was right. Horribly right. Who would want him on his crew? If he had been an officer they would have quietly posted him off to a desk job; there would be no loss of rank, no "LMF" stamped in his records. What was lack of moral fibre in an NCO was a temporary lapse of good judgement in an officer.

The village bustled about him, intent on its business: housewives and their baskets, a self-important type puffing along in suit and waistcoat, an aproned shopgirl hurrying across the street, hair fanned by the wind, boys from the grammar school in their blazers and caps, a couple of soldiers from the nearby REME camp, a smattering of air force. No one paid him any attention. Even his boots seemed subdued now; he didn't belong here any more.

What next? Home? He winced at the thought. His parents thought he was still a sergeant, still a member of a Halifax bomber aircrew. Some weeks earlier he had written telling them that he would be on the move for a little while and wouldn't be able to write; not to worry, though, he wouldn't be on ops; it was a special job, something hush-hush. An insane thing to do; he realized that now, but at the time it had seemed a good idea, a way to buy a little time, a breathing space in which he might work things out. But some things couldn't be worked out; once done they became irreversible; like setting off an avalanche. God, what a stinking mess he had made of everything! Sometimes he wondered if the real reason he wanted to fly again was because he hated the Tin Room more than he feared ops. Would he feel the same urge to fly again if he were in some cushy, safe admin job with his old rank and pay? He shook his head, wondering. A passerby glanced at him and shrugged.

He had met another LMF type at the Transit Camp. Aircraftman Snell, he of the broken nose and toothy smile. Snell made no secret of his delight at being safe and sound on terra firma. He had been in Coastal Command, a gunner on Hampden torpedo-bombers, an occupation he considered only slightly less suicidal than being one of the Christians in the lions' den. "We lost three out of five on one op, two out of four the next, and four out of eight the next time, and I said, 'Thanks very ruddy much but that's quite enough for yours truly.' And so here I am, a skivvy, cleaning bogs. But the war will be over one day and after a little while no one will give a tinker's cuss what you did in it. People forget. It's one thing you can rely on 'em to do. Just about the only one, in my experience."

Bryce tried for a few days to reason the same way. He was better off where he was. He would survive the war. He could make plans for his future. He should in fact be happy that things worked out the way they did. But he wasn't. Shame burned like acid. He had soldiered on through scores of hazards: near misses, engine trouble, icing, fog and flak. But his courage hadn't failed until that frightful night over Stuttgart.

Ferocious flak. A Hally flying on a parallel track became a torch that for a few terrifying moments lit up the night revealing a score of bombers. Seconds later, while Joe Hobbs, the bomb-aimer, was directing Neal on the bomb run, they were hit. Bryce was lucky; protected by a partition, he suffered no injury. But Hobbs was dead, inert, eyes staring. Caldwell, the navigator, was a raving lunatic, spewing blood, with a jagged bone sticking through the remains of his sleeve as he groped for God knows what. His face was a hideous red pulp behind his oxygen mask. Bryce tried to ease Caldwell's agony. Ray Mitchell, the flight engineer, brought the first-aid kit. They tried morphine. But Caldwell was a man possessed, still alive, still struggling, clutching, uttering blood-bubbled screechings as the kit sagged its way back to England. He was still semi-conscious, still writhing and groaning, when Neal flopped the kite down on an emergency strip near the coast, one engine out, bits of engine cowling and bomb doors falling off as the wheels made contact. The Hally went careering off the runway because one of the tires was shot through. The undercarriage collapsed. Bouncing, bucking, disintegrating, the bomber skidded across the grass, finally coming to a halt beside a petrol bowser. Caldwell was dead when the orderlies came aboard.

That was the night Bryce refused to fly. They could do what they liked to him; he would never set foot in an aeroplane again. There were interviews, exhortations, threats, appeals to his patriotism and pride. Then it was over. Case closed. Within hours he was reduced to AC2, "remustered to non-flying duties," and on a train heading for the Transit Camp and the Tin Room. His uniform bore oddly discoloured patches where his aircrew badge and his sergeant's stripes had once been positioned.

The cricket practice was still in progress at the grammar school.

Bryce watched it for a few minutes as he tried to collect his thoughts. A Halifax roared overhead, flaps and undercarriage down; the rear gunner looked out of his turret, his face framed in the brown leather of his helmet. The aircraft touched the runway with a puff of smoke from the tires; with a roar the engines picked up and the bomber sped away down the runway to take to the air again. Circuits and bumps. A sprog crew, probably, getting in lots of practice before going on ops.

Bryce watched the Halifax climbing. He wished the crew luck. They would need it.

God, how he had buggered up everything. The truth was, he had been in a state of semi-lunacy when he had refused to fly. Unable to think. Unable to reason. He was like a frightened animal, instinctively trying to get away from what frightened him. Couldn't they understand that it was a temporary condition, a reaction to a terrible situation? He was better now; he had recovered; it wouldn't happen again.

Another Halifax came taxiing along the peri track. A fair-haired crew member sat on the edge of the dorsal escape hatch; he raised a hand in greeting as he passed. Bryce returned the wave. The aircraft was brand new by the look of her. A pale blob of a face could be seen at the small window beneath the pilot's cabin. Bryce knew that position well: the tiny compartment, the array of radio gear, the dials shivering as the pilot ran up the engines. A quickening of the pulse: excitement and fear battling inside.

The Hally moved out onto the runway, the blast from the four propellers battering the grass flat.

"Crash," Bryce commanded. "Do a circuit and crash on landing – I'll jump over the fence and run to the wreck and pull the crew out one by one." That would make that bastard Stevens change his opinion. He would apologize, profusely, offering half a dozen crews from which Bryce might choose . . .

Idiotic, childish fantasies.

The Hally's engines bellowed. A gale rocked Bryce. He clutched his cap. With a wagging of rudders the bomber began its take-off run, its great wheels rolling over the patterns of black rubber streaks, mementos of umpteen landings.

Braced against the gale, Bryce watched through narrowed eyes. The Hally picked up speed. Its tail rose. Balanced on its two main wheels it went bounding over the hump in the runway, disappearing momentarily, then reappearing, airborne. The square-cut wings, the jutting Merlins: the assembly formed a whole as recognizable as a face, a shape that evoked a hundred memories. Conflicting memories. Of terror. And of happiness. The trepidation of preparation, the gut-twisting strain of the op itself; it all gave way to delicious relief, an extraordinary sense of worth. Life had never meant more than in those times after ops when the weary airmen gathered to be debriefed, their faces branded by the outlines of their oxygen masks, hair flattened by hours under close-fitting helmets, ears still ringing from the din of the Merlins. Clutching mugs of cocoa laced with generous tots of rum, they told their stories to the intelligence officers who nodded and made notes, as impassive as bank clerks taking particulars for new accounts.

Bryce used to join with the others in yawning and carping about being kept from his bed, but secretly he revelled in the sense of belonging at such moments; it imparted a curious significance to every word, every gesture. It had been a privileged world. True, memories of that world still jarred him into sweating, heart-thumping wakefulness in the middle of the night. But it was the price of membership. Everyone had to pay. He ached to get back on a crew. On ops.

The prop blast from the Hally blew dust in his eyes. He dabbed at them as he turned away. Through the blur of tears he saw a bicycle wobbling along the road from the village, a Flight Sergeant in the saddle. He looked familiar. Sharp features. Longish nose. A firm little line of mouth. Ernie Thwaites, a gunner on Nigel Pettigrew's crew. Not a friend exactly, but an ally, you might say, someone you could talk to, discuss your problems with – and, more important, someone who knew the system and how things worked.

He raised an arm. "Got a minute, Flight?"

The Rear Gunner

"COMING UP TO THE TARGET, SKIPPER. STEADY AS YOU GO."
Charlie's voice. Until the bombs had gone he was in
virtual charge. The Skipper did what he was told.
This was the point of it all, the reason that they were all here
at this place at this time. Geoff kept swivelling the tail
turret, from side to side, searching.

"Left-left . . . right a bit . . . bit more . . . steady . . ."

It was the worst part of every op. It seemed to him that he
had spent much of his adult life on endless bomb runs. You
had to keep flying straight and level, no matter how much
flak was popping off around you, how many searchlights
were probing the sky about you. Keep an eye on the blue-
tinted jobs, the master lights, radar-controlled. No fun getting caught by those bastards. Once, on a trip with Ross
Sinclair's crew, Geoff had seen a Lanc coned over the Ruhr;
the kite wriggled and struggled like a fish on a line. After a
couple of minutes it went down in flames, spinning, whirling
its way to destruction.

Monica, the radar warning device in the tail, was bleating.

Monica couldn't be trusted. Always going U/S. Some
blokes claimed it led to bombers shooting each other down,

mistaking friendly bombers for Jerries. Some blokes said the Jerries could home in on Monica.

"Bombs gone."

Relieved, the Halifax leapt upward. It was the halfway point in the trip. Before that moment everything had been devoted to getting the load to the target; now the object of existence was getting home in one piece.

They were well clear of the target area when the trouble started.

Geoff glimpsed the faintest glimmer of light on whirling propeller blades.

An instant later he saw the shadowy shape.

"Fighter. Port quarter. Corkscrew port! *Now!*"

He was fast, this skipper; not a moment's delay. The words were barely out of Geoff's mouth before the Hally was plunging, rolling, turning, heaving, straining every rivet, every strut and former, bouncing Geoff around in his narrow turret like a pea in a rattle. It went on and on, a frantic ballet in the inky sky, punctuated by flashing pinpoints of light as the fighter sent burst after burst after his prey.

"I think you've shaken him, Skipper," said Ben.

"Geoff?"

"No sign of the bugger."

"Well done, gunners," was the Skipper's response. "Sharp eyes and good shooting. Very professional."

Professional. It was the Skipper's highest praise.

A toff, the Skipper, related to Lord Somebody-or-other; he had a house in Mayfair and a Bentley, a 6½-litre monster, it was said.

Geoff kept rotating his turret, searching the black sky while he listened to the navigator telling the Skipper to steer half a dozen degrees to port. Sounded a bit breathless. No doubt he'd been clinging on to his navigation table during the corkscrewing, trying to keep his charts and pencils from flying all over the place. Geoff didn't envy navigators at such times. Poor buggers, they could only sit and hope for the best; at least a gunner had something positive and important to do.

The crew reported no significant damage.

Geoff glanced at another aircraft going down streaming flame. A long way off, too far to identify the type. And important not to stare. It'd ruin your night vision; eyesight was more important than gunfire where fighters were concerned. Bastards, they had all the advantages: speed, manoeuvrability, and about ten times the fire-power. They could streak out of the darkness and blow you to bits before you knew what was happening. Sometimes they worked in pairs. One fighter would come stooging along, perhaps even showing a navigation light to draw attention to himself. Then, while you were busy lining up your guns on him, his mate would come nipping in from the other quarter. You had to keep your eyes open and your wits sharp in this lark. But it wasn't easy. The cold always got to you no matter how much clobber you put on – lambswool underwear, Shetland wool sweater under the battledress, electrically heated Taylor suit with its built-in Mae West, three pairs of gloves, silk, wool, and leather. Geoff always put strips of sticking plaster on his face at the points where the metal studs held his oxygen mask in place; at lofty heights the studs could turn into little lumps of freezing hell. The cold dulled your senses, the monotonous hiss of the oxygen hour after hour half hypnotized you so that for moments you forgot why you were staring into the blackness. Sometimes the Benzedrine tablets that were supposed to keep you alert had just the opposite effect.

Geoff hadn't seen any of his crew-mates since they had waddled out to the crew van in their clobber; Mae Wests unbuttoned and untied, tapes and microphone flexes trailing, hands clutching parachute bags, helmets, goggles, thermos flasks, packets of snacks, satchels, more luggage than you saw on the Sunday School outing on August Bank Holiday. Funny how no one seemed to look you in the eye during the trip out to the aircraft. Everyone had his own thoughts. Mostly about life expectancy.

The voices of the crew were his only companions on ops. Intercom voices, they were, not the real thing. Geoff had done two trips with this crew; he could put faces to the voices. The Skipper with his moustache and his protruding front teeth. The navigator, Cecil or Neville or something, studious, serious, looking as if he belonged in a lawyer's wig. The mid-upper gunner, a country lad, cherubic, an innocent pretending to be a man of the world. The Cockney wireless operator, perky like a Brylcreemed sparrow. Charlie, the gruff, businesslike bomb-aimer, the only married bloke on the crew, always looking as if he was worried about meeting the next never-never instalment on the piano, which he probably was. And Ben, the burly, fiery Scottish flight engineer. A good crew. But not his crew. Not like Ross's. But Ross's crew didn't exist any more. So here he was. Until the regular rear gunner recovered from his scarlet fever. Important to have a crew of your own. The blokes you flew with became the most important people in your life. One leave, he had started to explain it all to Angela. Barmy thing to do. She got that tight, hurt look. Laboriously he had tried to explain that his crewmates weren't important in the same way that she was important. He might as well have saved his breath. There were some things you should never discuss with women. In fact, the list of don't-discuss subjects was a ruddy sight longer than the okay-to-discuss, in Geoff's opinion.

After a lengthy trip there would be a moment of faint surprise at meeting the lads in person; in an odd sort of way they became more real to him as voices than as people. On one op with Ross they had to take a replacement navigator because Roland had a toothache. It was disquieting to sit in the tail and hear a Belfast accent telling the Skipper what course to fly. Silly, of course, but the truth was, you became particular about the voices you flew with.

The Skipper: "Geoff, check in, please. Things are well with you?"

"No problems back here, Skip."

One by one the voices responded.

Some blokes claimed that the ride home was more dangerous than the trip to the target. Probably true. Outward bound, the stream was usually good and tight. But on the way home crews were tired and beginning to relax. Lots of crews got the chop over the North Sea when they thought the worst was over.

A dazzling flare to starboard. Another poor sod had had it. Down he went, twisting, writhing. Peculiar, and not very commendable, the feeling you had on such occasions: an uneasy combination of pity and a smattering of relief because you could look on his bad luck as improving your own. Some aircraft always got through, so every casualty shifted the scales of chance in your favour. Sort of.

Search. Side to side, a segment of the sky at a time. Probe the shades of darkness, peering and yet not looking directly at the shapes that were real and the shapes created by his imagination.

He had given up cigarettes a month before; the Gunnery Leader had claimed that smoking spoiled your night vision. Geoff would have given up plum duff if he had been told it detracted from his efficiency. Being a rear gunner was a sacred trust; the crew depended upon him to protect them from the rear and below, which was the way most of the bastards chose to attack. Some even seemed to be able to fire vertically; Geoff was sure he had seen an Me 110 firing up through the roof of its cabin and destroying a Lancaster over Essen. The bomber disappeared in a gigantic explosion, a sickening blossoming of fire, of streaking sparkling darts in the night, then nothing. Seven bods blown to bits. But at debriefing the intelligence officer had shaken his head at Geoff's report; no, Jerry night-fighters didn't shoot upward, he must have been mistaken; the prim sod had that know-it-all, pursed-lip look that Geoff remembered so well from his school days.

Cecil-or-Neville instructed the Skipper to steer half a dozen degrees to port.

The world erupted.

A flash. Blinding, numbing; a clattering of shattered metal.

"Flak," someone reported. "I saw it go off just behind the tail. You all right, Geoff?"

All right? Of course he was all right.

He lifted his hand to flip the intercom switch. A simple action but it triggered the pain – an avalanche of pain, grinding, tearing pain. For an instant he seemed to lose consciousness; he didn't know where he was; only the pain was real, only the pain mattered.

Dimly he heard the Skipper's voice crackling in his earphone, asking if he was alive and kicking.

Got to answer. Got to.

He raised a gauntleted hand again. Steeling himself, he switched his intercom. He managed to utter a couple of words to tell them he was alive. But they couldn't hear. He was receiving. But he couldn't transmit.

He tried again. And again.

The pain was concentrated somewhere in his middle. He didn't know where. It moved. It spread itself around as if it were alive. He touched his body and his legs. A few minutes ago everything had been so bloody cold – now he didn't know whether he was hot or cold – the pain overwhelmed every other sense.

The kite rocked as it flew through cloud. In the clear again, Geoff could see searchlights criss-crossing the blackness. At this distance the target looked like the remains of a fire in the kitchen grate.

He had to get out of the turret. The sliding doors were at his back. He had to turn the turret so that it sat along the line of the fuselage, creating enough room to get out. He steeled himself for the effort. But the turret wouldn't budge.

The Skipper's voice again: "Ben, go and check on Geoff, there's a good chap."

Unhurried, as usual.

Ben responded: "Okay, Skipper. Going off intercom."

Again Geoff tried his intercom.

Nothing. Intercom not working. Turret not working. He couldn't get out; he was trapped.

Impossible to do much more than move a finger. Legs immobile. Were all the connections gone? Cut through? *Jesus Christ.*

"Can you hear me?" he bellowed.

His voice was a rumble inside his skull.

The crew reported some holes in the fuselage and wings but nothing more significant; engines still functioning, controls still operating.

Am I dying? I don't mind dying as long as the bloody pain stops.

It was like having a pneumatic drill working inside you.

One of the four Brownings had gone. The barrel terminated just beyond the breech mechanism. The flak had snapped it off clean as a whistle.

"Geoff? Soon have you out of there, old son."

Encouraging to hear the Skipper saying such things, even when you knew bloody well that the Skipper had no idea whether you were alive or dead, or indeed whether the turret was still on the aircraft. Plenty of turrets had been blown away by flak with the gunners still inside.

The din of the Merlins had become part of the throbbing pain, a maddening, malevolent rhythm. Now the cold was fighting for its share of the agony.

Ben: "Can you hear me, Geoff? Hang on, laddie. We'll get through to you."

Geoff swore at him. *Hurry up, you lazy bastard. Turn the bloody crank. Get me out of here.*

Ben was on the intercom, this time talking to the Skipper: "The sodding handle . . . it broke right off."

What?

The Skipper asked what could be done, as if there was all the time in the world. Ben said he was going to use the axe.

The pain and the cold had become a mad animal and you had to keep fighting it off because it was biting, snapping, tearing at you, trying to rip you to pieces while you sat helpless . . .

The flak should have done the job and got it over with. God only knows what had happened to him. Geoff had seen the results of flak hits on turrets, the occupants reduced to something that belonged on a butcher's block.

"Skipper." A call from the mid-upper turret. "Aircraft behind us. A bit below. Fighter, I think."

"Keep an eye on him."

"I'll do that."

"Ben, how are you coming along?"

"Having a go with the axe."

"Good man."

The rotten bastards sounded as if they had all the time in the world. Damn them.

He felt as if his body was splitting down the middle an agonizing inch at a time. Christ only knew what they would find when they examined him. His body. . . . He had been proud of it; he had looked after it, running regularly around the peri track, taking walks, doing physical jerks. Now what state was it in? Even if he survived this trip he would probably become some pathetic something in a wheelchair. Damn it, he wouldn't let it happen. He would end it all. Somehow.

A voice jarred in the intercom:

"*Fighter!* . . . corkscrew starboard . . . *Go!*"

Darts of light came streaking out of the night, wobbling, curving, streaking past.

Geoff could only watch. One of them had to get him. Had to. The Hally kept staggering. Something cracked into the torn metal of the turret – a bang and a streak of light that seemed to pass through his head . . .

He thought he was dead. Thought it was all over.

But the pain and the cold were still there, still grinding away at him.

God, it hurt like all the fires of hell when the Skipper wrenched the kite into the corkscrew. The manoeuvre threw him from side to side in the turret, banged him against the Perspex walls with the busy little rivulets of water reflecting odd glimmers of light from the gunfire.

Sorry, Mum, Geoff found himself thinking. Your prayers didn't work. Useless bloody things, prayers. God doesn't give a damn. Why should He? What was so worthy about dropping bombs on cities? God should worry Himself about the poor sods on the ground . . .

The Hally quivered. Bullets and cannon shells smashed through her flimsy skin, carving her up, killing her bit by bit.

Geoff bellowed as the kite went twisting and diving; his voice sounded as if it belonged to someone else, someone far away. Still the specks of fire came darting. Sod the fighter. Sod everything.

Ben's voice crackled:

"Port outer's on fire!"

"Feather it!"

"Feathering port outer!"

He saw the streaky flame fluttering past his turret, illuminating the tail fin.

Christ!

The kite was on fire . . . and him still trapped in the bloody turret!

He heaved, strained with all his might, but the turret refused to budge. It would be his tomb . . .

Then he heard the bale-out order.

"God . . . don't leave me!" he screamed.

But only he heard his scream.

They had forgotten about him.

Swine! God . . . bloody swine!

Down onto one wing the kite went, the flames still streaking back, fragmenting in the darkness.

A glimpse of a figure, arms and legs splayed, whirling away into the blackness. It vanished.

God, the bastards, they were *jumping*!

Abandoning him!

And there was nothing, absolutely nothing, he could do about it.

Not fair . . . not bloody fair . . .

It would be over in a moment, he told himself. A few seconds. One awful bloody instant of impact. Then nothing.

I'm sorry . . . for everything.

He felt the remnants of his self-control snapping like the last few strands of an old, rotting rope.

The kite plunged, half rolling, engines roaring.

Primeval screams rose in his throat, but they emerged as sobs, sobs of terror, sobs of regret.

The end of it all. The moment he had dreaded so long.

Mum, Dad, Angela, faces he knew as well as his own, places, happenings, a cup of tea and the Sunday paper, learning to drive an Austin Seven, shaving before the op . . .

He squeezed his eyes shut.

Braced himself, instinctively huddling himself, trying to pull his head into his shoulders.

Cowering, defeated.

Then he became aware of a change in the noise of the engines.

He opened his eyes. Stared in disbelief. Tried to comprehend the significance of the shadows outside. Something had happened. The kite was levelling out in a funny, uneven way . . .

No flames now. Had the dive blown the fire out? It was possible. It sometimes happened.

A weird half a barrel roll and a turn so tight that he felt as if he was being pushed out through the floor . . .

Was that ground? Or cloud?

What the hell was happening?

"Still with us, Geoff?"

Christ, the Skipper! Lean face twisted into that funny grin of his, brown eyes twinkling; Geoff could *see* him.

"Yes, I'm still here!" Geoff yelled. It hurt.

But the Skipper couldn't hear. Sod the intercom.

"Didn't think we'd abandon you, did you?" The Skipper chuckled, actually bloody chuckled. "A couple of the lads have baled out. But Ben and I are still here. Ben's still working away on that rotten turret of yours. Thought you were supposed to keep the thing in working order. Bad show!"

Typical Skipper, bless him!

He heard the Skipper and Ben on the intercom, talking about switching fuel tanks and leaning out the remaining engines.

"The kite's a bit banged up," the Skipper said. "But she's still flying. More or less."

To hear him, you'd think he was talking about a copy of *John Bull*, tattered but still readable.

"Can you hear me in there?" Ben called. "Hang on, be through to you in a jiff."

God, those marvellous voices! He loved them. They were *life!*

He had an idea. Perhaps the emergency warning lights were still working. The lights were there in case the intercom failed, a means of telling the pilot which way to turn to evade fighters.

It hurt. But he managed it, quickly, so that the Skipper would know it wasn't a warning: Left, right, left, right, left, right, left, right.

The Skipper understood at once.

"Message received, Geoff old son. Knew you were alive and kicking in there. Never doubted it for a moment. Just sit tight and we'll see this little episode through. In a little while we'll be laughing about it all over a pint in The White Rose."

"Only if you're paying," said Ben.

Lovely voices. The Skipper, a bit la-di-da, but a hell of a good sort nonetheless. Ben with his throaty burr.

The kite wallowed from side to side as if it were on a string. Geoff screeched in pain.

"Sorry we can't make things a bit smoother," said the Skipper. "Wretched controls aren't quite up to scratch. How are you coming along, Ben?"

"It's coming, Skipper. Like bloody Christmas."

A treat to hear them babbling away. He wished he could tell them how much their voices meant, what it was like to think you'd been left alone to die in the kite and then to find that a pair of your crew-mates were still aboard, working like hell to get you down in one piece.

"Bloody chopper's busted," Ben announced. "What sort of bloody quality is that, I ask you? Handle busted right off."

"They'll make you pay for it," said the Skipper.

"Sod 'em," said Ben. "I'm going to try a fire extinguisher. Won't be a jiffy."

"Hang on, Geoff," said the Skipper.

"I'm not going any-bloody-where," Geoff grunted as the pain assailed him again, applying itself, a fresh layer of agony upon the torment of the cold.

The kit skidded; a drunk might have been at the controls.

It kept turning, sliding, wobbling. Geoff winced. How long could it stay in the air?

"Never fear, Geoff," said the Skipper.

"Hell, no."

"You keep on practising, Skipper," said Ben. "You'll get the hang of how to fly this thing, don't worry."

Now the kite seemed to be circling, but the glimpses of cloud and sky weren't enough to place the earth in position. God only knows where it was supposed to be. What did it matter anyway? Gravity would take care of the problem in the end.

"This bloody turret is a disgrace," said Ben. "I think you should reprimand the rear gunner, Skipper."

"I shall. Making any progress back there?"

"Slow."

"Good man."

It seemed as if the kite had been wobbling around for hours. Over enemy territory, for Christ's sake. Asking for trouble. And bound to get it sooner or later.

If I'd been bleeding to death, he thought, it should have happened by now. Perhaps it already has. Perhaps this is hell.

The kite lurched.

Geoff gasped; the pain enveloped him, wracking his very being, every nerve on fire anew. He felt himself drifting, as if he was no longer trapped in the turret.

"All right, Geoff, old son?"

"Soon be through to you," Ben declared. "This sodding thing isn't going to beat me."

Good blokes. None better.

Odd, the sound of the engines. Uneven. Labouring. One of them kept roaring, then fading, as if the throttle was faulty.

The pain eased to a dull ache – rapture of a sort. What was it like to be without pain? He couldn't remember. He could hardly imagine life outside this damned turret. What was it like to walk? To run?

Come on! Hurry!

God, the bloody controls must be in a bad way. The kite kept wallowing and dipping.

How long had they been flying? Minutes? Hours? Weeks? This seemed to have been his prison for a major part of his existence.

"Everything's going to be all right," the Skipper said in that decided way of his.

"I wonder if Geoff thought we'd bale out and leave him," said Ben.

"No, Geoff would never think that, would you, Geoff?"

Geoff shook his head.

"Good man."

"Won't be long," said Ben. "A couple of minutes."

"Thank you, Harry Lauder," said the Skipper.

You had to smile, you had to, in spite of being in this bloody torture chamber and feeling yourself being pulled apart . . .

"I think we've got it," said Ben.

Silence. Sudden, startling.

The aircraft lurched, staggered.

Air washed past, whispering, moaning. He could hear the creaking of the aircraft's structure, like a ship under sail.

"Ben!" he yelled.

His voice sounded oddly metallic.

No reply from Ben.

The air sounds intensified. The kite was going down, picking up speed. The intercom must have conked out when the engines stopped.

The tree swept into his line of vision, silhouetted against the glimmer of a distant searchlight, swaying, branches outstretched as if trying to touch the bomber . . .

Christ, too low to start banking! *Watch it, Skipper!*

The tree tilted.

He heard someone yell: "Hang on, Geoff!"

Distinctly.

The Skipper's voice. No question about it.

The bang was a bellow of pain, of metal twisting, fracturing, crumpling. The distant searchlight turned upside down. A hundred hands pummelled him, jammed him against the back of the turret. For a crazy instant the pain was taken by surprise. Revolving, he felt nothing but the impact of sound. Tumbling into a kaleidoscope. Riding on a hurdy-gurdy gone mad.

The flak gunners saw the bomber approaching, its propellers stationary, one wing dragging. With a whoosh of startled air, the big aircraft swept over the gunners and smashed into the trees five hundred metres to the rear. The fuselage rolled over three or four times, looking, as one of the gunners said later, like a playful dolphin, as it shed its wings and engines. There was no fire; the fuel tanks were found to be bone-dry. The *Feldwebel* led a squad of half a dozen men to investigate. They held their rifles at the ready, but there was no sign of movement in the twisted wreckage. A weak whimper led them to the remains of the turret and the gunner. Poor devil, he was in a bad way. Two wounds in the chest. A miracle he still breathed. A medical officer hurried to the scene and did what he could for the gunner. An ambulance was on its way, he assured the young man in uncertain English.

A soldier announced that more crew members had been found. The medical officer followed him to what was left of the forward part of the aircraft. There were two bodies. Even the doctor, to whom death had become a familiar sight in recent years, recoiled at the sight of them. Both had taken direct hits from cannon shells, which had distributed parts of them about the cabin like offal in an abattoir. Both had died instantly, about three or four hours ago, the doctor concluded. The man in the pilot's seat still grasped the control column, his feet firmly planted on the rudder pedals, as if even in death he was determined to fly the aircraft home. The bomber must have travelled in great circles until the fuel was exhausted.

It proved difficult to convince the gunner. He kept insisting that the two men – the Skipper and Ben, he called them – had been talking to him until moments before the crash. Delirium, of course. No question about that.

The Adj

THERE WASN'T THE SLIGHTEST DOUBT THAT GUY Venables *existed* before Dorothy came on the scene. The records proved it. But for the life of him the Adj couldn't recall ever laying his eyes on the fellow. Of course, it was probably the fault of the man himself: a retiring sort, Venables, always reading some book or other or scribbling God knows what in a note-book, never entering into the life of the squadron in a wholehearted way. He was tall and slim with a dreamy manner and a pale complexion and prominent cheek-bones that gave him a slightly undernourished look.

Certainly no Clark Gable.

Which made the whole thing that much more remarkable.

The Adj had spent much of the day compiling a report for the CO, a tedious dissertation on the cost per mile of operating various types of squadron motor transport. After the evening meal, he strolled down to the village with Fawcett, the Admin Officer. A moderately amusing companion, Fawcett, as long as you kept him off the deep stuff. Before the war he had been a house master at a public school and there was the ever-present danger of him starting on the wars of Carthage and chaps with names like Hamilcar Barca and

Hanno; he always talked as if he were personally acquainted with them and they were as relevant as Churchill and Hitler.

They went to The White Rose and settled down with pints. Fawcett rambled on about a peer of the realm who was notoriously delinquent in the settlement of his accounts; at one point the fees for his two disagreeable sons were a full six months in arrears. A meeting of the Board of Governors sat to discuss the dilemma, debating whether they dare send a reminder to so august an individual. After three hours the Board had risen, still undecided.

It was during this seemingly interminable story that Venables walked into the Saloon Bar with Nigel Pettigrew, a flight sergeant gunner named Thwaites – and Dorothy.

"Good Lord . . . " breathed the Adj.

"Whatever's the matter?" Fawcett looked concerned.

"Don't you recognize her?"

"Should I?"

"I'm sure that's . . . "

Young Venables, all smiles, brought the lady over.

"Gentlemen, I'd like to introduce my wife, Dorothy. Darling, this is Squadron Leader Simon Coombs, our highly esteemed Adj – that's short for Adjutant – and Squadron Leader Roderick Fawcett who looks after all sorts of vital administrative matters."

"Mainly making sure that we've ordered enough soap and toilet rolls and things like that," said Fawcett. "I'm awfully pleased to meet you."

"You're . . . I'm sure . . . " For the moment, the Adj couldn't form a coherent sentence. He found himself biting his upper lip.

Venables grinned. "Dorothy Miles. Is that the name you're trying to think of?"

"Of course!" The Adj squirmed, embarrassed; he felt his face glowing. "For the moment I just couldn't think of it. So sorry."

"My wife used to be known as Dorothy Miles," Venables explained to Fawcett. "She was an actress."

"How interesting."

"Recognized her the moment she . . . er, you both came in," said the Adj.

"You're so kind to remember," said Dorothy. What a voice she possessed, silky yet curiously powerful. And her diction! A pleasure to listen to her, sounding every "t" and "d" in such a delightfully unselfconscious way, as if it had never occurred to her to run words into one another like the rest of the human race. And that smile, and the charm! She held herself like a queen – no wonder they had put her in those period pictures with Ronald Colman and George Arliss. Blue eyes, oval face, delightfully sensuous mouth, a thick mane of silvery blonde hair pulled back in careless perfection.

"I must write and tell Grace about this," said Fawcett on the way back to the airfield. "She goes to the cinema sometimes. Perhaps she will remember the name. Dorothy Venables."

"Dorothy Miles."

"Of course."

Never in his pottiest meanderings had the Adj ever dreamed of chatting in a pub with Dorothy Miles. The memory still thrilled him. He squirmed when he remembered not being able to recall her name. Idiotic! Bloody brain seized up. Excitement of the moment. "She was marvellous in *Royal Intrigue*, wasn't she? With Flynn, wasn't it? Better looking than Madeleine Carroll, I thought. Always beyond me why she didn't become one of the really big stars. Like Garbo. Or that Crawford woman. Perhaps she got tired of it. People can get tired of films just like any job, what?"

"I'm afraid I haven't the slightest idea."

The Adj clicked his tongue. Old Fawcett was so out of touch with the real world; typical academic. "She met Venables at a party, she said. What would Venables be doing at a party with people like Dorothy Miles? And what would she see in him? Nice enough chap of course. But . . . "

"He's a very pleasant young fellow."

"Pleasant? Yes, that's it: *pleasant*. But I wouldn't have thought pleasant was enough for someone like Dorothy Miles. I mean, she's had her *pick* . . . the Jack Buchanans, the

George Brents, Donat, Richardson, *everybody* . . . and she marries Venables."

"Possibly his youth was a factor. I fancy the lady has ten or twelve years on her husband."

"The remarkable thing is that she looks just the same in person as on the screen."

"Did you expect a transmogrification?" chuckled Fawcett.

"I'm not at all sure what I expected," said the Adj with a sniff. Fawcett was too fond by far of such words as transwhatever. Irritating at times. "She's taken a room at The White Rose. Imagine Dorothy Miles staying at a dreary little place like that. Not for long, I fancy. The CO doesn't like wives close by. He's told me so several times. *Venables*, of all people! He wasn't an actor in civilian life, was he?"

"Something to do with banking, I believe."

"Banking. Imagine."

The Adj sighed. When he had talked to her about being a star, she was quick to deny it. A supporting player, she called herself. She was always the "other woman" or the one who died tragically. She lacked whatever it was that stars had, she said. "Amusing, wasn't it, when she talked about how they tried to make her into another Deanna Durbin."

"Deanna who?"

Dorothy Venables was an instant hit at Officers' Mess gatherings. Witty, charming, she answered questions with endless patience and good humour. No, she told anyone who asked, she didn't miss acting a bit. She had already had more luck than her talent entitled her to and she certainly wouldn't be missed in films or the theatre. Besides, it was far more important to be a good wife to her navigator husband than to star in *Gone with the Wind*, darling. She called everyone darling. All actresses did, according to Coates, the MO, who claimed to know.

Which prompted more than a few puzzled glances at Venables. Such a quiet type, self-effacing, you might say. He habitually wore a look of utter adoration in her presence, putting the Adj in mind of a Doberman puppy. What on earth did she see in him? He was so *ordinary*, just another bod in the squadron. Sometimes Dorothy would sit down at the piano to play and sing a song or two. Her voice was far from exceptional but she used it with skill and verve – professional "business," she explained, courtesy of the patient drill-instructors at MGM.

It couldn't last, the Adj concluded. Marriage and operational flying were utterly incompatible. For Dorothy Venables it was bound to be particularly hard, living as she was within a stone's throw of the airfield. She would soon tire of being stuck in a shabby little pub in a thoroughly deadly part of Yorkshire – she who had hobnobbed with the mighty in London and Hollywood. Inevitably she would depart for more glamorous surroundings. And who could blame her? The Adj's heart quickened whenever he saw her. So statuesque, so graceful, so utterly, totally delectable. Beside her, the Yorkshire lasses were like cart-horses. She had a fund of show business stories, talking about "Marlene" and "Erroll" as if they were ordinary human beings, mere co-workers. If she included herself in any of the stories it was always in a charmingly self-deprecating way; she recounted how she had been brought up in a village in Northumberland, one very much like Rocklington; she had worked countless hours to rid herself of the local accent – and in her very first speaking role she was required to play a North Country peasant girl. Freeman, the catering officer, had dug up an old fan magazine containing a photograph of Dorothy on a yacht with Robert Taylor. The caption hinted at a romance between the two. Nothing but studio press relations, Dorothy said; in fact, she had never left dry land with Mr. Taylor; the photograph had been taken on a film set at least ten miles from the Pacific shores. A certifiably crazy world, that of films, she was fond of declaring. What an extraordinary life she had led; the Adj found himself shaking his head whenever he gave the matter any thought, which he did with increasing frequency. It was still a puzzle to him why she married Venables. If he had *done* something, if he had been a Cheshire or a Gibson, then it would have been understandable, there would have been something to attract Dorothy. But Venables was so average. Actually, because of his introverted ways, a trifle *below* average, in the Adj's opinion. A bit of a bore, when you got right down to it.

Venables requested permission to live at The White Rose. The Adj had to say no. Regretfully. CO's orders. Aircrew had to be billeted on the field, available at all times.

"But I'd only be half a mile away. A telephone call and I could be back at the field in a matter of minutes."

"Orders are orders," said the Adj.

"Exceptions can be made," Venables pointed out.

The Adj shook his head. "If the CO granted you permission he would have to do the same for the next officer who made the same request. Look here, I don't mind asking him. But I know what he'll say."

The Adj was wrong. The CO smiled when the name Venables was mentioned. He stroked his starboard moustache.

"Magnificent woman."

"Absolutely, sir. She's taken up residence at The White Rose and Flying Officer Venables has asked permission to . . . well, to live there with her."

"Don't blame him," said the CO. "Don't blame him at all."

"I explained your feeling about officers living off the station . . . "

The CO caressed his nose. He said,

"But it's only half a mile or so. The chap is just as available as those men we billeted in that farm on the other side of the river. I think we can make an exception in Venables's case. Remember her in that thing about the Spanish Armada? Always a wonder to me that the censors passed the film with that *marvellous* dress she wore. God knows how she kept the thing up. Remember those . . . er . . . that figure of hers."

"Outstanding, sir."

"That's the word," said the CO.

In no time Dorothy Venables was appearing at ENSA shows for the airmen and at concert parties in the village and nearby. She sang a song or two and recited bits of suitably patriotic verse from Shakespeare and performed excerpts from modern drama (*This Happy Breed* went over particularly well). She invariably did a number or two at dances with the RAF Rocklington Dance Orchestra under the direction of Corporal Cuthbert Hardy. She brought the house down one evening by introducing him as "a maestro of exceptional talent" and demanding a "big, enthusiastic hand" – then embracing him there and then on the stage in front of everyone and crying, "Kiss me, Hardy!" The audiences adored her.

It was at about this time that she received the offer from Korda. He was planning a major feature on the Indian Mutiny; he wanted Dorothy for the Viceroy's wife, a leading role. She refused it. She had retired from the profession, she said. Korda caused a sensation at The White Rose when he arrived in his Rolls Royce and had dinner with Dorothy and Venables; he attempted with upraised voice and flamboyantly Continental gestures to get her to change her mind about the film. The White Rose had seen nothing like it since the visit of Oscar Wilde in 1894. But Korda's journey north was in vain. Dorothy said she simply wasn't interested in acting any more.

"He took it awfully well," Venables told the Adj. "I rather fancy he blames me for her decision. The truth is, I thought it might be a good idea; poor girl, she must get frightfully bored. But no, she said she couldn't care less about films."

She did a little acting, however. An amateur group asked if she would play Mrs Erlynne in *Lady Windermere's Fan*. A local butcher, Clement Plunkett, played Lord Windermere. He had fortified himself with one or two whiskeys before going on stage. Although he remembered all his lines, his balance suffered; during one intense speech he toppled over backwards, glanced off a table, and finished up sprawled on the stage. The consummate professional, Dorothy made a remark about it not being necessary for him to get down on his knees to her; no one in the audience seemed to notice anything awry.

Everyone remarked on how happy she was – which continued to puzzle the Adj; by now she should have been insane with boredom, in his opinion. During the days she was often to be seen strolling in the village and on the Wolds to the south. Within a week or two she appeared to know everyone; she invariably asked about husbands, wives or children, seldom getting a name wrong. Of course her theatrical training helped, everyone was agreed on that; learning all those lines would make anyone's memory sharp. But it was good of her to take the trouble; everyone was also agreed on that.

She and Venables would often be seen having a drink or two in the Saloon Bar of The White Rose. A crowd would gather; new aircrew would be introduced; if they were Canadians or Aussies she would be able to tell them about engagements in Toronto or Sydney, winning them all in her effortless way. The young men could hardly take their eyes off her. Venables would sit on the sidelines and take it all in, puffing away on his Dunhill and smiling beatifically.

The pair of them went to London on his next leave. Their pictures appeared in the *Illustrated London News*: "Noted Film Actress and Airman Husband Are Seen Strolling in Hyde Park." When the leave was over Venables told his crewmates how Dorothy had done the washing-up at his widowed mother's flat while various friends gazed on in wonder.

"Jolly good type," said Nigel Pettigrew, Venables's skipper.

"Does she have a sister?" enquired Glossop, the flight engineer.

"Just a brother," said Venables.

A reporter from one of the dailies came up from London to interview her. She chatted with him for an hour. No, she kept assuring him, there were no plans for films or plays; yes, she intended to continue living quietly at The White Rose, just another service wife. The reporter returned to London, somewhat disgruntled.

One morning an invitation arrived for the Adj. It was from Dorothy. Would the Adj be able to attend a small party she was arranging to celebrate her husband's twenty-sixth birthday on the 20th? RSVP.

The Adj gazed at the note for minutes. Only a year or two before he had watched her on the screen, magnificent in eighteenth-century attire; he had thought her the most desirable creature he had ever seen. God knows why she wasn't the star of the picture. And now he was holding a note written in her own hand, a note addressed to him, Simon Coombs! It made one think that life must have other delicious surprises up its sleeve.

The Adj telephoned The White Rose. Yes, he told Dorothy, he would be most pleased to accept her kind invitation. She was genuinely pleased; you could tell by the sparkle in her voice, that marvellously expressive voice that was a joy to listen to – such a joy that he was losing track of what she was saying about it being a small, rather *special* group: just the crew of Q-Queenie, Squadron Leader Fawcett, the MO, a couple of WAAF girlfriends . . . and himself. Such fun, because Guy knew nothing about it. He thought the two of them were going to York to celebrate privately . . .

The next night Pettigrew's aircraft went missing.

The Adj drove immediately to The White Rose.

Dorothy kept nodding as the Adj told her what he knew. Her left hand was white as she gripped a chair back.

"I suppose I have been secretly rehearsing this scene ever since we were married," she said, her voice husky. "We often talked about it . . . *this*. We've always known that it might happen. What hope is there?"

"There is a great deal of hope," the Adj replied with more confidence than he felt. "The very fact that we have no news is encouraging. The Jerries are usually quite good at reporting the names of aircrew who crash in German or occupied territory. So we can look at a number of possibilities. The crew might have baled out and evaded capture. If they are caught we'll hear about it in short order. If not, well, they might link up with one of the Resistance groups. That could mean a long time without news. On the other hand, they might have experienced difficulties over the sea. They could have ditched. They could be bobbing about in a dinghy at this very moment. The moment they're picked up we'll get news . . ."

"But how will the rescue people know where to go to pick them up?"

"It depends . . . sometimes the wireless op sends out a distress signal to help the rescue boys get a fix, you see . . . "

"But no signal was received from their aircraft?"

"Not that I know of."

"So we wait."

"I'm afraid so. We will of course be in touch the moment we hear anything . . . " Dismal banality, yet anything was better than silence.

"It's awfully good of you to come to tell me personally."

"My pleasure," said the Adj – and immediately regretted the remark. Idiotic thing to say. Damn it, it just slipped out. Poor woman, stuck there alone in that room, just waiting. Perhaps the Station Commander's wife would go and spend a little time with her. He would talk to the CO about it that very afternoon.

He went back to the airfield. There was no word on Queenie. The kite might have vanished from the face of the earth. Which it may have well done if hit fair and square by flak. An 88 mm anti-aircraft shell exploding in a fully loaded bomb bay could reduce a thirty-ton bomber and its crew to a handful of unrecognizable, unspeakable bits of rubbish. On the other hand, Queenie might have gone straight into the sea before the wireless op could transmit. God only knows how many kites lay in crumpled repose on the bottom of the Channel and the North Sea. Their crews were classified as "Missing" and often remained so for months until the sea gave up a body or a fragment of the aircraft.

The Adj called on Dorothy every couple of days. She seemed glad to see him, inviting him into her small room overlooking the square. She indicated a chair in front of the empty fireplace. On the mantel there was a framed photograph of Venables in battledress holding a tankard of beer. Dorothy said it had been taken a couple of months ago, downstairs, precisely seventeen days before she had met him. The Adj had the odd feeling that grief had made

Dorothy physically smaller; poor girl, how vulnerable she looked, how he longed to tell her something to bring that marvel of a smile to her lips. But all he could tell her was that there was nothing to tell her. Which was really something to be grateful for, wasn't it? The Jerries had made no mention of Queenie or any members of her crew; no news was almost certainly good news.

"He's alive," she declared. She punched the palm of one hand with her fist. "I know it. I feel it. I shouldn't worry; no more tears – because crying puffs up my eyes; I can *hear* Guy saying it." She smiled, a little brittle on-again-off-again smile. "Forgive me, babbling on. It must seem to be an awful lot of nonsense for someone like yourself who's seen so much of all this."

"Not nonsense at all," said the Adj. "Terribly important to keep thinking... er, positively. Do you intend to stay on here at The White Rose?"

"Naturally," she said. "This is our home." Then she looked up. "I wonder if I might ask your advice."

"Of course."

"Before all this . . . I accepted one or two engagements at concerts and dances. Naturally I'm not accepting any more; and I've cancelled the three or four that were outstanding. But a certain Mr Bickle is kicking up a tremendous fuss, threatening to cause all sorts of trouble if I don't honour my obligation, as he puts it. I explained the circumstances but his response was that business is business."

"The wretch," breathed the Adj. "God, some people really make you wonder if the country is worth fighting for. Let me have this Bickle's address and telephone number. It will give me more than a little pleasure to deal with him."

"I can't thank you enough."

"Think nothing of it, Mrs Venables."

"Please call me Dorothy."

When the Adj called again he was able to report that Mr Bickle had been taken care of. "Piece of cake. Explained that since your husband was an officer on active duty you were protected by all the resources of the Royal Air Force, and I mentioned that if he didn't toe the line he would be visited by a squad of Service Police who are experts at handling awkward customers. I don't think you'll have any more trouble from Mr Bickle, but if you do, be good enough to let me know."

"I'm most grateful, darling." Eyes slightly downcast: it was exactly the same look that she had given Gary Cooper when he rescued her from Indians in *Prairie Fire*.

The Adj glowed. "Look, I have to drive into York tomorrow afternoon – a little job for the CO. Won't take long. If you'd care to come along – for a change of scenery, you know – we might have a spot of tea at Betty's."

To his surprise she nodded. Yes, it would be a pleasant change; how kind of him to ask.

All the following morning, the Adj sat in an agony of anticipation; it would be typical of the CO to wreck the arrangements at the last moment by deciding to come along or go himself. But no, the CO was busy inspecting the repair work on the bomb dump; he hadn't returned by noon. Thankfully the Adj departed.

The sun came out while they droned along the main road to York in the grey Humber. Dorothy said little; she seemed to be engrossed in the countryside. The Adj wished the journey would go on for ever; marvellously peaceful, bowling along in a fine car with a stunning woman like Dorothy Venables at one's side.

An hour later they were comfortably installed at Betty's, munching on scones and talking, talking, talking. Mainly about him. Absolutely miraculous how she could make one open up. It was like digging into a trunk and dragging out old memories about the days on the Western Front; the frightful FEs and DH-4s – sluggish and inflammable as the very devil; and, the Adj pointed out, airmen had no parachutes in those far-off days. Delightfully feminine, how she caught her breath and bit her lower lip at the thought of him at fifteen thousand feet without a brolly. And how she inveigled him into recounting how he won his MC. Every detail. He told her about the peacetime years in Mesopotamia and India. The unfriendly denizens of Kurdistan and Northern Waziristan. The weary old aircraft left over from the war. His accident. The three-month spell in hospital that put paid to his flying career. A succession of administrative jobs. The disquieting certainty that if it hadn't been for Adolf he would have been out on the street by now having been heartily thanked for his years of service and deluged with any number of good wishes for a jolly successful career in civilian life.

"But you're much too young to retire," she declared. God, what eyes! Hard not to gaze into them and imagine heaven knows what.

The Adj blushed. "Not a spring chicken any more. Have to make room for the younger chaps."

"You're in the prime of life, darling," she asserted. "The thing that puzzles me is that after all these places you've been and all the things you've done, you've remained single. It's quite disgraceful. Have you never even been engaged?"

More blushes. Damn it, like a bloody schoolboy. "I was engaged once," he admitted.

"What was her name?"

"Daphne."

"Very beautiful?"

"Very pleasing. And such a nice disposition."

"Why didn't you marry her?"

"She told me she'd been divorced. Married a Rhodesian during the war. It didn't work. So they divorced. And my CO thought it would be detrimental to my career to marry her. They were still jolly particular about that kind of thing at the time."

"She was a fool to let you go."

"Oh, I say . . . "

"I mean it. Women see the rights and wrongs of these situations far better than men." She smiled: a good, wide smile that revealed the tips of her teeth; the first complete smile the Adj had seen from her all day. "Never mind, there's still lots of time."

"For me?" A hoarse chuckle – and still more blushes. "I'm an old confirmed bachelor now. Far too late."

It was a perfect afternoon – and for the next couple of days the memories of it kept intruding, dancing about him like playful elves: the way she shook her head – a decisive shake it was – and how she informed him that it was never too late; and in his case it was obvious that the clock was still ticking merrily, she said. Lord, she could put a saucy tone in her voice when she fancied. Shaving, he found himself holding his head up a bit to smooth that suggestion of a sag under the chin. Still, he was in pretty vigorous form for a chap within spitting distance of fifty. Hair – or most of it – still in place; spot of grey about the temples probably an improvement on the original. The middle needed a little more holding-in than in years of yore. But it wasn't unsightly, definitely not unsightly. A spot of running every day would soon tone him up. He could still wear a uniform well; Daphne used to say that some men seemed born to wear uniforms; he was definitely one, according to her. Poor Daphne. Where was she now? It was hard to recall her features; fragile things, memories. For years he had carried a small photograph of her; it had vanished during some move or other. Would that photograph of Guy Venables vanish one day too? Did Dorothy gaze at his photograph by the hour? When would she finally come to accept the fact that he had had it? He had, of course. One developed an instinct for death; Adjs on all operational squadrons did.

The days passed. Dorothy seemed to have no plans for moving out of The White Rose. She spent her time in her room or walking in the village and on the Wolds. Sometimes she encountered aircrew who had known Venables. But already she was finding it necessary to learn new names. Pilot Officer Dalgleish, Warrant Officer Newman, Sergeant Adams. Fresh young faces to replace those who had "failed to return" – the official term that seemed to embody a hint of criticism of the unfortunates who didn't try hard enough to evade the flak shell or the night-fighter or the ice that hung suspended in tiny droplets in the clouds.

She went down to London for a few days. Someone said that she was going to see Korda about that film. But the someone was wrong. Dorothy was making her presence felt at the Air Ministry. She had connections – and she used every one of them to find out if news of Venables's fate was being withheld for some reason. The effort was in vain; no one, however exalted, knew what had happened to Queenie or its occupants.

The squadron lost five crews on four ops. A sixth crew was lost when a Halifax on a training flight took off, climbed away from the field, rolled onto its back, and spun into the village, destroying four small houses, killing six civilians as well as the crew of seven. The following day an explosion in the bomb dump obliterated two aircraft and three ground crew. It was the grimmest period anyone could recall. Already there were references to the "hard-luck squadron" of the Group. The replacements kept arriving, each batch pinker and softer-cheeked than the last. A young Canadian pilot said he was having a beer in "that funny old pub near the station and this good-looking broad – older, you know, but still a dish – got talking about a guy named Venables." Who was this Venables? The Adj told him.

The weather turned. Grey days and raw winds. And longer nights. Deeper penetrations into Germany. Distant targets. Frankfurt and Darmstadt, Hannover and Berlin.

At take-off time, the Adj always joined the well-wishers at the end of the active runway. Each kite had to be sent on its way with a cheery wave.

Engines bellowing at full bore, the heavily loaded bombers would roll away, along the mile of asphalt. N-Nuts had travelled two thousand feet when it developed a swing, veering from one side of the runway to the other. The undercarriage collapsed. A fuel tank burst. The fire started as little more than a flicker. Then with an ugly *whoosh!* it engulfed the Halifax while the aircraft clattered along on its belly.

"Spot of bother last night," the Adj told Dorothy over a glass of sherry at The White Rose the following day.

"I know," said Dorothy. "I was there."

The Adj raised an eyebrow. "Really?"

"Watching from the road. It looked bad."

"It was."

"Oh, God," she sighed. "I try to be there when they're taking off on ops. Guy used to talk so much about the preparations, the briefing, the dressing-up in all the gear, collecting the charts and equipment. And the waiting. He had a lot to say about the waiting. How it eats at your courage. How it seems to consume energy like violent exercise, so that when at last it's time to go you're already exhausted. He's written a couple of poems about the waiting."

"Poems?"

"Yes, didn't you know that Guy writes poetry?" She beamed. "The critics consider him one of the brightest of the younger British poets. His latest book has been getting quite marvellous reviews. *Allusions*. Perhaps you've seen it . . . "

"*Poetry!* My goodness . . . " The Adj shook his head. "I'm afraid not . . . Not much in my line, poetry . . . "

"You'll like Guy's poetry," she said confidently.

Someone saw her two nights later when the squadron went to Berlin. She was at the north-east corner of the field, standing by the fence, watching the aircraft as they taxied along the peri track and turned onto the runway. From time to time she would be seen during the day, trudging the lanes that flanked the field. Fawcett, the Admin bloke, drove by her in his jeep. He stopped. Could he give her a lift? It looked rather like rain, didn't it? Awful the winds in this part of the world, weren't they?

She declined Fawcett's offer. She liked to walk, she said.

An Aussie navigator named Finlay saw her plodding through the puddles near the main gate.

"She remembered my name," he reported wonderingly. " 'Hullo, George,' she said, just as if we'd met that morning. 'How's Nancy?' Nancy, the wife. She remembered her name too. And it's been weeks. Weeks and weeks. I'd even forgotten Venables. Gone out of my head, the way they do, the blokes who get the chop. He was in Nigel Pettigrew's crew, wasn't he?"

"Did she ask if there was any news?" the Adj enquired.

"Sort of," Finlay replied. "Wanted to know if we'd heard

anything of the crews who'd been shot down recently. I said Potts and his crew all baled out and were taken prisoner in good order. She said what splendid news, that they were alive even if they were prisoners."

A sergeant pilot saw her when he taxied his Halifax to the runway for take-off from the south end of the field. She stood in the teeth of a frigid wind, arms folded, watching. When the sergeant landed after more than an hour, she was still there.

"P'raps she's a spy," suggested someone.

A sergeant gunner shook his head. "She's waiting for her husband to come back. He was a navigator. Got the chop weeks ago."

"Perhaps he will come back."

"And p'raps Adolf will see the error of his ways and want to make friends with Winston."

As the weather worsened, she was seen more frequently, trudging along the main road that was the field's northern boundary and on the little lanes that meandered about its flanks. She gazed at the bleak slashes of runways and the black-bellied Halifaxes squatting on their hardstandings, waiting.

The CO sent for the Adj.

"Not happy about that actress woman. The newer crews are talking about her. Not good for morale, not good at all."

"I don't think she's breaking any laws, sir."

"What?"

"Well, she's confining her . . . er . . . activities to public roads."

"Not the point. Not the point at all. She's like a bloody wraith about the place. Watching. Morale is wonky enough without her. Wretched woman should have had the decency to buzz off when her husband . . . uh . . . "

"Venables, sir."

"Quite. When Venables went for a Burton she should have taken herself off. Imagine if all the bloody widows kept parading around the field. Marvellous way to buck the sprogs up, wouldn't you say?"

"I'll have a word with her, sir."

"There's a good chap."

The Adj went outside. In the course of his career he had been ordered to do many unpleasant things. But none as nasty as this. It simply wasn't possible to carry the order out without causing the most frightful offence. In all probability Dorothy would pack up and leave the village the same day. And who could blame her? But the mere idea of her leaving Rocklington was sufficient to plunge the Adj into despondency. How incredibly dreary life would be without her. Her presence made everything worthwhile.

He decided against the telephone. Cold, impersonal things, telephones. Face to face contact was absolutely essential on a mission of such delicacy.

He put on his cap and greatcoat and walked to the village against a biting wind. His stomach rumbled all the way. Blast his stomach; it always rumbled when he was nervous.

Sam Borthwick, the proprietor of The White Rose, met him at the door. Yes, Mrs Venables was in her room. Was there news of . . . *Mr* Venables?

The Adj shook his head.

Sam sighed, as much from relief, it seemed, as from disappointment. No news was still a sort of good news.

Dorothy appeared a few moments later, looking as lovely as ever. But pale and tired. How much sleep was she getting?

She invited the Adj to her room. He sat facing the picture of Guy Venables.

"Mr Borthwick tells me there's no more news."

"I'm afraid not." The Adj groped for the right words. "I do wish we had something to tell you. Something positive. I know it's awfully hard on you . . . always the same when you're facing a situation that you can't do anything to influence. And particularly difficult for you . . . here, alone. We've been concerned about you."

"About me?" She gazed at him, the hint of a smile shading her lips. "Surely you have infinitely more important things to worry about than me."

The Adj kept groping. "I've been through this sort of thing

many times over the years. Too many times by far. In France in the first lot. Now this. The point is, I know how important it is to ... well, to try to make a fresh start ... "

"A fresh start? Whatever do you mean, darling?"

The Adj felt the sweat gathering around his collar. The words hadn't emerged quite as he had intended. He cleared his throat.

"What I mean is, well . . . for example, do you think it's good for you to stay here at The White Rose?"

"Why shouldn't I stay here?"

"The associations . . . and everything . . . can't be a good thing ... on the whole."

"The associations are a comfort to me."

"I see."

"Besides, I intend to be here when Guy comes back."

"I see," muttered the Adj again. The home fires thing. God.

She got to her feet and went to the window. A heavy lorry went by, rattling the glass in its frame. She watched for a moment, then turned.

"You don't think Guy's coming back, do you?"

The Adj found it necessary to clear his throat again. He stared at Venables's picture; couldn't help himself. "I wouldn't say that. . . . But the truth is, they've been missing too long. We should have heard something by now. The fact that we haven't . . . now, after all this time is . . . in my experience an indication that they've almost certainly had it."

"Almost certainly isn't certainly," she said, as if repeating an article of faith.

"It's just that . . . we felt it might be . . . better for you not to . . . well, spend so much time around the aerodrome . . . with all its . . . well, its memories."

She gazed at him, touching the point of her chin with her forefinger. "It's very kind of you to be concerned." She frowned. "But that's not the real reason, is it?"

"No," he admitted.

"I thought it was still a free country and a citizen was entitled to go walking where she wished."

"Yes, but . . . "

"Am I looking at something secret?"

The Adj shook his head miserably. "No, of course not, but . . . the new crews . . . they've been asking about you . . . "

A mirthless little chuckle. "It was only a few weeks ago that your CO told me what a splendid job I was doing to bolster everyone's morale! Now my presence is apparently having the opposite effect!"

The Adj squirmed. "I feel frightful about all this . . . "

She nodded thoughtfully. "I'm sure this visit wasn't your idea. Did your CO order you to do it?"

The Adj nodded.

"He should do his own dirty work."

"He's quite a good sort really, the CO . . . but he's very concerned about morale. The squadron's been having a bad time of it recently."

"I know," she said. A quick little sigh. "Very well, I will keep away from the aerodrome during my walks. Do you think your CO will object to my taking my constitutional on the Wolds? There's always the terrible danger of one of your pilots spotting me from the air."

"You're very understanding," said the Adj.

And lovely, he wanted to add, but didn't.

The next morning there was a report from Group. The navy had picked up the body of an airman. A Flight Sergeant E.F. Thwaites.

Thwaites. Pettigrew's rear gunner.

The Adj went back to The White Rose.

"Sad news, I'm afraid. They've found the body of a member of your husband's crew . . . the rear gunner . . . in the North Sea."

"Ernie Thwaites," said Dorothy, turning toward Venables's picture, as if to seek his verification. "I remember him. Very good-natured young chap. Engaged to a girl in Gateshead. I liked him." The Adj saw her take a bracing breath. "But it was Ernie's body they found, not Guy's; that is correct, isn't it?"

"Quite correct. But it does tend to suggest – "

"I don't listen to suggestions," she declared, a little too brightly. "Only facts, incontrovertible facts, if you please, Squadron Leader."

The Adj nodded uneasily: the poor dear woman seemed to be trying so frightfully hard not to break down.

"I'm awfully sorry," he murmured.

"I know you are," she said. "But it's Ernie Thwaites you have to be sorry about, not Guy." She managed a smile; it was quickly gone. "Nothing has changed. That's the important thing. Guy is still only missing. The situation is just as it was on that first day. I think I shall write a letter to Ernie's parents. Do you think it would be appropriate? I can't see how it could possibly do any harm, do you? After all, I did know Ernie. I remember, we talked about *Charley's Aunt*. He'd seen it a dozen times or more. I told him I had once done the part of the silly girlfriends – both of them; we used to exchange parts to relieve the monotony; he was convinced he had seen me in it. But I rather think we missed each other by quite a few years . . ."

The Adj let her chatter on; perhaps it would help her recover from the shock of Ernie Thwaites. At last he rose. She extended her hand; he took it – and was startled when her free hand clasped his, almost fiercely.

"You're such a pillar of strength, darling."

"Well . . . one does what one can."

"You don't know what it's meant to have you *here*."

"You only have to ask."

A smile, lovely though fleeting. "Thank you. And please tell your CO that I promise faithfully to keep well away from the airfield. You might also tell him that if he had sent anyone else to do this I would probably have rung up by now and given him a piece of my mind. But you were so nice about it that I was disarmed. I just hope that this won't mean that we see any less of you."

The Adj went back to the airfield in a state of mild euphoria. A positively intoxicating feeling, to know that one was actually *valued* by someone like Dorothy. Imagine him, Simon Coombs from Watford, a *friend* of hers, a *confidant*, you might say. Unbelievable. And unsettling. Hard to concentrate on all the absurd Adj-type duties that had once seemed so important.

But what now? It couldn't go on like this much longer. Soon she would be compelled to come to grips with reality. Her husband had gone for a Burton; he'd bought the farm, he'd got the chop; no matter what euphemism you chose the end result was the same. He wasn't coming back. Ever. Eventually she had to face the truth. What would she do? Go back to London? There was absolutely nothing to keep her here, in the wilds of East Yorkshire.

Except one Simon Coombs, he found himself thinking. Couldn't help himself. The thought intruded and refused to budge. No matter how he tried.

Idiot! At his age, imagining a lot of romantic bilge, like some soppy Ivor Novello character.

He told himself in the strongest terms that it was absurd to think for one moment that she entertained *that* sort of feeling for him. It was simple gratitude that impelled her to clasp his hand in hers. Possibly a spot of affection in there somewhere, but mainly gratitude. She had come to rely on him; he was someone to turn to in time of trouble.

But he wasn't at all sure that he believed himself.

He took her to York to see *His Girl Friday* with Cary Grant. Afterwards, they had a drink and a bite to eat in a pub near the Minster; she reminisced about Grant; she had met him at a party. "He kept on talking about England and how he intended to return in a few years. He said there was something unreal about Southern California; it was unhealthy to stay too long. You lost touch with the real world. Really rather a nice man," she said. Which struck the Adj as funny, a bit like saying that the King was quite royal. The contrast between her former life and her present existence was bizarre. She had taken a part-time job in the local Food Office, sitting at one of those plain wooden tables with metal legs, issuing ration cards and answering endless questions. She still refused to move away from Rocklington; to move would presumably be to admit that Guy was indeed dead and would never return.

"I sometimes see aircrew in the bar," she said. "So young and trying so hard to be grown up. But I hardly ever see anyone I recognize."

"They come and they go," said the Adj. "New crews arriving every week. They do their tour or – in any case, they don't stay more than a few months at the most."

"I talked to a young Australian pilot," said Dorothy. "He'd done twenty trips – and he didn't know Guy. He'd arrived after Guy went missing. Amazing."

"Incredible," murmured the Adj. It wasn't. Venables had got the chop back in the summer; now the winter winds were blowing again; the early morning frost gave the aircraft and the buildings a vaguely festive look. "The important thing," said the Adj, "is to live a day at a time. Things sort themselves out."

She smiled. "A day is far too much. I divide every day into at least eight bits. I seldom think in longer terms."

"Time will help to heal the wound," murmured the Adj with the best of intentions. But she reacted sharply. There was no wound, she informed the Adj, because there was nothing but uncertainty.

The Adj had a private word with Sam Borthwick, the proprietor of The White Rose. How did she seem to be managing?

"Moderately well," Sam reported in his guarded way. "Keeps to herself of course. Reads a lot of books. Always going to the library. Then she has her little job. Has her meals here most days; sometimes she goes to the station café. Depends."

"Depends?"

"What we've got on. Take our shepherd's pie. She's fond of it; but she doesn't like our fish. Fond of bread and butter pudding, hates porridge. See what I mean? Lovely lady, she is. Very glad to have her here; nice to have the room let more or less permanently, at least, permanently for as long as she wants it, if you get my meaning."

The Adj talked to the padre.

"Worried about her, living alone. Unhealthy, wouldn't you say?"

"People do manage to live alone. My father, for one."

"Yes, but she persists in believing that her husband is still alive when it's quite obvious that he isn't."

"People cope with crises in their own ways," said the padre. "I'm perfectly prepared to have a word with her if you think it might help."

"It might," said the Adj, trying not to sound doubtful.

"Does she have any relatives?" asked the padre.

There was a thought. "I seem to recall something about a brother. In the BBC, I think. Producer or something."

"It might be sensible to apprise him of the situation. In the meantime if there's anything I can do, don't hesitate."

The following Friday morning Group telephoned.

"The navy found one of your chaps. Body had been in the water for at least three months, they said. Name of Betts."

"God," said the Adj. Betts was Pettigrew's mid-upper gunner.

"And another bod."

The Adj's heart tripped.

"This one's name was Bryce. According to our records he went LMF ages ago. Remustered to non-flying duties. So how did he finish up in the North Sea?"

"Haven't a clue," said the Adj, breathing again. He vaguely remembered Bryce; pathetic little bugger, fell apart when things got a bit too rough. Why he was on Pettigrew's aircraft was beyond the Adj – and he hadn't the time or inclination to puzzle it out at the moment.

It was obvious that Pettigrew's aircraft had crashed in the sea, taking the whole crew to the bottom. Now, one by one, the bodies were working their way free of the wreckage and coming to the surface, bloated, obscene . . .

When the Adj telephoned The White Rose he was told that Dorothy was working at the Food Office until half past five. He walked to the village, bought stamps at the post office, then went and stood outside the empty-windowed shop that provided space for the officials and their stamps and ration cards.

Her brows knitted the moment she saw him.

"Something's happened."

"They've found another body . . . a member of your husband's crew."

"Where?"

"In the North Sea, just like before."

"Who?"

"Sergeant Betts."

"I remember him. Rather a shy boy."

"Was he? I'm afraid I don't recall."

"No word on Guy?"

"None."

"So nothing has changed." She said it firmly but her voice had a reedy quality; her face was tight as if every muscle was strained to breaking point.

The Adj walked with her back along the High Street. A Halifax roared overhead, its undercarriage nestling into the inboard nacelles. Only one or two pedestrians bothered to look up; in Rocklington aeroplanes were as common as buses.

"Do they keep you busy at the Food Office?"

"At times," she said. "At other times it's a most awful bore."

"I still can't get used to the idea of you working there."

"Why not?"

"Well, after your career . . . "

She half smiled. "There was a woman this afternoon, a rather overpowering type. Recognized me, she said. Knew me from somewhere. Did I go to the Chapel? Had I ever lived in Huddersfield? Did I swim at the Municipal Baths? Was I a friend of Mrs Fisher's? She had *definitely* seen me somewhere but she couldn't place me."

"She would have been thrilled to know who she was talking to."

"Not necessarily. Another woman last week said I was Wendy Hiller and when I assured her I wasn't, she became quite annoyed. She knew Wendy Hiller when she saw her!"

It was a tonic to see her smile. He suggested a glass of sherry; to his delight she agreed. There was a merry fire blazing in the Saloon Bar; Sam Borthwick himself was behind the counter. With a conspiratorial wink he murmured something about his best sherry that he kept for special customers.

And very good it was. From their chairs beside the fire, the Adj and Dorothy nodded their thanks. It was really all most pleasant, positively homelike. One might be relaxing in front of one's own fire with one's own wife.... Hell's bells, there he went again, day-dreaming.

"You've been in touch with my brother," said Dorothy.

The Adj sat up. "How did you know?"

"He telephoned me. You told him where I was."

"Yes, I did actually – "

"It was presumptuous of you to contact him."

The Adj gulped. "I suppose it was but – "

"How did you find him?"

"You said your brother worked at the BBC. So I simply telephoned and said I had to speak to Dorothy Miles's brother. On official business, I told them. It usually helps."

"Clever of you, darling."

"Thank you."

"But naughty."

"I thought he should know."

"The less Gilbert knows the better. He bullies me. Always has. He means well of course, has admirable intentions but ... he's always so *right!*"

She smiled. Sweetly. Adorably. She wasn't angry with him, thank God. In a moment she was chatting about the CO and Fawcett and the other permanent staff types, remembering all their names as effortlessly as ever. It seemed to help her to talk, to ask about this person and that, to recall parties and shows. She often mentioned Guy, always talking about him as if his absence was temporary; soon, inevitably, he would be back and everything would be as before.

The Adj said, "I bought a copy of his book. The poetry."

"Splendid, isn't it?"

"Oh quite." He had waded through half a dozen verses before giving up. Couldn't grasp what Venables was getting at. If anything.

"One day Guy will autograph that book for you."

To hear her talking, you'd think Venables was spending a few days in the next village and would return on Wednesday at ten a.m. sharp. Steadfastly, expertly, she kept her gentle eyes shut to reality. Perhaps it was her theatrical training that made her so good at it. Laughing, she recalled how she had met Guy at one of those Mayfair parties: "No one seemed to know why anyone had been invited or why it had been organized in the first place. Actors and writers and producers all huddled together nursing gins, trying to impress each other, blathering on about how marvellously they were doing and what incredible things they were working on. Guy had been invited by his publisher – who didn't show up himself. Guy, poor darling, hated it; there wasn't a soul he knew; I'm sure he wished he could have been anywhere else, even over Germany in a bomber, I expect. I saw him edging towards the door. Charming, the way he was doing it; he didn't want to offend the host or hostess even though he probably hadn't the foggiest idea who he or she was. Typical of him. Anyway, a director friend of mine introduced us just as Guy reached the door. Another thirty seconds and he would have escaped. 'This chap writes good poetry,' said the director. 'You should read him; he says important things.' He was right, wasn't he?"

"Rather," said the Adj in what he hoped was a suitably enthusiastic tone.

"My brother did his best to dissuade me from marrying Guy. Too young, he said. And in too dangerous an occupation. And, worst of all, a poet. Bad types, poets, in my brother's estimation. Irritating and irrelevant, he says. I said that described the BBC perfectly!"

"I'm sure your brother has your best interests at heart."

Her eyes were gentle and lovely with amusement. "Have you noticed how no one ever talks about having your best interests at heart when he's agreeing with you?"

The Adj ached to reach out and touch her; what an infinitely desirable creature she was and what an appalling waste that she should be living in a dream world, believing that her husband would return to her when it was obvious to anyone who had the least experience of such things that he would never return. Day-dreams were all right in their place, but eventually one had to wake up.

She put her glass down. No, she wouldn't have another. She had things to do, some letters to write, some bills to pay.

"Thank you so much," she said, the simple, everyday words assuming new significance because she uttered them so superbly. "You are most kind and thoughtful."

Why was he incapable of simply accepting the gracious words and making some equally gracious response? No, all he could do was splutter a lot of inanities, sounding like a hippo in heat.

He cursed himself all the way back to camp.

A *crush*.

That was what he had, he declared. At his age. Almost indecent. But there was no denying the delicious tingles when he thought of her and the very definite pangs when he left her. Not to mention the heart-thumpings when she said "darling." Was it possible, he wondered, that she was becoming just a little bit . . . *interested*? It wasn't beyond the realm of possibility. There was, after all, little more than ten years' difference in their ages. A mere bagatelle these days. After a young chap like Venables she was probably beginning to appreciate the stability and wisdom of someone more mature. It was clear, quite deliciously clear, that she enjoyed his company. He shook his head in wonder; Dorothy *Miles* had become a *close friend*! It still took a bit of believing. Soon she might become even closer, incredible as it seemed. Sometimes the Adj had to kick himself mentally to make sure he wasn't day-dreaming.

But nothing really significant could happen until she accepted the fact that Venables was dead.

The very next day the Air Ministry reclassified Venables to "Missing – Believed Killed."

"It's a question of probability," the Adj told Dorothy. "The finding of Thwaites and Betts – and Bryce of course – made a difference, you see, an important difference."

"Not to me."

You had to admire her dogged courage. She told him about a dream in which Guy Venables was found alive having floated for days in his life-jacket to end up on a tiny spit of land with a lighthouse. The lighthouse keeper, his wife and son, fed and looked after Venables – and made him play endless games of bridge. "Guy hates bridge," she chuckled.

The Adj sighed; still she refused to face the truth.

Eventually she would have to. It was vital. God knows what long-term effects might result if she didn't. How could she ever hope to . . . well . . . to make a fresh start until she came to accept that the old life was over?

One evening over a glass of sherry, the Adj told her a lie. He hadn't intended to lie to her. It slipped out.

"They've found bits that . . . look as if they belonged to Nigel Pettigrew's kite."

She said nothing for a moment. Her eyes roamed his face. She took a breath.

"What . . . bits?"

"A section of the fuselage. The rear . . . with part of the serial number still visible, not all of it, but . . . "

"It matched Nigel's number."

The Adj nodded. "But, as I say, it was only part of the number, not the whole thing."

He hated lying to her; indeed, he experienced a slight nausea as he uttered the words. But it was necessary. He was doing it for her, to rescue her from the uncertainty that was consuming her. Poor dear woman, you could see her *diminishing* day by day. She couldn't get her life in order until she came to terms with reality – the reality that her husband was dead and would never come back to her.

But still she clung to threads of hope. Miracles did happen. As long as there was no news there was still hope. She kept saying it, and the Adj kept nodding and agreeing; it was expected.

Early in December he lied to her again. A helmet had been washed ashore, he told her. The name *Dunc* was still visible: Duncan Glossop, a member of the crew.

"But no sign of Duncan himself?"

"Not so far, but . . . "

"But what?"

The Adj shrugged. "I fear the pieces of the puzzle are coming together."

She said nothing. Sadness gave her features a special loveliness. She was as pale as ivory. The Adj had the feeling that if he reached out and touched her she would be ice-cold.

His mind was in a torment as he walked back to the field. At last she was beginning to acknowledge the truth; the weight of evidence was simply too great for her to ignore any longer. It was progress – but at what cost? What agonies of grief was she suffering? Could he have been less cruel? How? Was there a nice way of convincing a woman that her husband was dead?

He had to go to Group for a couple of days of meetings. When he returned Dorothy greeted him warmly enough. But she had been suffering; you could see it in her eyes and in the way she held herself. At first the Adj thought she had come to accept Guy's death. But he was wrong; she talked about Guy all evening. She had been reading escape books; they had filled her with a renewed confidence in his survival. Somehow he would get back to her; she didn't know how, she only knew that he would manage somehow.

The Adj trudged back to the field. All his efforts seemed to have been in vain. Perhaps her theatrical background was to blame; perhaps if one spent one's life in a world of drama and marvellous twists of fate, one started to think that real life would be as satisfactory.

The only thing that made it all worthwhile was the fact, so absolutely beautifully crystal clear, that she was fond of him. You could see it in the way her eyes lit up when she saw him, in the way she held his hand a moment longer than necessary when they said good night. She called him Simon now, as well as darling; she could have no idea how thrilled he was.

But the relationship couldn't gather momentum, so to speak, until Guy was dead, to her as he was to everyone else. The Adj couldn't help himself: he kept seeing Venables as a sort of ghostly apparition blocking the gate to paradise.

The following morning the Adj was at his desk when the Guard Room telephoned. There was a gentleman to see Squadron Leader Coombs. A civilian gentleman. A Mr Coleman.

"Never heard of him. Yes, I have. Ask him to wait. I'll be there in a jiffy."

Coleman. Dorothy's brother. He remembered getting the name from the BBC switchboard and thinking that it should be Miles not Coleman. Odd the way film people changed their names. Did she choose Miles because Coleman was already taken?

Coleman was a slim man in his forties wearing a well-tailored overcoat in the casual manner of someone accustomed to the best.

"Thank you for seeing me without an appointment, Squadron Leader. I was on my way to see my sister." A hand indicated Bert Rogers's Austin taxi waiting by the main gate. "Then I thought I should perhaps see you first to find out if anything had developed since we last communicated."

Coleman had the same penetrating gaze as his sister, but his voice contained stronger traces of their northern antecedents.

"He's still missing, I'm sorry to report. He's dead, that's the fact of it."

"Does she know that?"

"I think she knows it but I'm not sure she fully accepts it. Yet."

Coleman nodded like a doctor hearing familiar symptoms.

"It's always been difficult to shake a notion once it's taken hold of her." He shrugged, reminding the Adj of the way Dorothy had shrugged the evening before. "Pity the parents aren't still around. Useful, parents, at such times. By the way, I hear you've been most kind."

Coleman had a way of eyeing one as he spoke. Did he fancy there was more to the Adj's feelings than just sympathy for a widow?

"She's been . . . remarkably gallant through it all."

"I take it there's no hope."

The Adj shook his head. "It's been too long. They found two members of the crew, plus another chap who seems to have got on board unofficially. God only knows how. Or why. What is clear is that the rest of the crew are down on the bottom of the sea with the aircraft. The sort of thing that's happened countless times. I've tried to convince her and I do think I've made some progress. But I'm afraid she still believes there's a hope. It's quite vital in my opinion that she stop believing such things as quickly as possible."

Coleman buttoned his overcoat up to the throat.

"I tend to agree. I'll do what I can. We'll have a good long talk about things. She's a sensible girl. She'll listen to me. Always has."

"It's good of you."

"I want to do what's best for her. Incidentally, she speaks highly of you."

"Of me? Well . . . "

He watched the taxi rumbling away toward the village. Coleman sat bolt upright in the back seat. Offhand sort of cove, but he had his sister's best interests at heart and that was what mattered.

So Dorothy spoke highly of him, did she? The Adj glowed.

That evening Coleman telephoned from The White Rose.

"Thought you'd like to know that Dorothy and I had a good chat. I think she's seeing things a little more . . . realistically. You paved the way; I simply had to put the finishing touches, so to speak. Greatly appreciate what you were able to do. Frightfully important to have someone to lean on at such a time. You've been a real friend."

The Adj went back to the Mess. The aircrew types were indulging in one of their absurd games, a lunatic version of bullfighting in which chairs became bulls, their legs the bull's horns and their tablecloths the matador's cape. Then it was time to roll up various unfortunates in the Mess carpet and stage a tug-of-war with the victims still inside. All rather childish and quite dangerous; those over thirty-five years old were well advised to retire to their rooms and settle down with a copy of *Picture Post* or a good book (Edgar Wallace in the case of the Adj – no more of that unfathomable poetry by Venables). Soon after one a.m. he was roused by his batman. A message from her? No, a couple of squadrons of Lancasters were being diverted to Rocklington, their bases in Lincoln-shire being fog-bound. No sooner had the Lancs put in an appearance than one of their number undershot runway number 1 and crashed into trees bordering the runway, spreading its remains on the landing strip. The runway had to be changed. The wreckage had to be cleared; the survivors had to be cared for; the rest of the Lanc crews had to be fed and accommodated. It was after four before the Adj finally got to bed. At nine his batman woke him with the news that ops were on for that night. Then, bless Butch's heart, he wanted the squadron to participate in the next night's activi-ties too. And the next. The Adj forgot what day it was; all that mattered was staying awake to face the next crisis. He had meals not knowing or caring whether they were lunch or dinner.

Then the squadron was stood down. The Adj slept for twelve hours; his batman woke him with a cup of tea and news.

The Adj had a headache; irregular hours, not enough sleep, then too much sleep. It played havoc with a fellow's systems.

The Adj's batman, Shufflebotham, stood there with that silly little smile of his. Sometimes the Adj thought Shuffle-botham wasn't all there.

"Well?"

"News, sir, like I said."

"What news?"

"Flying Officer Pettigrew and Flying Officer Venables and Sergeants Glossop, Carter, and Morris, sir. They've found them, sir. Alive."

It took a moment to sink in. Pettigrew? *Venables!*

"*Alive!*"

"Yes sir, wizard, isn't it?"

The Adj managed a nod. He got up and dressed. The whole damned place was talking about Pettigrew and Co. The Adj had to keep nodding and smiling and saying what a good show it was. He heard the story half a dozen times. Pettigrew's aircraft had been attacked by a night-fighter and badly damaged. Off course, Pettigrew had tried to reach neutral Sweden. Over the Skagerrak between Denmark and Norway, the gunners had baled out, misinterpreting intercom signals apparently. It had to be presumed that Bryce had gone with them; a further presumption was that he had persuaded one of them to smuggle him aboard. The rest of the crew had stayed on board while Pettigrew attempted to nurse the faltering Halifax across to Sweden. But the Hally had gone down on Norwegian territory. The crew had survived the crash and had made contact with the Norwegian Underground, with whom they had remained until it was considered safe to make the journey to Sweden. As far as was known the Jerries still hadn't found the wreck of the Halifax.

"Bloody marvellous, what?" said the CO.

"Splendid news," said the Adj. He felt dead inside.

"Does Mrs V know?" enquired the CO, cheeks ruddy with delight.

"Mrs V, sir?"

"Venables, old chap, Venables."

"Well, not that I'm aware of . . ."

"Pass on the glad tidings, will you. There's a good fellow. Tell her he's in Sweden and will be home in no time."

The Adj telephoned The White Rose. Mrs Borthwick answered.

"Is that Squadron Leader Coombs speaking? Thought I recognized your voice. Lovely morning, for a change. Just a mo', I'll pop upstairs and see if Mrs Venables is in. Haven't seen her yet this morning."

The Adj sat back, a dull, rhythmic ache in his chest. Was the pain heart-break or a common-or-garden attack? He didn't care. What a fool he was to have thought for an instant that someone like Dorothy. . . . The Simon Coombses of this world never got the Dorothy Mileses; things were arranged that way. And the sooner he got used to the idea the better. Back to the old life. This would be something to remember and perhaps prattle about at a dinner party, if he was ever invited to one.

He became aware of Mrs Borthwick's voice in the distance. High-pitched, urgent, calling for Sam. Sam, Sam, where was he? What the hell did she want Sam for? God, what a silly woman she was at times. The Adj sighed as a door slammed and something clattered. The Adj was about to hang up, thinking Mrs Borthwick had forgotten him, when Sam picked up the phone.

"I'm afraid there's been . . . a sort of accident."

She left a note written in her neat hand beside the empty bottle of sleeping pills. She hadn't acted impulsively no matter what people might think. The simple truth was that she just didn't want to go on living without Guy; he meant far more to her than her own life. Therefore her own life was not worth living without him. She deeply regretted any pain her action might have caused, particularly to her brother, Gilbert, and to Squadron Leader Coombs, such a staunch ally in a terrible time. She had worked so hard to convince herself that Guy might still be alive. But in the end she had been forced to see the truth. And so there was only one thing left for her to do . . .

The Mid-Upper Gunner

ANDY SHAW SWIVELLED HIS TURRET METHODICALLY, searching the night sky sector by sector. But after hours of straining to glimpse the shimmer of a propeller, a glint of metal, the glow of exhausts, imagination started playing tricks. It had happened before. Horses and boats. Lots of them. At eighteen thousand feet above sea level. They were at the extreme right of his vision. But they vanished the instant he shifted his gaze in that direction. Perhaps one day they wouldn't vanish; they would be there, large as life, cruising along with the bombers.

That would be the day to give up this lark once and for all.

He glanced over the side of the Halifax.

For once the Met man had it right. The cloud cover was breaking up. He could see a river far below wending its way through the darkened countryside. A light winked. Did someone turn on a light without pulling the blackout curtain? Was a Jerry ARP warden giving them what-for? Off to his left tiny flickers of light erupted in the sky. Flak. Andy hated flak. His turret offered little protection. A near miss would blow the thing off the top of the fuselage like an egg off a wall.

"Target in five minutes, Skipper."

"Thanks, Navigator."

They didn't use first names, this crew. All very by-the-book, they were. Nice enough blokes, but strangers. The skipper's name was Swann. His regular mid-upper gunner was off on compassionate leave. Grandmother's funeral or wedding. Or something. Awfully decent of Andy to join the crew at short notice, Swann had said. As if Andy had had any choice in the matter.

The flak stopped over the target. Which was as good as the fighters sending a postcard saying they were on their way. It was only a matter of time.

Time up. A kite got it in the neck off to starboard. The quickest of glances in that direction. Fire gobbling up one wing, greedily. Someone tumbling out of the nose hatch. A moment later another bomber got itself blown to bits immediately to the rear. Andy winced, anticipating more casualties. But nothing happened. Ops were like that. Intense activity, then nothing. After one trip the BBC had said that thirty-four kites had got the chop, but Andy had seen no sign of trouble from take-off to landing.

The bomb-aimer seemed to take a lifetime to drop his bombs. Andy's nerves tautened one by one until he felt like one of Granny's old boots, all strung up. It was at times like these that he wished he had joined the navy. Asking for trouble, this lark.

A relief when the kite bucked; you could almost hear it sigh with relief.

"Bombs gone."

No need to tell us, mate.

Ten minutes from the target the Skipper found the cloud again. Straight down into it he went. It made for a bumpy ride but you could put up with a few bumps if it helped keep you out of Jerry's way.

It was like driving too fast in a London pea-souper, grey-ness streaming by on all sides. You tried not to think of all the other aircraft that could be doing the same thing. A couple of times the turret would peep through the cloud layer, like the periscope of a submarine piercing the surface of the sea. For a few weird moments he would be alone, the solitary occupant of a strange little vehicle whizzing along backwards at incredible speed on a road of fog with nothing but a couple of fins and rudders to keep him company. Then Swann would edge the kite down and the world would be dark again.

The cloud began to break up near the Belgian border. Down went the nose; the Hally was going flat out for the sea and home. No ditherer, Swann.

"Gunners. Keep your eyes open, chaps. We'll be over the coast in a jiffy."

The kite was fairly shuddering as the speed picked up. Don't overdo it, Andy silently cautioned Swann. Hallies had a nasty reputation for shedding bits of themselves. It was said that Butch Harris had threatened to put Frederick Handley Page up against a wall and have him shot at dawn if he didn't correct the Hally's faults. Forthwith.

They were over water when Andy saw the fighter. A single-engined job. An FW 190, by the evil look of it. Off to port, stalking its prey. Andy reported the fighter. The skipper told him to keep watching it. Andy didn't need telling. The thing at night was that you couldn't look directly at anything if you wanted to keep it in sight. You had to make yourself look to one side of it so that you saw a ghostly half-image . . .

Christ!

"He's coming in, Skipper! Corkscrew port . . . go!"

No delay from Swann. The Hally wrenched itself into a violent plunging turn, then, suddenly, brutally, into a bellowing climb.

No time to wonder about structural weakness now.

The fighter's fire streamed past Andy's turret in tiny darts of light. The rear gunner fired back. Stupid sod. Giving the Jerry a target. A form streaked across his twin guns. More bursts. More misses.

The FW turned, banking vertically.

"I think we've shaken him off," said the rear gunner.

I don't, said Andy; but he spoke to himself, leaving his intercom off.

The Skipper got the kite back straight and level and checked with the crew. Everyone all right? Any damage?

The wireless op said the evasive tactics had made the coffee flask fall on the floor and break.

Silly bugger, Andy thought, using the intercom for chit-chat . . .

A shadow cut across the darkness.

"He's coming in again!" Andy yelped. "From the starboard quarter! Prepare to corkscrew starboard . . . *now!*"

Again the world turned topsy-turvy. The velvet sky rolled over on its back. Gravity smacked you in the face. You could hear the kite groaning, complaining.

"Christ . . . look . . . "

At that moment everything disintegrated.

A cataclysmic explosion of sound. The Hally seemed to stop dead. Andy felt his head crack against the side of his turret. Metal crumpling, ripping, an engine in frenzied, un-controlled roaring; a torrent of frigid air screaming around him. Andy felt it snatch at his flying boots, like icy, im-mensely powerful fingers. They grabbed him and tossed him to one side; he saw something spinning by, something with arms and legs but no head.

He couldn't move. Couldn't think. Couldn't help himself. More frigid hands pressed him against the floor of the air-craft. Beat him in the face. Flung him against the side. He rolled, helpless. Waiting for the end, wanting it to be quick.

His parachute pack was somewhere near. But God knows where. And what did it matter now? No time left. No hope either.

The night was whirling about him. Crazily. In a moment would come the final, awful thump . . .

He heard the bang.

Knew it was the end of everything. Opened his mouth – then closed it, astonished as grey light flooded in on him and bits of wreckage went past him, spinning, tumbling, burning, a nightmarish merry-go-round.

He heard voices. God only knows whose.

Was he dead already?

No. Something cold and hard struck him across the face. A sword. Was he being sliced up like bacon?

Then came the splash. A sharp, slapping splash. It sounded far away, too far away for him to worry about.

For a strangely leisurely moment he revolved, clutching at air, wanting to cry out but not knowing what to say . . .

An instant later he was struggling for breath wrapped in hellish cold. Clutching something. Pushing something away. Trying to see, trying to breathe. It took long moments to realize that he was in the water, and he had to get out in a hurry . . .

Something was trapping him. Something unyielding. Part of the aircraft, probably. Felt like the ammo tracks to the rear turret: simple straight channels of metal, yet the bloody things were contorting themselves like snakes, starting to wrap themselves around him and trap him for ever down here in the freezing blackness . . .

But suddenly it didn't matter. And it wasn't cold. The world had become pinkish and the ammunition tracks were pretty pink ribbons that danced about him, playfully stroking his face and darting away when he tried to reach out . . .

But now something was disturbing it. Bloody intrusive fingers. Clutching. Pulling. Hurting. He tried to pull himself away from them. In vain. They kept grabbing at him, insistent . . .

His chest burned. It was red hot. Glowing, searing.

"*So.*"

God . . . please . . .

Suddenly, mercifully, delicious air flooded into his lungs. Then a quantity of sea water. Stinging, choking, coughing . . .

Those hands again.

He tried to grasp one of the hands but his own hand didn't function. It simply didn't obey his commands.

Neither did the other.

Christ, what's the matter with you? he asked them as if addressing two old friends who were suddenly exhibiting unfriendly characteristics.

Hands grabbed him by the collar of his flying jacket. He was being pulled, torn to bits.

A grunt, a gasp, and he found himself lying on something. Something wet. Something flexible.

"Hold on."

Can't, he wanted to reply but couldn't. More air flooded into his lungs. It hurt. Hurt like hell. He was a carcass on display in the butcher's. Paroxysms of coughing. Gasping. Spitting. Sucking in air, great dollops of it.

"Something is wrong with your arms?"

Funny, the voice seemed to come from a distance. He half turned and felt himself sliding. An arm clutched him and pulled him back onto . . . onto what? A dinghy, that's what it was. But a dinghy no bigger than something you'd frolic about on at the Municipal Swimming Baths.

Now Andy managed to turn his head without going over the side. In the darkness he could just make out a broad-faced young man in flying gear. Bit of luck, being picked up by one of the crew.

"Ta . . . very much," Andy managed, his voice croaky and uncertain.

"You are welcome."

Odd accent, the bloke had.

Dazed, Andy tried to recall a Dutchman or a Pole in the crew. Without success. He coughed, spitting out more salty water.

Then it struck him.

Crikey!

Again he almost fell off the raft; he put out his left hand to catch his balance and it went into the sea up to the elbow.

The other man grabbed him quickly.

"You . . . you . . . "

"What is it?"

"The Jerry . . . the bloke who shot us down."

"I did not shoot you down. I hit you. I apologize. An error of judgement. We are both lucky to be alive, I think."

It sounded like "sink."

"Was it you . . . pulled me out?"

"Yes . . . it was I."

Andy gulped. "Ta."

"Ta?"

"Thanks. Very much."

Felt wrong, saying ta to a Jerry.

"I think you have an expression in English, 'Both in the same boat.' Amusing, no?"

"A riot," said Andy. He tried to manoeuvre himself into a more comfortable position. But the dinghy wobbled, threatening to overturn.

"Your arms are hurt?"

"I think they're broken. They don't work. Don't do a thing."

"Let me see."

Whereupon Andy was sick, horribly, violently sick.

"Sorry about that. Bloody salt water."

"Of course."

Andy was sick again. It hurt. It felt as if all his innards were being ripped out one by one. When the spasms were over he could only lie gasping, dimly aware of the German's arms about his shoulders and waist. Without those arms he would have slipped over the side.

"I think that's the lot," Andy gasped.

"I am glad."

A moment later Andy was sick again.

"Spoke too soon. Did it over the side though. Didn't muck up your dinghy."

"Most thoughtful of you. I think your arms are indeed broken. They are hurting?"

"Christ, I'll say."

"We need a . . . what you call . . . something to hold them . . . like cloth."

"A sling."

"That is the word, is it? Sling. But does that not also mean to throw?"

Andy nodded and gazed bleakly into the windy darkness. Water kept splashing in his face. Was this really happening? Was he really sitting in a dinghy with a Jerry pilot? Discussing the finer bloody points of the English language? Wasn't it treason or something? Consorting with the enemy? No doubt there was a King's Reg about it.

"You speak good English."

"Thank you. I liked languages at school."

"They didn't teach languages at my school," said Andy, wondering why he bothered to tell the Jerry such a thing. He felt as if he had gone ten rounds with Joe Louis. Everything ached. His arms were like two leaden weights attached to his shoulders.

The Jerry took off his scarf and improvised a sling for Andy's left arm. Then Andy's sodden scarf became the sling for his right arm. The pain eased.

"Perhaps if we get you in the centre you will be a little more secure." The Jerry tugged on Andy's collar, dragging him along like a sack of spuds. Andy was more or less sitting in the Jerry's lap like a babe in arms . . . a babe who'd wet himself from head to toe.

"You sure this thing'll float with both of us on it?"

"No," said the Jerry. "But we shall see."

"It's a tiny bugger."

"It is intended for one occupant only."

The Jerry's head was higher than Andy's; he could feel the movement of the man's jaw when he spoke. A bloke felt at a disadvantage in such a position, yet what could he do to improve it? Throw the Jerry overboard? Take command? Sail in triumph to Dover? Fat chance.

"You were flying an FW 190."

"Correct."

"Thought so. Caught a glimpse of you."

Funny, up till now the Jerry fighters had always been *things*; you seldom thought of them as having human beings inside.

"And your aircraft was a Halifax?"

"Right. Was."

"You were the pilot?"

"Mid-upper gunner." With a shock he thought of the others. "Did you see anyone else?"

"No one. It was lucky I saw you. You bumped into the dinghy. At first I thought you were dead."

"Me too."

His nose itched; he had to twist his neck to rub it against his wet collar. Bloody miracle if any more of the crew got out alive. Besides, how many more could they squeeze on the dinghy?

"Did you bale out?"

For some reason it seemed important to keep talking. As long as you were still talking you were alive.

The Jerry said his aircraft had crash-landed in the water after the collision.

"Any idea where we are?"

"I estimate perhaps thirty kilometres from the coast."

"Your coast."

"As you say."

All right then, if they did get rescued it would be by the Jerries. So what? Bloody sight better chance of living to a ripe old age in a POW camp than going back on ops.

"You have been flying on bombers for much time?"

Nosey sod, the Jerry.

"This was my nineteenth op."

"Op?"

"Operation. Operational sortie."

"So."

"Did most of my trips with another crew. Had a Canadian for the skipper. Nice bloke. But he got an arm knocked off. So they broke up the crew, what was left of them. I've been a spare bod for a while. Now this crew – this was my first op with them. Hell of a bloody fresh start. The skipper's name was Swann. I didn't know any of the others."

The dinghy tilted. Andy squeaked, scared. The Jerry's arm tightened about him. Andy found himself trying to explain it to his father – how he went boating on the North Sea squatting in a Jerry's lap. Poor old Dad would have heart failure just thinking about it.

"The sea seems to be rougher."

Andy nodded. His stomach was in knots. Another couple of minutes and he would be sick again, he could feel his innards preparing themselves for the next upheaval.

The Jerry said, "I think it is the time we introduce ourselves. I am Ernst Müller. I am from Köln."

"I'm Andy Shaw. From Bristol. I'm a sergeant. Are you an officer?"

"A *Leutnant*."

"Thought so," said Andy.

And vomited again.

The retches almost dislodged him from the absurdly tiny dinghy. The Jerry had to cling to him, patting him comfortingly. Andy expected him to murmur, "There, there," like Mum used to do.

"Feeling a little better?"

"On top of the world," said Andy bitterly, teeth chattering. His arms throbbed as if they were on fire despite the fact they were freezing.

The Jerry was right; the sea was getting rougher. The dinghy was going up and down monstrous hills of water, tilting alarmingly as it was carried up one side, lurching, tottering, then plunging down the other.

"Jack and Jill," Andy muttered. He wished he hadn't. The Jerry wanted it all explained.

You couldn't maintain any sort of balance without your arms. You just had to hope the Jerry wouldn't get tired of holding on to you. God knows how long you would last if you slipped over the side.

Cold ached into every bone. He kept remembering the warm, clammy evening before take-off, how they had sweated in their flying togs. He would never complain about the heat again. Never.

"Any idea how long till daylight?"

"Two hours perhaps. You are married?"

"Married? No. Why?"

"When I was a small boy my father taught me that if I should ever find myself in a dinghy with a stranger I would be well advised to find out something about him."

Odd bird, the Jerry, you never knew when to take him seriously.

"You married?" Andy enquired, since the Jerry had asked him.

"On Saturday I will marry."

"*This* Saturday?"

"Indeed. Civil ceremony on Saturday. Church ceremony on Sunday."

"You got to go through it *twice*? Blimey."

"You do not?"

"No. Registry office or church. Not both, not so far as I know. Why d'you do it like that?"

"Two ceremonies make the marriage last twice as long."

If you weren't careful you'd think he was serious. Andy grimaced. Just his luck to be stuck on a dinghy with a German Bob Hope.

"Congrats," said Andy. "Er, congratulations."

"Thank you."

"What's your intended's name?"

"Maria."

"That's nice."

"You like the name?"

"I do. Definitely. One of my favourite names."

That seemed to please the Jerry. He said Maria was petite, only twenty-three centimetres tall, which made her sound like a specimen in a laboratory. She was a nurse, the Jerry said.

"Always fancied nurses," Andy said. "Something about that white uniform."

"You find it provocative?"

"Provocative. Yes, that's the word."

"Me also," the Jerry said with a chuckle. "I will tell Maria that we sat in the middle of the sea and discussed her uniform! And she will shake her head and say what silly creatures men are! And she will be right of course. But we are what we are, no?"

"Can't argue with you there."

Salty water splashed into Andy's open mouth. He spat it out. He had a touchy tooth on the starboard side. It had been jabbing him whenever he drank anything hot or cold; for a week he had been putting off going to the dental officer. Now the tooth didn't hurt a bit. Everything else hurt too much.

How would the Jerries treat him? There were stories about bomber crews getting beaten up – even lynched – when they baled out. More than one poor sod was said to have ended up hanging from a lamppost.

"You have brothers and sisters?"

Andy shook his head.

"I have a younger brother," said the Jerry. "His name is Martin. He is waiting until he is old enough for the *Luftwaffe*. I tell him to be patient. His time will come soon enough."

The dinghy almost toppled. Andy felt himself going; only the Jerry's firm grip saved him. Andy heard himself whimper with fright. And pain. It swept through him like a living thing, a gnawing, writhing thing. A relentless, tireless thing.

The dinghy's bottom slapped the sea as if chastising it.

"How are you, Sergeant Shaw?"

"Having a marvellous time. Wish you were here."

Pause. "But I am here."

Andy sighed. "See, if you go away to the seaside you send postcards to your friends and say, 'Having lovely time. Wish you were here.' Sort of a tradition, you might say."

"Of course," said the Jerry.

An exhausting, terrifying business, trying to anticipate the waves when you couldn't see them coming in the darkness. You could hear their angry rumblings as they gathered strength for another try at swamping you. You had to tense yourself for the impact, but when it came it still caught you by surprise, almost tipping you over as you tried to stop yourself from blubbering, silently begging the Jerry to hold on tight, then half wishing he'd let you go so you could get it over and done with.

How Mum used to go on about changing into dry clothes if you got caught in a shower; delay meant being crippled by rheumatism, probably before the day was out.

"It will be light soon," said the Jerry.

"If we last that long."

"We will last . . . "

"Sure?"

"Two men who survive a mid-air collision could not possibly be defeated by a dinghy."

He sounded so bloody sure of himself. Had all the answers. Typical officer. They were the same all over.

Numbly he kept thinking about surprising the Jerry, pushing him overboard, taking command.

Some hope. In his condition he couldn't take command of a wet flannel.

The dinghy lurched. Helpless, terrified, Andy slid to one side. His right leg went into the sea. In a trice he was half off the dinghy, unable to stop himself going overboard. The Jerry was quick, you had to hand it to him. And strong. He had to be; it must have been as awkward as bloody hell dragging a grown man back onto that little bit of puffed-up canvas; it had about as much stability as a pregnant jellyfish. But he managed it. He was puffing afterwards.

"Thanks . . . again."

"A pleasure, Sergeant Shaw."

"I'm lucky I ran into you."

"No, I ran into you." Another guffaw. He was his own best audience, this one.

The peculiar thing, Andy thought, was that he knew this Jerry better than he knew any of the Hally crew. Apart from Swann the only one he remembered was the bloke with the carroty hair, the flight engineer. God knows what his name was, but Andy remembered the way his pink brow had been beaded with sweat just before they boarded the aircraft; he looked as if he'd been left out in the rain.

Andy tried to think of his parents. But they didn't seem real. Shadowy beings, they inhabited another world, an almost forgotten world. Andy couldn't feel sorry for his parents who would soon receive the dreaded telegram. At this moment he didn't care about them. All he cared about was the throbbing burning within him.

Why did he survive the crash? Why couldn't he have bought it then? What purpose was served by making him go through this? Did it amuse some bloody-minded angel up there?

"Are you well?"

"Never better."

Andy tested the surface of the dinghy with his knee. Was it his imagination or was the dinghy losing air?

How long had they got?

The cold added a vicious edge to the pain. Someone had told him that just before you died from exposure you felt hot. You tore off your clothes. You had to get cool even though you were freezing to death . . .

"Try to sit in the exact middle," said the Jerry, shifting Andy bodily an inch or two. "It's important, I think, not to upset our balance."

The Jerry's hands were bare. And white with cold.

The wind moaned about them, sending little drops of spray into their faces, stinging like hail.

The dinghy dipped. Andy gasped out a gurgle of sheer funk, feeling himself going.

The Jerry held him.

"It's all right. I have you."

The Jerry's voice was strong and calm, as if he was used to this sort of situation and was ready for any emergency. He said it was far worse for Andy because of his broken arms; he understood.

Andy closed his eyes. God, he wished he was dead, wished he'd been dragged down with the kite, wished the bloody understanding Jerry had left things well enough alone and let a bloke die when his time was up . . .

A sudden lurch and he was over the side. The frigid water embraced him, blinded him, paralysed him. The dinghy had collapsed. It was all over. No. His head was against the dinghy. The *bottom* of it. Panic streaked through him, galvanizing him into a frenzy of struggling, his useless arms flopping, dead weights that would drag him down to eternity when his Mae West became waterlogged as it would in the end, inevitably . . .

He surfaced. Fresh, sweet air flooded into his lungs.

"Here. I help."

Christ, a beautiful voice. Andy had never been so glad to hear anyone.

The Jerry's fingers clutched at him, digging, scratching like some mechanical device gone mad.

Andy tried to say something. And swallowed Christ only knows how much of the North Sea. The fingers closed on his collar.

"Come, my friend. You are safe."

"Like bloody hell," he spluttered as more water sloshed into his mouth.

Now the Jerry tried to haul him bodily into the dinghy.

Helpless, Andy watched. When the Jerry managed to get a good grip the dinghy would dart away like a playful pet.

But the Jerry wouldn't give up. He produced a length of cord and passed it beneath Andy's arms. Then he tried to attach it to Andy's feet.

All he succeeded in doing was upsetting the dinghy. Arms flailing, the Jerry tumbled into the water. When he re-emerged he was smiling.

"Now we are no longer in the same boat," he said.

Tommy Handley should have you on bloody ITMA, Andy thought.

"You should not worry."

"Christ, no."

"Here, I have a good hold. I will not let go."

The waves kept washing right over Andy's head. Horrible bloody waves, they splashed into his eyes and mouth and nose. The Jerry was muttering something about the line. And guiding his hand.

"I attach this to you while I get back on board . . . "

A nightmare. Of angry sea and utter confusion. He was so bloody tired. Utterly shagged. Never in the history of the human race had anyone ever been so bloody . . . *whacked*.

But the Jerry was pulling him again, tugging at his shoulders.

"Come on . . . you can do it . . . "

"No . . . " Andy gasped.

But he had done it. He was half on the dinghy again, one leg trailing in the water. The Jerry pulled him again and turned him over. A strong bloke, the Jerry.

"Safe again," said the Jerry. His arms encircled Andy.

"Ta . . . thanks."

"My pleasure."

"Now you're as wet as I am. Bleedin' water babies, that's us."

The Jerry laughed. Uproariously. Hooting as if Andy had told the funniest story ever.

Just as bleedin' scared as I am, Andy thought. Poor sod.

The dinghy was like a ride at the Hampstead Heath Fair. Up one side of the swell, almost capsizing on the crest, then tumbling, sliding down the other side. A wave hit him fair and square in the face.

"All right?"

"Never better," Andy managed to reply. He realized that his teeth had stopped chattering. He wondered why. Perhaps rigor mortis was setting in already.

"Good fellow."

The Jerry still held him, protectively, as he might have held a child.

With his knee Andy tested the resilience of the dinghy. It was softer, definitely. How long before it was just a hunk of canvas floating in the water?

"In a few minutes it won't be dark any more."

"And in a few minutes we won't be afloat any more."

"The dinghy will be all right. If not we send it back and ask for another. Good?"

Funny, the Jerry managed to reassure him for a moment, because he wanted to believe so much. Then the Jerry said:

"And we have our life-jackets. So we shall be all right even if the dinghy goes down. I will not let you go, I promise." The Jerry pointed. "There."

Yes, a faint glow on the horizon, like the first glimpse of the target on a clear night. Daylight! A glimmer of hope in the distance.

"I think we have drifted west. Soon we shall see the sky-scrapers of New York." The Jerry chuckled. A laugh a minute with him.

A pretty good bloke, though, you had to admit – even if he

was a Jerry. Made you wonder if you would have worked so hard and risked your own life if the roles had been reversed. Who could have blamed the Jerry if he had left Andy in the water? The dinghy was designed for one man, not two.

"The wind is weakening, I am sure."

"Yeah?" Another wave sloshed over Andy; frigid water dribbled down his neck.

The glow of daylight grew. Pale droplets of light danced across the restless sea like tiny glowing jewels.

But the light revealed the enormity of the sea. It stretched away in every direction, grey and restless and utterly disinterested in the fate of the pathetic little creatures bobbing on its surface.

The wind seemed to ease. The waves were still big but they were gentler than before. The dinghy rode them without those heart-stopping lurchings and pitchings.

The Jerry loosened his grip, rubbing his hands together. Andy turned. It was light enough now to make out the man's features. A wide humorous mouth, broad cheeks, deep-set eyes beneath unusually thick eyebrows. His dark hair was pushed straight back from his brow.

"Good morning."

"Morning," said Andy. "And . . . thanks."

The Jerry shrugged.

"Well," said Andy, "I mean, you didn't have to . . . what with you being who you are and me . . . well . . . "

The Jerry smiled. "For the moment we are just two men on a tiny boat in a large sea."

"Christ!"

"What is it?"

"Just remembered." Andy indicated a pocket in his flying suit. "It's in there. Can you reach?"

"I will try." A moment later the Jerry produced it with a triumphant flourish – a bar of milk chocolate, sodden and bent but still edible.

"A feast!" chuckled the Jerry.

"Should be all right. Have some."

"Thank you."

The Jerry broke the bar in half, carefully collecting the fragments in the wrapper. He fed a couple of squares to Andy.

"'Cadbury's.'" The Jerry read the label in the interested way of an archeologist studying hieroglyphics in King Tut's tomb.

"What do you call chocolate?"

"*Schokolade*."

"How d'you like this stuff?"

"Excellent. I shall write and tell Herr Cadbury how tasty his chocolate is when eaten in a dinghy in the North Sea." The Jerry chuckled to himself, enjoying his own jokes again.

"You a regular?" Andy enquired.

"Regular?"

"A regular is a bloke who's in the military all his life. A career man."

"Ah, so." A brisk shake of the head. "No, I intend to be a lawyer. And you?"

"Never thought about it," Andy replied. "Went straight into the air force from school. Haven't had to think about afterwards."

"But you should, my friend, you should."

Nosey sod. "What's the point? How many of us are going to be alive and kicking when this lot is over?"

"I do not know."

"Well then."

"Not a satisfactory answer, Sergeant Shaw, not satisfactory at all."

Andy managed to turn to look at the Jerry.

"You're a funny bugger, y'know that?"

"Bugger?"

"Never mind. The way you go on, anyone would think we're a couple of old cronies. But we're not old cronies, are we?"

"It depends," said the Jerry.

"On what?"

"On what *cronies* means."

Andy laughed. Couldn't help it. Even with the pain throbbing within him like a pneumatic drill.

"You are all right?" enquired the Jerry, sounding concerned. Did he think Andy was going to have a fit?

"I'm all right." Andy looked down. "But this isn't."

The dinghy was settling in the water, its plump surface now wrinkled and sagging.

"We're going to get our feet wet again."

The Jerry shrugged. Then he cocked his head to one side. "*Ein Flugzeug* . . . an aircraft."

"What? Yes."

"There."

It appeared from the port side. A wondrous sight. A sight to make you forget the pain and the cold for a moment.

A high-winged job with fixed undercarriage.

"A Lysander," said Andy. "One of our air-sea rescue boys."

As if hearing the remark the Lysander dipped a wing and did a circuit around the dinghy. The pilot could be seen, in blue battledress with a brown leather helmet. He waved.

"He's seen us. Thank Christ. Won't be long now, shouldn't think."

The Jerry shrugged. "It would seem that your people will get to us first. The fortunes of war."

"I'll tell them what you did for me. They'll treat you all right," he told the Jerry, "I'll see to that."

The German nodded, a sad little smile on his lips as he watched the Lysander flying past once more. Another wave from the pilot before he turned away.

Now that rescue seemed close at hand there was nothing to say. The two men sat in silence gazing out on the restless waters. The sun was bright, but it did little to warm them through the chilly wind.

Another aircraft flew by, high, a mere dot in the blue. It sped away in the same direction as the Lysander.

A few minutes later they heard the throbbing sound of a boat. Then it appeared, long and sleek, carving a foamy path through the water. A lovely sight. Except for one thing. Andy frowned. The boat's flag bore a great big bloody black and white cross with something in the middle that looked suspiciously like a swastika.

"Oh Christ," said Andy.

"So," muttered the Jerry, sitting upright.

"Looks like your lot got here first."

"It does appear so."

A bloke could burst into tears, he really could. A few minutes ago it had seemed so certain that the air-sea rescue boys would be picking them up in no time at all . . . Now this. Just his flaming luck. Typical.

What now? What could he do? What would Biggles have done? Out-manoeuvred the Jerry boat single-handedly? Taken command? With two broken arms?

A couple of Jerry sailors stood on the deck, machine guns at the ready. A third was busy with a coil of rope. An officer studied the dinghy through binoculars.

Andy said, "I always wanted to have a ride on one of them."

The Jerry smiled. "Here is your opportunity."

Which was when they heard the first shot. It came from behind them. Then a second, a third, then a burst of rapid fire.

Andy turned, mouth dropping open. A British destroyer – no, not as big as a destroyer – a corvette perhaps. Whatever it was, it packed plenty of fire-power. The air seemed to shudder from the boom-boom-boom of cannon and the rattle of machine guns. Caught by surprise, the E-Boat took a moment to respond. Then both boats blazed away; bullets snapped past like angry insects.

There was nowhere to hide, nowhere even to huddle down.

"Silly bastards," Andy yelped when something came particularly close. "We're *here* . . . "

He kept shaking his head; he couldn't stop himself. Typical navy. Go out to rescue a bloke and then blow him to bits in the bleedin' process . . .

The vessels kept circling, firing. It was as if they were using the tiny dinghy as a reference point, the dead centre of their manoeuvring radius.

Andy cursed sailors for their stupidity. They were all the same. Shoot first and wonder about the identity of the target afterwards.

He turned to the Jerry. Was it the same with his navy?

He didn't ask the question. He stared, aghast.

The Jerry's head lolled to one side, loosely, like the head of a broken doll. Blood oozed from his throat; it had formed a great dark patch on the front of his flying jacket.

But he was alive; his mouth moved; he breathed in little gasps.

Andy yelled at the British ship.

"You stupid sods . . . " And at the E-Boat. "For Christ's sake, can't you see what you've done . . . " To the Jerry he kept saying that everything was going to be all right; a scratch, nothing more.

Dimly he was aware that the smaller vessel, the German E-Boat, was retreating, trailing smoke.

The firing had ceased.

Andy kept telling the Jerry that he would be all right. Repeated it endlessly. Right as rain. Right as could be. Right, right, right . . . The dinghy was half submerged now, limp and floundering.

Andy pressed his shoulder against the Jerry's wound and held it firmly. "Got to stop the bleeding."

The Jerry managed a thin smile of appreciation.

"The navy'll be here in a jiffy. A jiffy's a minute. Or a moment. Whatever you like."

But now the dinghy was almost completely under water.

"You hold on to my harness. Tight. There. That's it. Keep hanging on."

Like an animal's cast-off skin, the dinghy folded and floated away.

The water splashed up to their necks; only their life-jackets kept them above the surface. The Jerry's face was white, but still he clung to Andy, his grip tenacious.

"Hang on, mate. Hang on. Keep on hanging on."

Where was the bloody navy? Late as usual . . .

The sea heaved about them, creating hills and valleys that

suddenly seemed immense. All too easy to lose a couple of blokes in there . . .

A sound. Jesus! The bloody navy was going off after the E-Boat! The buggers cared more about it than *them*!

But he kept reassuring the Jerry.

"It's all right, mate. Just keep hanging on. They'll be back. I promise. Soon have you looked after . . . "

Bastards. Blue bastards.

"Where are you? Ahoy!"

Funny, metallic voice.

Andy managed to twist his head. Another lovely sight. A lifeboat with half a dozen matelots and an officer with a revolver strapped at his waist, Wild Bill Hickok-style.

In a moment they were alongside, peering down at the airmen as if they'd discovered an interesting new form of marine life.

A sailor reached out his hand for Andy to grasp.

"Can't," said Andy. "Arms busted."

"All right. Stand by."

Stand bloody by.

Typical.

It took a week. A week of searing pain. Of panic. Of lapses into feverish unconsciousness.

But at last they were in the boat, flopping, like freshly caught fish. Someone wrapped a thick blanket about him.

"Look after the other bloke first," Andy gasped. "He's wounded."

"You're a bit banged up yourself," said the officer. "But we'll soon have you fixed up."

"Look after him."

"Will do, old chap."

Andy watched as the officer moved to where the Jerry lay, pale and oddly shrunken.

"Shot down, were you?" said a sailor, standing, legs spread wide, swaying with the movements of the boat.

"No, we always come home like this," grunted Andy, still keeping his eyes on the Jerry. He saw the officer's eyebrows arch in almost comic surprise when he saw the uniform beneath the Jerry's sodden flying suit.

"Is he going to be all right?"

The officer shook his head.

"You sure?"

"This man's dead."

"He can't be."

"But he is."

"He was going to be married on Saturday."

The officer sighed and adjusted his cap. "Why all the fuss? He was only a Jerry."

The Leading Aircraftman

THE TELEPHONE'S SHRILLING STARTLED MRS SWANN. HER heart thumped, drumlike. For an hour or more she had been sitting at the kitchen table, head down on her arms, neither fully asleep nor properly awake. She got to her feet, trying to shake herself alert. She had to think: Was it morning or afternoon?

"Is that Speedwell 3442?" A man's voice, confident, well-educated. "I appear to have a message to ring you."

"Appear to have?" Mrs Swann kneaded her forehead, harshly, as if to force some sense into it. "I'm not sure I understand . . . "

"Nor me," the man replied cheerfully. "The note says, 'Ring Speedwell 3442.' Do I have the correct number?"

"Yes."

"So far so good, what? By the way, my name's Weston. Edmund Weston. The rest of the note says, 'Tell them about the match with Arnold.'"

"Arnold?"

"That's what it says. But don't ask me why. I'm afraid I haven't the foggiest."

"A match? What sort of match, Mr Weston?"

"Couldn't say. Haven't a clue. Except for a couple of numbers; four actually: 6–1, 6–0. At first I thought it was another telephone number . . . "

"*Richard* Arnold?"

"Could be. Just says Arnold here."

Mrs Swann clasped her hand to her mouth. The maddest ideas came flooding into her brain. But she had to be calm, *had* to –

"Can you describe the handwriting?"

"Describe it? Rather a pleasant, flowing hand, I'd say. Letters well rounded. Ah, here's something a trifle unusual: The top of every 'd' and 'b' has got a little tail out to port . . . sorry, to the left."

Mrs Swann bit her lip. What did it all mean? What was happening?

The man Weston said, "Are you still there?"

"Yes, I'm sorry. Would it be possible . . . for you to post the note to me?"

"Yes, of course. May I ask why?"

"I'm not sure. But . . . the handwriting you describe is very much like that of our son Patrick. He had an important tennis match a few years ago, against a young man named Arnold. He won it six-one, six-love."

"How very curious. But one wonders why on earth would your son write a note on my pad? And how? Perhaps you would be good enough to ask him."

"That will not be possible, Mr Weston. Our son was killed last month . . . with the RAF."

She heard him catch his breath.

"Killed? God, how awful – I'm most terribly sorry. Please accept my sincere condolences – "

"Are you sure you didn't know our son, Mr Weston? Patrick Swann?"

"Patrick Swann? I don't think so. No, I can't remember anyone of that name. But . . . I wonder . . . "

"You wonder what, Mr Weston?"

"Mm?" He sounded distracted, as if he was thinking of something else. "Nothing, Mrs Swann, nothing at all. Look,

I'll pop the note in the post . . . if you'll be good enough to give me your address . . . and . . . "

"Yes?"

"I'll include my card . . . if you feel I might be of some further service please don't hesitate to ring . . . "

Leading Aircraftman Slattery swallowed the last of his morning tea. Horrible, metallic-tasting muck. As usual. He got to his feet. It was always a relief to get out of the Airmen's Mess, away from those dreadful tables, great slabs of bare wood, with their disgusting pong of boiled cabbage and body odour that seemed to be embedded deep in the grain. And away from those ribald wretches who were forever poking fun, cruel fun. One had hoped to meet a reasonably nice type in the air force; but one had been bitterly disappointed. Thank the Lord there was but a few hours of this *purgatory* to survive before ten blessed days of leave, ten *precious* days. Slattery washed his "irons" – his knife, fork, and spoon – in the hot-water tank at the door and made his way outside. It was chilly, the air heavy with drizzle.

"Wotcher, Prim, m'dear."

That nasty corporal, Minden, with his leering mouth and his pimply skin.

"Good morning," said Slattery with as much dignity as he could muster. Minden had called him Primrose that first day at Rocklington; the wretched name had stuck. The only response was no response. Slattery had learnt that lesson at school years before, from a boy named Schneider, a Swiss or Austrian or something of the sort. Saucy little blighter, but an expert at being different yet managing to survive.

No sooner had Slattery sat down at his desk in the Orderly Room than Fawcett called him into his office. Another morning: The Mornings-After-The-Ops-Before, Slattery called them. The squadron had lost two aircraft during the night: R-Robert, skippered by Sergeant Kincaid, and L-London, skippered by Pilot Officer Dickenson.

"Start on the paperwork, will you."

"Right away, sir."

The Admin Officer always seemed to take the losses personally, as if he were somehow to blame. "Bad business. Dickenson was on his last trip but one. I thought he'd get through."

"So did I, sir."

"Isn't it today you go on leave?"

"Yes sir." Something in Slattery's forehead started pounding. He would *scream*, he really would, if Fawcett delayed his leave. "I was thinking of catching the 5:12, sir."

To Slattery's relief, Fawcett nodded absently, his mind apparently still on the missing crews.

Slattery wanted to withdraw discreetly, without drawing attention to himself. He pushed himself half onto his toes. But that action only succeeded in drawing the most hideous squeals and squeaks from those ghastly boots he had to wear. Fawcett raised an eyebrow, glanced at Slattery, then, thank *heavens*, returned to his papers.

A distasteful business, poring over the men's records, akin to going through the contents of a corpse's pockets – although there was no proof that the airmen were dead. So far they were simply missing. But in about three cases out of four, "missing" meant "dead." You could place a bet on it. Name. Rank. Serial number. Age. Home address. Next of kin. Civilian occupation. Dickenson was a New Zealander, therefore of no immediate interest. But the crew's navigator came from Bromley, Kent. A possibility, very definitely a possibility. Slattery already had a few jottings on him. Studying law before joining up. Positive indications there. Pretty standard handwriting; no trouble at all. Address, telephone number. Father, retired solicitor. Slattery made hurried notes, his hand trembling. It simply didn't bear thinking about, what they would do to him if they found out.

The train plodded into Town more than two hours late. Slattery had spent the entire trip in the jam-packed corridor, squatting on his suitcase, anxiety gnawing at his vitals like half a dozen hungry rats. Would Edmund wait all these interminable hours? One could hardly blame him if he didn't, could one? What to do if he wasn't there? GodGodGod, could nothing in life go smoothly, as planned, as advertised?

But he needn't have fretted. Edmund was there, as immaculate as if he had stepped out of a De Reske cigarette poster, a broad smile of welcome on his lean, patrician features. Slattery was limp with relief. How marvellous of Edmund to wait so long! Edmund shrugged; it was nothing, the least one could do for a gallant fighting man returning to civilization from the wilds of East Yorkshire. He found a taxi – easily, as always – and in no time they were at the flat near Marble Arch. Bliss, pure bliss. Was it possible for anyone to experience more profound contentment? Were there any pleasures still to be experienced? Slattery pondered these questions as he fell asleep. What an utterly fascinating individual Edmund was, so complex yet so thrillingly elemental . . .

It was close to noon when Slattery awoke to the exquisitely appetising aroma of kippers in the frying pan and to the sound of Edmund chanting "Roll Me Over." He claimed to know eighty-one verses of the song. Slattery wriggled his toes, revelling in the sheer delight of being.

Edmund brought breakfast on a tray.

"You're spoiling me," said Slattery.

"Of course. It is *de rigueur* when one has a guest of honour in one's humble residence."

Slattery grinned. "I wish I could stay for ever."

"So do I, dear boy."

Edmund had a way of gazing directly into one's eyes when he said such things; there could never be the slightest doubt that he meant every word he uttered.

"But I have to put in an appearance at Ilford."

"I understand." Edmund sighed. "Mater and Pater."

"Three days."

"Then you'll be back here until the end of your leave."

"I can't bear to think of it ending."

"Neither can I, dear boy. So let's not. Let's discuss vital matters such as this evening."

Edmund had tickets for *Sweet and Low* at the Ambassador. After the show they would go to a party given by Frederick

Somebody-or-other for an up and coming artist who was about to make "a very big mark for himself, another Picasso, perhaps. Truly *significant*. And an utterly fascinating individual. You'll adore him, I promise." The following day there was to be an expedition, an attempt to corner a few items of wearable clothing. "Sixteen bloody coupons for an overcoat, eight for a shirt that looks as if it was styled at Dartmoor. Shoddy *utility* muck, the sort of rubbish that would never be given wardrobe space in the old days. Yet those rogues in the shops act as if they are doing you a favour letting you have the beastly stuff. It's a grim battle, keeping up any sort of appearance. By the way, have you come across any promising candidates recently?"

Edmund always made it sound as if it was like spotting likely horses in the racing papers. It never seemed to occur to him that there could be risks in unearthing personal data on dead aircrew.

"Twelve more," said Slattery.

"Twelve! Heavens, we shall be busy."

"Three officers, the rest NCOs."

"Strategic locations?"

"Bexley Heath is the furthest."

"Splendid, dear boy." He ran a hand over his smooth dark hair. "You've done most awfully well."

Slattery smiled, warmed by the compliment. "I did my best."

"Quite bowled the Swanns over, I can tell you. Couldn't wait for me to drop over to see them. Lovely house. Finchley Road. By the by, how did you dig up the gen on young Swann's tennis ambitions and that match with what's-his-name?"

"I overheard the Adj talking to him a couple of weeks before he got the chop – was killed. I made a note of it in case . . . and it happened. It does, to two out of three of the aircrew, you know."

"Well done." Edmund beamed. At times he looked like a mischievous boy with a secret. "Unlike most eavesdroppers, you get the facts straight. You're clever, dear boy. So am I. A good combination, wouldn't you say?"

Slattery wished he was an artist, capable of capturing those magic moments when the affection fairly brimmed in Edmund's eyes.

Edmund said, "Can you find out anything more about young Swann? I fancy there is considerable potential there. The father is on the board of some shipping company. The mother is well connected. Banking. I think another item or two would work wonders."

"But his records have gone to Group."

"You're such an ingenious fellow. Surely you can make a few discreet enquiries among his friends."

Slattery wished Edmund understood what a vast social chasm existed between an LAC and commissioned aircrew types. It was laughable, his idea of sidling up to pilot officers and flight lieutenants and striking up casual conversations about long-dead comrades.

"They wouldn't talk to me. Why should they? I'm not one of them, I'm just a lowly LAC to them, an erk, a nobody. Besides, they would start talking. Why is he so interested? What's he after? You do understand, don't you? I have to rely on the official records and on the notes I've already made. There's a chap called Tuttle. Quite well connected. I think he'll get the chop. I'll be able to give you heaps of gen on him when it happens."

Edmund shrugged as if the matter was no longer of the slightest interest to him. Muttering something about everyone having to make *do* these days, he flung himself into an easy chair and started reading *Picture Post*. Slattery winced. He had disappointed Edmund. Tight lips, slightly flared nostrils; the signs were unmistakable.

Slattery didn't know what to say; he never did at such times. Why did the most perfect moments have to turn sour? It was his fault; he should have said something positive. Now he had to wait. Edmund would thaw. But it would take time. It always did.

Edmund flipped the pages of the magazine, but he was thinking, Slattery fancied, not reading; God knows what ideas were dancing around in that extraordinary mind of his.

A genius, Edmund, but a restless genius, impatient with details, contemptuous of difficulties. He lived by his own rules,
and his world was a thrilling place. Slattery was intensely
grateful to be a part of it. How tedious life was *before*. He
shuddered when he thought how tenuous was the web of
chance that led to their meeting. It happened during a particularly boring mid-winter leave. Strolling in civvies one morning because he had nothing better to do, Slattery
encountered Oswald, an acquaintance from his school days.
A medical student at Guy's, Oswald was a strutting peacock
of a fellow who appeared to have an unlimited allowance
from his father who manufactured uniforms. Slattery indulged in a few minutes' desultory, disinterested conversation; he was on the point of remembering an appointment
when Oswald mentioned the coffee shop. It had become *the*
place, he said. All manner of interesting people met under its
pink ceiling. Slattery accompanied Oswald, and met Edmund. There were others, too, but Slattery later only remembered Edmund. Oswald introduced them, pointing out that
Slattery was on leave from the air force. Within minutes the
conversation had drifted to the air war and the dreadful casualties being suffered by Bomber Command. Slattery mentioned a certain Flight Lieutenant named Montague, an
Honourable, with a house in Mayfair and a 6½-litre Bentley.
Poor chap, he had been lost with most of his crew on the
nineteenth trip of his second tour. Such a *congenial* and
informed person, Slattery said, the sort of individual with
whom one might have had a truly *rewarding* friendship if it
hadn't been for the ghastly officer/other ranks thing. He
told Edmund about the long conversation he had had with
Montague on the subject of Aubrey Beardsley's art and its
fascinatingly suggestive qualities. Edmund nodded understandingly, one eyebrow raised in that charming way of his.

During his next leave, Slattery went back to the pink ceil-
inged coffee shop six times. On the sixth visit – heaven be
praised! – Edmund was there. Smiling. Debonair as ever.
Clearly as delighted to see Slattery as was Slattery to see
him. They talked for hours, eye to eye. Afterwards Slattery

felt as if he had exchanged souls with Edmund. They had discussed *everything*. Edmund was an absolutely intoxicating personality! Marvellously well informed. Cultured in every sense of the term. Did Slattery remember the conversation with the Honourable Archie Montague? Slattery nodded. Did he perhaps recall Montague's address? Slattery did. He had an exceptionally good memory; when he wanted to, he could study a man's service record and recall it all weeks later as if it was imprinted on his mind.

Three or four weeks after he returned to Rocklington, Slattery received a letter from Edmund – exciting enough in itself; but to his astonishment a crisp five-pound note was enclosed. Edmund explained that it was "an honorarium" for his "professional services" in respect of "our mutual acquaintance." Slattery was mystified. What on earth was Edmund talking about? What professional service had he rendered? He wrote to Edmund asking him to explain. But it was clear that Edmund had no wish to put more on paper. Slattery had to wait until his next leave to learn more.

"I dabble in one or two things," Edmund explained. "Investments. Property. Insurance. I counsel. I explore. I'm awfully good at it. Even in wartime there are ways to put money to remarkably profitable use; indeed, if you know what you are doing, wartime offers even more potential than does peacetime. The key to success in my profession is getting to know the right people, the people with the sort of money necessary to make all the effort worthwhile. When you were talking about poor Montague I had a notion. It struck me that Montague's family might be grateful to hear from him."

"Hear from him? But he's dead."

Edmund shook his head, a gentle smile playing on his lips. "His earthly being may have passed to the other side but his spirit still exists and wants to communicate with the loved ones he has left behind."

Slattery stared. "Really?"

The smile broadened. "No, dear boy, it's a lorry-load of utter codswallop. But who am I to ruin nice people's day-dreams? I telephoned the Montagues. Took a deuce of a lot of talking to get through to the old man, I can tell you. Told him I found a note on my desk, telling the family about one or two good Beardsleys on sale in a spot on Bond Street. I assured them that I was utterly mystified by the note. I had never had the pleasure of meeting the Honourable Montague and I was therefore a trifle miffed that he managed to get into my place to write the note. And puzzled as to why. You get the idea?"

"I do indeed," breathed Slattery, enormously impressed.

"In all modesty," said Edmund, "I must say I think I handled everything quite brilliantly. I declared myself totally without psychic powers; indeed, I dismissed the notion as absurd, so that in the end it was the Montagues who were trying to convince *me* that I had the power to communicate with the departed, instead of the other way around. In no time they trusted me absolutely. And I have reinforced that trust by making a considerable amount of money for them. Everyone has profited. No one has any complaints. Now it seems to me that the concept might be put to further use. Do you agree? I do hope so. You told me that two out of three aircrew people eventually become casualties. Most of them are better educated than your average soldier or sailor. It therefore follows that their families are likely to be more *comfortable* than most. It will be necessary to work in the closest harmony, dear boy. Not an unpleasant prospect as far as I am concerned ... "

Edmund didn't come to the Tube.

"Loathe goodbyes. Even goodbyes of short duration. Do hurry back."

"Tuesday. As early as I can."

"Until then. Chin up, dear boy."

During the journey to Ilford Slattery tried to convince himself that he would enjoy a few days at home. The familiar streets and shops. Home cooking. His old room. His stamp collection. Grey flannels and a sports jacket. Privacy. In his first few months in the air force Slattery had longed for those things so desperately that he wondered if he might do himself mental damage. Now home and family were tiresome obligations. He ached to return to the flat at Marble Arch and to Edmund with his mercurial moods and his intensity, his unthinking cruelties and his unexpected kindnesses. Compared with Edmund, the rest of mankind seemed only half alive. But it was a frightful task keeping him supplied with gen; Slattery hated it. Day after day he had to keep the precious notes from God only knows how many prying eyes until he could get to the village to post them to Edmund. He dared not use the camp post office facilities because of the ever-present danger of the CO or someone deciding to censor everything. Edmund simply didn't understand the limitations of life in the services. To be in uniform was to enjoy about as much dignity and consideration as an inhabitant of the Regent's Park Zoo. But it was worth it. Every jab of panic, every knotted nerve was worth it, because it made him an important part of Edmund's life, a person of privilege, an *intimate*. At various times Edmund had admitted to having been a chorus boy in a seaside concert party, the assistant manager of a Soho club of dubious reputation, a host at a holiday camp, an actor in a repertory company, an advertising salesman for a nudist magazine.

Edmund never mentioned family. How typical of him to exist without the usual encumbrances of mother, father, brothers and sisters. Even if he did possess relatives, it was doubtful that he wasted any of his valuable time on them. The constraints of everyday existence seemed not to apply to Edmund. To follow conventional paths was to miss the true *essence* of life, he always said; besides, it was *boring*, quite the most heinous of crimes. No wonder he revelled in this elaborate method of developing new clients. How often he had told Slattery that the real joy of every human endeavour was in the developing drama, not the dénouement.

Slattery's parents and twelve-year-old Stephanie greeted him with the usual effusion. Had he had a good journey down? Terrible, he told them. Had to stand the whole way. His mother was of the opinion that was a disgrace, the air force giving him a mere seventy-two hours' leave. He said he was lucky to get away at all, with ops on almost every night;

the pace was frightful. Even in the Orderly Room? asked Stephanie. Cheeky little bitch. For ten minutes they wanted to know all about him and his life "up there" in Yorkshire. But in no time the conversation was about the tribulations of the home front. Rations. Queues. Raids. Shortages. Mr Loomis from number 12 dropped in to borrow some flour. And made himself comfortable the moment he saw Slattery: a splendid opportunity to chirp about his years on the Western Front, which he could do for hours on end. At one time Slattery had found Mr Loomis's ramblings moderately interesting; now he saw how trivial and unimportant they were. The ritual exchange of banalities, in Edmund's words: hours of dross for hours of drivel. Thus did the vast majority of people spend most of their waking hours.

Why did time drag by so slowly here when in London it pranced away so rapidly? Three days; an eternity. How would he keep his sanity? He wanted to telephone Edmund but the family never seemed to leave him alone.

Over breakfast on the first morning Stephanie asked him about his love life. His mother clicked her tongue and told her daughter not to be silly. There was plenty of time for that sort of thing, she declared. One day the right girl would come along. She seemed to have a mental picture of "the right girl" for Slattery: a cross between Shirley Temple and Queen Mary. Stephanie was of the opinion that he had a secret love – and she strayed chillingly close to the truth when she conjured up a story about him having two weeks' leave but spending only a few days at home because he wanted to spend the time with his lover. Fortunately his parents never paid any attention to her chatter.

On Sunday evening his parents and Stephanie went to church. They wanted him to join them in his uniform; no, he told them, he got enough of that sort of thing at Church Parades. He wanted to work on his stamp collection. They went out. He telephoned Edmund. Damn! No answer. Dejected, he listened to *Hi, Gang* on the wireless. Then he had the idea.

"They just phoned from Rocklington," he told his parents when they got back from church. "Emergency or something.

I've got to go back tomorrow instead of Tuesday. First thing. Rotten, isn't it? But there's nothing one can do about it. You do what they tell you, or else. But they said they'd make it up on my next leave."

It was painful, seeing the tears glistening in his mother's eyes but, mercifully, she recovered, murmuring something about it being better than him having to go to the front line. His father slipped a couple of pounds in his hand, calling him "old man" in that slightly self-conscious way of his. Dad meant well, but the truth was Slattery didn't need the money; he had more than twenty pounds in his wallet – the rewards of more professional services for Edmund.

God, what a relief to get away! As he settled himself into the Tube seat he could have chortled with sheer delight. He'd done his duty. Now he had an extra day with Edmund. A bonus twenty-four hours. They would pack a lifetime into the rest of the week, enough memories to last him through the dreadful months ahead. He loathed the air force. God knows how long he would have to stay in uniform; the war could last for years. In a way it was worse knowing that he had it in his power to get out. Perfectly simple. All he had to do was admit to certain tendencies. He would be out in no time. But at what a price! To be different was to be condemned. Instantly. It was the system. If one was not what society wanted one to be, then one had to pretend and keep on pretending, no matter what. Once Slattery told Edmund that he was ashamed of his feelings – to which Edmund said there was only one thing to be ashamed of: regret, because it was such a monumental waste of time. He had an amusing way of making such pronouncements, head angled, lips slightly pursed, hands outstretched, palms up. Edmund had a splendid voice and he used it skilfully. It was a pleasure to listen. And to watch. His hands created fantastic patterns around himself; the more outrageous the statement, the wilder the pattern. He outdid himself when he theorized that Christianity had all begun when an unfaithful wife had concocted an excuse for an embarrassing pregnancy, an excuse so totally, utterly outlandish that it was believed and had continued to be believed by umpteen millions for nearly two thousand years. The bigger the lie the more likely it would be accepted as the truth, Edmund claimed; he advised Slattery never to waste himself on trifling mendacities or cheap gin. Slattery longed to stay in London with Edmund. Desert? An intriguing possibility, but Slattery couldn't see himself lasting long as a fugitive. But he *would* desert if they charged him with purloining gen from aircrew records; he had already made that decision. He couldn't face the glasshouse, that place of evil reputation where, it was said, they made you move at the double all day long, even at meals and at your ablutions, where suicides and so-called accidental deaths were everyday occurrences, and where they had special treats in store for anyone they categorized as "pansy."

Edmund claimed the fear of discovery usually led to discovery. Ignore the possibility and it would go away, he said. Typical Edmund. "The important thing," he always claimed, "is never to admit to yourself that you are doing anything wrong. You must get into the habit of seeing life and living it as it is, not as the world tells you it should be." He had an original way of looking at everything – "from politics to pederasty," he would add with a wink.

Heart thumping with excitement, Slattery got out at Marble Arch. There was a cool wind but the sun kept peeping through the scattered cloud. He breathed deeply as he stepped out onto the pavement, anticipation tingling within him. It was only a few minutes' walk to Edmund's flat. Along Oxford Street. Pushing through the throngs of people. Left turn. It was quieter here; he hurried along, past a hotel with a supercilious-looking doorman. Two more minutes brought him to Edmund's place; once an imposing town house, it now contained half a dozen flats "of character." Interesting people lived there, according to Edmund: an actor who was often heard on BBC dramas, an illustrator whose work appeared in several magazines, an old chap who seemed to occupy himself writing letters to the *Times*, advocating sterilization for the Germans, Japanese, and Italians, occasionally the Irish and French too.

Slattery trotted up the stairs. An odd smell hung around number 4; the illustrator liked to experiment with exotic cooking.

He rapped on Edmund's door.

Was he out?

A movement! Relief! Slattery started to smile in anticipation of Edmund's surprise.

The door opened.

Edmund, resplendent in his scarlet and gold dressing gown. Uncharacteristically dishevelled. Startled.

Mouth slightly open.

"You're not due back until tomorrow."

It wasn't the welcome Slattery had expected.

His stomach lurched uneasily.

"I came early," he mumbled.

There was a frightful moment of silence. Why didn't Edmund welcome him? Ask him in? Smile with joy?

"Who the hell is it?"

A voice from within the flat. An unfamiliar voice, throaty and foreign-sounding.

Something snapped within Slattery. He felt it. Heard it too. It propelled him, mindlessly. He pushed past Edmund. Fingers touched his arm.

"No, don't be a fool . . . "

A voice from far away, a voice echoing in emptiness . . . footsteps jarring his frame, thudding . . . a glimpse of the man, stretched out on the cushions that Edmund was fond of scattering all over the floor, stark naked, great white limbs outstretched, propped up on an elbow, cigarette in hand . . . a fringe of fair hair falling to one side of his loathsome face.

"You don't understand . . . "

But he did. All too sickeningly, maddeningly well.

He hurled himself at the intruder. The limbs twisted and turned in instinctive self-protection. Vainly the man tried to roll out of reach.

"Christ . . . !"

The cigarette smashed against his hand. Burning embers

bit into his skin. He heard a voice screeching in fury. His own voice. A hand clasped his wrist. He tore free of it.

Even the sight of the knife in the man's hand didn't deter him. The man's arm swung and the blade glinted as it flashed at him.

He watched the blade streaking toward him, disappearing into his mid-section. He felt nothing.

Then he saw the blood welling, spurting.

The light dimmed; the voice faded.

The telephone rang at noon. Mrs Slattery answered it, her voice still tight and uncertain from the hours of crying.

The man's voice was confident, well educated.

"Is that Mrs Slattery? My name's Weston. I appear to have a note to ring you. Something about stamps. But I must confess that I have no idea why . . . "

The Navigator

H IS MOTHER'S JAW JUTTED DISAPPROVINGLY.
"Unwise, I call it. Unwise. You'll just open old
wounds."

Roland said, "There are some things a chap just has to do."

He recalled the hero in a Hollywood epic saying something of the sort. In the film everyone had nodded approvingly. But here in real life, home in London, the words seemed to have the opposite effect.

His father and mother started discussing the matter, ignoring him as if he were still a child incapable of making a worthwhile contribution to the conversation. When would they accept the fact that he was a man now and capable of making his own decisions? His mother kept on about his leg. About his leg not being right yet. About how a journey to an outlandish place like Edgware could do it harm, set it back, even do it further injury. His father nodded, glancing at his *Mail*; he had been nodding and glancing at his *Mail* at breakfast for as long as Roland could remember.

"Your mother's right, you know," was his father's eventual contribution, as Roland knew it would be. "Got to go," he said just as inevitably. He pushed his chair back, got to his feet, stooped over the table and gulped down the last of his tea, another essential part of the morning ritual. "Probably better to let sleeping dogs lie, old fellow."

"He saved my life."

"Not denying it, not at all. But . . . well . . . "

"You wrote his wife – well, widow – a very nice letter," said his mother. "It's enough, I think, I really do."

"I'm going, Mother."

It was a relief to get off the bus. But the instant he started walking his leg flared up with the fierce throb that always made him think of bones disintegrating, muscles and ligaments unravelling. Perhaps he should abandon the journey. A stumble on the bus platform had done it. Always the same. Some wretched little thing would set it off. He wondered if his leg would be like this for the rest of his life. The doctors said no, but they could be wrong, couldn't they?

He waited until the traffic had eased before crossing the street to the Tube station. So far so good. Press on regardless.

At the foot of the escalator he paused again, feeling wobbly. Perhaps his mother was right. Perhaps he wasn't ready for trips to exotic destinations like Edgware.

"Want a hand, buddy?"

A GI. Bland, boyish features topped by a cropped fringe of corn-coloured hair. Chewing, of course. Always chewing, the Yanks.

"It'll be all right in a minute."

"I can wait," said the Yank.

"It's not necessary, really . . . "

But the GI seemed to have no intention of leaving. He asked how Roland got himself wounded. His pale blue eyes opened wide when Roland told him about the shell exploding in the wireless compartment, blowing poor Gordon to bits.

"I sat right in front of him, you see. I was the navigator. I was lucky, awfully lucky. If it hadn't been for all the wireless equipment in between us I don't think I would be here today."

"Son of a bitch." The American shook his head in wonderment. "So where are you headed now?"

It was none of his business of course, but how could you be stand-offish in the face of such genuine interest?

"I'm going to visit the widow of the man who saved my life – and who got himself killed doing it."

The GI's mouth dropped open. He had perfect teeth like someone in a Kolynos advertisement.

"Jeez. That's really somethin'. You know her?"

"No, I've never met her. I wrote her a letter a few weeks ago. I said I'd like to visit her when I was on my feet again."

"And she said okay?"

"She didn't reply."

"But you're going anyhow. I like that."

"I'm not looking forward to it."

"Did you call her? Say you were coming?"

"She's not on the telephone. I looked in the book. To be honest, I'll be glad if she's out when I get there. I'll write her a note and say I was there. I'll feel I've done my stuff."

More sober nods from the GI; he put Roland in mind of a businessman agreeing to the finer points of a complicated business deal. He liked it, he said again. Liked it a lot. He insisted on taking Roland to the correct platform and waiting until the Edgware train arrived.

He saw that Roland was safely seated – and he advised the other passengers that Roland had been wounded in action and they should look out for him. It was acutely embarrassing.

Roland thanked the GI as the door closed. "No sweat," was the response. The Yank meant well, but did he have to be so *public* about it?

Roland wished he had bought a paper. He had nothing to do but stare at the other passengers and the floor and its assortment of cigarette ends and tickets and various unidentifiable items wedged in the crevices between the wooden slats. The leg was on fire now. What would happen when he reached Edgware station? Would he fall full length in the carriage?

The journey seemed endless. He felt sick from the angry burning of his leg. Would he disgrace himself here, in front of all these people?

The train suddenly emerged from the tunnel between Hampstead and Golders Green. Pale sunlight flooded the carriage; the passengers blinked disbelievingly as if they had forgotten that there was a world outside.

The territory was as unfamiliar to Roland as Rocklington and East Yorkshire had once been. It was a different world up here north of the river. A vaguely foreign world. The houses looked grander, the people flashier – for instance, the be-furred woman with a bright red gash of a mouth and that chap in the tweed suit with the brogues. Twenty-quid shoes, was the way old Harry used to describe them; hand-made jobs made especially to fit one person. Until he went into the air force Roland had no idea that it was possible to have shoes hand-made. It still staggered him that anyone would part with twenty pounds for one pair of shoes. The lads were right. After the war it *had* to be different. The wealth had to be redistributed. Too few had too much. The system needed a modification or two.

"Most awfully sorry," said a man who brushed against Roland's leg.

"No sweat," said Roland, wondering why he used the GI's term; he wasn't even sure what it meant.

The man sat opposite him. Classy mac and shoes; tie looked like silk. Why should upper crusters be able to put silk around their necks when everyone else had to make do with wool and cotton? Another instance of the gross unfairness of things that Harry was always on about. But Roland had long ago decided that if the country's wealth was indeed redistributed he would never be caught wasting any of his share on ties made of silk.

Edgware station at last. Roland heaved himself to his feet, grasping the vertical rail beside the doors. He winced as his leg sagged; for a sickening instant he thought it was going to collapse. But no, thank the Lord, he was airborne and proceeding on course. Through the sliding doors on to the platform. Nice to smell the fresh air after the musty and dusty Tube train. Tummy settling down. A tug on the tunic, an angling of the cap; everything in good order. Odd how some civilians deliberately avoided catching his eye, as if they pretended to themselves that they couldn't see him. Perhaps they were afraid of being touched for a few bob. A bloke at the hospital swore that an old geezer thrust a fiver in his hand during a stroll in Green Park. And an Aussie gunner named Banning had been stopped by a woman near the hospital. How did the gallant Colonial get his wound, she wanted to know. Falling out of the CO's wife's bed, was what Banning told her. Typical Banning.

A bobby directed Roland to Peel Street. A nondescript-looking area, not a bit like some of the avenues he had seen from the Tube. He made his slow, plodding way to number 88. For a moment he gazed at the place; Harry had talked at length about this house and how he had negotiated so cleverly with the landlady. He had made it sound like number 10 Downing Street, which it most certainly wasn't.

Roland walked up to the front door and pressed the bell. Nothing. He waited a moment, then rapped on the door. Silence.

He felt in his pocket for the piece of notepaper he had taken from his mother's box of stationery, a Christmas present from Aunt Freda, blue writing paper and envelopes held together by purple ribbon; it was used only for epistles of importance. He knew what to write. He had worked it all out at home: "Sorry I missed you. I was looking forward to meeting you. Harry told me so much about you." Which was not quite true, strictly speaking, but it seemed the right sort of thing to say. "It was a privilege being on the same crew as Harry and if there is anything I can do please don't hesitate . . ."

A step within. His heart tripped.

The door latch rattled. A squeak and a creak and the door opened. A plump middle-aged woman stood there, cigarette dangling disconsolately from chubby lips. She had an incongruously sharp chin for someone carrying such weight. It gave her an inquisitive look.

"Is Mrs White in, please?"

The woman sniffed. "No." She glanced at his uniform, her eyes narrowing. "Are you the bloke . . . the bloke her husband knew?"

"Yes, my name's Hibbert. Roland Hibbert."

"You wrote to her . . . after it happened."

"That's right."

"Thought so." She sounded pleased with her deduction. "Best come in. You can wait. She'll be home any minute. Any minute at all."

Roland followed her into the house. There was a bicycle against the wall in the hall, a brace of empty milk bottles outside a closed door. The woman led him to a sitting room at the rear.

"You can wait in there."

"Perhaps I'll just leave her a note," said Roland.

The woman shook her head, firmly, removing her cigarette and pointing it for emphasis. "You've come now. Only a few minutes and she'll be home. Sit down."

The chair emitted a weary croak as Roland settled himself.

"Lost your leg, did you?"

"No, it's just an . . . injury. It's almost better."

"Were you there when . . . her husband . . . was . . . ?"

"Yes . . . And he saved my life."

"Did he, by God!" Her eyebrows arched over her glasses. "Mind you, I only met him a couple of times. When he was on leave, you know. Mrs White has been living here, eighteen months it'll be at Christmas."

"Does she work nearby?"

"Place that makes wireless and radar stuff. In Cricklewood. She's a foreman. Or forewoman, I s'pose it should be." A mechanical little smile. It quickly vanished. "Where have you come from?"

"Putney."

She nodded knowingly. And mumbled something about having a friend there. Or near there. She shrugged and puffed on her Woodbine. She leant on the back of a well-worn easy chair, looking past him and rambling on about a neighbour's son who was in the air force and got himself killed, just like Mr White. She shook her head as if inferring that both Mr White and the neighbour's son should have had more sense than to join the air force. Her head jerked to one side; she looked like an overweight ferret.

"I think that's her now."

Roland's heart pounded. Why hadn't he left a note and gone? What on earth was he going to say?

The woman raised a don't-move-a-muscle finger in Roland's direction, then she went back into the hall as the front door opened.

"He's here," Roland heard the woman say.

"Who's here?" a younger voice responded.

"The air force chap. The one that wrote to you."

No response. Roland got to his feet. The woman came back; a younger woman was with her, a plain, tired-looking person wearing a bandanna.

"Hullo," said Roland.

"You must be Sergeant . . . er . . . "

"Hibbert."

"Yes. I remember." She had a pleasant voice. "Did you have to wait long?"

"He came not ten minutes ago," chimed in the older woman.

"I just got back from work," said Harry's widow. She smiled. "Your name's Roland, isn't it? I'm Doreen. Let's go up to my room."

She led the way up the stairs. The house seemed to contain half a dozen flats. Hers looked out on the street. It was neat and plain, like her. She indicated the solitary easy chair. Would he like a cup of tea? Or something stronger? She thought she had some brandy left, or possibly a spot of gin.

"Tea would be lovely, thank you," he said. Then he found himself thinking about the time it would take to boil the kettle and make the tea. It would mean being stuck there at least half an hour. And what could he possibly talk about for half an hour with this woman, a total stranger?

"I see you got a bit bashed up," she said.

"It's quite all right. I was lucky."

She nodded as she went to the stove in the corner and lit the gas. Roland massaged his ankle. It stung as if a bee had been to work on it. He glanced about the room. No picture of Harry. Too painful, he presumed.

"I hope you didn't mind me coming here," Roland said. He had been practising the line for days. "I know it must be difficult for you . . . with everything that's happened."

The soft warm smile again. "I fancy it might be a bit more difficult for you than me."

Roland didn't know what to say to that, so he said nothing.

While she made the tea she asked him where he lived, about his family and his hobbies. He listened to himself chattering on about himself; all of a sudden he seemed to have a lot to say.

"There." She brought the teapot to the table and placed a pink cosy over it. "We'll let it stand for a couple of minutes, shall we? Were you and Harry very good friends?"

"He was a marvellous pal," Roland said.

"I'm glad."

"He sort of . . . looked out for me, being older, you know."

"Of course."

"And such a terrific sense of humour."

Doreen poured the tea. "Funny, I don't remember him saying many funny things."

"He told stories well." Dirty stories mostly, he might have added, but didn't.

"We weren't together long, you know. Less than a year. And a lot of that time he was away."

She seemed able to talk about him without getting teary, which was a relief. You never could tell how women might react to this sort of situation, all the boys were agreed on that.

"He was a wonderful bloke," said Roland. His voice had become husky. He had to clear his throat. "Have you heard anything about a gong?"

"Gong?"

"Medal."

She shook her head as she opened a biscuit tin.

Roland said, "Everyone said he should have got a gong. A VC, just like Willy did, although I've never heard of two VCs in one crew . . . mind you, some chaps said it might happen if we were in 5 Group. Harris's favourite, 5 Group, so they say . . . "

"That's interesting," she said, although her voice didn't seem to agree. "I got a very nice letter from a Wing Commander Somebody-or-other. He spoke very highly of Harry. At the time I wondered, did he really know Harry? After all a Wing Commander is quite senior, isn't he? Would he really be on friendly terms with a flight sergeant?"

"That would've been the CO who wrote to you. Wing Commander Davis. I expect he knew Harry . . . quite well, I'd say."

"And there was a letter from a Ross Sinclair."

"He was the skipper. Lost an arm. He's back in Canada now. A good skipper. Good pilot, too. We all liked him."

"What was your job?"

"Navigator. I did sums all the time trying to sort out where we were and where we were going."

"That's a very responsible job for . . . well, you're very young, aren't you?"

"Almost twenty-one," Roland told her. Another seven months and twelve days to be precise, but why bore her with details?

"Ah," she said, "that's different." That soft smile of hers touched her lips. A nice woman, Mrs White, but the way she spoke to him reminded him a bit of Aunt Freda.

"Harry used to sit next to me. He helped me sometimes, map-reading and that sort of thing. Some of the fellows called him Chalky. In the services if your surname is White you're automatically Chalky. But I don't think Harry liked being called Chalky. So I always called him Harry."

"Was he good at his job?"

"Terrific. One of the best."

"He said he liked it," she said. "I remember him telling me that. 'Serve the bastards damn well right. They started it, now they're getting a taste of their own medicine.' Is it very frightening, flying on bombing raids?"

He glanced at her. "Didn't Harry tell you?"

She shook her head, slowly, thoughtfully. "He never admitted to being frightened of anything that I can recall." She looked up at him. "Will you tell me what happened?"

"Don't you know?"

"Only what the letters and telegrams told me."

"Well." Roland tried to collect his thoughts. He told her how he, Gordon, and Harry occupied the confined space of the nose compartment, wedged in between the radio receivers and transmitters, the navigation table and the bomb-aiming equipment. In that narrow area the effect of the direct hit was devastating. Only the radio equipment had shielded Roland from the full effect of the explosion. But he was knocked out. The fire had started immediately.

"Flames and sparks everywhere. I was only half conscious; it was like a mad sort of fireworks display. I can remember looking at it and wondering what it was and where I was. But Harry knew. And he got to work at once. He could have jumped and saved himself, but he didn't. He stayed and made sure I was all right. He got all that wireless equipment off me. And he clipped on my chute. By then it was too late."

He didn't tell her about the fire blistering Harry's hands, about the way his face was distorted with pain, about his flying suit smouldering, then erupting in flame, while he struggled with the heavy radio. When at last the job was done Harry was in mortal agony, screaming, as he tried in vain to clip his parachute pack on with those blackened claws of hands. He hurled himself out through the emergency hatch in the floor. And fell to his death.

"The thing was, I was able to put the fire out with the extinguisher. Willy, the flight engineer, took over the controls and got the kite home. He got the VC. Harry should have too. I told the CO. He said he'd see about it. That's why I wondered if you had heard anything."

She shook her head, smiling a wry little smile as if it really didn't matter much one way or the other.

They drank their tea and munched biscuits. He asked about her job; she enquired about his ambition to become an engineer after the war. Then the conversation started to lag; they had little else to say to one another. Soon it would be time to leave.

It had all gone far more smoothly than he had dared hope. A nice person, Harry's wife. Or rather, widow. Easy to talk to. Now it was time to deliver the little speech he had rehearsed so often. He turned to her.

"It was kind of you to spend such a lot of time with me. I came to tell you I count myself lucky having been in the same crew as Harry. I owe everything to him. He was the bravest man I've ever known. If it wasn't for him I wouldn't be here now. I just want to add that if there is anything I can do for you, anything at all, I hope you'll ask ... and it will be my privilege to do it ... "

She nodded slowly, thoughtfully, her eyes downcast. God knows what memories were tumbling through her head.

"I can't tell you how much I appreciate your coming all this way. It can't have been easy."

"I wanted to do it."

"I know you did. And I'm very grateful." She smiled her gentle, tired smile. "I'm glad Harry saved your life. I have a feeling it's going to be a worthwhile life."

"I'll try," he promised, embarrassed.

Ten minutes later he was on his way back to the Tube station, weary but elated. He had done his duty by Harry.

From her window, Doreen White watched the slight figure in blue. A nice young man. Incredible, Harry having the good taste to save such a life. She pulled the blackout curtain and went back to her seat by the gas fire. She chuckled; couldn't help it. Imagine how young Roland would have reacted if she had told him the truth. That she hated Harry. Feared him. Dreaded his coming on leave. A vindictive bastard, Harry, a bully and a braggart. Her cheek-bone still ached where he had hit her the last time he was home. What would poor Roland have said if she had shown him the heavy penknife she had purchased only a week before the telegram came? The knife still lay in the left-hand corner of her undies drawer. She had practised reaching for it in the dark. She had become adept at opening it rapidly. She knew how to hold it. How to use it.

But now she wouldn't have to. Harry was dead. Heaven be praised.

The Marksman

THE TRUTH WAS, GIVEN ANY CHOICE IN THE MATTER, Chris would never have selected Cornelius. He looked too *forbidding*. Dark-complexioned, with eyes the colour of coal, he had an expression that told you in no uncertain terms to keep your distance. But Chris wasn't given options. Mike Ballard came down with an obscure form of ear trouble the day after the crew arrived at Rocklington. The MO, Coates, sent him off to the Group medical people. The next day a replacement rear gunner appeared. At first Chris thought he was from the Far East or the Caribbean.

But the flashes on his shoulder said CANADA.

"Welcome aboard. My name's Chris Warren."

"Cornelius Brand."

"What part of Canada are you from?"

"Attawapiskat. Northern Ontario."

"That's interesting."

"Is it?"

Not a suspicion of a smile.

Chris introduced him to the rest of the crew: Bob King, the flight engineer; Ted Buckman, the wireless op; Roger Birch, the navigator; Norman Sims, the bomb-aimer; and Marty Finch, the other gunner.

They did their best, smiling and saying hullo; in return Cornelius merely nodded at each man and studied his features as if looking for something.

Chris wondered if the fellow knew how to smile. He had observed glances from one or two of the crew, glances that asked why he, as skipper, couldn't have found a more congenial gunner. But, according to his log book, the fellow could shoot – and, Chris reasoned, couldn't that prove to be far more important than a winning personality?

"They're really an awfully good bunch of chaps," Chris told Cornelius that evening. No response. "Of course, you have to get to know them. Marty's rather a clever cartoonist. He wants to work for one of the dailies after the war. Roger is quite an expert on the Middle Ages: he's planning to teach history. Norman Sims makes model aeroplanes. As a hobby of course. Do you have any hobbies?"

Cornelius shook his head. Subject closed. Not exactly verbose, friend Cornelius. One might as well have a conversation with a pillar-box. Were all Indians like him?

"Tell me about that place you come from. I'm afraid I've forgotten the name."

"Attawapiskat."

"That's it. Must confess I've never heard of it. Where did you say it is?"

"Maybe a hundred miles north of Moosonee."

Chris smiled.

Cornelius's features hardened. "What's so funny?"

"No offence. It's simply the kind of thing an Englishman might say if he comes from a tiny village in the Cotswolds that no one has ever heard of . . . and it's near another place that no one has heard of. Get the idea? It's the English sense of humour, I suppose you might say."

Cornelius clearly didn't think much of it. He was not the easiest of fellows to get to know. He looked at you with a forbidding, disconcertingly direct gaze, the sort of gaze that said you were guilty until proved innocent. A powerfully-built fellow, Cornelius looked to Chris rather more Oriental than the Indians he had seen in films. He was good-looking in his own singular way, with a prominent, well-shaped nose and a broad brow; his thick black hair was as sleek and shiny as a horse's mane. He had a purposeful walk, shoulders and head thrust forward as if he was about to break into a run. During the next few days Chris did his best to make Lo welcome in the tight little brotherhood of the aircrew. But Cornelius seemed to prefer his own company; off duty, he went strolling for countless miles around the airfield. In the billet he would lie for hours staring at the ceiling. With some difficulty Chris persuaded him to visit the camp cinema; unfortunately, the film was a Western featuring a particularly unsociable set of Indians. Cornelius walked out after twenty minutes.

It was Marty who christened him Lo.

"Cornelius is too long. Let's call him *Lo*-awatha. Instead of Hiawatha. Lo for short. Get it?

"Clever," said Roger, nodding in his precise, rather prim way. "To be honest I thought the only literary character you knew about was Jane in the *Mirror*."

"Just goes to show you," said Marty. "You shouldn't underestimate your fellow man."

"I usually find it quite impossible," Roger responded.

Cornelius didn't react when they told him about his new name. His dark eyes surveyed each man in turn. Why, he seemed to be asking, would they waste their time thinking up a name for a man who already had one?

"It's a special name," Chris explained. "Just for you. Like Dusty for people called Rhodes. And Chalky for chaps called White."

Cornelius frowned, shaking his head, apparently finding the whole business incomprehensible. He went for a walk.

"I say let's get rid of him," said Bob, his thin features dark with irritation, "He doesn't like us, that's as obvious as the nose on his face."

"How do we get rid of him?" Roger asked. "Drop him overboard?"

"They don't trust white men," said Norman. "I saw it in a flick; the Redskins were complaining about the white men coming and taking over their land. Do you think Lo's still cheesed off about that?"

"We haven't touched his bleeding land," said Ted.

"I wonder if he's ever scalped anyone," mused Marty.

Bob said he wouldn't be the least bit surprised and that the sooner Brand was out of the crew the better.

Chris said, "I can't refuse to have him on the crew just because his attitude is a bit . . . distant. After all, you might be a trifle ill at ease if you were stuck in a crew full of Indians." Rather apt, that, he thought. "We'll have to wait and see how he does on ops."

They flew G-George to Mannheim. Five minutes before they reached the target, Lo spotted a fighter.

"Two hundred yards!" he announced. "One fifty. Skipper, prepare to corkscrew port. *Go!*"

The dry rattle of machine gun fire sent shivers through the aircraft; the stink of cordite penetrated oxygen masks.

"You got the bugger!" shrieked Marty.

He had indeed. The fighter – a Junkers with an array of radar antennae sprouting out of its nose like some sort of metallic growth – went skidding by, wrapped in a cocoon of fire; with a twitch of its wings it broke up and went spinning earthward.

"Wizard, Lo!" hooted Chris. "Good shooting."

Lo didn't respond.

"Are you okay?" Chris enquired, concerned.

"I'm okay," said Lo shortly.

At debriefing, Chris claimed one night-fighter definitely destroyed.

"My rear gunner got it. Clean as a whistle. Two-second burst, that's all it took. A Ju 88. We all saw it. Fell to bits in the air. Bloody marvellous!"

The intelligence officer noted the fact with all the warmth of a solicitor preparing for a difficult case.

At the post-op meal, Marty said to Lo, "Where did you

learn to shoot like that? Do a lot of hunting and stuff like that, did you?"

"Some," said Lo. And that was that.

An odd one, Lo. But he could shoot and that was what mattered. Chris went off to write a letter to Anne. He intended to tell her that he had had an interview for a commission and things looked encouraging; and he might mention that he was growing a moustache, although the wretched thing was pretty feeble so far; not a bad collection of dark hairs, but all so ruddy soft! Positively *downy*. Perhaps he wouldn't tell her about the moustache after all. Difficult to know how she would take it. Difficult to know lots of things with Anne. At one time he had thought that he was making splendid progress with her. Now he wasn't sure. Her recent letters seemed to lack intensity.

They flew to Milan the next night. A long trip. Then to Leverkusen. And Berlin. A nasty one, the Berlin trip. Fighters all the way to the target and back. Chris saw a Lanc coned by half a dozen searchlights, poor devil. Once the lights had you coned it was time for the Lord's Prayer, everyone said. But the Lanc's misfortune was like the proverbial ill wind. With most of the lights concentrating on one writhing, twisting victim, it was possible for scores of other aircraft to slip by unscathed. The Lanc exploded, smearing fire across the darkness; it was as if someone had emptied a bucket of flames into the night sky; a vivid flash, a few fluttering bits of wreckage, then blackness. A quick end, that's all you could say for it. The lights were on the prowl again, probing the scattered clouds, traversing, following the lead of the blue-tinted light, the radar-controlled job.

"Fighter port beam. Prepare to corkscrew to port."

Lo. It was the most he had said all day.

"Go!"

As Chris wrenched the bomber into a diving turn, Lo's four Brownings opened up.

"Christ, you got him!"

"There he goes!"

"A flamer!"

"Marvellous," Chris called out. "Well done, Lo. But keep your eyes open, gunners, sometimes the blighters work in pairs."

"Still going down," reported Marty from the mid-upper turret. "Still burning like a lovely torch. That'll teach him! Splatter! He's hit the deck, Skipper. I saw him! That'll teach the buggers to mess about with us!"

Chris shook his head, smiling to himself. You couldn't accuse Marty of lack of enthusiasm. But the amazing one was Lo. Two kills to his credit already. Most gunners went through a tour without hitting a thing. Many never fired their guns. A phenomenon, Lo; an unsmiling phenomenon, it was true. But who cared if he smiled when he could shoot like that?

The CO congratulated Lo. Bloody marvellous show. Lo nodded; yes, he supposed it was. But still it didn't call for a smile. The CO declared Lo to be a natural. He made it sound like a benediction.

For once the air force seemed to have found just the right job for a chap, what? Lo shook his head; no, he would have preferred to be a pilot.

The following evening the squadron was stood down. Someone suggested visiting The White Rose. Chris asked Lo to join the others. He shook his head.

"I don't like drink."

"Have a lemonade or something. No one has to drink if they don't want to. The idea is just to sit down in a nice chummy place and have a good old jaw."

"A what?"

"A chat. Come on, you'll enjoy it."

It was busy at The White Rose. It was always busy when the squadron was stood down. Chris bought the first round of drinks, a lemonade for Lo, beer for the others. Marty immediately launched into a story about a barmaid he had met during his last leave.

"Married, she is. Husband in the navy. Having it off in every port. So why shouldn't she? I said to her, 'Fair is fair.'"

Marty had an impish face and bright blue eyes.

"And she chose you?" enquired Roger incredulously.

"She knows a good thing when she sees it."

"And did she see a good thing?" chuckled Ted.

"At least a dozen times," Marty replied with a smug smile.

"You want to watch yourself, messing about with married women," was Bob King's advice. The flight engineer was an old chap of twenty-six, remustered ground crew, a family man.

"Too busy watching her," said Marty.

Bob sighed, declaring that more blokes had got the chop for shagging married women than had got the chop on all the ops since the war began.

Chris glanced at Lo; the Indian seemed bewildered by the exchange; he looked as if he was wondering how to extricate himself from these lunatics.

"Hey, aren't you the bloke who's shot down two Jerries?"

An Australian Pilot Officer asked the question, a blond giant of a man with a wide grin.

"That's him," said Chris. "Cornelius Brand in person."

"Good on you," boomed the Aussie. He thrust out a large hand which Lo regarded dubiously before taking. A moment later the Aussie had returned with a double whiskey, which he placed in front of Lo. "With my compliments."

Lo shook his head.

The Aussie stared.

"He doesn't drink," Chris explained.

"Well, he'd better bloody learn. Come on, chum, down the hatch!"

Again Lo shook his head.

The Aussie grinned. "You've got to. King's Regulations. Page 56, Paragraph 22. Anyone who shoots down two Jerry night-fighters has to drink a whiskey to celebrate!"

"He doesn't want to," said Chris.

Still the Aussie grinned. He picked up the glass and held it within an inch of Lo's mouth. "Come on, chum. You'll like it. I promise."

A peculiar look entered Lo's eyes, a hunted look, a cornered look.

"That's enough," said Chris, sensing trouble.

It was too late. With a sudden movement, Lo took the glass out of the Aussie's hand and threw its contents in his face.

"Oh, Christ," said someone.

The Australian staggered back, startled. Then, enraged, he took a step in Lo's direction. Fortunately another Aussie grabbed him about his sopping chest. It was all right, he said. A misunderstanding. A mistake.

Chris clutched Lo's arm. No time to think the matter over. No time to do anything but push Lo through the throng of wide-eyed patrons and out into the cool evening.

"That's better," he said for some reason.

"What's better?"

"Being out here instead of in there. The Aussie didn't mean any harm."

"But I did," Lo muttered, nostrils flaring.

His dark eyes kept bouncing from Chris to the pub and back again. There was something frighteningly elemental about his anger. Chris wanted to turn and head back to the field at a brisk trot. But he stayed.

"He was just having a bit of fun," he said, dismayed at how lame it sounded.

"Fun? Pushing that stuff at me?"

Chris tried to explain. "It's a sort of tradition, you see. When a chap gets married or shoots down Jerry fighters, everyone wants to share in the thing and the custom is for the chap to have a few drinks. Usually far too many. Don't ask me why. I don't know. But it's expected."

"*Expected*," said Lo. Remarkable, the scorn he could inject into a single word.

"Well, aren't there some traditions that you have that are a bit pointless?"

"Huh?" Lo peered at Chris as if seeing him for the first

time. Then his shoulders relaxed. Unexpectedly he half smiled. A warm smile. But it quickly vanished.

He began to walk in that emphatic energetic way of his. Chris fell in step beside him. In silence they strode across the village square and down the main street, past the post office and the little cluster of shops. Most of the pedestrians were air force personnel; Rocklingtonians tended to keep to their homes in the evenings.

"We must be a strange lot to you," suggested Chris.

"Mm?" Lo turned, apparently slightly surprised to find Chris still beside him. "A bit, I guess."

"But you've got to remember that you're not, well, a run of the mill chap to us. Actually, you're the very first Indian I've ever met; the first *non-Indian* Indian . . . if you get what I mean."

"I get it. Will that officer bring charges?"

"The Aussie? I doubt it. They're pretty good sorts, the Aussies. But perhaps you should send him a note, apologizing."

"*Apologizing!*"

Lo looked incredulous.

"You could express your profound hope that his uniform didn't get stained."

"I hope it did."

"Yes, and he knows that. But still it would be a good idea to hope it didn't."

"Is that the *right thing* to do?" Again that scornful edge in his voice. "You say you hope it didn't when you hope it did – and the man you're writing to knows you hope it did. Sometimes I wonder."

"So do I, old chap. But it's the way of the world. Tell me about that place you come from, the one with the unpronounceable name."

"Attawapiskat?"

"That's it."

Lo turned and gazed at Chris as if asking why this Englishman would want to know.

"Just interested," said Chris. "Does your family live there?"

"My mother and my sister," Lo replied in his own time. "My brother lives in Kapuskasing. My father is dead."

"I'm sorry."

"He drank until he died. Killed himself . . . committed suicide, in a way."

"That's why you don't touch the stuff? Very sensible."

"The Aussie didn't think so."

"I'm sure he would have understood if he'd known your reasons. In fact it might be an idea to tell him."

Lo nodded thoughtfully. "Will you help me with the letter?"

"If you'd like me to."

"I would."

They didn't have to send the letter. The Aussie went missing the next night. Lo was dejected; he seemed to feel responsible, no matter what anyone said.

They flew to Nuremberg. An endless trip. But no fighters came near. When they landed Lo was still silent and morose. He cheered up the next morning when the news came in: The Aussie and his crew had survived their crash and were POWs. Then it was Berlin again, and he shot down yet another Jerry.

"Bloody amazing," said Marty. "This kite comes flashing across our line of flight. Looked as if he'd been attacking someone else off to starboard. Lo pulls off this unbelievable deflection shot. Quick burst. Bang-bang-bang. The next thing you see is the Jerry going down in flames. Anyone else and I'd have said it was just luck. But not with Lo. I don't know why you bother taking me along, not with him on board."

"We keep you for your charming personality," Chris told him.

The CO informed Lo that he was getting the DFM. The next day a Canadian war correspondent arrived for an interview with the "wonder gunner." A chain-smoking man in his mid-thirties, the correspondent talked to Lo for half an hour; then while a photographer was taking pictures, he asked to talk to Chris. They met in a conference room next to the Adj's office.

"Cal Myers," the Canadian announced, lighting a fresh Sweet Caporal.

"My name's Warren."

"You're Cornelius's skipper, eh?"

"Cornelius? Yes, I'd forgotten that's his name. We call him Lo. Short for *Lo*awatha. Awful pun, I'm afraid."

"Cute," said Cal, scribbling in his note-book. "Pretty good gunner is he?"

"Good? He's bloody marvellous. Fantastic eyesight."

"Uh huh," muttered Cal, as if he wasn't the least bit surprised. More scribbling.

"The thing is, he seems to have the ability to compute everything in an instant. Very tricky, shooting in the air, particularly at night. Nothing stays still and targets seem to skid about all over the place. But once Lo spots a Jerry he usually gets him. It does a great deal for my self-confidence, knowing he's back there, looking after my rear end."

"How do the rest of the guys get along with him?"

"Pretty well on the whole. He was a bit shy when he first joined the crew but now he's got used to us – "

"And you guys have gotten used to him, eh? What does he do for kicks?"

"Kicks? You mean fun?"

"Sure. Girls, booze."

"I don't know anything about his adventures with girls. But I do happen to know that he doesn't drink. I gather his father had a drinking problem – in fact it killed him. So Lo won't touch the stuff."

"You're lucky. They can't drink, Injuns. In fact, there are lots of places that won't sell booze to them. Something about them, they just can't handle liquor like a white man."

Chris stared. "You talk about them as if they're a different species."

The Canadian nodded. "That's about the size of it."

"Surely not. Mind you, I haven't known many Indians before – "

"I have," said Myers. "Lots of 'em. And, believe me, they are different. Something about their heritage, their ancestry, I guess. We're all the products of what's gone before, right? You must have noticed things about your buddy Brand . . . "

"He likes to go for long walks by himself and he doesn't smile much. But I don't think – "

"Truth is, he probably doesn't smile because he doesn't see

anything funny. Never yet met an Injun with a sense of humour. It's just the way they are. When you deal with Injuns you got to understand their limitations."

"Limitations?"

He shrugged. "Face it, they're not the sharpest guys in the world."

"Lo seems intelligent enough to me."

"Maybe you got lucky. What matters is that the guy can shoot, eh?"

Chris was beginning to dislike the correspondent; the fellow talked about Lo as if he were simple. An arrogant sod, Mr Myers.

Myers's photographer came in, his beefy face pink with indignation.

"I can't get any co-operation from that Injun. Stubborn s.o.b. Does he think he knows better than me?"

Cal Myers got up. "You'd better come," he told Chris.

They found Lo sprawled on the grass beside a dispersal, his mouth set in a grim line, his eyes like two black stones.

The photographer said, "I just want him to stand there, by the tail turret of the airplane. And smile. Is that too goddam much to ask?"

Chris went over to Lo. "What's the matter, old boy?"

Lo said, "He said I was to put my arm around the guns like they were buddies."

"Just to add a bit of zip to the shot, that's all."

Lo said, "I told him he could take a picture of me in the turret, that's all."

"But we can hardly see anything of you when you're stuck in that thing."

"That's the way I want it."

Myers said, "Look, friend, we're not playing games. We got our orders. This isn't snapshots at the picnic. We're on official business here."

"Me too," said Lo. "I'm here to shoot at the enemy, not to grin for Popeye here and his Brownie."

"Who the hell're you calling Popeye?"

Lo turned to Myers. "You want him to take me in the turret or you want to go home?"

Myers sighed, teeth clenched. He told the photographer to take Lo in the turret.

As Lo climbed into the aircraft Myers turned to Chris. "What did I tell you? Sons of bitches, all of 'em."

It was Remscheid next. They dropped the bombs on the ground markers on the eastern flank of the city, then turned for home. A minute later the searchlights found them. More lights joined in. The cockpit windows shimmered in the unholy glare. Chris wrenched the Halifax into a plunging turn, his head down, concentrating on the instruments, compass, airspeed indicator, artificial horizon, rev counters, boost gauges, turn-and-bank . . . shuddering needles that were the only means of knowing whether the aircraft was upside down or the right way up, diving or climbing. No use looking outside because the world had become a blinding dazzle. Dive, turn, climb, roll . . . desperately trying to evade the pitiless glare that by now would have ruined the gunners' night vision . . . knowing how sickeningly slim the chances of escape were; once the searchlights had you coned, you had just about bought it . . .

That was when he heard Lo say, "Ted, fire a green flare, then two reds."

"What?"

"Do it! Green. Then two reds!"

"All right."

Ted did as he was instructed.

At once the lights dimmed. Blessed darkness cloaked the bomber.

Chris levelled out and resumed the course for home.

"Lo, how did you know what flares to fire?"

He replied, "I saw a Jerry fighter caught in the searchlights about ten minutes ago. He fired a green then two reds one after the other. The lights went out so I figured they could be the colours of the day for the Jerries. Anyway, it seemed worth a try."

"Well done. Good work." Chris felt his tensed muscles

relax; relief washed over him like a balm applied by a certain nubile maiden about whom he occasionally dreamt. So Myers thought Lo wasn't sharp!

The following morning the Gunnery Leader recounted the story for the benefit of the squadron's other gunners. A really splendid show, he declared, which just went to show what one could accomplish when one put the old noggin to work. Lo clearly found the whole thing intensely embarrassing. He seemed not to know how to accept praise. He had a funny way of contorting himself, twisting his shoulders and arms as if the words caused him physical discomfort.

The Guard Room telephoned. A Mr Patchett wanted to see Sergeant Brand.

"Patchett? I don't know any Patchett," said Lo. Then he bit his lip. "I bet he's the guy who owns the pub. I didn't think I broke anything but maybe I did. Do you remember?"

Chris shook his head. "Would you like me to come along?"

"Sure. Thanks."

Mr Patchett greeted them warmly. He was of middle age, tall and thin with a remarkably small mouth and a minuscule moustache to match.

"Grand of you to take a jiff to consider my request. I know you're busy lads. I hear you buzzing about at all hours of the day and night. Not that I'm complaining, mind. Grand work you're doing, simply grand."

Chris said, "Just what is your request, Mr Patchett?"

Mr Patchett peered at him. "Didn't I say? I don't think I did. I really don't. The excitement of the moment, that's what it was. Quite put me off my stroke." A dry chuckle emerged from his miniature orifice. "You see, lads, my troop have all heard about Mr Brand here – or should I say, Sergeant Brand – and they want to meet him without delay."

"Troop?"

"Aye, the Rocklington troop." Mr Patchett beamed.

"Salvation Army?" Chris enquired.

Mr Patchett stared. Then smiled. He had a surprisingly warm smile.

"Scouts, gentlemen, Lord Baden-Powell's finest. I thought you knew that. But how could you? Just goes to show you, right?"

Lo frowned, still perplexed. "You've got the wrong guy, mister. I don't know anything about Boy Scouts."

"Ah," said Mr Patchett, raising a remarkably long forefinger and wagging it three times. "Now I'm more than willing to agree that you may know nothing of Boy Scouts. But" – another two wags – "the Boy Scouts want to know about you, sir."

"Me, sir?"

"You, sir."

"Why?"

"Because of your background, your upbringing, your unique qualifications. You, sir, are a true son of the wild, just the sort of fellow my young lads would love to hear from. I fancy you could tell them a lot of simply grand tales about the prairies and – "

"I don't come from the prairies."

" – all the animals and the customs of the Indians."

Lo shook his head. "No way."

"Think it over."

"I don't have to."

"You can bring a breath of real adventure."

"Thanks but no thanks."

"We'll talk about it again," said Mr Patchett, unperturbed.

There was a letter from Anne, the first in nearly a month. Reams of stuff about visits to the West End, this theatre and that ballroom. Having a wonderful time – but not a single mention of how desperately she was missing him. Was she doing any longing at all? It made one wonder. A peculiar lot, females. Did they ever say what they actually meant? Sometimes they all seemed to be playing an infinitely complex game; Chris wished he could get hold of a set of the rules.

A couple of days later the Flight Commander told Lo to report to the BBC studio in Leeds. They wanted to record an interview with him for broadcast on the BBC and later on the Canadian Broadcasting Corporation.

Lo said no. Chris was sent for.

Afterwards he told Lo: "It'll be a day in Leeds at *their* expense. Have a meal out and perhaps see a film."

"I don't want to," said Lo.

"Why not?"

"Another guy like that jerk Myers. Asking questions. Sticking cameras in my face. Makes me feel like a performing monkey."

"There'll be no cameras at the BBC. It's wireless. You'll be in a little room talking to someone, answering a few questions. Easy as pie. The only reason they're doing it is because of what you've done. You're exceptional, old man. You've done great things. You have to tell the world about it. It'll be a piece of cake – a big line-shoot."

"If you go I'll go."

"But I wasn't invited."

"If you don't go I don't go."

Lo said little during the bus ride to Leeds, but from time to time he would turn to study a tree or a bush. What was its name? How long had it been growing in this part of England?

Chris had to admit to an almost total ignorance of the trees and bushes.

"City man," Lo commented with his soft smile. "It's a good job you know something about the air. You sure as hell don't know anything about the ground."

They encountered the brown jobs on the walk from the bus station. Royal Artillery. Three of them, ruddy-faced and full of beer, judging by their rubbery gait. The tallest of the trio stopped in his tracks.

"Bloody lovely! Brylcreem boys!"

"Ignore them," Chris grunted in Lo's direction.

"Oo, I do wish I was a Brylcreem boy," hooted the soldier. "Don't you, Charlie?"

"I do . . . not 'arf. They're so . . . pretty."

Lo turned. "What?"

Chris urged Lo on. They mingled with the pedestrians, losing sight of the khaki figures. Chris heaved a sigh of relief.

"What were they talking about?"

"Nothing. They weren't talking to us."

"I thought they were."

The interviewer was a plump fellow with a lisp, a mass of blond curls, and extraordinarily thick glasses through which his eyes looked like green marbles. He was effusive about the combination of ordinary English lad and full-blooded Indian from the pwaiwies of Canada – in spite of Lo pointing out yet again that he had never been on the prairies in his life. The blond-haired individual seemed to regard that as a minor inconvenience; the story was the thing, the story of partnership, the Empire at war, democwacy in action, white wace and wed fighting shoulder to shoulder to defeat the common enemy. Lo regarded the man warily. His answers were monosyllabic. Yes, as to whether the bombing was causing the enemy serious damage; no, as to whether he knew of any other Indian gunners in the air force. The ordeal lasted half an hour, after which Blondie said it had been a most rewawding expewience, a memowable moment, one that he would always wemembew.

It was a relief to get away from him. They had a meal of egg and chips near Lewis's after which they made their way back to the bus station.

Where they met the Royal Artillery again. The same three. Even more wobbly and shiny-faced than before.

"Is it? Chwist, it *is*! The Brylcreem boys! Back again, now ain't that nice . . . "

"You know them?" Lo asked Chris.

"Not well."

"Going our way, are you, gents?"

"Don't reply," said Chris quietly. "Pretend they're not there."

"Why?"

The army came nearer, swaying.

"What? Can't 'ear them? Can you 'ear them, Charlie? I can't. Such soft-spoken gentlemen in the air force. Beautiful manners, all of them."

The civilians were stirring uneasily, moving out of the immediate area.

"Not only do they 'ave beautiful manners, they're 'eroes, all of 'em, all Brylcreem boys. Like at Dunkirk. Bloody Luftwaffe bombing the 'ell outa us and where was the bloody air force? Back at 'ome 'aving tea and crumpets in front of the fire – "

Lo turned. "Are you talking to us?"

"Oh, God," breathed Chris, who always felt slightly sick at the prospect of physical violence.

Someone said something about getting the police.

The biggest soldier pushed his way through to Lo.

"Bloody right I'm talking to you, cock."

"Well, don't," said Lo. It all happened with bewildering speed. The big soldier drew back his right arm. And in a flash he was over Lo's shoulder and floundering on the pavement, blood streaming from his nose. The second soldier moved forward and then went tottering back to collapse in a heap against the wall.

The third soldier shook his head as if declining the offer of combat; he went wandering away on uncertain legs.

The bus arrived. Lo picked up his cap and asked the big soldier if he was okay, receiving an adenoidal gurgle in reply.

"You were *tremendous*," Chris said when they were safely on their way back to Rocklington. "How did you learn to fight like that?"

Lo shrugged, caressing bruised knuckles. "You pick up a trick here and a trick there. Those guys weren't much of a problem. Drunks never are, not in a fight."

"You're an amazing fellow."

"You think so? You should meet my mother."

"I hope I will one day."

The thought seemed to please Lo.

Lo got his next Jerry over Mannheim. There wasn't any doubt about the claim; the 110 blew up like a speeding firework, one wing breaking away with its engine still functioning, the propeller revolving as industriously as before.

Back at the base, the Station Commander and the CO came over to congratulate Lo personally. Bloody marvellous show. Magnificent example to all the other crews, superb demonstration of what could be accomplished with a quartet of

Browning .303s. The ground crew wanted to paint a row of Iron Crosses on the fuselage close to Lo's turret. But Lo wouldn't hear of it. Roger suggested scalps. Lo wasn't amused.

Chris had borrowed a copy of *The Good Companions* from the station library. Roger was of the opinion that he should have chosen a book of more modest proportions; he stood a distressingly good chance of getting the chop before he finished it.

They flew a night-flying test during the early afternoon. The sun came out while they were in the circuit. Afterwards Chris made himself comfortable on the grass outside the Crew Room with Priestley's hefty work.

"Skipper."

He looked up. Lo.

Lo glanced about. There was no one in earshot. He spoke quietly: "Got something to tell you." He took his time continuing. Then: "I've got a feeling we're . . . going to have trouble this trip."

"What sort of trouble?"

"Beats me. You'll maybe think I'm nuts, but the fact is, at home we take dreams and . . . *feelings* . . . very seriously. In the old days it was no disgrace if a brave stayed home because he had bad feelings about the battle that day."

"You're joking," said Chris. "You're having me on, you sly blighter."

"I am perfectly serious."

He was, too. His eyes had that motionless intensity that Chris had come to know.

Chris said, "I have feelings every time we fly. I'm scared bloody stiff."

Lo didn't smile. "I thought I should mention it."

"Of course," said Chris. But what was he supposed to do with the gen? "We'll be getting some leave soon. Do us all good to get away from flying for a bit. I'll bet you had too much fish and chips last night. Make you dream like hell, fish and chips. But, honestly, I don't think dreams mean anything."

"Most don't."

"How can you tell the difference between the dreams that mean something and those that don't?"

"How come you think it's all right to have twelve people for supper but not thirteen?"

"Touché," Chris said. "Why not report sick or something if you're ... well, uneasy."

Lo shook his head. "I'll fly the op if you do."

"But you think we're going to get the chop."

"I didn't say that. I said I think we'll have trouble."

"But you can't be more specific?"

"Sorry."

"All clear at the back of the bus?"

"All clear," Lo responded.

"Right. Stand by for take-off."

Chris eased the four throttle levers forward. The aircraft shuddered as the spinning propellers took the evening air in their angled blades, twisted it, contorted it, and hurled it behind in a blast strong enough to blow a man off his feet. The blades' power fought the inertia of thirty tons of aircraft and payload; the floor vibrated beneath the crew's feet; needles shivered behind the glass of a score of instruments. The propellers won; the bomber rolled forward, reluctantly at first, then with a certain ponderous enthusiasm.

Bob King, perched on his fold-up seat, positioned his hands behind Chris's, ready to take over the throttles when Chris let go.

With speed the airflow gained strength, enough to lift the thirty-foot-wide tailplane. The bomber accelerated, the runway swirling by on either side of the cockpit. Now Chris was able to steer with the rudders alone; he let go of the throttles and Bob's hands immediately took over, ensuring that the vibration didn't make the levers slip back.

A fine throaty bellow from the engines. All forty-eight cylinders banging away in good order. The Hally, balanced on its main wheels, picked up speed with every foot, the airspeed indicator needle quivering past sixty, sixty-five ...

Then the bomb fell out.

A 4,000-pound "cookie," it tore loose from its shackles in the bomb bay, ripped through the bomb doors, and hit the runway with a bang that could be heard in the control tower. Like a monstrous sausage, it bounced on the concrete, half turned and neatly removed the port tailplane complete with fin and rudder, missing Lo's rear turret by a matter of inches.

In the cockpit Chris didn't know what was wrong. There was no time for anyone to tell him. No time to calculate how much of the 6,120 feet of runway remained before the barbed wire fence and the ditch and the York Road. No time for a rational decision. Instinct took over. Chop throttles. Brakes. A bang and a bounce and the aircraft was slithering off the runway onto the grass, dragging the remains of its tail unit along, a disconsolate collection of wires and tubes.

The crew wore the bemused expressions of men who weren't at all sure why they were alive.

"We nearly got blown to kingdom come," declared Ted Buckman in aggrieved tones.

"I saw the sod bounce," said Marty. "Turned over and over. Had a big dent where it landed on the runway."

"Suppose we'd just become airborne when the thing fell out."

"Then the Skipper's landing would have been even worse than usual," said Roger.

"But not much," said Chris. One had to treat such happenings as lightly as possible. It was expected. No matter that one's heart still pounded like a pneumatic drill and one's hands had a disturbing tendency to wobble even when parked in one's pockets.

There would be a full investigation, said the Flight Commander. But he couldn't believe it was the result of anyone's sloppiness. The armourers were such good types, weren't they? Gremlins, no doubt; little swine.

"You *knew*," said Chris over a cup of tea in the Mess.

"Not exactly," Lo replied.

"Did you know it was going to be on the take-off run?"

"Of course not. Like I said, it was just a feeling . . . a sort of uneasiness."

"Do you ever get feelings about which horses will win races?"

Lo shook his head, not smiling.

The station dance band roared into "Bugle Call Rag" to enthusiastic applause from the audience.

"They're terrific," said Marty.

"The saxes are out of tune," said Roger. "It's the first tenor, I think."

Poor Roger, his ear was too good. He admitted it. Quite spoiled his enjoyment of all but the most excellent of musicians.

Chris had a dance with a somewhat hefty local lass who kept humming the tune in his ear and whose hands were hot and damp. Then he danced with a WAAF who was marvellously adept at keeping herself a safe distance from him, as if afraid that he was suffering from some communicable disease.

"Not much in the way of crumpet tonight," observed Ted, taking a drag at his Woodbine, then picking minute fragments of tobacco from his lower lip.

"A dearth of delectable darlings," said Roger.

"All the best-looking popsies go in the Wrens. I've always said so."

The band slowed the tempo down with "Long Ago and Far Away."

Chris saw her and the Warrant Officer at the same instant. He had to move fast to beat the WO.

"Care to dance?"

She smiled and her eyes sparkled. Chris liked that; some girls smiled with their lips only, as if just the bottom half of their face were alive.

Grand, the way she fitted into his arms; one couldn't help but think she was pleased to be there.

"The band's in fine form tonight," Chris observed. He wished he could think of something more original to say.

"They're awfully good."

Pleasantly modulated voice with a charming hint of huskiness.

Quick breath to bolster his courage.

"My name's Chris Warren."

"Phoebe Webb."

"Would you like a drink?"

The funny thing was, she glanced down at the pilot's wings on his chest, as if she was having the conversation with them. Then she looked up and smiled.

"All right. Thanks."

The slightly out-of-tune saxes wheezed into silence.

Chris and Phoebe made their way to the refreshment counter.

"Champagne? Cognac? Dear me, all they have is lemonade."

"War is hell," she said.

"Have you been here long?"

"About half an hour."

He laughed. "At the station, not the dance."

She smiled, a broad, generous smile. Delightful, how those intriguing little wrinkles appeared at the corners of her eyes when she smiled. "About four months. You?"

"Nearly two months. It seems longer. I feel as if I've been here all my life."

She nodded. "I've heard other people say that . . . aircrew types."

"Something to do with flying ops, I suppose."

"Perhaps."

"Can I have another dance when you've finished your lemonade?"

"If you like."

"I do like."

Dancing to "South of the Border," "Ida," and "42nd Street" he found out that she worked in Sick Quarters, that she liked Bing Crosby's singing and Harry James's trumpet, that she had had her tonsils out three years before, that her cousin Dave was in the Tank Corps, that she was reading *Crime and Punishment* and finding it hard going, that her favourite colour was brown, that she had a pound note stolen last week in the Waafery.

The following evening they went to the camp cinema and had a few drinks in The White Rose and The George; they spent a Sunday in Scarborough five days later.

Chris wrote to his parents about the "simply wizard" girl he had met; he hoped they would meet her one day (that would make them sit up and take notice; he'd never suggested that they should meet any girl of his acquaintance – not that there had been that many).

Lo came down with the measles.

It seemed mildly funny until they were briefed to go to Leverkusen with a lugubrious individual named Vernon Snook occupying the rear turret.

Fortunately, no Jerry fighters came near. The Jerries kept their distance the next night too when Berlin was the target and where Bomber Command lost 56 four-engined bombers, the worst loss of the war to that date.

In the morning Chris went to Sick Quarters to see Lo. And Phoebe.

She said, "Your friend's coming along nicely. But you can't see him; he's in quarantine."

"I've never heard of a Red Indian getting measles."

"You have now."

"How long will he be in?"

"About a week, I believe."

"Tell him we've got a chap called Snook taking his place."

"Snook?"

"Snook. Somehow it's hard to have confidence in a rear gunner called Snook. Care for a film this evening?"

The camp cinema was playing an Abbott and Costello comedy. Chris didn't pay much attention to the screen; he was content sitting in the darkness beside Phoebe and listening to her laugh. She had a distinctive laugh, clear and compelling, a challenge to anyone within earshot not to laugh along with her.

It was a fine evening. They walked hand in hand beyond the hangars along the gravel path, which must have been put down to go somewhere, but now simply disappeared in the long grass near the barbed wire that separated the aerodrome from a turnip field.

They kissed. She told him about once being engaged to a bomb-aimer named Don Flinders. About him getting the chop.

"Too bad," said Chris, glad that Flinders had got the chop and ashamed of being glad.

"I thought I should tell you."

"I'm glad you did," Chris lied.

"Then there was a Canadian. He got banged up pretty badly and they sent him home. I swore I'd never get involved with an aircrew type again. For obvious reasons."

"Of course. I understand."

He wondered; was she telling him this to say she regretted getting involved with him? Or was it that she had no intention of getting more deeply involved? He didn't pursue the point. Let nature take its course. A singular girl, Phoebe, she always seemed to be thinking about something. She thought more than she talked. Which was a change from the norm, in Chris's experience. Babble machines, most of the girls of his acquaintance.

Nuremberg, Mönchengladbach, then Berlin again. Forty-seven bombers went down on the Berlin trip, the poor old lumbering Stirlings suffering the most. Chris's aircraft was unscathed. But it made you wonder. A couple of dozen Berlin trips and Bomber Command might cease to be.

Chris called in at Sick Quarters. Lo would be out of quarantine the next day, he was told.

Phoebe was at her desk; a male orderly was in the office too, sorting through file folders, looking as if the files had a disagreeable smell.

She smiled in a tight, guarded way.

"We've been rather busy," Chris said.

"I heard."

"But we're stood down now," he added quietly.

A touch of colour at her cheek-bone. Sorry, she was on duty this evening. She didn't know how she could get out of it.

Damn and double damn. How sorry was she? Did she ache like he ached?

He had a couple of beers too many at the Mess and got into an argument with a Jamaican gunner, about socialism of all things.

Afterwards, Chris couldn't remember whether he had been for or against.

In the morning his eyes were heavy-lidded and his tongue furry. He couldn't face breakfast; Ted promised to bring him a cup of tea from the Mess. While Chris was lying in bed, waiting for his tea, Lo walked in.

"Feeling all right now?" Chris enquired.

"Fine," said Lo.

"Fit for ops?"

Lo nodded.

Chris nodded too. The last few ops had been nerve-wracking with friend Snook in the tail.

Bob said, "Someone in the Mess was saying that they're pulling Hallies and Stirlings off the Berlin raids."

"Thank Christ for that. The Lancs can have Berlin and welcome."

"You didn't miss much," Chris told Lo.

"Five trips," said Lo. He would have to make them up with other crews; it was the system. Ted returned from the Mess with a cup of tepid tea and the morning's *Express*. He thrust it in front of Chris.

"We're famous. Or Lo is."

A typical morale-booster of a story, designed and fabricated for the home front consumption: BOMBER COMMAND'S WONDER GUNNER IS RED INDIAN. The story had been reprinted from a Toronto paper, the work of one C. F. Myers.

"That was the bloke who came and interviewed Lo."

"The all-wise one," Chris murmured. "Let Lo read it. It's all about him."

Lo was lying on his bunk. He shrugged, apparently not interested.

Chris tossed the paper to him; it opened up and fluttered to the floor like a wounded bird.

"Here you are, old chap. The gospel according to Saint Cal."

Lo took the paper. He read the story, shaking his head once or twice as if embarrassed by the flamboyance of the press. Then, abruptly, his face darkened. He glared at Chris.

"How did the son of a bitch find out?"

"Find out what?"

Lo didn't reply. He sprang to his feet and went storming out of the hut, slamming the door behind him. Chris saw him hurrying past a window, bareheaded, black hair tangled by a stiff breeze. He went off toward the hangars, half walking, half running.

"What's the matter with him?"

"Did they misspell 'Wigwam'?" enquired Roger.

Chris picked up the paper. Had he missed something the first time he had read the article? It was the usual stuff: miraculous eyesight, incredible ability to compute the angles and deflections instantaneously, one-in-a-million aim; Myers said all the things that had been said God only knows how many times before. Then it made sense. Myers concluded the story: "He's a dedicated man, this native son of Canada, dedicated to the destruction of the German air force. But if he's a terror in the air, he's the model of sobriety on the ground. No wild sprees for Cornelius Brand. He never turns up for briefing suffering from a hangover – for one very good reason: he never touches alcohol. Cornelius has no intention of letting John Barleycorn destroy his life as it destroyed his father's, a hopeless alcoholic . . ."

Bloody hell. Chris remembered the chat with Myers.

He scrambled into some clothes and went off in pursuit of Lo.

He caught up with him outside the Armoury.

"They'll be after you for being improperly dressed."

Lo turned. "What?"

"You forgot your cap. I brought it . . ."

Lo took the cap and turned away.

"I had no idea he was going to write . . ."

But Lo wasn't listening. He strode away, his tie flapping behind him like a pennant.

Damn and double damn. Chris cursed himself. Idiotic of him to babble about Lo's father to someone like Cal Myers. They loved a bit of dirt, those wretched newspapermen. It didn't matter to them what troubles their stories caused.

With a sigh, Chris retraced his steps. On the way a voice hailed him, a strident voice. It belonged to the Station Warrant Officer, a bristly old sweat who, it was said, had once occupied a bed-space next to Lawrence of Arabia when the latter was Aircraftman Ross.

"You're improperly dressed, Flight Sergeant. Your head's bloody *naked*."

"What?" Chris touched his head. "So it is – "

"Bloody poor example for the men."

"You see, I was actually taking another fellow's cap to him – "

It didn't seem worth explaining.

The SWO grumped something about sloppy bloody aircrew disgracing the King's uniform.

Chris said he wouldn't let it happen again.

After lunch Chris made his way to Sick Quarters. There she was, busy with her files as usual. She looked up as he entered.

"I was wondering if you'd care to step out somewhere tonight."

The touch of colour had returned to her cheek-bones.

"I'm sorry, Chris. I can't."

"Are you on duty again?"

She shook her head. A quick breath. She looked straight at him. "Actually I'm going out with someone else."

His innards seemed to slump, as if a supporting membrane had snapped.

He tried to nod matter-of-factly; it was expected. The luck of the game. All's fair, etcetera.

He heard himself talking about some other time.

She said something non-committal. He turned and stumped out of the building into a heavy shower.

Bloody women. Bloody weather.

The clouds dispersed late in the afternoon, revealing a serene panoply of blue; the air was soft and sweet.

Chris went down to the village with Ted Buckman. They had a pint or two in The White Rose, then went to the Rialto and saw *Foreign Correspondent*, Chris for the second time, Ted for the third. On the way back to the field they passed the bus stop. A bus was just pulling in from York.

Lo and Phoebe got off, hand in hand.

The Flight Commander scratched his neck; his collar seemed to be irritating him. "They're asking us about Brand."

"They?"

"The Canadians." The Flight Commander found another bit of neck to scratch. "They seem to be awfully interested in him. They want to make a big thing of him at home." He sighed as if the notion distressed him. "Red Indian comes off the prairies to fight in European skies; that sort of bilge."

"He's never been to the prairies, sir."

"He hasn't? I thought that was where Indians came from." The Flight Commander's fingers drummed on his desk top. Someone in the Mess had said that the poor blighter was beginning to get the twitch. It was to be hoped that he would stop flying before it was too late. "Anyway, prairies or not, the feeling is that he's good for the war effort. Visiting factories. Talking on the wireless. You know the sort of thing."

"Yes, sir, and I'm sure he'd do it admirably."

The Flight Commander raised an enquiring eyebrow. "But I think they're a bit concerned."

"Concerned, sir?"

"About how he might, well, *behave*."

"You mean, they're afraid he might disgrace them?"

Another sigh. "I wouldn't put it like that." The Flight Commander sniffed. "But yes, that's the general idea."

Chris shrugged. "Do they want our opinion?"

"More or less. You're his skipper. You seem to know him better than anyone else. And he regards you very highly, I'm told."

I wonder, Chris thought. He said, "I can't pretend to be an expert on Indians. Lo is the only one I've ever met. And as far as I'm concerned he's a very bright type indeed. He handles himself with a great deal of natural dignity. He's shy, though; I think he still finds some of our ways rather odd. But that's not a drawback, is it? Far better to have a chap who's a bit shy than someone who's spouting off all the time. I'd say he would handle any publicity duties admirably."

And, Chris added to himself, if he gets sent off to do publicity he'll be out of the picture as far as Phoebe is concerned.

Lo damaged a 190 over Hannover. There were no ops for a few days while fog shrouded the field. Chris had an interview for a commission; the interviewing officer seemed only interested in knowing what sports he enjoyed and whether any members of his family had been commissioned officers.

The next morning Chris was summoned to the CO's office. The Flight Commander and Simon Coombs, the Adj, were already there.

"This bloody man Brand," said the CO, "is rapidly becoming a pain in the neck."

"Sir?"

"Well, what the blazes would you call it?"

The Adj interjected, "Sir, I wonder if Flight Sergeant Warren is aware of what has happened?"

The CO glared at Chris. his expression seeming to indicate that if Flight Sergeant Warren didn't know what had happened he bloody well should know.

"Brand was involved in a fight – a *brawl* – with a civilian. Know anything about it?"

"No sir."

"*Christ*." The CO shook his head, emitting a vast sigh. "A reporter from the local paper, the Rocklington Weekly Bloody *Clarion*. I mean, the cretin can't just have a fight with a dustman, no, he has to take on a newspaper reporter. Does our cause no end of bloody good with the community, wouldn't you say?"

"Sir, may I ask what happened?"

The CO referred the question to the Adj with a flick of his hand.

The Adj said, "Sergeant Brand had been addressing the

local scout troop. He's talked to them on two or three occasions, I understand. Apparently he's most popular. Indian folklore and all that kind of thing. I spoke to a Mr Patchett. He's full of praise for what Sergeant Brand has done. This man Patchett thought it would be a good thing to get the local paper involved. But Sergeant Brand objected when the reporter wanted to take his picture."

"He doesn't seem to like having his photograph taken."

"Who does?" snapped the CO.

"Who indeed?" asked the Adj.

The CO clicked his tongue, fingering his moustache. "What is it with Brand, Indian voodoo or something? Bad luck to have your picture taken?"

"I don't think North American Indians are interested in voodoo," said Chris. "It's simply that Lo – Sergeant Brand – has had a couple of bad experiences with photographers recently. He's got the idea that they are all trying to make fun of him. Sergeant Brand is really an awfully good type. But he flares up when he thinks his dignity is being jeopardized."

"*Dignity*," hissed the CO, apparently finding it inconceivable that a mere sergeant should concern himself with dignity. "Where is Brand now?"

"In the police station, sir."

"*Christ*." Another tug at the moustache. He turned to the Adj. "Go down there and talk to them, there's a good fellow. And perhaps Warren should go along. Let's see if we can settle the thing, nip it in the bud before it's blown out of all bloody proportion."

It took hours. The police were willing to forget the incident, but the reporter, one Wilfred Moon, was less amenable. He kept dabbing at his bruised eye and declaring that in *his* day such a vicious assault on a civilian would have been a court martial offence. He was a skinny man with large ears.

"Sergeant Brand has been under an awful lot of strain recently," said Chris.

"So has my Wilfred," chimed in Mrs Moon, who was as well-upholstered as her husband was lean. "Deadlines, day after day, it's cruel, I can tell you."

Mr Patchett materialized from time to time to click his tongue and say how regrettable it all was.

"Actually," said Chris, "I think it can truthfully be said that you, Mr Moon, have a lot in common with Sergeant Brand. You have to contend with tremendous pressures, abnormal strain. It's not just the members of the armed forces who suffer war wounds, Mr Moon. It might truthfully be said that that bruise is as much a war wound as the trauma suffered by Sergeant Brand since that cannon shell so nearly ended his life just a couple of nights ago. Such happenings take their toll, Mr Moon, just as your deadlines do."

Mr Moon nodded. "Aye, you're right there, lad."

"But it's no excuse," said Mrs Moon.

"Heavens, no."

"After all, I only wanted him to slink – "

"*Slink!*"

"Aye. He'd been doing it not five minutes before, showing the lads how wolves slink between the trees. I thought to meself: That'd make a grand picture. But I'd no sooner mentioned the idea than he was getting nasty, quite nasty, telling me to butt out or some such thing. Then this. Assault and ruddy battery."

"Unprovoked," added Mrs Moon.

"Most regrettable," murmured Mr Patchett.

In the end Mr Moon decided not to press charges, but he asked that Sergeant Brand be informed in no uncertain terms as to the identity of the enemy.

"I was just doing me job, nowt more or less."

Lo was released. He was sullen and uncommunicative all the way back to the field.

An odd bird, Lo. When Mr Patchett had first proposed the idea of his addressing the local scouts he had refused out of hand; the very thought of it seemed to appal him. But now it became apparent that he had been talking at scout meetings for several weeks and enjoying himself no end, regaling the Yorkshire youngsters with stories about Indian life and legends about the glory days before the white man came. Typically, he hadn't mentioned it to anyone on the crew.

Nor did Chris's intervention in the Mr Moon crisis help heal the rift between them. Lo behaved as if Chris had ceased to exist. In the air he addressed him as "Pilot" rather than "Skipper."

Chris's commission came through at last. He was given six days' leave to get kitted out.

He telephoned Anne and told her about his commission.

"How nice for you," she said. She might have been talking about winning a raffle at the local hop.

"I just got home on leave. I was hoping we might see something of one another."

"Ah."

"Ah?"

"If only you'd told me earlier."

"I didn't know I was coming. The air force is like that."

"Godfrey Ramsay is on leave. A captain. You know him of course. No? Such an amusing fellow. You'd like him enormously."

"I'm sure I would," lied Chris.

He met a girl named Marigold at a dance. She had a sexy mouth and heavy-lidded eyes that Chris found stimulating. She liked him, there simply wasn't any doubt about that. The way she nestled in his arms, the way her hand worked against his; in fact it was more than just liking; it was a definite *yen*. She invited him back to her place "for a night cap." He said yes, thrilled by the promise of the words "night" and "cap." An expensive taxi ride later he discovered that she was the mother of two with a husband in the Tank Corps serving on the Western Desert.

He was a failure with women, that was the truth of it. Perhaps Bob King was right; it was a great big propaganda campaign with the entire female sex advertising themselves as cuddly playthings when the reality was that they were simply following nature's dictates, cynically using every one of their not-inconsiderable store of wiles to trap providers for their offspring. It was time males woke up and protested, Bob said.

Back from leave, Chris moved into the officers' accommodations, sharing a room with a South African navigator who had a surfeit of girlfriends. The fellow got perfumed letters in every post; Chris guessed that he was corresponding with at least a dozen of them. Every spare moment was occupied in letter-writing, brows furrowed as he tried to remember what he had promised to whom. Chris found the whole business of sex quite bewildering and distressing. Perhaps the monks had something after all.

They bombed the marshalling yards at Cannes in bright moonlight. On the way home a Jerry attacked but Lo warned Chris in time; a violent corkscrew confused the fighter. He disappeared in the darkness.

"Thanks, Rear Gunner," said Chris.

"Okay, Pilot," said Lo.

The next day a Canadian war photographer arrived to take more pictures of Lo. But Lo wasn't to be found. The photographer went away, muttering about the awful consequences of insulting the fourth estate. But he was back the next day and clicked away at Lo and the others as they prepared for an op.

The target was Mannheim, the next night Leverkusen. Every op was different yet grindingly the same. The same cycle of briefing, testing, waiting, flying, being scared, being thankful, being bored. Emotions seemed to blend like colours on an artist's palette, intermingling until there was only one. Opsession, Chris called it, a state just a few shakes short of the twitch.

He was sleeping badly. His dreams were full of blazing aircraft and foggy runways. He found himself becoming resigned to death, asking only whether it would come on the next op or the one after that. Yet one could never reveal such fears; they were secrets for the empty minutes at night when one was alone, unprotected by the collective courage of the others.

Then, suddenly, there were only two ops to go.

He encountered Phoebe one windy afternoon on the cinder path leading to Sick Quarters.

She saluted and smiled.

"Congratulations, sir."

"On what?"

"On your commission."

"Oh, that. I think the food was better in the Sergeants' Mess."

"I was hoping I'd run into you, sir."

His heart skipped a beat. "Well, here I am."

"It's about Cornelius."

The heart that skipped now slumped. For an instant he had thought she wanted to pick up things where they had been so unceremoniously deposited.

"What about him?"

"He's awfully worried about these plans for publicity, travelling all over Canada. Perhaps he's mentioned it to you."

"Not so far."

She nodded. An errant curl bounced in the wind.

"He keeps things to himself. Very intense, isn't he?"

"Very."

"I was hoping you might talk to him, sir."

Irritating, the way she kept saying "sir." Was it her way of keeping the conversation on a strictly official basis?

Chris said, "Lo and I don't talk."

"Pardon?"

"A difference of opinion. Hasn't he told you about it?"

"No."

"That's what you get with intense types. What was it you wanted me to talk to him about?"

"He hates this whole publicity business. It's an insult, he says. They're talking about sending him back to Canada and making him into some sort of national hero. He says it's the guilty conscience of the Canadian government; they want to cover up the rotten things they've done to the Indians for generations by making a fuss of one just because he happens to be a good shot."

"Better than nothing, isn't it?"

"What do you mean?"

"Well, surely it's preferable to the government ignoring him and what he's done."

"He doesn't see it quite like that."

"He wouldn't."

"It's a serious thing with him. It's a worry."

"He'll get over it. Celebrities do."

She frowned. "Thank you for your time, sir."

"Don't mention it."

A snappy salute and she went on her way, striding along with that beautifully balanced rhythm of hers.

Chris sighed as he watched her. He had handled the encounter with all his customary skill and aplomb.

There was a lull of almost a week while rain pelted down, turning the airfield into a quagmire. Two ops were scheduled, then cancelled, making everyone irritable and frustrated.

Then they flew to Berlin and narrowly escaped extinction by collision. A Lancaster swerved suddenly, its rear guns scraping the Halifax's nose. The Lanc disappeared into the darkness.

When they landed the crew examined the scars in the conical Perspex nose. A near thing. Hideously near.

"Wonder what happened to the Lanc."

"Easy to find out. Ring all the Lanc squadrons and ask who got back with bent tail guns."

"Probably didn't get back at all," said Roger. "I'd wager the pilot got hit. That's why it swerved. Kites don't swerve if their pilots are okay."

"Another few feet and he'd have gone right into us," observed Bob.

Marty said, "No, Lo would've shot him down before he hit us, wouldn't you, old cock?"

He turned but Lo was nowhere to be seen.

"Not very matey these days, is he?"

Roger said, "It's because he and the Skipper are competing for the same woman."

Chris felt his cheeks flush. "Nothing of the sort. Lot of rot. Can't imagine what put that idea in your head. Pure flight of fancy."

"Wasn't there a lady in *Hamlet* who protested too much?" enquired Roger as they went to the Crew Room.

The next morning Chris's name was again on the Battle Order.

The last trip. *If* the weather held. *If* the aircraft remained serviceable. *If* Butch Harris didn't change his mind at the last minute.

They did their night-flying test and found trouble with the Gee set. The radar mechanics promised to have the repairs completed in a jiffy.

Chris collapsed in an easy chair and finished *The Good Companions*. It took him an hour. He wished he had more to read. He would miss Priestley's characters; they had become good and reliable friends who had seen him through some trying moments. But if he got the chop he would at least have the satisfaction of knowing what happened to Jess Oakroyd, Miss Trant, and Inigo Jollifant.

He wandered down to the Flight Office.

Roger was there, talking to an Australian navigator who had just arrived on the station.

Roger introduced Chris to the new arrival. The Aussie seemed to find it incredible that he was talking to airmen who were about to depart on the last trip of their tour.

"Just take them one at a time, old chap," said Roger.

Does one have any choice? Chris wondered silently.

"By the way," said Roger, "Lo had to go and see the CO."

"What for?"

"Haven't a clue. Another gong perhaps."

Bob came in. The bowsers were filling the tanks to the brim. It was going to be a long trip.

Chris stood up, intending to go for a walk. Walks were good when you had too much time before an op.

The door burst open and Lo entered, brows dark.

"Bastards," he hissed.

"Can we take it you're not entirely pleased about something?" Roger enquired.

"Son of a bitch."

"The CO?"

Lo shook his head. "Another one. A Wingco. I hate guys like him. He wouldn't have said hullo to me back home. Wouldn't have known I was alive. But now it's all goddam smiles. What a hell of a time we're going to have travelling all over the place together, talking on the radio, meeting the press. Now all of a sudden we're buddies! Makes you sick!"

"Never mind, old son," Roger said, "you'll be far too busy fighting off all those adoring females to worry about that chap."

"Will you send your rejects over to me?" Norman enquired.

They ran up the engines. The aircraft quivered as if eager to be on its way. Pressures and temperatures okay. Chris shut down. The engines spluttered into silence. The crew clambered out and stood on the concrete hardstanding.

"I shall miss these little gatherings," said Roger, "but not very much."

Bob said he heard of a fellow who waited two months to do his last trip. "He got ill. Flu or something. The rest of his crew went off without him. He had to wait behind until someone needed a spare wireless op. It took two months. The poor chap was almost a mental case by the time he finally did it."

"He got back all right?"

"I never thought to ask."

"Who's this?"

They turned as a pair of staff cars arrived at the dispersal.

"Jeez, it's him," hissed Lo.

The CO's companion was a Canadian, a Wing Commander, a burly man with a wide smile. He met each member of the crew in turn, wishing them good fortune on their last trip. A pretty harmless-looking type in Chris's opinion, even if the smile was a bit mechanical. A couple of NCOs unloaded camera equipment from the second car.

"I'm sure you won't mind if we take a couple of shots while you're getting set to take off. It'll make a real fine piece of footage for the newsreels. And I shouldn't think you fellers will mind being seen over half of the world."

"Only half, sir?" asked Roger.

"Tell you what, if it turns out real well we'll go for Russian, Chinese, and South American distribution too. What d'you say?"

The CO had the mechanics look busy tinkering with the engines and polishing windows while the aircrew stood in a self-conscious little group and pretended to discuss the forthcoming trip. The camera turned.

"Seems like quite a nice bloke," said Norman, nodding his head sideways toward the Canadian Wing Commander.

"He's a parasite," said Lo.

"He's only doing his job," said Norman.

"So's Hitler," Lo replied.

Bob said, "They're just showing you off a bit. Can't see the harm in that."

"You would if you were standing where I am."

Marty said, "You're a puzzling sod, Lo, you know that? If I were you I'd just relax and enjoy it."

"But you're not me."

"Anyway," said Ted, "it's nice to think that our families could be going to the pictures and could see us, all of us, standing here, chatting. Makes you think, doesn't it?"

Roger said, "I can hear the announcer now: 'Intrepid aviators prepare to do battle with the King's enemies.'"

The white flare went wriggling into the sky.

"Go get 'em, guys," exhorted the Wing Commander, grinning.

Chris glanced at Lo. His innards lurched. Was it his imagination or did Lo have the same wary expression he had the evening the bomb fell out during take-off?

Up through the pitch-black night, navigation lights blinking on wingtips as they passed through the scattered cloud that had persisted all day. Everyone aboard was on the lookout for aircraft from the airfields that dotted the Vale of York. On ops nights far too many kites wallowed about in the darkness overburdened with fuel and bombs. God knows why there weren't more collisions. Perhaps one night there would be an enormous smashing-together of umpteen Hallies and Lancs. What a hell of a bang there would be as all their bomb loads went off simultaneously.

The target was Frankfurt.

Greyness flowed past the cabin windows. One hoped it was unoccupied greyness. The aircraft was just back from a major overhaul. X-X Ray. A good kite. Senior crews got the best kites. Soon the squadron would be re-equipped with the new Hercules-engined Hallies, faster and capable of flying higher than these old Mark IIs. No longer would the Lancs have the top spots all to themselves. X-X Ray had done more than fifty ops. Strange, how some kites survived only a few trips. Others kept soldiering on, accumulating rows of bomb silhouettes on their flanks, each signifying a raid (ice cream silhouettes signifying Italian targets). Some aircraft, like X-X Ray, acquired reputations for invulnerability. It was a major blow to everyone's sense of the order of things when such a kite went for a Burton.

The cloud dropped away. The Hally's nose thrust itself at the panoply of stars. After the fear of collision, total loneliness. No – another kite ahead, a vague shape in the darkness off to port. Chris relaxed. His world was in good order. For the moment. Kite functioning well. Her controls were light and responsive – as light and responsive as a Hally was capable of being. Odd how individual aircraft varied. One might tend to fly with a wing slightly low (or it would *feel* as if it was low) no matter how diligently the fitters adjusted ailerons and tabs. Another kite might have controls that felt oddly "soft"; movements of the column or rudder would have no effect for a fraction of a second, invariably creating disquieting visions of control cables stretching, fraying . . .

Although Lo had missed a few trips mid-way through the tour, he was to be screened with the rest. Then a commission and off to Canada and the hero treatment. Poor blighter, he hated the thought. Most chaps would revel in it. But not Lo. Typical of fate to choose the wrong chap.

Chris checked with the crew. Everyone present and correct. Already Ted was passing new wind gen to Roger. The

Met blokes had cocked up the job. As per usual. The aircraft at the head of the stream were calculating winds and sending the data back to England; diligent clerks were working out averages and sending them out to the stream for all the navigators to use; important to keep the stream intact. Once the aircraft began straying they became more vulnerable.

They crossed the North Sea without seeing it. According to the Met man, the cloud could break up near the target.

"Enemy coast in five minutes, Skipper."

A tightening of half a dozen nerves somewhere down in the region of the solar plexus. Sometimes the most wearying part of ops seemed to be the constant battle with fears real and imagined. Curious, the stages of an operational tour. For the first few trips you were almost resigned to the chop; there seemed no chance of surviving this lunatic business. Then with experience came a modicum of confidence. Quickly followed by over-confidence. You had got the hang of it all. You knew the ropes. You thought. Then came Opsession, a sort of numbness, a zombielike state in which you felt resigned to the inevitable, oddly disconnected with events. But towards the end of the tour you started to know the old fears all over again. A second operational virginity, someone called it.

Flak. Familiar crackling sores in the darkness ahead, each telling of the operation of a clockwork fuse setting off an explosion that converted an eighteen-pound 88 mm shell into a couple of thousand chunks of shrapnel. Any one of them was lethal up to a hundred yards – or even more if your luck happened to run out that night.

"Coast coming up," Roger announced.

The tour seemed to have taken a major part of his life. In reality it had only been a matter of months, yet pre-tour life had a strangely shadowy quality in his memory. It was as if it hadn't been completely real, just a sort of rehearsal for the real thing. This.

Tomorrow night there would be a party. The end-of-tour party. The White Rose would probably be the location; the ground crew would be invited as would be any and all girlfriends. Perhaps Lo would bring Phoebe. No, he might invite her, but she would refuse. Almost certainly.

Crew check. Everyone present and accounted for.

Dangerous to start thinking about end-of-tour parties. A hell of a long way to go before this trip would be over and done with. A bugger, getting Frankfurt for a final trip. The squadron usually lost at least one aircraft per Frankfurt op.

"Aircraft going down to port."

"Poor sod."

Poor sod indeed; the flames seemed to bubble out of the kite as it plunged.

"No chutes so far."

One kept hoping.

Roger provided a change of course. Another thing to keep hoping was that all the navigators in the stream were providing their skippers with the same course at the same time.

"Right, everyone, I'm turning now. Eyes wide open, if you please."

Look until your eyes hurt because the sky is full of aircraft and we don't want to wander into any of them.

The intercom was silent as they headed across Germany.

Yet another thing to hope for was that the diversionary activities, if any, were brilliantly successful. What had they said about it at briefing? Chris couldn't remember. He had attended so many briefings that he automatically shut out the gen that wasn't of direct concern.

The minutes ticked by.

All quiet at present. A stately procession through the night sky. Hundreds of aircraft all around, yet as a rule the only ones you saw were the poor blighters in trouble.

"Ten minutes to target."

Crew check. Everyone still present and accounted for. The endless scanning of the instrument panel: bottom left to top left, then across to the right and back down to the bottom left to start the process all over again.

Ted called over the intercom; did Chris want him to come back to the astro dome?

Chris said yes. Over the target area it was a good idea to have an extra pair of eyes on lookout duty.

Ted's slight figure, bulky in flying gear and parachute harness, emerged from the depths of the nose. His gloved hand signalled thumbs-up as he squeezed past.

The clouds were thickening again.

"Target ahead," Roger announced, managing as usual to sound slightly bored. Roger seldom moved from his navigation table; he said he preferred not to see what was going on outside. He said, in his dry-as-dust way, that by concentrating on his sums he would keep his sanity twenty-three per cent longer than those who looked outside.

The fighters swarmed in, dropping flares that lit great avenues in the sky. A Lancaster broke up ahead, burning fragments fluttering earthward like bits of fireworks on Guy Fawkes night. A moment later another reared up, apparently undamaged; it hung on its props as Chris's aircraft sped by, then went tumbling away to disappear in the clouds.

The Pathfinders' markers sparkled then vanished into the cloud. Frankfurt was down there somewhere visible only to the aircraft with H2S sets, flickering green images on cathode ray tubes representing rivers and built-up areas.

A gentle weaving and banking to port and starboard to give the gunners a good view in every direction. Chris's mouth was dry; the oxygen tasted flat and sour. He could hear his heart thumping. At times of extreme vulnerability it seemed as if he could feel the functioning of every organ, liver, kidneys, pancreas . . .

"Hullo, Skipper." Norman's voice crackled in Chris's earphones. Norman was prostrate in the nose, eyes glued to his box of bomb-aiming tricks. "A couple of degrees right . . . hold it . . . now left-left . . . steady . . . nice."

A sort of relief to relinquish control. A time for obedience, for following the bomb-aimer's instructions. And hoping. Hoping that the flak didn't get a bead on X-X Ray while it was cruising along straight and level. Hoping that if anyone suffered a direct hit it was someone else, someone he didn't know. Not an admirable aspiration but an honest one. *Let me get through this trip. Please.*

"Steady ... that's it ... good ... "

Norman sounded like someone commenting on form at a horse show.

Chris had to fight the impulse to yell. Drop the bloody bombs and get it over with! Same old impulse; he knew it well.

How long could you continue to ignore the law of probability?

"Left-left a bit more ... "

Concentrate on the instruments. Ignore the lights, the explosions, the gunfire. Flak *and* fighters at work. Usually the flak packed up if fighters were around, and vice-versa. A mistake? A cock-up? Was some *Kapitän* frantically trying to sort out the mess?

"Steady ... yes ... bombs gone."

A marvellous moment, when the kite bucked, relieved of the weight of the bombs. The signal that duty had been done. The midway point of the trip. But before they could turn homeward, they had to fly straight and level for half a minute to give the photo flare time to fall until barometric pressure detonated the magnesium, emitting a flash of umpteen million candlepower. The resulting photograph was proof that the crew had indeed been to where they were supposed to go and had dropped their bombs more or less in the right spot.

"Okay ... let's go home."

They turned as yet another bomber was hit and went whirling earthward, shedding burning bits of itself.

So far so good. Not even a bang on the fuselage from a fragment of spent shrapnel. Crew check. Everyone okay. No problems with oxygen or intercom. It remained to be seen if the guns would work if needed. The Brownings had an unpleasant habit of freezing up when the combination of temperature and humidity was just right. The turrets had been known to freeze too. Didn't anyone mention to the designers that bombers sometimes had to operate on nasty nights in winter?

A mighty explosion to the rear. Some poor blighter got a direct hit before he'd dropped his bombs. But there was much to be said for going that way. One moment you were breathing, worrying, hoping; the next you'd got all your problems solved and you'd become a collection of bits of pulp and froth and you didn't know a thing about it.

Darkness enfolded the aircraft. Blessed darkness.

Now the whole purpose of life was to sneak home through the blackness, like a cat-burglar after his night's work.

A change of course from Roger. Six degrees. Precise type, Roger.

Bob changed fuel tanks: no doubt he was diligently noting the fact in his log.

The crew was going about its business in its quietly professional way. A grand crew; he was lucky to have joined up with them. Back in those early days he seldom let himself think that one day he might be flying the last trip of his tour. Yet here he was, the crew still intact.

He recalled Lo's expression just before take-off. Another presentiment of trouble? Or just a spot of indigestion?

Would the crew have survived this long without Lo? Probably not. He deserved all the accolades they would be handing out. The irony was he didn't want them. He just wanted to be left alone – which didn't seem an unreasonable request, did it?

Another kite going down ahead. A couple of miles away by the look of it. Pretty, the way the flames carved a path through the blackness. But singularly unpretty for any poor devils still inside.

Crew check. Everyone present and correct.

"We'll hit the coast in twenty minutes," Roger announced.

"Not too hard, I hope," said Marty.

"The strain's getting to him," said Ted. "You'd better toss him overboard."

End of chatter. Good. No need to tell them.

The automatic scanning of quivering needles and gauges. The minutes ticked by. They would breathe a little easier when they reached the coast. Over the sea they would have a cup of that revolting coffee . . .

The clouds were solid below. Good friends, the clouds, for bombers trying to get home unobserved. More than once he had flown all the way to England in clouds rather than stay with the bomber stream. But clouds could be enemies, too. Once over Nuremberg the bombers unloaded over thin cloud cover. The fires and searchlights created a sort of translucent area against which the bombers were silhouetted, dangerously visible to the fighters above. That was a near-thing night, one of God knows how many.

Lo's voice cut through his mental ramblings: "Fighter . . . let's corkscrew to port . . . *now!*"

Instant, automatic obedience. No time for questions. Time only for a heaving of the heavy controls, rudders and ailerons thrusting the kite into a violent diving turn.

"Another one!"

Marty's voice this time.

Chris heard the clatter of Brownings. He winced. Far better to evade the Jerry night-fighters than to engage them in combat. Hell's bells, things had been going so well . . .

Too well.

Little darts of light went sailing past his window to disappear in the gloom. No doubt some bastard was watching from a Lanc or Hally, thankful that the fighters were busy with some anonymous unfortunate.

"Christ, *Lo!*" Marty sounded almost hysterical. "You got 'em *both!* I swear to God . . ."

And yes, there was a glimpse of two separate plumes of fire spiralling down into the cloud. Chris saw them. Distinctly.

"You can straighten out now, Skipper," said Lo.

Skipper. Good to hear Lo say it again.

"He got *two*," said Marty. "I saw both of them. One attacked right after the other. And he had 'em both in about five seconds. Bloody beautiful!"

"Is it all clear behind now?" Chris enquired. "Any damage? Casualties?"

The crew checked in; as far as could be determined the fighters hadn't succeeded in hitting the Hally with a single shell or bullet. And both had gone down in flames to Lo's guns.

"Nice work, Lo," said Chris.

"*Nice!*" Marty squealed. "It was incredible! I've never seen anything like it!"

Roger said, "But if you get three, Lo, we'll be obliged to consider it showing off."

"Let's keep our eyes peeled," Chris told them. "How long to the coast, Roger?"

"Six minutes."

They flew in silence for a couple of minutes.

Then Ted said, "Christ, Lo, wait till you tell 'em what you did. That Wing Commander will go bonkers! You'll be all over the front pages!"

"Okay, let's cut the chatter," said Chris.

He knew how they felt, but it was dangerous to clog the intercom; there could still be fighters in the vicinity.

Far to the left a couple of searchlights pierced the night sky. The clouds were starting to break up now. Which was a change; usually when the weather was reasonably good over the target it was far worse over England.

"Coast in two minutes."

One hundred and twenty seconds.

Chris heard a crackle in his earphone.

"Skipper?"

Lo's voice.

"Yes, Lo."

"I wanted to tell you. My Mom saw that story. She wasn't mad. She said it was the truth."

"What?" For a moment Chris thought he was dreaming, hearing things.

"It's been nice knowing you, all of you. But I'm not sticking around for that publicity crap. I won't give 'em the satisfaction. Know what I mean?" He sounded cheerful, almost light-hearted. "Marty can watch out for you the rest of the way home. You guys were okay. So long."

"Lo . . ."

He felt the kite shift its stance in the air.

Marty said, "I think he jumped."

"You think he *what?*"

"I saw him. Just for an instant. Then he was gone."

Chris gulped. He told Bob to go back to the tail and check on Lo's turret. He thought momentarily of diving and turning. But what would it achieve? Even if by some chance they saw Lo dangling at the end of his parachute they could do nothing; they couldn't communicate with him or snatch him back into the aircraft.

"Roger, have we crossed the coastline?"

"Just going over now."

There was a good chance that Lo would get down on dry land. But there was an equally good chance that the bloody fool could drift out to sea.

Bob's voice came over the intercom.

"Tail turret's empty, Skipper."

Chris nodded. He wondered how he would break the news to the CO and the Canadian Wing Commander.

The Bomb-Aimer

PRECISELY AT MIDNIGHT, WHEN THE ENGLISH COAST WAS only a matter of minutes away, the Skipper called Taffy:

"Priority message!" He sounded tense and urgent. Then he chuckled. "Happy birthday. And many of them!"

All the crew followed suit, one after the other, laughing and wishing Taffy many happy returns – which for a member of a bomber crew was just about the warmest wish there was, they all agreed on that.

Mike, the navigator, turned and patted him on the back; Ken, the wireless operator, raised his coffee mug in salute.

From his perch in the tail, Jake said, "You're a man now, mate. Twenty-one years old. And that means you can't leave your wick-dipping any longer."

Taffy grinned. Wicked lads, all of them, particularly Jake. But he loved them like brothers.

The coastline slid below. Only a few minutes more and they would be back at Rocklington, number twenty-four over and done with.

Taffy always stayed in the nose during landings. He enjoyed landings. He had a splendid view through the great transparent nose cone – it was like a bloody monstrous tit, Jake always said. Typical Jake. Everything reminded him of tits and other female parts. A terrible fellow, Jake, but a good soul in his own odd way. It was hard not to like him even when one's conscience gave one quite specific instruction to the contrary.

The field rolled like the deck of a ship as the Skipper banked to line up with the runway. The lights sparkled, tiny jewels in the darkness. A magical business, returning to the familiar world of shops and streets after hours of existence in a metal tube high over the world, one's very breath dependent on the oxygen system, communication courtesy of the intercom; it made one see one's world anew, gratefully, every familiar sight somehow fresh and full of interest.

"Undercart down and locked. Brakes off. Rad shutters open."

The standard litany.

The airfield was all lit up to welcome its brood back to the nest. Ahead, a Hally settled on the runway. Toylike, it went trundling along, then turned off at the first taxi-way.

Taffy yawned. It had been a long trip, the third in five nights. A bit much by anyone's standards. He would sleep for a week.

The canal slipped below, glinting dully like old pewter. A farm house, a pub – The George – favoured by some over The White Rose; the York Road along which a lone figure cycled. A bobby perhaps. Or a farm worker going off to work just as the aircrews were coming home from theirs.

It happened smoothly as if it were all intentional. A sudden tilting of the runway ahead. A burst of power. An exclamation over the intercom.

Like an enormous wall the world was on its side.

And it came straight at Taffy.

"About time," he said.

The rescue bloke looked startled. His thin-lipped mouth dropped open. "Jesus H. Christ."

Taffy forgave him. "I'm jammed. Can't move."

"Don't worry, mate. Have you out in a jiff. Injured, are you?"

"I don't think so. Just stuck. I wonder why there was no fire."

"Just be thankful."

"What about the others?"

"Shouldn't worry about them, mate. Just relax. Hey, over here, Bert! I've got one of 'em – and he's *alive!*"

The CO had visited him in Sick Quarters. Awfully bad show about the rest of the crew. Especially after twenty-four ops. Luck of the game and all that. The experts still weren't sure what had gone wrong. The most promising theory was that a flap had been the culprit, retracting on one side, stalling one wing on the round-out just before touch-down. Battle damage possibly. Full investigation of course. They would get to the bottom of it eventually. No question. In the meantime, Taffy was to take a couple of weeks' leave. Wasn't his home in North Wales? Penrhyn Bay? Splendid. Wizard part of the country. Lucky chap, going there.

But Taffy didn't go there. At York he caught the train to London. He had something to do. And London was the best place to do it. Everyone said so. The mere thought of it gave him the shivers. Shivers of delight. Shivers of guilt. And fear. This time he was definitely going to do it. Nothing would deter him. It was now or, in all likelihood, never. A prang served to remind a fellow of his mortality.

Why was he spared? It made no sense. Jake in the tail turret was killed instantly. Yet he, stuck up in the nose, of all places, came out with nothing but a few bruises and scrapes. The Skipper, Paul, Jake, Ken, Mike, and Doug . . . dead, every one of them. He still hadn't fully accepted the fact; he still expected to see them, chattering into the billet, boisterous and smelling of beer. What would happen when he got back from leave without a crew to rejoin? No doubt they would keep him around as a spare bod. Anyone whose bomb-aimer was ill would get him. Not a comforting prospect, flying with strangers. But it was the price of surviving your crew.

Dear old Jake. A good and true friend, dreadful blasphemer though he was.

"Whosoever curseth his God shall bear his sin."

He didn't mean it, Taffy explained silently.

The carriage began to fill up. A pretty Wren sat in the opposite corner of the compartment reading *Picture Post*. Perfect, heart-shaped face with delightfully bonny cheeks that looked good enough to carve up and eat. What a wonder she would look in nothing but a diaphanous nightdress . . .

No! He wouldn't permit that secret lustful self to harbour such thoughts. It was dreadfully wrong. Didn't the Bible say that whoever looked on a woman to lust after her had already committed adultery in his heart? How many times had he been guilty in his heart? If only one could discipline one's thoughts, ordering them to keep to safe, wholesome subjects. Sometimes it seemed to him that he was close to being obsessed, his evil impulses held in check by only the narrowest of margins.

An RASC corporal sat beside him and offered him a Woodbine.

"No? Sensible bloke. Coffin nails, my old woman calls 'em. On leave, are you? Can't get enough of it, can you? Stationed in these parts, are you, Sarge? Can't say it appeals to me much. Raw, that's what I call it. Raw . . . "

The corporal rambled on as more passengers boarded. At last the train pulled away.

Taffy watched the countryside rolling by and imagined himself engaging the Wren in conversation. Charming her. Winning her. Delicious imaginings. But hardly practical. Apart from the RASC corporal there was an old codger opposite, puffing on a sour-smelling pipe, and a prim-looking lady, a bit like Miss Evans, the teacher who lived on Llanrhos Road just around the corner from his parents. In order to talk to the Wren he would have to lean across the lot of them. The alternative was to step out into the corridor and suggest that she join him, perhaps by means of a cheeky toss of the head. He sighed. She didn't look like the sort of girl who would jump to her feet and go and talk to a perfect stranger. A girl like her would have dozens of boyfriends, all officers probably. Besides, it was silly, him thinking about engaging her in conversation. He was incapable of it. His brain simply would not operate at such times. It seized up.

He dozed. And dreamt that the Wren was sitting opposite him, stark naked. Beckoning. Her expression could only be described as imploring. The rattle of the train became a sort of jungle rhythm as he reached out and took her warm breasts, one in each hand . . .

He awoke suddenly, cheeks burning. Realistic, appallingly, frighteningly realistic, that dream. For a moment he thought it had actually happened. He could still *feel* the Wren's breasts. In fact, his hands, resting so innocently in his lap, were still cupped. Quickly, before anyone could see, he clasped them as if to keep them under control. Jake used to say that some breasts were like paper bags half full of water and other were like perfect peaches, soft but firm –

Shame coursed through him; if these good citizens even guessed what he was thinking, they would throw him off the train.

But no one was looking in his direction. Clearly he had only disgraced himself in that seething cesspit of a mind of his. Jake used to joke that he could tell when Taffy was having erotic dreams. Something about mumblings and tent-like projections in his bunk. The extraordinary thing was, Jake seemed to regard it all as perfectly natural, just a bit of a chuckle.

"The flesh lusteth against the Spirit, and the Spirit against the flesh."

How many times had he heard his father quoting the line? Taffy wasn't sure precisely what it meant, but the general drift wasn't hard to grasp. Whatever the details, he *felt* guilty.

Sometimes it seemed that his entire life had been a never-ending struggle with guilt. He *tried*, God knows how hard he tried to control those appalling thoughts that kept invading his mind. And yes, he felt genuine guilt. He knew it was wrong. But guilt didn't solve anything, he had discovered.

The thoughts still danced into his mind at the slightest provocation. The bewildering thing was, he felt more guilt about dropping bombs on human beings than he did about sex. But no one else seemed to think there was anything wrong with dropping bombs. Even his father.

He knew where to go in London. Jake had often talked of the place. Soho, it was called. Look for Shaftesbury Avenue. Then nip up one of the side streets. Whatever you fancy you could get there. As long as you could pay for it. It was waiting on the street. All you had to do was say what you wanted, then agree on the price. So Jake said. For the life of him Taffy couldn't imagine how one could talk business about such things.

"Got family in London, Sarge?"

"I was just . . . No."

Taffy shook his head. For the next half an hour he had to hear all about the corporal's relatives including first and second cousins and an Uncle Percy who was doing time for something done by a bloke who ran a garage in Mill Hill. The fly in the ointment was proving it, said the corporal.

At last the corporal fell silent; his head nodded, bouncing gently on his chest as the train rattled along. Only an hour to London. *"One sinner destroyeth much good."* Another favourite line of his father's. His father could look into a fellow's soul. Perhaps he sensed the sin there, seething, bubbling like something in a great iron cauldron.

Deep breath. Not far to London now; the passengers were collecting their belongings from the overhead racks. The corporal insisted on shaking hands as if they were warriors who had come through a battle together.

London teemed with people. Taffy had to push his way through the throng to get to the Underground station. He watched as the Wren was swallowed up by the mob.

He had a meal of powdered scrambled egg and chips in a café near the station. He bought an *Evening Standard* and read about the battles in Sicily and Russia. Bomber Command hit Cologne again, losing thirty aircraft. Crafty, the reporters always talking about "large forces" so that thirty didn't sound that many. But perhaps they only sent sixty. Or only forty.

A family sat at the next table: dad, mum, and a cheeky-looking lad of thirteen or fourteen with a mop of parchment-coloured hair.

"On bombers, are you?"

Taffy nodded.

"Thought so. You being a bomb-aimer. Lancs?"

Taffy shook his head.

"Halifaxes?"

Taffy nodded.

"Good kites," said the boy knowingly.

His mother shook his arm and hissed something about not troubling the gentleman. Taffy winked at the boy to tell him that it was all right and he wasn't the least bit troubled. But the boy had turned away, pouting.

He found a room in a boarding house off the Euston Road. It smelt of cabbage. The ancient landlady said he was lucky to get the room; it had been booked for weeks but had been cancelled because of a death in the family. How long would he be staying? One night only, he told her. Her heavy-lidded eyes narrowed suspiciously. For a gnawing moment he was sure she could read his mind and all the sinful thoughts within. How many airmen, soldiers, and sailors had come to her place with just such thoughts? It was a relief to get away from her and into the privacy of the little room with the single bed and the wobbly dressing table decorated by a row of cigarette burns along its edge. In the next room a man laughed, a huge, booming laugh, the sort that Paul used to emit when told a particularly juicy dirty joke.

Poor Paul. Poor Jake. And Mike. Poor all of them. How long would it be before he stopped feeling incomplete without them, as if he had lost a part of his own body?

He took his towel along the dark corridor to the bathroom. It was chilly and not very clean; the basin felt as if it had a film of grease. A spider was slithering about in the bath; experiencing difficulty in getting up the steel side. Taffy picked it up and put it on a pipe. It made off at top speed, disappearing into a crack.

Taffy turned on the tap. Plenty of cold water but nothing emerged from the hot tap. He put his tunic on and went downstairs. He explained the situation to the ancient at the desk. She nodded; quite correct. No hot water for baths until tomorrow. And then only between seven and nine in the evening. There was a war on.

He trudged upstairs and doused himself in cold water.

"Wash me thoroughly from mine iniquity and cleanse me from my sin."

The passages kept emerging from the past like old ghosts.

He brushed his hair. It was dark and thick with a neat little wave just over the forehead. He was, he supposed, a reasonably nice-looking chap. Nice-looking but so *young*. How he longed for a rugged face, a man's face, like Gary Cooper's or Humphrey Bogart's. How pleasant to earn respect instead of pats on the head. A proprietor of a pub actually had had the cheek to ask him his age, him with his aircrew badge and sergeant's stripes. For some peculiar reason the uniform and the badges only seemed to accentuate his youthful appearance; sometimes he looked like a child dressed up for a part in a play.

It was Jake who discovered that Taffy was a virgin. A very serious condition, was Jake's diagnosis, something that should be cured without delay. Did he realize that atrophy could be a problem; one couldn't leave vital organs unemployed for too long; they were liable to shrivel up and fall off. Very painful, atrophy, in that particular area. Besides, a chap couldn't get his flight-sergeant's pips without adequate proof of wick-dipping. The remarkable thing was how Jake could keep the joke going for months without ever becoming obnoxious. In an odd sort of way, Taffy felt as if he was doing this for Jake and the others as much as for himself.

He changed his underwear. The occasion seemed to call for clean. Would he have to undress with the woman looking on? He shuddered at the thought. It would be as excruciating as trying to urinate in that little container during his first medical . . .

"Going out, are you?"

Meaningful, the way the old woman asked the question.

"Whoremongers and adulterers, God will judge."

His father preached like a man possessed. Some in the parish were said to be in actual terror of him. Perhaps it was the fervour in his eyes and the way his voice crackled with righteousness. As he spoke his right forefinger probed and pointed, as if indicating where every last vestige of sin was to be found.

It was a fine evening. He made his way along the Euston Road, taking his time. No hurry. Tottenham Court Road was up that way. He could catch the Underground there; he had ascertained that much from a helpful bobby that afternoon.

He walked past the Tube station. He had plenty of time. No hurry, he told himself. Lots of shop windows to look at. He chided himself; he was lying; walking instead of taking the Tube was nothing but a cowardly device, a way of postponing the inevitable. Fear groped around his innards, poking and pushing, not in the wrenching, tearing way that it did in ops, but naggingly, persistently, never giving a fellow a moment's peace.

He had spent little time in London before today; half a day here, a couple of hours there on his way from one training establishment to another. Funny to think that at one time Chester and Bangor had seemed immense and frightening. In comparison with London they were mere villages.

His father hated the city. Any city. To him they were all evil; as a boy Taffy had thought "evilcity" a proper word.

Jake claimed to have sampled every variety of female from Polynesian to Pygmy. Jake spoke highly of Orientals; they had the right idea, he used to say; they had been trained from childhood to please the male of the species. You've got a choice, Taffy told himself – a thought that sent the umpteenth quiver of panic coursing through him. How could one *choose*? It wasn't a bakery shop, was it?

"Got a sec?"

Taffy turned, surprised. A man stood in a shop doorway, a short fellow with a wide-brimmed trilby and a twisted smile.

"Pardon?"

"Looking for a good time, cock?"

Taffy thought he said "time-clock."

"Thanks, but I have one."

He extended his wrist to display his watch.

"Gawd." The trilby shook from side to side. An impatient click of the tongue. "Welsh, aren't you? Thought so. What I'm saying, cock, is are you looking for a bit of crumpet? You know what a bit of crumpet is, don't you?"

"Yes, but . . ."

"I can put some very fancy goods your way."

"No, no thank you, no."

The padded shoulders shrugged.

"Just asking."

Taffy had hurried twenty or thirty yards before he slowed down and asked himself why he answered the man as he did. Wasn't a "bit of crumpet" precisely what he did want? Perhaps if the man hadn't talked about "fancy goods" he might have felt differently . . . no, he wouldn't. He was afraid to admit the truth, that was the fact of the matter. So he denied it – he pretended to be better than he really was. It was hypocrisy pure and simple.

"Woe unto you, scribes and Pharisees, hypocrites!"

He stopped in front of a tobacconist's and considered going back to the man. He decided against it.

He shook his head, causing an elderly lady to cast a curious glance at him as she walked by.

Soho wasn't far now. A few more minutes.

Jake claimed to have worked in a private club in Soho before the war, a hideaway for society types with time on their hands and money in their pockets. There were hostesses who would dance with you and – according to Jake – do anything you fancied for a price. A wealthy Greek used to hire three of them at a time; one woman at a time didn't satisfy him, he said. Jake recalled watching the Greek's performance through a tiny secret knothole in the panelling.

Disappointing, was his appraisal. More show than substance. Taffy had longed to ask what Jake had meant. In detail. But he didn't.

He reached Oxford Street. His pulse quickened. Charing Cross Road dead ahead. It would lead him straight to Shaftesbury Avenue. And hell perhaps. Hordes of people. Uniforms everywhere. Yanks by the million. Laughing, talking, chewing. One thing you had to say for them: they knew how to have a good time.

Taffy felt as if he was being carried along on a tide of humanity. There were, he reckoned, more people on this little stretch of pavement than in the whole of Penrhyn Bay. Faces blurred by like photographs in an album when the pages are flipped.

Dean Street. Jake had talked about Dean Street. The heart of Soho. Deep breath. Right turn. Out of the babble into the comparative quiet of dark doorways and shadowy, disreputable-looking buildings with mysterious windows. *Sin . . . the transgression of the law.*

A movement. A whiff of cigarette smoke.

"Feel like a fuck, darlin'?"

An over-painted face with an absurd little hat stuck on golden curls that looked for all the world like wood shavings.

"I do a little extra for the air force, darlin'."

He hurried on, pretending again. Pretending that he hadn't heard the woman. Pretending that he was going for his evening constitutional. Pretending not to have a mind preoccupied by carnal thoughts . . .

"Hullo, sweetheart."

Another one. Pretty face but the eyes had died years ago.

He turned a corner. An American officer was negotiating with a yellow-headed tart who had her arms crossed across an ample bosom. The Yank sounded as if he had had too much to drink. He declared loudly that for a tenner he should get her and Sadie all night, not just for a crummy hour, and he was going to call a cop if she didn't stop hassling him.

Another corner. A tall woman, nearly six feet of her, stood in the middle of the pavement. She wore a loose-fitting dress; as he approached she reached in and pulled out her left breast like a grocer producing a plump grapefruit. Did he fancy a bit of that? There was more where that came from, she added, thumbing her nipple as if priming it.

Shaking his head, Taffy crossed the street. So crude. . . . He felt a trifle sick.

Yet another corner. More women plying their trade. More lurid slashes of mouths, glowing cigarettes, lifeless eyes. A travesty. Taffy turned away.

A woman stepped out of a doorway. A young woman, less violently made-up than her colleagues.

"You look sweet," she said. She had warm eyes. "We could have a lovely time together."

Nice voice. Pleasant smile. She took his arm.

"What's your name?" she asked.

"Gwyr but they call me Taffy."

"I wonder why."

"Because – " He stopped in time. She was quick, this smiling one. He cleared his throat. "How . . . ?"

"Two pounds ten. And you'll feel like a new man, I promise."

"All right." Quickening of breath. He had done it. The die was cast.

"Give you five, baby."

It was the American officer, beaming, rocking slightly, grasping a huge white fiver between thumb and forefinger.

"Done!"

And off they went, leaving Taffy standing in the street.

He shook his head in disgust and frustration. He needed a drink. He found a pub around the next corner. He pushed open the door and was instantly enveloped in a suffocating blanket of sound and smoke. Half of London's population seemed to have jammed themselves in here. It took an age to penetrate to the bar and order half a pint of brown ale.

"Permit me."

"What?"

Taffy turned. A middle-aged bloke. Moustache decorating smooth, untroubled features. Tweed suit.

"Please let me buy you a glass, my dear chap. I want to. It's the least I can do for you."

"Me?"

"Rather."

The middle-aged man turned to a silver-haired woman holding a slim glass. He raised a questioning eyebrow.

The woman smiled at Taffy. And nodded.

"You've been through it, haven't you?"

"Through it?"

"You've had a terrible experience."

Taffy stared. "How do you know?"

"A sort of gift, you might say." He pressed a brimming glass into Taffy's hand. "We're seldom wrong. We see it in the eyes. Very informative, eyes. But most people don't trouble to look." Big smiles from the two of them. Taffy wasn't offended at being offered a drink, was he? No, Taffy supposed not.

"Marvellous. We love Wales, don't we, Marigold?"

"Indeed we do."

The man edged closer to Taffy. "Feeling better now, old man? After everything that's happened?"

"I wasn't hurt," said Taffy. "Not really. I was lucky. We crashed coming in to land. Went straight in."

"Ghastly. There were casualties?"

"The whole crew . . . except for me."

"How frightful. And now you're celebrating your lucky escape."

"In a way." Taffy swallowed his beer in great gulps. The sooner he got out of this place the better. He shouldn't have told the civvies about the prang. The powers-that-be had made that amply clear umpteen times.

"Are you enjoying your stay in London?"

"Yes, thank you."

"Awfully pleased to hear it," said the man. His eyebrows arched. "If only it were true. The fact of the matter is, you're having rather a miserable time. You wish you'd never come."

"I wouldn't say that."

"I'm sure you wouldn't, old man. It's one of the curiosities of our species that we spend so much of our time pretending. You don't know a soul here in London, do you?"

"Well . . . no."

"You do now. George and Marigold Lee-Swinburne. Awfully pleased to meet you."

Taffy permitted his hand to be shaken with vigour while his new acquaintances told him how delighted they were to meet him. He wondered why.

"At this point," said George, "you're probably saying to yourself 'What on earth are these two up to?' Correct?"

"Well, I wouldn't say that – "

"Of course not. Far too polite. But it's true, isn't it?"

"Perhaps – "

"Don't blame you. Not in the least. I'd be asking myself the same question if our positions were reversed. But let me set your mind at rest. We're not engaged in any sort of under-hand activity. Our motives are quite altruistic. We want to do something for you. We can afford it. We're comfortably off."

"That's nice," said Taffy. Some response seemed to be called for.

"We live on Palmerston Square. Quite close by. It's a re-markably pleasant part of town. Perhaps you'd like to pay us a visit."

"Yes . . . er, one day."

"Today," said Lee-Swinburne. "In fact now."

"You'll be glad you did," put in his wife with a smirk.

"We recognize the signs," said the man.

"Signs?" Taffy wondered if he had strayed into the company of a brace of dangerous lunatics. You heard of such things.

The man edged himself an inch closer.

"Randiness," he half whispered.

Taffy wasn't sure he heard correctly. "Beg pardon."

"Perfectly natural," smiled Marigold.

"Rather," beamed her husband. "At your age I remember – well, no one's interested in ancient history."

"Certainly not," chuckled Marigold.

"I think I'd better be on my way . . . " Taffy started to move.

"Hear us out first," said the man. He raised a forefinger. "Point number one: We only have your best interests at heart. Point number two: We want nothing for ourselves. Point number three: This is our way of repaying you brave lads for what you are doing on our behalf. And point number four . . . " He had to depress his little finger with his left hand. "You'll have the time of your life."

Marigold had linked her arm through his; she grinned conspiratorially.

"Let's get out of this frightful place."

"Let's," said her husband.

Taffy found himself being propelled through the pub; a moment later he was on the pavement with a Lee-Swinburne on either flank.

It was raining.

"Typical!"

"English weather, m'dear."

"Appallingly unpredictable," Marigold informed Taffy.

"It is in Wales too."

"Really? How very interesting."

Taffy decided to run for it at the first opportunity.

"Perhaps we can get a taxi here," said the man as they approached Shaftesbury Avenue.

"Jolly good," said his wife.

They paused at the curb.

Now! Taffy told himself.

But at that precise moment a taxi pulled up with a shrill squeal of brakes. Taffy found himself inside, collapsing into a seat as the engine roared and the taxi pulled away.

"Brilliant," said Marigold.

"Lucky," said her husband. "Just happened to glimpse it as it came around the corner."

"But most people wouldn't have glimpsed it."

"I'm sure you're right. In any jungle a chap develops certain instincts to help him survive, what?"

He beamed at Taffy.

"Yes . . . yes . . . "

Completely off their rockers, these two, Taffy decided.

The curious thing was how the Lee-Swinburnes chatted so casually during the journey. Somthing about wines for next Friday. And arranging for Clarence to be met at King's Cross. All very business-as-usual. They might have been going for an afternoon drive in the country.

They didn't appear to be dangerous, as far as one could tell. Just eccentric, Taffy decided. The only positive thing to be said was that he was getting a free tour of the back streets of the West End. And a proper maze they were. Endless twisting, turning streets, miles of them; you could lose Llandudno in them.

They arrived, abruptly, the taxi thumping to a halt in front of a row of imposing houses. Taffy looked about him. They were in a square with a small park in the middle. It reminded him of a historic painting he had seen somewhere. You expected to see the Prince of Wales and Beau Brummell out for a stroll. Except that it was still raining.

"That didn't take long, did it?" smiled Mr Lee-Swinburne, opening the taxi door. "Just follow Marigold, old man, while I settle up with Malcolm Campbell here." Chuckle, chuckle.

Should he run the moment he set foot on the pavement? He thought about it a moment too long. He felt Marigold's arm sliding through his again. Then he was across the pavement and going up steps to a white front door with a gleaming kick-plate and a door knob that wouldn't have looked out of place at Buckingham Palace.

One sharp rap and the door swung open. An elderly maid peeped cautiously around it as if anticipating small-arms fire. She seemed relieved to see the Lee-Swinburnes.

Taffy wasn't prepared for the interior of the house. It was enormous. All polished wood oak flooring and walls festooned with paintings; a colossal staircase swept upstairs like something out of a Hollywood musical. He was vaguely aware of the maid whisking his cap away and Lee-Swinburne's beefy hand guiding him into a room the size of a Tube station. A library, apparently; there were books from floor to ceiling, books of every conceivable size and colour, books of leather, books with paper jackets, old books, new books, and vast sets of identical volumes, encyclopaedias or dictionaries or something equally weighty. The chairs were all soft leather, the sort that look better with age and use, not worse.

A glass of whiskey was thrust into his hand.

"Welcome, old man. Jolly glad you could visit our little place."

"*Little?*"

An indulgent chuckle. A good chuckler, Mr Lee-Swinburne. "Figure of speech, old man. Cheers."

The whiskey traced a bracing path down his gullet. Before Taffy had left home to go into the air force, his father had talked at length about the horrors of alcohol; but since he had started operational flying Taffy had come to the conclusion that the stuff had its uses.

"Care for another?"

Taffy shook his head. "Thanks, but I'd better not."

"Then what about a swim?"

"A what?"

"Swim, old man. All the facilities downstairs. Come."

"But I haven't got a costume . . . "

"Good heavens" – chuckle, chuckle – "we don't bother about such things. Much nicer without anyway. It's all quite private down there."

Taffy followed the man back into the hall, then down a flight of stairs. The house seemed to be as vast beneath the ground as above. There was a corridor and a door with a circular window like a porthole. The air down there had the faint tang of disinfectant, reminding Taffy of the Town Baths.

"Here we are, old chap."

Taffy gaped. The pool was huge, like some incredible subterranean sea. Steam rose lazily from the tranquil surface.

"Temperature seems about right," observed Lee-Swinburne, dipping his hand in the water. "You can hang your things on the hooks over there. Enjoy yourself, old man. Stay as long as you like."

"That's very good of you . . . very good indeed."

"Think nothing of it. Have a good time. That's all that matters to us. See you later."

And off he went, leaving Taffy shaking his head. A peculiar pair, the Lee-Swinburnes. Filthy rich. Filthier-rich than anyone he had ever heard of before. His father would rant at length about the fundamental evils of a system that permitted two such people to have so much when so many had so little. War profiteers perhaps. Taffy shrugged. May as well help them enjoy the profits.

He took off his clothes and hung them on the gold-plated hooks.

Then he took a deep breath and dived in.

Perfection! The warm water embraced him, caressing his limbs. A bit of all right, this, and no mistake! Gleeful, he hooted; his voice bounced about the great room as if it too were enjoying itself no end at all.

The old boy was right. Swimming in the buff was just the job! He rolled over and over, cavorting like a sea lion at the Regent's Park Zoo, naked and unashamed.

Until he saw the girl.

For a moment he thought he was imagining things, conjuring up a sort of mermaid out of bits of mist.

She waved at him.

His mouth dropped open. He stared. Incredible! It was the Wren from the train! And she didn't have a stitch on!

While he stood and gaped she swam to him.

"I'm so glad you decided to come."

"Er . . . yes."

His mouth must have remained open, for he swallowed a couple of mouthfuls of water.

"Like it?"

He nodded, speechless again. She laughed and swam away, effortlessly, superbly. Never had Taffy seen anything or anyone quite so totally lovely. But who . . . and what . . . ? Now she was at the other end of the pool, still laughing, still beckoning. His brain felt as if it was spinning, like a top, sending thoughts flying in every direction. He couldn't concentrate. And he knew he had to concentrate. But on what? He couldn't remember. He half swam, half waded. She was resting an arm on the diving board, water still dripping from her hair, running across her shoulders, trickling between magnificent breasts. He tried not to look at them.

"I saw . . . you on the train."

"Of course you did," she replied. "It's nice to see you again."

"Are the gentleman . . . and lady . . . your parents?"

Another dazzling smile. "In a way."

"I see." Quite untrue. "I wanted to speak to you in the train."

"You should have."

"I realize that now."

"Do you want to swim more or would you prefer to sit and rest for a minute?" Without waiting for an answer she took his hand and led him to the steps. "We can go back again later if you feel like it."

"I'm sure I will, " he said.

She smiled and turned to the steps. Still dripping delightfully, she climbed out of the water, superbly unconcerned by the fact that she had not a stitch of clothing on. What a breathtaking creature she was. So supple, so svelte, so absolutely perfect!

It took a moment for him to pluck up his courage to follow her. It was made easier by the fact that she seemed not to see anything odd about a naked young man sitting on the edge of the pool with her, drying himself and attempting with only limited success to look as if he did this sort of thing every day of the year.

"This is . . . a marvellous place."

"We like it."

"Do you . . . have lots of people in for swims?"

"No, only special guests."

"Of course."

"You're very nice."

"Thank you."

"But rather shy."

"Yes . . . I suppose so."

"I find some shy young men wonderfully appealing. Not all. Just some."

"Ah."

"One gets so tired of brashness and all that goes with it."

She opened a panel in the wall and pressed a couple of buttons. In a moment the sound of an orchestra filled the room.

"The Duke," said the Wren.

"Pardon?"

"Duke Ellington. Like it?"

"Grand."

"Care to dance?"

She asked the question as she turned away from the sound panel, perfectly formed breasts stirring as if in time with the music. She extended an arm in his direction.

He gaped at her and looked down at his nakedness. "Dance? Like this?"

She nodded. "It's nice. Have you never tried?"

"Lord, no."

"Time you did. Come on."

His fingers slipped off the arm rest as he tried to push himself to his feet. He almost fell, great white limbs angling grotesquely. She grinned at his discomfiture and reached out to him.

"I don't dance very well," he heard himself say.

"You'll learn."

She took his hand and drew him to her, her arm encircling his neck.

"Lord," he breathed as their bodies made contact. A delight beyond belief. A sort of electricity. Pounding through him. Galvanizing every fibre of his being. In all of human experience had greater pleasure ever been known? He felt as if he was melting into her, his skin blending with hers to form some totally new, utterly sublime substance.

They began to dance, slowly, while Cootie Williams

carved his patterns high over the Ellington orchestra.

"Just let the Duke take you," she whispered, her lips touching his ear.

It was easy. And heavenly. The rhythm commanded. He obeyed. Suddenly, magically, there was no need to wonder where to put the next foot; he knew; it came to him as naturally as if he had been doing it for years. The music seemed to be a part of him, pulsating through his very being like some new-found life force. Every step intensified the pleasure. Touching her body, feeling her body touch his: his secret imaginings had never conjured up anything to compare with this sublime reality. How magnificently unashamed she was, apparently indifferent to the possibility that this kind of thing might be categorized as unusual. The rich had different standards, it was a well-known fact. Dreadfully sinful, this, it couldn't be denied, but what did it matter? It was pleasure, pure and simple. Which was what he had come to London for. But it might have been a brief coupling in some grubby Soho room followed by a nasty, shamefaced retreat into the dark streets. Instead he had found this. And her delight was as real as his. You could tell, watching her nods of pleasure when he touched her beautiful breasts, feeling the nipples harden just as the boys said nipples did.

The music ended.

"Let's sit down."

She took his hand and led him to a corner strewn with plump orange cushions.

"Would you like to make love?" she asked.

"Yes, please."

She smiled, gently.

"It's your first time?"

"Yes."

"It's going to be a privilege to teach you. You are a very attractive man."

"I am?"

"Didn't you know?"

"No."

"Firm body, a kind, good-humoured face. You are quite

adorable, my dear, in fact it's becoming increasingly difficult to keep my hands off you. So I don't think I will be able to for a moment longer. You like me to touch you there?"

He felt himself dancing along a tightrope between pleasure and pain. Her fingers were electric, galvanizing every secret sense.

"Important, terribly important, to know the right spots," she said with her soft smile, the smile that seemed to bespeak such affection and tenderness.

Dimly he heard the disconsolate wail of the air raid siren.

He pushed himself up on his elbows and kissed her. She tasted of warmth and love with a subtle hint of peppermint.

"Will they come down here?"

"Who?"

"The others. Didn't you hear the alarm? I thought they might use this as a shelter, and find us like this."

"Don't worry. They wouldn't be so unkind. They remember, you see."

"Remember?"

"How demanding the senses are at our age. I want you."

"I want you too."

"Then place your hands here. Gently please. That's it. Lovely. You have such a wonderful touch. Just *there*."

Passion suffused him, drawing him into a world of warm reds and blues that turned somersaults of sheer delight.

The thuds sounded distant, mere punctuations in the night.

"Beautiful ... beautiful ..."

"You are perfect ..."

More thuds, nearer now.

A battering ram of sound smashed through the room.

And heat, searing, blinding heat.

Instinctively he recoiled. A wall of fire sprang up between them.

He thrust out his arm to her. Their fingers touched. Then parted.

She tried to say something. He saw her lips move, those soft and lovely lips he had just kissed; then, with a sickening twitch, she erupted in flame. Flesh blackened and blistered before his eyes. Hair sizzled as it ignited. Her beauty dissolved, melting.

He had to save her.

Had to, though the heat snapped at him like a savage hound.

He pushed himself into the searing flames.

They found him under the twisted remains of the nose.

"This is the last of 'em, Bert. Gimme a hand."

They had to use the rescue hook, the heat was still so intense. While they were still working an aircraft landed and taxied past, the crew grimacing as they regarded the wreckage.

It was a relief to get the job done, to see the meat wagon carting the pathetic sod away, or what was left of him. The blokes carrying the coffin at the funeral would have a pretty easy job of it.

A cigarette helped to kill the stink.

"The only thing you can say is it must have been quick. Bet the poor bugger never knew what hit him."

The Replacement

FROM THE START, FLIGHT SERGEANT CROCKER WAS A PAIN IN the neck. And elsewhere, in Tuttle's opinion, although it would not have been like him to voice such a thought. But Crocker's presence pushed him close to the brink; the man was like a chilly wind at a picnic.

"I'll tell you straight," said Crocker, "I don't like it. I don't like it a bleedin' bit."

Tuttle said he understood. Understood perfectly. Crocker shook his disagreeable head. Tuttle couldn't understand. Not *really*.

"Anyway," Tuttle said, "I do want to say how fortunate we are to have someone with your operational experience on the crew."

Crocker sniffed. He was an expressive sniffer. "Twenty-eight bleedin' ops and they stick me with a bunch of bleedin' *sprogs*."

He uttered the word as if it was a curse.

The wretched man should have been a Jerry. He had a square head, narrow and slab-sided, terminating in a prominent chin of mournful aspect. To make matters worse, there was so much of him. Six feet two or possibly three. The blighter *towered*.

Crocker met the rest of the crew when they took J-Jig for its night-flying test. He wasn't impressed. He had his doubts about Johnny Pitt, the navigator.

"He's got that look," he told Tuttle.

"Look?"

"In the eyes. Jumpy. Jumpy eyes. I've seen 'em before. He'll come to pieces, that one, when things get nasty. Just like a gunner we 'ad. Same look. On the bleedin' edge, 'e was. I told the skipper. Warned 'im. But 'e wouldn't listen. Thought 'e knew better. Sure enough, that very night, off 'e went."

"Off?"

"Off 'is rocker. Carried 'im away on a stretcher when we got back, they did. Your navigator's got the same look."

"I'm sure you're wrong," said Tuttle.

"No, I'm bleedin' not," replied Crocker.

Which was the whole trouble with the man. He knew it all. Even then he might have been bearable if he'd been content to do his job as flight engineer without trying to take command.

The aircrews gathered in the briefing room. The CO declared with evident relish that this was to be the *coup de grâce* for Hamburg. The city was reeling after two cataclysmic raids; now Bomber Command was going to put the place out of its misery. The clouds that had produced a couple of light showers earlier that afternoon had moved east. Of more significance was the cumulus that Met said was developing over the North Sea. Cu was the breeding ground for thunderstorms. The veterans sniffed the air and shook their heads. Ten to one the op would be cancelled.

It wasn't. The airmen garbed themselves in their flying gear, collected their rations and parachutes, and boarded the crew vans.

Tuttle and his crew clambered out at J-Jig's dispersal. The aircraft loomed over them, black wings outstretched, bomb door agape. Tuttle once again experienced that odd little feeling: that the whole thing was a mistake, that the authorities would suddenly wake up to the fact that they were entrusting this immense and incredibly expensive piece of machinery to Thomas J. Tuttle of St Albans.

They ran up the engines and then shut them down. They got out for a final smoke and a pee before take-off.

Tuttle wished he could think of something suitable to say to the crew. Something memorable, a neat blend of confidence in their ability and wisdom to help them face the coming ordeal. This was their first *real* op, after a couple of "gardening" sorties, dropping mines in the waters around the Frisian Islands. It was soon after landing from the second that his flight engineer, Phil, had started complaining of the stomach pains that led to him being in hospital with appendicitis. Which in turn led to Crocker being on board, a temporary "spare bod" because of illness in his own crew.

"Don't bleedin' chatter on the intercom every time you see a bleedin' searchlight," Crocker told the crew. "There's more bleedin' sprogs got the chop because the gunners couldn't tell the pilot about a fighter because some twerp was yappin'."

"Yes . . . thanks," Tuttle muttered. Blast Crocker for saying what he, the skipper, should have said.

His innards felt as if they had been tied into a series of knots. He fancied he saw a couple of the ground crew shaking their heads. Over him? The crew? Some of the ground wallahs were said to have an uncanny ability to calculate aircrews' chances.

He kept glancing at Flying Control. If the op was cancelled they would fire a red flare; then all innard-wrenching preparations would have been for nothing.

"Five minutes," he announced.

Whereupon Johnny Pitt rushed toward the rear of the dispersal, clasping his hand to his mouth.

"Lovely," snorted Crocker. "Just as I bloody thought."

"He'll be okay," said Tuttle with more confidence than he felt. Poor Johnny had been on edge all day, getting paler and quieter as the hours rolled by.

"Better scrub right now," said Crocker. "Good excuse, having to scrub because your navigator is heavin' up his guts."

He had a charming way of expressing things.

"The navigator is quite fit," said Johnny Pitt, emerging beneath the nose of the Hally, dabbing at the front of his flying suit with a handkerchief. "I'm perfectly capable of flying. Must have been something wrong with the bacon. I'm fine. Piece of cake."

Perhaps it was the further mention of food; poor Johnny had to rush to the tail again. Tuttle followed. Johnny coughed and spluttered. Then said he was fit. His face looked as if it had been shaped in wax.

"You're sure?"

"Positive." They rejoined the others.

The last few hurried drags at cigarettes. Sid, one of the gunners, dragged too enthusiastically; he started to cough. Another gunner thumped him on the back. The coughing stopped but hiccoughs took its place. He was still hiccoughing when he clambered aboard the aircraft.

Crocker said, "I got serious doubts about you lot."

"I haven't," said Tuttle. He wished the hiccoughing didn't resound so within the aircraft. From the ground it sounded as if a small animal was loose inside.

"Luck, Chiefie," said the corporal fitter.

"We'll bleedin' need it," Crocker was heard to mutter as he clambered aboard.

Tuttle followed Crocker, making his way up the angled interior of the fuselage with its innumerable projections and angles. You could do yourself serious injury if you didn't look where you were walking in a Hally.

Tuttle settled into the pilot's seat; beside him, Crocker planted himself on the spring-loaded jump seat; he sighed as he sat down, his thin lips set in an I-told-you-so line. Ready for any catastrophe, was friend Crocker.

Harness. Intercom. Oxygen. Ground/Flight switch. Pressures, fuel tanks. Flaps, landing light, brakes, controls, oxygen capacity. Undercart lever down. Flap and bomb door levers neutral . . .

The green flare shot skyward. The signal to start engines.

Crocker shook his head again, a little melancholy movement, an abandoning of any hope.

Switch to ground; master engine cocks on.

"Tanks one and three," Tuttle grunted.

He set the throttles just off the rear stops, adjusted the mixture control, and set the supercharger to the "M" ratio.

As each engine burst into noisy life, the aircraft trembled, the floor shivered beneath the crews' boots; Johnny Pitt's navigation instruments and pencils bounced and danced in their holder. One by one, the crew members reported in, testing the intercom system. No wisecracks this time.

From every corner of the field the bombers waddled out from their dispersals, heavily, awkwardly, engines emitting angry little bursts of power as pilots negotiated turns on the perimeter track, big tires groaning, tails bumping along on their small wheels, the faces of gunners pale behind the Perspex panels of their turrets.

"Stand by for take-off."

The green light from the control van. Brakes on; open up, throttle back, release brakes and then give her full power. Reluctantly the Halifax began to roll.

Tuttle's gaze was fixed on the centre line of the runway. It was like one of those fun fair games to test your driving skill; the line kept rolling no matter what; it was up to you to keep the line in the middle of your field of vision. You had to lead with the two left-hand throttle levers; if you didn't, the kite would wander off to port as it picked up speed. For long moments the engines were the only means of steering the kite. Then with velocity the rudders became effective. But your corrections had to be sparing. Too much rudder and you'd have to correct the other way. In a flash you'd be zigzagging down the runway. Your undercart would probably collapse and that would almost certainly be that.

Beside Tuttle, Crocker crouched forward, holding the throttles forward, lest the vibration make one or more slip back, cutting power at a critical time. Now the kite's tail was up; the runway was hurtling below, unwinding like a gigantic roll of carpet. Tuttle held her down until the York Road came speeding into view, a handful of citizens' heads visible behind the fence. A gentle easing back of the control column. She fairly bounded into the air; the rumbling of the wheels ceased. The runway dropped below.

Relief flooded through Tuttle. He was off . . . and on his way! In a crazy way he felt as if this was the end of his responsibility; now he was nothing but a tiny cog in a mighty aerial machine, simply following orders.

Kite climbing well. Almost enthusiastically. ASI steady. Altimeter needle turning steadily. Engines doing their stuff. Up through a layer of murky cloud, the aircraft jogging and rocking in the uneven air. He had an almost irresistible urge to glance at Crocker and grin, a sort of there-I-managed-it grin. But such behaviour would be definitely unskipperish. A skipper had to earn the respect and confidence of every member of the crew; they had made that point at OTU half a dozen times.

"Right, everyone keep an eye out for other aircraft, if you please."

Not bad, that, brisk and businesslike. From the corner of his eye Tuttle could see Crocker peering ahead, mouth set in a grim line. In a little while the crew would have to go on oxygen; then most of Crocker's unsmiling face would be concealed by his mask. It would be an improvement.

They would hit the coast south of Bridlington; from there they would strike out across the sea, joining up with the rest of the bomber stream at some unnamed spot over the waves.

Johnny announced a correction of a couple of degrees.

He sounded better. Definitely better. A thoroughly good sort, Johnny, accurate and reliable. Friend Crocker simply didn't know him.

"A Hally dead above us," reported Roy Gilpin from the mid-upper turret.

Tuttle eased J-Jig to port, putting breathing space between the two aircraft. The experts were said to have predicted losses of between one and one and a half per cent due to collisions. It was an acceptable rate of loss, they said. Acceptable to whom?

"Navigator to skipper. Coast in two minutes."

Good. Two minutes precisely. No "about two minutes" or "any time now." A veteran of twenty-plus ops had told Tuttle that vagueness on the intercom fostered uncertainty. And uncertainty spawned lack of confidence between crew members. Which invariably meant the chop.

J-Jig climbed better than the other Halifaxes Tuttle had flown. She handled well too. Some of those weary old things at HCU wandered all over the sky, and their engines kept overheating and cutting out; more dangerous than the Jerries, those HCU jobs.

Tuttle's eyes roved the instrument panel. Everything in good order. Needles quivering industriously. Pressures nicely up. Revs right. Piece of cake.

"Coast dead ahead," reported Fred Boxley, the bomb-aimer.

"But which sea?" chuckled Roy from the mid-upper turret.

"Very amusing, I must say . . ."

"See? You're doing it already," declared Crocker. "Yapping. A lot of bleedin' yap about nothing. Nervous yapping, that's what it is. What if a Jerry fighter had come along? The bleedin' intercom would've been busy with a lot of yap and the gunners couldn't have told anyone about it. And you'd have all got the bleedin' chop like Christ only knows how many sprogs before you."

"Er . . . precisely," added Tuttle.

Blast Crocker for sounding as if he was in command. A couple of telling remarks were needed to put him in his place. A couple? He couldn't think of one. He told himself that it would be a poor thing to start indulging in verbal jousting over the intercom. Particularly poor when it was more than likely that Crocker would come out ahead.

Look here, I'm the captain of this aircraft. Besides, I'm a Pilot Officer and you're a mere Flight Sergeant. So let's have no more of it.

Quite devastating, the way it sounded in his head. He

reminded himself a bit of Basil Rathbone in a particularly cutting mood.

Ahead was darkness, and Germany. When next it grew light, this op would be over and done with and he would be safe and sound back at Rocklington – or a statistic, one more to add to the list of Bomber Command casualties.

If it happens it happens, he thought, and there really isn't a lot I can do about it. Peculiar, the sense of resignation. He wondered if it would last.

"Look at that clag ahead."

Crocker's gloved hand pointed forward. Tuttle almost replied that he knew which way was the front. Almost.

In the fading light the dark clouds formed a mountain range, a gigantic wall barring their path. It was cumulonimbus, the stuff that spawned thunder and lightning, icing, and air turbulent enough to rip the wings off a bomber. The Met boys had talked about a relatively innocuous cloud formation. This lot looked terrifying.

"We're not going through that muck," said Crocker.

We are if I say so.

"My thoughts exactly," said Tuttle.

"If you ask me – "

"We're going around it," said Tuttle.

He edged to port seeking a break in the wall. But in the twilight it was hard to estimate distance. The angry clouds seemed to come forward to meet the aircraft. One moment the air was clear and kind; the next it was a nightmare of invisible fists that punched the Hally as it passed, a maelstrom of lunatic lifts of air that hurtled up and down in a perpetual frenzy of activity.

Why weren't the authorities cancelling the op? This was madness.

"We're picking up ice," Crocker reported. "Bleedin' fast. Best go back now."

Tuttle gulped. In the catalogue of aerial terrors, icing came right after fire. Ice had lots of ways to kill you. By coating propeller blades so that they could no longer pull the aircraft. By accumulating in carburettors and choking the life out of your engines. By building on wings, tailplanes, and rudders, sticking tenaciously, breeding layer upon layer of itself, adding tons as it industriously set about the task of changing the shape of your flying surface so that your aeroplane could no longer function and fell out of the sky, transformed into frozen scrap.

"Flew right into it, didn't you?"

Precisely as I intended.

Tuttle said, "I'm sure we'll find better conditions lower down."

Crocker muttered, "I've seen stuff like this before. I know what it can bleedin' do. Better scrub."

Tuttle didn't respond. He eased the control column forward. With any luck they would encounter drier, warmer air lower down.

It was as if they were going down stairs, bouncing from one step to the next. The angry, roiling cloud swept past, occasionally crackling with eerie flashes of light that revealed glimpses of huge dark caverns of purple-hued clag. Rain and hail battered the metal flanks of the Hally. An aerial Dante's *Inferno*.

Typical Tuttle luck to run into this kind of weather. Life never ran smoothly for Tuttles. It was ordained. During elementary training, only a day or two after his first solo, he had an engine failure. Tuttle reacted admirably. Nose down to maintain flying speed. Open space dead ahead. He recognized it: the local golf links. He swept over a tiny pond. Past a sandtrap. Crikey! Two players suddenly appeared, heads swivelling in alarm. Lord knows how he missed them. He landed. He scrambled out of the cockpit to the sound of approaching footsteps. They belonged to the CO and to the Chief Flying Instructor. The latter's golfing cap was a tangled, torn lump attached to Tuttle's tailskid.

He heaved back on the column. It budged only a fraction of an inch. Ice! The elevator was jammed with ice! For a moment he gazed at the hand grips as if pleading with them to do something. *Anything*. Ten thousand feet . . . nine thousand five hundred . . .

He pulled. And kept on pulling. And prayed. *Please*.

No joy with the trim tabs. Iced up too.

The grey clag seemed endless. And infinitely malevolent, swirling past him, leaving damp mementos of its vile self on the windows. Six thousand . . . five thousand five hundred . . .

Bit by torturous bit he was winning. He could feel the column edging back as its force crushed and dislodged the ice.

But, he told himself elaborately, we're running out of air with appalling celerity. His mind seemed numb, capable of accepting the fact but incapable of responding.

Suddenly, shockingly, he saw the sea. Black and angry.

A final heave on the column. The restless surface sped beneath the Hally's nose. Too bloody close for comfort. Another few seconds and they might have gone straight in . . .

But they didn't. And that was all that mattered.

Beside him, Crocker's head shook slowly from side to side. Like an instructor expressing disapproval of how a pupil performed a particular manoeuvre.

"Christ, that was a bit close," said someone.

"Miracle the wings are still on," said someone else.

The crew reported in. Everyone okay. The air was tranquil now. Throttle levers forward. Time to climb back to operational height. The ice broke away from the wings in great clattering chunks.

The sea was like a sheet of glass now. Black glass. It was hard to believe that the air had been so hostile a few minutes earlier.

Crocker went aft to change fuel tanks.

Tuttle stared into the darkness. The world had vanished. The Hally was suspended in infinite blackness, a throbbing little world of its own, its inhabitants connected by umbilical cords that permitted them to breathe and to communicate. A total population of seven.

"Enemy coast in five minutes."

Poor old Johnny, the wobble in his voice was evident even through the crackle of the intercom. A sensitive type,

Johnny, with ambitions to get into theatre production after the war. How was his stomach behaving?

The sky seemed to be deserted. Perhaps all the other skippers had had the sense to turn around and go back.

"Listen," rasped Crocker's strident tones, "we'll be over enemy territory soon. Everyone keep your eyes peeled. And no yapping. Talk only if it's important."

"Right you are," added Tuttle lamely. Why didn't he have the presence of mind to say that instead of leaving it to Crocker?

Leave the question until later. Flickering lights ahead. Flak! And occasional flashes of lightning revealing brooding clouds piled high into the heavens, an Everest of bad-tempered clag.

The flak drew nearer, little flashing eruptions in the darkness, a silent fireworks display. The experts declared that flak was at its least dangerous if the shell burst above you because the speed of the shell going up tended to cancel out the speed of the fragments coming down. Similarly, those bursting behind you were less likely to do you serious damage because your speed helped to reduce the velocity of the bits of shrapnel. It was the shells that burst in front and below that were particularly dangerous – but even those didn't compare with the shells that hit you fair and square. Some veterans said that over heavy flak areas it was a good thing to indulge in tiny changes of course every twenty seconds or so. The theory was that if the gunner on the ground had lined you up in his sights it would take approximately twenty seconds to fire the round, plus another fifteen for the shell to reach your altitude, by which time it was to be hoped that your subtle manoeuvre had placed you out of harm's way. Some pilots advocated flying a little higher or lower than the bomber stream, but that tended to make you a better target for the fighters. Theories galore. The best plan was to be consistently lucky.

Flak burst nearby. Fragments pattered against the aircraft's flanks. Harmless fragments, those, their impetus spent. If they hit when they were fresh they would go through the aircraft and its occupants, hardly slowing down.

"Searchlights ahead," reported Fred Boxley from the nose.

Great fingers of light, the searchlights probed the night sky for prey. The purple-tinged jobs were the master lights, radar-controlled, the ones to avoid, for if one got you the others joined in; they trapped you in a cone of lights and your chances of getting away were about one in ten. So said the experts.

The clouds were breaking up. Tuttle glimpsed a river winding through the shadowy land far below. He almost called up Johnny Pitt to ask him what river it was; for some reason it seemed important to identify it. He would look it up on the map when he got back. *When*, not *if*.

"There's an aircraft off to starboard. Below us. Could be a fighter."

Roy Gilpin's voice.

"Dip your wings," said Crocker, "so the gunners can see down."

Tuttle obeyed. Idiot, he should have known enough to dip his wings without being told.

"Can't see anything," said Sid Partridge from the tail.

"Must have gone," said Roy. "But I did see something. I definitely did. I wasn't mistaken."

"Belt up," Crocker snapped. "Watch."

The intercom fell silent.

The air was rough and getting rougher. It felt as if the Hally were bashing into things, staggering from collision to collision. Tuttle wondered how much the kite could take. There had to be a limit. Structures could absorb only so much punishment; one more bang could be the aerial last straw . . .

Germany was invisible beneath cloud. The course had looked so neat on the briefing room blackboard: it angled into the Reich on a southeasterly heading, passing between Hamburg and Bremen, then turning abruptly to port before heading due north to the target.

A moment's respite from the battering. The kite flew in gentle calm between sheer cliffs of black, sullen clouds.

Dead ahead lay Hamburg. Were the sirens wailing? Were

parents shepherding their children into shelters? The city had almost been destroyed by fire a few nights before. Now Bomber Command was returning to add to the misery of the citizens. What a hell of a way to fight a war.

"Target in ten minutes," announced Johnny.

"Thanks, Navigator. Everything in good order in the nose?"

As if in reply the kite flew into turbulent air again, bouncing, yawing, wallowing.

"More searchlights ahead," said Fred Boxley.

Twinkling lights probed the murk.

Alistair left his radios and made his banging, bruising way back to the astro dome to watch for fighters.

"We'll be there in a jiffy," said Crocker. "So keep on your bleedin' toes, every one of you."

"Right . . . thank you, Flight Engineer," muttered Tuttle. Some skipper.

In the nose Fred would be setting up his sights, playing with the graticle light, adjusting for wind speed and direction, checking bomb selector and fusing switches.

"Someone bought it," reported Alistair. "Port. Three o'clock."

Ours? Theirs? Dark red fire, so it was a bomber; the Jerries used a lot of magnesium in their kites, so they burned with a white glow. Down it went, twisting, trailing flame until it disappeared in the dark, seething mass of cloud.

Green target indicators wobbled in the sky ahead. They too vanished into the clouds.

To all intents and purposes Fred was now in control of the aircraft, crouched over his bomb sight like an Arab at his devotions.

"Steady," he murmured, "steady. Right . . . Bit more, Skipper."

Tuttle's eyes kept scanning the instrument panel. Better to concentrate on dials and gauges than look at the flak and the fire outside. You were at your most vulnerable at this point. Flying straight and level over a hotly defended target. It was hard to think of a barmier pursuit.

"Christ - look!"

A bomber became a ball of fire.

"Belt up," said Crocker.

"Right a bit more," said Fred. "Left-left now . . . steady. Hold it there, Skipper."

Tuttle felt his nerves stretching, straining – if one broke would he go beserk? The kite rocked. It felt fragile. No wonder the Air Ministry were concerned about the phenomenon of "creepback." If one faint-hearted bomb-aimer released his bombs short of the target in understandable haste to get out of the way of the flak and fighters, the next one might drop his even earlier. And so it might go. And often did.

"Steady . . . steady . . . " The aircraft leapt. "Bombs gone."

A 4,000-pound "cookie" and bundles of incendiaries tumbled away.

A flash.

A sharp, shuddering bang.

The Halifax skidded, swerved, tilted onto one wing. A ribbon of flame sprang from the port inner engine. They'd been hit! The horror he'd imagined so many times. Now it was reality. Finger on the feathering button. Throttle lever back. Master fuel cock off.

Automatically, instinctively, Tuttle corrected the controls to compensate for the loss of power. Rudder, ailerons, elevator, trimming and retrimming.

The fire went out.

Crocker shook his head. Tuttle wondered why.

Then he knew. The intercom was dead. Bloody hell! But there were other more urgent problems. Mentally Tuttle shoved the U/S intercom to the back of the priority queue.

Alistair appeared at his side and bellowed in his ear. God knows what he said, something about mending the intercom, it was to be hoped. Fervently. Too late to ask him; he had vanished aft.

The aircraft seemed to be flying well enough for the moment. All controls working. Three out of four engines still running. One wing hung low as if in utter fatigue. Tuttle corrected. The wing tilted again.

Now they were back in cloud. Angry, violent cloud. It was hard work keeping the kite the right way up. The poor battered thing kept shuddering. But the cloud was welcome; it provided cover; they could slip away unobserved.

A familiar crackling in the earphones.

"Intercom test," came Alistair's voice. "Everyone receiving me?"

The crew reported in one by one. Everyone was okay. But the mid-upper turret didn't work. Neither did the radio. Hydraulic fluid was sloshing around on the floor. Fuel was leaking from number 3 tank on the starboard side. Crocker busied himself with the fuel cocks, transferring the precious petrol.

Out of the cloud. An instant of awe. And fear. A gigantic black wall of mist loomed over the puny little Hally. It looked solid. A precipice of gargantuan proportions, a bottomless canyon, a narrow passage between great, rumbling masses, purples and greys, blending in terrifying beauty.

Darkness swallowed them: angry, noisy darkness that kicked and punched, jabbed and tripped, darkness alive with sudden, crackling flashes of light, darkness that bellowed in a voice loud enough to be heard above the engines' din. Tuttle worked madly, correcting, trimming, recorrecting. The instruments were useless. Before they had settled down from one reeling, staggering gyration, the kite was off again, at the mercy of immeasurable forces.

God knows how long it lasted. Time had no significance in that storm-tossed world. Only the moment mattered, struggling to survive from one instant to the next.

At last they found themselves in relatively calm air.

Tuttle's arms were aching. He trimmed the kite for the umpteenth time. A miracle the wings were still on. He called the crew. Everyone responded.

But Johnny sounded odd.

"Who's calling?" he wanted to know.

"What the hell do you mean?"

"What the hell do *you* mean?"

"Johnny? Are you all right?"

"I'll thank you to call me by my proper name, John Wellington Pitt, to be precise."

He sounded drunk. Absurd. Could he have been having a nip in that little compartment in the nose?

Crocker cut in. "Bomb-aimer, what's the matter with that bleedin' navigator? Have a look at him and be quick about it."

Johnny said, "I'll thank you to keep a civil tongue in your . . . h . . . h . . ."

He seemed to lose interest in the statement before he had completed it. A moment later Fred Boxley provided the explanation.

"Oxygen," he announced. "Bloody connection's got a leak in it. I'm patching it up. Poor sod isn't getting enough."

"Nor'm I," said Roy Gilpin with a lascivious chuckle.

Tuttle said, "Fred, be a good chap and get Johnny to work out a new course as soon as he's better. I think we're going in approximately the right direction but I need a proper course."

He looked about him but there was no sign of other aircraft. Or even of the target. Towering alps of cloud stretched away into the infinite darkness.

Fred said, "Skipper, I think he's coming around now."

Johnny said, "Hullo, Skipper, where are we?"

Tuttle said, "I was rather hoping you would tell us."

"I haven't the faintest foggiest bloody idea," Johnny replied with a sort of tipsy dignity.

"Hang on," said Fred. "Give him another moment."

"Of course," said Crocker, "We've got all the bleedin' time in the world, we 'ave."

A couple of minutes dragged by like hours.

"Skipper?" Johnny sounded weak but sober. "Sorry. I don't know quite what happened."

"Just get us a proper course for home," said Crocker. "And be quick about it."

"I'm sure he's working at it as quickly as he can," said Tuttle. "Isn't that so, Johnny?"

"Isn't what so?"

"That you're working on our course."

"Course?"

"For home."

Johnny was sounding vague again.

Fred said, "That bloody pipe. It's leaking. I'm patching it up. Should be okay."

Tuttle said, "Flight Engineer, why don't you go and see if you can mend that oxygen connection properly."

"A' right," responded Crocker without enthusiasm.

His leather-clad figure squeezed past the cockpit on his way forward into the nose compartment.

"Flak," said Roy Gilpin. "To port."

Desultory stuff. Half-hearted, as if no one was taking it very seriously. Was the rest of the bomber stream passing overhead at that point?

The only positive thing about the foul weather was that it discouraged the fighters. In normal conditions a limping straggler like J-Jig would have already become a casualty.

He scanned the instrument panel. J-Jig still functioned. More or less.

Crocker reported that Johnny's oxygen connection was serviceable.

"Should've been properly checked before take-off."

"I'm sure it was."

"I'm not."

He had to have the last word, friend Crocker.

"More clag ahead," reported Fred.

A moment later it enveloped them, a grey blanket packed with energy, an aerial gauntlet punishing poor J-Jig as it tottered and staggered through.

Crocker emerged from the nose, hanging on to a strut.

"You're getting icing," he reported.

"I can't climb any higher," Tuttle told him.

"Navigator," snapped Crocker. "What the hell are you doing about that course?"

"Just coming . . . " said Johnny weakly.

After which came the unmistakable sound of someone being violently, horribly sick. Johnny had left his intercom switched on. The crew had to listen.

"Sorry about that," said Johnny Pitt weakly.

"It's all right, Johnny," said Tuttle.

"Perfectly all bleedin' right," Crocker put in. "Just lovely. Where the hell are we, that's what I want to know? And what's the course for home?"

The Halifax gave an almighty lurch as it hit a fierce up current; an instant later a down draught sent it plunging, its structure creaking and bending under the strain.

"He's working on it," Tuttle said. "You heard him."

"Not at the moment he isn't," reported Fred Boxley. "He's heaving. Heaving badly."

"All right, thank you," said Tuttle.

Bits of ice kept hitting the sides and windows with impatient little raps. Ice was sheathing the leading edge of the wing and the engine nacelles. The immobile port inner prop was already covered; it looked like some absurd Christmas decoration.

Damn the Met boys. One heard of aircraft disintegrating in this sort of stuff, falling to bits, pulled apart by Mother Nature on a rampage.

"I warned you," said Crocker. "I warned you, didn't I? You can't bleedin' say I didn't."

Tuttle said, "I want the intercom used for essential messages only."

Frosty.

But Crocker was unabashed.

"I'd call it bleedin' essential, making sure we can find our bleedin' way home."

The last word again.

Tuttle possessed an affable nature; he was slow to anger; but his temper flared now. He was tired and scared and Crocker was so damned exasperating.

He started to tell Crocker to shut up. Once and for all. But he only got the first word out when the port outer engine stopped.

With a sort of snort.

Deprived of power on one side, the aircraft skidded, swinging drunkenly, sluggishly, heavy with ice.

I can't hold her, Tuttle told himself, calmly, numbly. She's going to spin in. This is it.

"Bet the bugger's iced up," said Crocker, reaching for the throttle and mixture levers. "Good backfire should do the trick."

And it did. With a bang and a frightening streak of flame, the engine roared back to life.

"Good show," said Tuttle, breathing again.

Beside him, Crocker shrugged. All in the day's work. He had his shortcomings, friend Crocker, but he knew his job, you had to admit that.

"Sorry, Skipper," said Johnny. He sounded weaker than ever.

"It's all right, Johnny. Just work out our course, will you?"

Silence.

"Johnny?"

"Give me a jiffy, Skipper."

"Your icing's getting bad again."

Wasn't it Crocker's icing as much as anyone else's?

The blackness still surrounded them. Great brooding masses of clouds had become their world, a world of angry winds and damp air that turned to ice the instant it touched the metal of the aircraft. Hateful stuff, ice. You couldn't fight it. Your only hope was to get clear of it before it killed you.

There was a dull sheen over the wing and the engine nacelles. The ice was encasing everything, burying the aircraft and its crew while they tried to stagger on through the night sky.

The controls felt as it they were no longer properly connected to the flying surfaces. Even the smallest corrections seemed to take an age to convert themselves to shifts in the aircraft's attitude. She was getting away from him, that was the truth of the matter. Soon she would ignore his silly fumblings altogether; she would simply fall out of the sky, an enormous, uncontrolled icicle.

Johnny came up with a new course to steer. But his tone troubled Tuttle. Was Johnny still feeling wonky? Or was he unsure of the way home?

Crocker's great brooding presence was still at his side, silent for once, thank God.

He asked Sid Partridge about the icing on the tail unit.

"Building up fast, Skipper."

He wished he hadn't asked.

Crocker was busy with the engines, nursing them. He knew his stuff, no question about that. Would Phil have coped so well? For a few crazy seconds he pondered the unanswerable question. His brain was getting iced up like everything else.

Then Fred announced that it looked clearer ahead.

Tuttle peered through the windscreen. Yes, indeed, the clouds were breaking up. Already the air seemed less violent. If they could just get rid of that ice . . .

"Saw the ground for a jiff," said Fred as if it was a matter of only passing interest.

Then a glimpse of stars. Wonderful stars – proof that there really was a world outside this vicious clag.

Crocker said, "Navigator, have you sorted out where the hell we are? And what's our bleedin' course for home?"

Silence.

"Johnny?" Tuttle called. "Are you all right?"

Silence.

"Fred?"

A moment later Fred's voice announced that Johnny was still indisposed but seemed to be improving.

"Told you," said Crocker. "Didn't I tell you? That bloke shouldn't set foot in a bleedin' aeroplane."

"I don't think this is an appropriate time to discuss it," said Tuttle. He gnawed at his lower lip. He was flying in approximately the right direction, but approximately wasn't good enough; in the darkness it was all too easy to miss England entirely and go wandering north. Next stop the Arctic Circle. How could anyone get a decent fix in these conditions? All one could do was make calculated guesses based on a pile of approximations.

Johnny's voice: "I'm all right now, Skipper. Sorry . . ."

"Nothing to be sorry about."

"Not bleedin' much," said Crocker.

Silence over the intercom. The aircraft quivered, swayed, the engines bellowing. Chunks of ice cracked against her flanks.

Crocker said, "I reckon we've got about an hour's fuel left. Maybe less. We lost a lot. And we've used up a lot wandering about."

Tuttle acknowledged the report matter-of-factly enough. But the bottom of his stomach was sinking through the cockpit floor. Was an hour's fuel sufficient to get them home? It was a question that couldn't be answered until it was sorted out precisely where the bloody hell they were.

"Town to starboard," Roy announced.

Yes, there! A place that could be identified, that could tell them without equivocation precisely where they were. Tuttle banked. As he did so the clouds closed in again.

"I'm going down to have a look."

No one objected. Even Crocker had no better ideas.

He eased the power off and retrimmed. The engines seemed to be whispering now; you felt as if you could talk above their noise. The altimeter unwound. Down, down, through the murk, wings rocking, flexing, absorbing the air's kicks and punches. A nail-biting business, this blind blundering through the cloud. One saw hills and church steeples, power lines and forests of Brobdingnagian proportions looming out of the darkness . . .

They flew into calmer air at seven thousand feet. The ground was a vague blanket of charcoal grey. No seas, no lakes, no hills to be seen.

And suddenly no clouds for the Hally to hide in.

"Searchlights off to port," said Roy.

"Flak, too," said Sid.

"You'd better go down to the deck or go back up to a decent bloody height," said Crocker. "Stick around this height and we'll get ourselves blown to bloody bits."

"Thank you, Flight Engineer, I'm aware of that."

"Then do something about it."

Tuttle muttered to himself as he shoved the throttle levers

forward. The engines roared, swallowing God knows how many gallons of precious fuel. The aircraft lurched and began to climb.

"There's a kite behind us," Roy reported. "Long way back. Can't identify it. One of ours perhaps."

A sitting duck, Tuttle thought, heart thumping.

He scanned the dark sky. No sign of cloud now that they needed one so badly. The kite was climbing at an agonizingly slow rate with one engine out and all the ice still clinging to its airframe.

Should have gone down, not up. But there was little chance of getting a fix at ground level. Unless you saw a sign.

Typical. What a rotten skipper. The crew deserved better.

Patches of ice still clung to the engine nacelles and parts of the fuselage but most of it had broken away from the wings, thank God.

"That kite is still there. Trailing us, if you ask me."

Lovely. Tuttle knew how a cornered rat felt. Nowhere to run. Just wait for the inevitable execution.

A few minutes later Roy reported that the other aircraft had disappeared.

"Keep watching."

"You bet."

"Looks like a town to port," reported Fred Boxley.

"What bleedin' town? That's what I'd like to know," said Crocker.

In vain Tuttle waited for Johnny to tell Crocker what bleedin' town it was.

"Johnny's working on it," said Tuttle. "Aren't you?"

"Yes," said Johnny. He sounded less than confident.

"We're lost," said Crocker. "That's the truth of it."

"I wouldn't say that," Tuttle replied.

"And what would you say, may I ask?"

God, what a grating, infuriating way Crocker had of talking. His voice had all the charm of a dentist's drill.

"Put a sock in it," said Roy. "Still don't see that other kite."

"We lost him," said Sid, from the tail.

"We bleedin' lost ourselves," said Crocker.

Johnny's voice came on the intercom. "Actually, I don't think we're lost," he said. "We're just coming up to Aachen. We passed over the Rhine a few minutes ago. That was Cologne, I'm sure – perhaps you caught a glimpse of it . . . "

He sounded like a tour guide. If the radio or Gee were working they would have been able to confirm the position. Tuttle shrugged. They weren't; so they couldn't.

"All very nice," said Crocker. "Except for one detail. You won't get home because you haven't got enough fuel."

He was right. Of course he was right, the bumptious overbearing oaf. It was an irrefutable law of the air: Engines won't run without fuel, and when engines stop, aeroplanes descend; the larger and heavier the aeroplane the more rapid the descent.

Bale out, Tuttle told himself. It was the only thing to do. Try to put the kite down in the darkness and he would kill everyone.

Abracadabra. It was their code word for abandoning the aircraft. When the boys heard the word over the intercom they would know what to do; they had practised the routine dozens of times with the kite safely parked at the dispersal. Everyone knew which emergency hatch to use. A bind, those practises, with full flying gear on; but perhaps all the effort would result in saving a life or two – or even seven.

Horrible, thinking about abandoning the Hally. She had served them valiantly, staggering along with her burden of ice, bashed about by hurricane force winds. She deserved better than to be left to die alone.

A ghastly emptiness seemed to have replaced his stomach area. He felt limp and sick at the thought of jumping into the darkness.

"No sign of that other bugger."

"Keep watching."

Were the boys cursing him for his incompetence? A typical Tuttle disaster, this. The luck of the Tuttles. His Aunt Penelope visited a friend in Dublin and drove her car into the middle of a gun battle between the IRA and British troops. His Uncle Wesley got into a card game in Marseilles and wound up in a Shanghai jail. A cousin named Gerrard went riding in Shropshire; the horse returned but Gerrard never did.

He explained the situation to the crew.

"There should be plenty of time to jump. You know the routine. With a bit of luck we'll all team up with the Resistance chaps."

"Some hope," said Crocker. "We'll be teaming up with the bleedin' Jerries, that's who we'll be teaming up with."

The clouds were thickening again.

Then, like nightmarish eyes from the Stygian depths, the searchlights came probing. peering, revealing weird cliffs and chasms in the murk. For a terrifying moment one of the lights snared J-Jig, illuminating oil-streaked wings and a few tenacious remnants of ice. But the cloud was an ally this time. J-Jig plunged into bumpy blackness.

"Keep turning," said Crocker.

His voice jarred like a sore. "That's what I'm doing," Tuttle snapped.

Flak burst innocuously to the rear.

"Nice work, Skipper," said Sid. "Missed us by miles."

They flew on in silence. How long before the engines coughed and fell silent?

Tuttle said, "I think we'd better go down and have a look around. Make sure we're over open country when we jump."

No one argued. Tuttle shook his head sadly. What a miserable way for the crew's first op to end. He eased the throttles back and adjusted the trim. The engines seemed to be barely whispering as the Hally sank through the cloud, rocking, swaying, shoved this way and that by the turbulent air. It was hard work, peering into the blackness, straining to see into its depths. Again eyes and senses played tricks, fashioning hills and houses out of mist. Every instinct screamed at you to pour on full power and haul the kite out of danger; and even as your muscles started to obey, your senses told you that you were being fooled, that there was nothing ahead but more greyness, wispy stuff that swept past your windscreen like unsavoury bits of cobweb.

Five thousand feet ... four thousand ... four thousand five hundred ...

This clag could go right to the ground. One heard of chaps flying straight into Mother Earth; this was one way it happened. Sod the Met boys and their miserable apology of a forecast ...

"Fighter!" yelled Roy, voice harsh and loud. "Bugger's following us. Just saw him in a break in the cloud. Twin-engined job."

"Don't bleedin' shoot," said Crocker. "Not yet."

"Wasn't going to," said Roy.

Tuttle's imagination painted one frightful picture after another, pictures of the fuselage shuddering under the impact of shells, of flames beaten to a frenzy by the screaming wind ...

"I see him too," reported Sid Partridge.

Phlegmatic as ever.

"You bleedin' shoot and you'll draw attention to us," said Crocker.

"I know. I know."

Tuttle felt his chest contracting as if fear was bringing his vital organs closer together, huddling for mutual protection.

At this moment the Hally was a blob on a vibrating, shuddering radar screen; the Jerry operator was no doubt chatting to his pilot, guiding him in for a visual contact. Line up the target; a burst of a couple of seconds into the wings where the fuel tanks were located; it would all be over and done with. Just another kite lost on ops. Telegrams to the next of kin. Letters from the CO. Paperwork for the Orderly Room clerks and the bods who organized for personal effects to be collected and packed and returned to the next of kin. For a time people would frown, trying to remember Tuttle and crew. Then an official stamp on the file and it would be closed. For ever and ever. Amen.

He remembered to keep easing the aircraft from side to side, dipping his wings to give the gunners as good a view as possible behind and below. Sod the Jerry pilot. Bastard, folowing them in a cloud, like some rotten little footpad in a

London fog. How he wanted to turn and look behind. But he could see nothing to the rear; the gunners were the eyes in the back of his head.

"Any sign of him?"

"Haven't seen him for a couple of minutes, Skipper. Cloud's closed in again."

"Keep weaving," said Crocker.

"I am," said Tuttle.

Left, right, wing down, up again.

Automatically, instinctively, he began to explain his actions, justifying his conduct of the operation before some beribboned symbol of authority. But with a shock he remembered that the only authorities he would be encountering in the near future were German. *Hauptmanns* and *Kapitäns*. There was a bleak, inverted comfort to be derived there . . .

Fred Boxley's voice announced that the cloud appeared to be breaking up ahead.

No, no, please no break in the clouds. The clouds are our only protection. Please . . .

He wanted to shrivel, anticipating the impact of the Jerry's bullets and shells smashing through the fuselage. The break was dead ahead; he turned to port.

Which was when the engines coughed. Spluttered. Stopped. One after the other, in quick succession.

"Damn," muttered Tuttle inadequately. He slammed the throttle levers back and punched the feathering buttons above the windscreen. Simultaneously he shoved the control column forward. The nose dropped. The aircraft plummeted. Head for the ground as rapidly as humanly possible. It was the only thing to do. And hope that it might confuse the Jerry, perhaps let them escape from his radar for a couple of precious moments.

"Get ready, chaps. Jump if you want. If not, take crash landing positions. Going straight in. No choice in the matter."

He wanted to say something else. But what?

Down the aircraft plunged, the sound of the wind suddenly deafening, wailing its way past the cockpit windows. Someone's voice to the rear. Shouting God knows what to God knows whom. Would the wings stay on? Were they capable of taking this kind of punishment? Wasn't it possible that they were already fatally damaged by flak and thus certain to collapse the instant he eased back the control column? Pity the poor sods who comprised his crew. Good types, but not too bright, choosing to fly with one Thomas J. Tuttle.

Better start easing her out. Altimeter unwinding. Two thousand . . . one thousand five hundred . . .

Please stay on, wings.

Hard work, hauling the big bomber out of its dive, forcing the elevators against the semi-solid stream of air. Nasty feeling that something would snap and everything would go loose in his hands.

Through the darkness the ground materialized, grey and ghostlike. It rolled below, a bland carpet. A glance at the altimeter. Five hundred feet, more or less. Too high. The Jerry could be on his tail at this very moment, preparing to blow the Hally and its occupants to eternity. Got to get lower . . . to plonk her down without delay . . .

At last, no words of wisdom from Crocker . . . Speed dropping off. The greyness sliding below like a sea of putty . . . faint impressions of trees and fields . . .

Where was the fighter?

Why didn't someone spot it? And tell him?

Sound of the wind diminishing as the speed bled off. Odd squeaks and creaks from the airframe; presumably there were such noises all the time but one couldn't hear them as a rule because of the din of the engines.

Small fields, lots of trees, a couple of houses, a curl of smoke at a chimney. No wind.

Can't waste time choosing the landing spot. Just wallop her down. And get it right the first time because there won't be a second chance.

A low wall rushed out of the darkness; it sped below . . .

trees ahead. How to avoid them? No, no need; they vanished. A biggish field ahead . . . a house . . . a fence . . . the images materialized out of the darkness like bits of film of appalling quality.

He heard the first contact with the earth. A crumpling, tearing, squashing bang. Oddly distant. Then he felt it. The harness trying to slice him up like bacon while he was being shaken; clearly an attempt to agitate him so violently that he would disintegrate and scatter his component parts to the four winds . . .

Then the world was still. And silent, but for a dripping sound.

A voice. Sounds of movement in the metal box.

A hand grabbed him.

"C'mon, Skipper. Let's get you out of this."

A strange sense of disbelief enveloped Tuttle like a warm cosy blanket. This wasn't real. It was a dream, a rambling collection of disjointed thoughts.

"What happened to the Jerry?" someone asked. What Jerry?

"God knows."

More voices, more sounds of movements. Tuttle yawned.

"Bloody good show, Skipper."

"Is he all right?"

"Bit dazed, that's all."

Why didn't they – whoever they were – come closer so that he could hear them distinctly?

They half dragged him, half carried him out through the emergency hatch. The night air was cold. He slipped and tumbled; more hands, more voices; the world had become a noisy, uncomfortable place again.

Tuttle sat down. He shook his head. And blinked. The great mass of the Halifax was a few yards away, flopped on the grass like a beached whale.

The boys were all around him. Still talking. Still saying that he did a hell of a good job, getting the kite down.

"Is everyone out?"

Crocker's voice. Crocker's grating, grinding voice.

"We're all present and correct." Roy's voice. Gentle little

hint of mockery there. Tuttle found himself chuckling quietly.

Crocker said, "We 'aven't got time to muck around 'ere. We've got to get going. And we've got to split up."

A circle of faces hovered around him, reminding him of a vocal group he had seen in a musical film. Astaire? Crosby? He couldn't remember. He wished he could remember. It seemed important.

"What are you eating?" he asked Alistair. He felt peckish.

"Wireless codes. Rice paper. Tastes like hell."

"I hear something," said Roy. "A motor."

"Christ, yes, so do I!"

"No one move," said Crocker. "I'm going to 'ave a dekko."

He darted away into the darkness. The sound of the motor became louder. A heavy vehicle, perhaps more than one.

"How are you feeling, Skipper?"

"Quite all right, thanks. Piece of cake."

"Bloody marvellous job, getting us all down in one piece."

"Lucky. Jolly lucky." For some reason Tuttle wanted to laugh.

Crocker came back, panting, fingers extended as if he were about to grasp something.

"Jerries!" he hissed. "I saw 'em. Sitting in them bleedin' lorries." He stared at Tuttle. "What the hell are you gigglin' about?"

"Was I giggling?" Tuttle giggled.

"How many Jerries?"

"Fifty at least. Maybe more. Bleedin' miracle they didn't see the kite already. We got to run for it."

"But we just arrived," murmured Tuttle. His head felt as if it were no longer properly connected to the rest of him.

Crocker threw him a despairing glance.

"Can you walk?"

Crocker snapped the question in Tuttle's face.

"Most certainly," Tuttle replied. "I learnt at an early age." He chuckled. What a jolly riposte.

Crocker didn't think so. He turned to the others.

"He's off his rocker."

"He knocked his head," Alistair pointed out.

"What was his bleedin' excuse before?" Crocker turned and disappeared inside the forlorn hulk of the aircraft. He reappeared a moment later carrying a Very pistol. He put Tuttle in mind of a highwayman.

"Stand and deliver," he said.

"What?" Crocker glared. "Listen, you lot, we got to make a run for it. You," he added, pointing at Johnny, "You're the navigator. Which way's the coast?"

Johnny indicated with his forefinger as if afraid of revealing the truth to too wide a public.

"Right, then we'll head that way."

"Who put you in command?" Johnny enquired.

"You want 'im?" Crocker grunted, nodding in Tuttle's direction.

"You've been doing your best to take over ever since take-off."

"Too bleedin' bad I didn't do it then."

He cocked the pistol and approached the Hally.

"I thought we ran out of petrol," said Roy.

"We did but there's enough fumes in those tanks to do the job. Soon as it's burning, run like hell!"

With a shock, Tuttle realized what Crocker intended.

"What do you think you're going to do?"

"I'm going to burn the bleedin' aircraft."

"I won't have it!" declared Tuttle. Unthinkable to burn the machine that had demonstrated such nobility of spirit, such gallantry in the face of adversities galore . . . "And since I am a Pilot Officer and you are a Flight Sergeant I will be obliged if you pay attention . . ."

Crocker bared his teeth. "It's our bleedin' *duty*, you twerp! We've got to burn it so the bleedin' Jerries don't get it. *Understand?*"

"Perfectly, but we mustn't act precipitately. . ."

The word absolutely refused to emerge as directed. Tuttle tried again. Unsuccessfully.

"You," said Crocker, "are a bleedin' nitwit."

He raised his pistol and fired into the wing.

The result was spectacular. A great whoosh of flame erupted, knocking Crocker off the wing. He tumbled, one leg jutting out before him.

"I really don't think you should have done that," said Tuttle.

"Run! Bloody run!" Crocker snapped as he pulled himself to his feet.

Alistair's fingers tightened on Tuttle's arm.

"C'mon, Skipper, gotta go."

"But the kite – "

The poor thing was blazing; you could see the metal squirming, contorting in agony. A dreadful sight.

"Come *on!*"

Someone took his other arm. Tuttle found himself being half carried, half dragged like some awkward bit of baggage.

"Look here," he began. But no one paid any attention. He had become part of a multi-legged creature that stumbled and cursed its way across the field, over a rough stone wall, into a muddy puddle, slithering, half falling, while behind them the flames soared higher, a monstrous beacon to attract every Jerry for miles.

The running seemed to shake the sense back into Tuttle. Reality hit him like a basinful of ice water. That fire was his kite . . . *his*. Another Tuttle failure, utter and abject, like all the others . . .

Through a hedge and into a narrow lane. Panting, they threw hurried glances to the left and right. All clear so far. Across the lane, then up a steep embankment. The grass was slippery. Tuttle fell. Fred helped him. Tuttle slipped again, clutching at air.

"Here." Alistair had grabbed a post that bore a large and imposing sign stating that the property was private and that trespassers would be prosecuted. "Give me your hand. Quick!"

"Just a jiffy," said Tuttle, blinking, his mind getting into a tizzy again.

"Hurry, Skipper!"

Fred was starting to push from behind.

Tuttle turned. "You know, we really don't have to hurry."

"What the hell are you talking about?"

Tuttle pointed at the sign. It was clearly readable in the light from the burning Hally.

"See what it says."

"*Says?*" Crocker seemed to think it an inappropriate moment to stop and examine signs in fields.

"Read it," Tuttle insisted.

"You're barmy . . . " But Crocker did turn to read the sign. Then his head described a kind of bounce as it went from the sign to Tuttle and back again.

"See what I mean?"

Alistair burst out laughing.

Crocker's mouth dropped open. Someone else emitted a huge sigh of relief.

"What's up?" Fred asked.

"See that sign? See what it says?"

"Of course."

"You know why?"

"*Why?*"

"Because it's in *English*!"

"I rather think I must have been mistaken about Aachen," Johnny Pitt murmured. "And possibly the tail winds picked up a bit . . . "

Crocker was still staring at the sign, examining each word; then he turned to the blazing Hally. His shoulders twitched into a nervous little shrug. "Well, what about the Jerries then? I *saw* them. With my own eyes . . . "

He was still shrugging when the trucks arrived, three of them, packed with soldiers carrying rifles and wearing steel helmets.

"*See?*"

Crocker wagged a lanky forefinger.

"Hi," said one of the GIs. "You guys from that airplane? You okay? Need any help?"

"Christ," said Crocker. He seemed to shrink.

"Awfully good of you," said Tuttle. "I'm glad to report that we all got out in one piece. By the way . . . "

"Yeah?"

"Did anyone tell you that those new tin hats of yours look a bit like Jerry helmets from certain angles?"

The Reunion

S CORES OF FACES. FACES IN TRANSITION. BEGINNING TO LOSE the firmness-yet-softness of youth. And unfamiliar, the lot of them. Not a friendly smile of recognition to be seen in any direction. Had he come to the wrong reunion? Why didn't he stay at home with the cat?

"Mr Fry, sir!"

As he turned, his hip dispatched a blazing rocket down his right leg. Or what was left of it.

A familiar face at last, pink and well-nourished. But the name?

HIBBERT, Roland, Sgt.

Thank God for lapel badges.

"Glad to see you again, er, Roland."

"I was in Ross Sinclair's crew. Navigator."

"Of course you were. I remember. You're looking on top line."

Was it significant that Roland Hibbert didn't ask after the state of health of his erstwhile Flight Commander? Was it so bloody obvious?

In engineering now, was Roland Hibbert. And engaged. To a girl from Twickenham. Four more times Colin and Roland said how good it was to see each other again. And wasn't it hard to believe that it had been ten years . . .

A firm hand clasped his shoulder. Chris Warren. He had become a captain with one of the airlines. Married, one son. A second infant on the way. A house in Hounslow. Colin was looking well, he said. Weren't airline pilots supposed to have good eyesight?

Colin asked him about the Red Indian gunner who baled out on the way home.

"Vanished," said Chris.

"Bad luck."

"I wonder. Knowing him, I wouldn't be the least bit surprised if he didn't manage to hide out somewhere until the war was over. Joined the Resistance perhaps. Then made his own way home. It would be just like him. One day I'm going to Attawapiskat. I have a feeling I'll find him there, large as life."

"Hope you do."

So far, thank God, no one had asked him about his profession. But it was only a matter of time. What to say? "Considering one or two interesting offers"? Or, "Pursuing something of a somewhat confidential nature"? Or the truth: "Living off my Uncle Andrew's bequest"?

Suddenly, as if by a sort of spontaneous verbal combustion, the subject erupted around him. In a moment everyone was involved. Voices were harsh and bitter. It had all been said umpteen times before but still it rankled: how Britain had so shamefully failed thousands upon thousands of Bomber Command aircrew. The bombing war was the longest battle of them all. Yet no campaign medal honoured its participants. The wretched politicians wanted to forget it had ever happened. None wanted to be associated with the beastly business of trying to burn and blast the Jerries into submission. Besides, Bomber Command had committed the unforgivable sin. It had failed. Butch Harris had promised to win the war with his fleets of cripplingly expensive bombers. He didn't.

Colin turned away. He couldn't listen to it all over again.

At one time it had troubled him, angered him. Now he didn't care any more. These days, what did a spot more injustice and a pinch more expediency matter?

Andy Shaw materialized – spiffy in a striped, double-breasted suit and a spotted tie with an inordinately large knot. His tie clip looked as if it weighed five pounds. He was in plastics, he said, whisking out a card that described him as Area Sales Manager.

"Plastics are the coming thing."

"I'm sure they are."

"What line are you in now?"

"I'm considering . . . well, nothing at the moment."

"You could do a lot worse than plastics."

"Selling? Hardly my line, old chap. Thanks anyway."

"If you change your mind . . ."

"I've got your card. How's the arm?"

"Get the odd twinge on damp days. You?"

Odd twinges all day every day, he nearly said, but didn't.

"Smarts a bit sometimes. But it could have been worse."

"Married?"

Andy sounded as if he was already interviewing Colin for a position with the plastics company.

"I was once," Colin told him. "It didn't work."

"Know what you mean. Know exactly."

A wink and Andy was gone.

The faces appeared and smiled and vanished. Old memories hung in the air like ancient dusty cobwebs. Best left alone, Colin was beginning to think. Nigel Pettigrew, he learned, was alive and well in Melbourne. Tom Tuttle was in hospital recovering from a broken leg suffered while out for a walk in Epping Forest. Chiefie Pudwell was recovering from a mild heart attack.

Willy Perkins. Respectful as if the old rank thing mattered still. He was the production manager at a printing company, married with two children and a house just around the corner from a laundrette; he said he was saving up for a television.

Colin said, "Bit late in the day now – but congratulations

on your VC. The only one the squadron ever got. We were all very proud of you."

A little blush and a shifting of the feet. "Ancient history now, sir. A bit of a nuisance sometimes. Some of the salesmen like to introduce me to customers and tell them about the gong. Good for sales, I suppose. But people are funny. They all know what to say when they hear you've lost your job or you've got the flu. But they're flummoxed when it comes to something like this. And there's a bit of resentment too, I'm sure. 'That little twerp doesn't look any better than me, yet he's got all the glory. Just lucky to have been at the right place at the right time.' And I suppose there's some truth in it."

He smiled in that wry way of his.

"I understand your sister married Ross Sinclair."

"Yes, sir, and they're living in Winnipeg. Great big house with a swimming pool. And they've got another house in Texas or somewhere like that. They go there in the winter. Ross plays golf and really does very well with his artificial arm." A quick glance down at Colin's leg. "He and Gwen have two nippers now. We went out to visit them, the four of us, Mum and Dad, Kath and me. Ross paid for everything. Even let me drive his De Soto! Like a tank! What line of work are you in now, sir?"

"I'm thinking of going into plastics."

More heated words. About inadequate defensive armament. About Fighter Command's failure to do more to neutralize the Jerry night-fighters. About pay. About leave. About food. About gongs. And memories: Don and Muggles, Neal and Gordon, Taffy and Jake. They should have got through if there was any vestige of justice left in the world. Full of promise, all of them. Better somehow than those who survived. Colin decided to slip away into the night.

Another familiar face. Older, a trifle more weathered, but still as genial as ever.

Fawcett, the Admin bloke.

"Colin! My dear chap! How very good to see you! So many people asked about you at the last do. Gave me a rocket for not inviting you. I told them no one knew where you were."

Wasn't too sure myself. "Is the CO coming?"

"He's in Singapore. Sends his regards. Quite a jolly turnout here, what?"

"Very jolly."

"You seem to be in good form."

"I'm much improved."

"I'm glad. Really."

"I haven't seen Simon Coombs."

"You didn't hear?"

"Hear what?"

Fawcétt raised a greying eyebrow.

"Poor fellow did himself in. In May, just a week or so after VE Day. Simon took his service revolver and went over to the far side of the field near the wood. Then he blew his brains out."

Colin winced at the thought. "Why?"

"We all asked ourselves the same question. Nobody had a clue. Perhaps he couldn't face civvy street. Or perhaps there was a woman somewhere. I remember he was frightfully upset about Guy Venables's wife, the actress. Terrible business. Heard from Venables by the way. He's in Hollywood. Place called Pacific Palisades. Writes film scripts, I understand. Seems to be doing very well for himself. Do you remember Bob Kendall? No, perhaps he came after your time. He was in journalism too. Poor fellow's not well at all. Cancer. Hard to credit, what? A chap gets through thirty trips for *that.*"

"It makes you wonder."

"And Michael Coates."

"Coates, the MO?"

"The same. Bought it in a head-on crash on the North Circular Road."

"God."

"I was just talking to his wife, or rather, widow, not too long ago. Awfully nice woman. In fact, it strikes me that you might remember her. Unless my memory completely fails me it seems to me she was once engaged to one of your crew."

"My crew?" He started to shake his head. Then he remembered. With a distinct thump of that weary old disillusioned heart. Yes, he remembered well. "There was a WAAF who got engaged to my bomb-aimer, Don Flinders."

"The same. Phoebe Webb."

Another thump at the sound of her name. "I do recall her." Vividly.

"Poor girl had an awfully rough time of it." Fawcett shook his head, frowning as if chiding fate for its cruelty. "She was involved with an Aussie pilot first. He bought it. Then there was Flinders. She was engaged to him. Then he got the chop. Then Ross Sinclair. He wasn't killed but he lost an arm and was sent home to Canada. After him there were a couple of others. All of them went for a Burton. By then the aircrew types were scared stiff of her. You know how it used to happen. The boys would tell each other that she was a Chop Girl. Take her out and buy her a drink and you'll buy the farm too."

"And so she married Coates?"

"Right. A safe, non-aircrew type at last. They lived Ealing way. He was in general practice. Doing well. Then eighteen months ago he had the accident. Killed instantly. Poor girl, it almost sent her around the bend. She had to have psychiatric care, she told me. She was quite frank about it. A Jonah complex, was the way she described it. But she's much better now. Just another casualty of the war, like you, old man. By the way, we talked about you the last time I visited her."

"Why on earth would you do that?"

"She was reminiscing about Don and the time he had to introduce her to the rest of the crew."

"At The White Rose."

"Yes. She remembered talking to you. And how kind you were – for a Squadron Leader. She asked what had happened to you. I said I hadn't a clue. You seemed to have disappeared off the face of the earth. Then a few months later we ran the advert in the *Times* about the reunion. And here you are."

"More or less."

"Why don't you write to her?"

"Me?"
"I think she'd be pleased to hear from you."
"Honestly?"
"Honestly."

THE END

SPY WARS
Espionage and Canada from Gouzenko to Glasnost
by J. L. Granatstein and David Stafford

The Cold War may be over but the "great game" of spy vs. spy will
continue, say the authors of this "path-breaking popular history."
"A fun read. Descriptions of the back-stabbing, blackmailing
politics of spying are admirably well done." – *Quill and Quire*
0-7710-3511-x $7.50 8 pages b&w photos

CHANGELINGS
by Tom Marshall

Fans of *The Three Faces of Eve* and *The Shining* will enjoy this eerie,
critically acclaimed novel about an estranged brother and sister, each
of whom suffers from multiple personality disorder.
"Fascinating fiction, controlled, assured … " – *Windsor Star*
"A chilling yarn … difficult to put down." – *The Gazette* (Montreal)
0-7710-5661-3 $6.99

KICKING TOMORROW
by Daniel Richler

The remarkable debut novel from Canada's hottest new literary star.
Four months on the national bestseller list.
"An exhilarating romp … It crackles with wit and insight." – *The
Globe and Mail*
"A gutsy *Catcher in the Rye* for the nineties." – Susan Musgrave,
CBC's *The Journal*
"Excellent … entertaining and ambitious." – *Calgary Herald*
0-7710-7470-0 $6.99

Hot titles from M&S Paperbacks

AFTER MANY DAYS
Tales of Time Passed
by L. M. Montgomery; edited by Rea Wilmshurst
Eighteen newly discovered classics penned by the author of the immortal *Anne of Green Gables*, collected by the editor of *Akin to Anne* and *Along the Shore*.
0-7710-6171-4 $6.99

CONSPIRACY OF SILENCE
by Lisa Priest
The powerful, award-winning best-seller about racism, murder, and apathy in a Manitoba community. Basis of the acclaimed CBC-TV movie. From the author of *Women Who Killed: Stories of Canadian Female Murderers*.
0-7710-7152-3 $5.99 Photos

ELIZABETH
by Alexander Walker
The definitive biography of Hollywood's much-married biggest star, Elizabeth Taylor, by the acclaimed author of *Vivien*.
"Informative, thoughtful, and understanding." – *The Listener*
0-7710-8781-0 $7.99 32 pages b&w photos

THE JACAMAR NEST
by David Parry and Patrick Withrow
Someone is out to bring corporate America to its knees and ex-CIA-agent-turned-insurance-investigator Harry Bracken is determined to find out who. Provided, of course, he isn't shot or blown up first.
"A fast-moving terrorist story leavened with sophistication and wit." – *The New York Times*
"The action never stops and the authors have a nice way with dialogue." – *The Globe and Mail*
0-7710-6931-6 $6.99